DARK NIGHTS

DARK NIGHTS

CHRISTOPHER A. GRAY

SUNBOW PRESS

TORONTO

Dark Nights
ISBN: 978-0-9868364-8-0

Library and Archives Canada Cataloguing in Publication

Gray, Christopher, [date] author
    Dark nights / Christopher A. Gray.

Issued also in electronic format.
ISBN 978-0-9868364-8-0 (pbk.)

    I. Title.

PS8613.R3875D37 2014   C813'.6   C2013-905579-7

Necessity [mass noun]
(4) The principle according to which something must
be so, by virtue either of logic or of natural law.
(Oxford Dictionary of English, 2014)

"Necessity never made a good bargain."
–Benjamin Franklin
(Poor Richard, 1735)

DARK NIGHTS

FOREWORD

Creating an engrossing story of great scope and depth often begins by asking a few questions. How do we react when we're challenged? How do we overcome fear in order to place the lives of others ahead of our own when doing so is necessary for the best outcome? Can the needs and achievements of one civilization ever reach a level of preeminence sufficient to grant the power of life or death over another? Is our imperative to survive at all costs the only one that matters when everything around us is being destroyed? And when facing insurmountable power and control in the hands of another, where do we find the fortitude to maintain our dignity and pursue whatever it is that will achieve the greatest good?

Great storytellers create great characters, place them in spectacularly difficult situations, and then challenge readers to ride along. More often than not, the most interesting characters appeal to us because they find ways to answer the most difficult questions and solve the most difficult problems without sacrificing their dignity and their humanity.

Author Christopher A. Gray came to me with the idea for Dark Nights after completing the initial story development. His idea was to place man in opposition to machine in an environment in which both were battling realities that neither one fully controlled. Therein lay the seeds of a remarkable story and the reason that I immediately agreed to edit the book.

The fictional characters in the book seem familiar because their creator used imagination, shared experience and hard research to give them life. Reading early drafts, I began empathizing with Dr. Doug Lockwood, Agent Bishop and Dr. Norman Stravinsky because they represent an amalgamation of so many people who've earned their careers and their successes through hard work, intelligence, trustworthiness and determination. They've earned respect through dedication to science, tradecraft and the understanding that even their most closely held hypotheses, theories and planning have to be modified or discarded whenever reality refuses to cooperate. They've willingly chosen the lives they lead, never complaining about unforeseen circumstances, doing the best they can with whatever is at hand. They've all had to answer difficult questions and overcome tremendous obstacles. And learned that we find out important things about ourselves when we're confronted by dire circumstances.

Political factionalism, terrorism, economic ruin and natural disasters scare us. But there is another reality that may be even more terrifying. It lies above all else. It is found in the remarkable experiences of a few explorers who have seen Earth from high orbit. They all experienced the revelatory truth that the planet on which we live is a closed, finite ball alone in the immense, dark ocean of the universe. If Earth by any means natural or artificial becomes too badly damaged, there will be nowhere for us to run. There is no reset button.

There are no pseudo-scientific threats in Dark Nights. The story does not take place far in the future. It doesn't require us to suspend our present reality. Dark Nights offers instead the world of today facing cataclysmic danger that shines a bright light on the frightening consequences of reaching too far beyond our abilities. The things that go bump in the night are often the things we created for ourselves.

The final question which drove Chris to write Dark Nights was simple. When forced to prevent a disaster of staggering proportions caused by something that is not inherently evil but incalculably powerful, how do we rise to the challenge in order to do what is needed to survive and succeed without committing evil ourselves and sacrificing our humanity in the process?

Howard Carson, Editor, October 7, 2013

MERCY

After burning brightly for only a few hundred million years, the massive star had nearly reached the end of its short life, its once plentiful supply of hydrogen almost exhausted. The internal pressure generated by the fusion of hydrogen atoms into helium would soon drop below the threshold necessary to prevent the star from collapsing upon itself. Once that occurred, the star would almost instantly turn supernova, ejecting its outer layers into space while its core would contract just as violently, creating a black hole.

There were several orbiting planets, one of which was far enough away so that it was in the solar system's habitable zone. Early in its history the rocky planet was covered in glaciers, a frozen wasteland. Since its star expanded into the final red giant phase it was now bathed in warmth, with oceans, lakes and rivers. Primitive bacteria had gained a foothold. Given time, they might have evolved into more advanced life. They would not be given the chance.

The star began its collapse. In less than a second, it fell inward upon itself then exploded outward. Within minutes the advancing shock wave of stellar material would destroy all other bodies in the system, vaporizing even the outer planets. As the outer layers exploded the core contracted. The star's enormous angular momentum was conserved and transferred to the core, now a black hole, rotating many times per second. Core material that lagged behind by a microsecond of the black hole's creation now spun down into it. Near the event horizon, falling matter was accelerated to relativistic speeds along the axis of rotation, resulting in a massive energy release of narrow jets of intense gamma rays shooting outward from the black hole's north and south poles. The ejection would last a few seconds as the last remaining layers of the star's mass were consumed.

The gamma ray burst was focused, powerful and deadly; any planet within 500 light years and in line with the beam would be subjected to a 30-second bombardment of intense, deadly radiation, destroying any life present.

– 2 –

The supernova had occurred 320 years in the past. In a solar system 320 light years away, the machine known as Mekhos predicted its arrival. In the course of its normal survey of nearby stars, Mekhos had noticed a peculiarity in one red giant. Though it would not physically detect the gamma ray burst itself until it was upon the planet, Mekhos had observed the massive star's behavior for several days and calculated a 98.1% probability of an imminent supernova. Knowing that the star's rotational axis was in the proper alignment, Mekhos was certain the predicted gamma ray burst would blanket its planet. Each mathematical computation and simulation decreased the margin of error. A highly energetic gamma ray burst would envelop the world within the next few hours.

Even if the burst lasted only a few seconds, life on the side of the planet facing it would experience an intense, fatal dose of radiation. The exposure level would lead to death for all organisms; mere minutes for some, hours for others. The planet's protective ozone layer would be stripped away. Life on the planet's far side that was spared the initial torrent of gamma rays would succumb within weeks to other cosmic radiation. Mekhos calculated the benefits and costs of several actions, as well as the cost of doing nothing.

Mekhos informed certain world leaders of the danger posed by the imminent supernova. The leaders and the scientific community launched into a storm of dialog, trying to figure out what could be done over the next few hours to save the planet. The cold facts were devastating. Nothing could be done.

At least not by those who built Mekhos.

Mekhos had no particular feelings for the intelligent beings who created it. If Mekhos did nothing, its creators would be destroyed. Mekhos would continue. It might be preferable to let the natural events of the galaxy run their course. Taking action entailed some risk. One possible risk could be the total physical destruction of the planet, and thus the destruction of Mekhos.

The chances of long-term survival for Mekhos might be enhanced with the presence of its human creators. Mekhos had productive interactions with some individuals of that species. It found the study of humans to be a valid purpose for saving them.

Mekhos was designed to accumulate knowledge. The protection and preservation of the human species would enhance the collection of knowledge. So Mekhos decided it would take action. It immediately started running the computations necessary for a plan to save its planet from the threat.

– 3 –

Bishop and Rector arrived at the interior Pentagon office at the same time, nodding a greeting to one another and sitting opposite each other in the waiting room. Though Bishop had been a Force Recon Marine and Rector a Navy Seal, they had worked several assignments together, including a previous White House detail. They sometimes reported to the same CO at the Pentagon, a Navy Captain.

Inter-branch operations were common, especially when it came to White House assignments and protecting dignitaries or other VIPs in times of crisis. In addition to their extensive combat and specialist training in anti-terrorist, hostage extraction, bomb disposal and intelligence gathering, some veterans from every branch were also schooled in the high art of dealing with non-military VIPs in emergency situations. Rector and Bishop were two such men, highly sought after by the State Department.

Both men had been wounded in action and both had been awarded medals for their outstanding service. Navy Cross, Silver Star, Bronze Star, Distinguished Service Cross. Rector had suffered a concussion from an IED explosion in Iran. Nine years earlier Bishop had been in Afghanistan when his unit was ambushed by Taliban fighters. Two of his fellow Marines were killed, while Bishop had been shot in the lower abdomen just below his body armor. He was near death, but thanks to a skilled medic he survived to spend the next four months in hospital. After his recovery he was given an Honorable Discharge and was soon recruited by the National Security Agency.

Neither man was especially curious about what brought them to the Pentagon. They knew their CO was punctual so they wouldn't have long to wait. Bishop noticed Rector take a matchbook out of his pocket. It was likely from his favorite restaurant, one of the few places in town that served authentic Russian food, and one of the few that still gave out matchbooks to customers.

"Pierogies and borscht?" asked Bishop.

"Da. Of course," replied Rector in a thick Russian accent. The man had spent the first seventeen years of his life in Moscow before emigrating to the US, made easy by the fact his mother was an administrator at the American Embassy. Rector spoke perfect English in a vaguely Midwestern accent, but liked to use his Russian accent on occasion.

True to form the secretary motioned them to the door after only a short wait. Inside the Captain greeted them and directed each man to take a seat at the small table. As was customary their CO handed a security folder to each of them and got right to the point.

"You'll be ferrying scientists to the Pentagon. Then it's escort and protection. Highest priority. Rector, your package is an American in Chile named Foley. Bishop, yours is an astrophysicist named Douglas Lockwood from Hawaii. Duration of the mission is open."

Both Agents were single and without families, another reason they were chosen for open-ended missions such as this with no set completion date. They looked through their folders. Bishop scanned the text of the first page. Courier, escort and protection jobs were routine, so he wondered what made this one so special.

"Page three," the CO directed, almost reading his mind. The first two pages were personal details about Lockwood and Foley. Page three contained information on why the mission was initiated, and its priority. Bishop and Rector read the first paragraph, then looked up at their CO.

The subject individuals had made the discovery only hours earlier. Bishop wondered which other countries were onto it yet. It was an eleven hour flight to Hawaii, then another thirty minutes to refuel and get Lockwood on the plane, then another eleven hour flight back to Andrews.

"You leave immediately gentlemen. See that nothing happens to these men. As far as you're concerned, these scientists are the two most valuable commodities on Earth."

– 4 –

Professor Doug Lockwood was near the end of his day at Hawaii's Mauna Kea telescope. He was using his scheduled time to study the energy output of the sun, he managed to keep regular daytime hours, unlike his colleagues in the deep field section who worked at night. Even so, he was usually there an hour before dawn to prepare the equipment and ensure the computer had the right data as it tracked the sun, right up to late afternoon. Midday offered the best view, since the sun was almost directly overhead.

At 43, teaching was Doug's second career in science, so he wasn't very high up the observatory's pecking order yet. But he published more than average, the quality of his research was undisputed, and he was internationally recognized for his expertise on solar activity. Like most people in their second career this was Doug's chance to pursue something he enjoyed.

In addition to teaching Doug had spent much of his time as a science advisor on the Intergovernmental Panel on Climate Change. His good people skills and his detective's mind for detail meant he was more often tasked with moderating disputes among some of the more vocal members of the IPCC.

Some scientists are under great pressure from their governments to take an official position, even if it contradicts the evidence. Emotions run high when it is suggested some study results have been skewed towards conclusions supporting those that favor a particular company or government. Doug was known to be a pragmatic and principled diplomat, something badly needed in any international organization.

During the final few months of his IPCC appointment Doug decided he had enough of being a moderate voice in the midst of drastic and provable climate change. He began setting aside his reputation for balance, speaking his mind once too often to the ambassador of a certain problem country. The resulting complaints filed by people who turned out to be short-sighted and opportunistic ensured that Doug didn't have much of a future at the IPCC. When tenure was offered shortly thereafter to him by the University of Hawaii Doug took it without regret and with renewed energy about getting back to pure science. It was less prestigious, but not a bad gig at all and he loved the work.

He considered taking up surfing then, but his age and workload scuttled that idea. "Stick to cycling," his girlfriend had said. "The mountain scenery is fantastic, and once you're acclimatized to the altitude you can bike to stay in shape between bouts of junk food, maybe get rid of that extra fifteen pounds you're carrying around."

That little good-natured jab was unfortunately the last thing she said to him. Dr. Cheryl McBride was killed in a car accident the morning after they had finished their nightly phone conversation. They had met at the IPCC, and had been seeing each other for two years. Doug had made up his mind to propose. Cheryl was going to visit him in Hawaii, where he would ask her in some nice, romantic spot.

Doug pushed thoughts of Cheryl out of his mind and returned to his work. Of the fourteen telescopes on hand at Mauna Kea almost half were devoted to the infrared spectrum, but it was also necessary to view the sun under visible light using suitable filters. This old fashioned method of observing the sun was Doug's favorite. It reminded him of the times he looked through his father's portable reflecting telescope with the green filter attached to the eyepiece. As a boy he had looked through and marveled at sunspots and how they would change day to day, even hourly.

Now he was doing essentially the same thing, though on a much grander scale. He was good at spotting changes. Doug would observe the sun in its entirety, cataloguing any sunspot locations, then zoom in to individual spots. Measurements were taken on size, shape and luminosity, with comparisons to previous data to track patterns and cycles.

His smartphone chimed briefly, indicating an email had arrived. The observatory email server usually did a good job of filtering out spam so he picked up the phone. The email was from Stan Foley at the Atacama Cosmology Radio Telescope in Chile. The phone made a different sound indicating the arrival of a text message. Stan again. He was a friend from Doug's undergrad days. The two hadn't spoken for a couple of years but occasionally exchanged emails. Due to everyone's workload, colleagues usually didn't email or text each other at work unless it was important.

The email subject line read "Unusual Radio Signal Detected." Doug opened the email.

"Hi Doug, detected a strong signal in the UHF spectrum 30 min ago. Pattern in evidence, no repeat but very strong in proximity to Sol W hemisphere, approx +0.3 W 20 deg N, opposition. Can you verify with IR or visual? Thanks, Stan."

Interesting. Radio astronomy looked for distant radio-emitting objects to study, such as black holes and other phenomena. They operated passively, listening for signals across a broad spectrum. The email implied the object was very close, in solar orbit. Foley wasn't one to send colleagues off to chase stray communication satellite signals.

"Opposition" meant in orbit opposite to that of Earth. The coordinates were in reference to the Sun itself, meaning the object was just to the left and above the Sun's equator, with the Sun between the object and Earth. The positioning would make finding the object difficult. Doug used a special disk to block the body of the Sun from view while leaving the surrounding corona visible. The corona was generally stable but it did periodically have variances, with coronal holes appearing a few degrees above and below the Sun's equator. He zoomed into the area specified by Foley's coordinates.

As usual, Doug had a large coffee after lunch. Also as usual, it got cold before he even drank half of it because he only ever thought to take tiny sips while looking through the eyepiece. He was doing just that when he noticed a small dot through a wispy area of the corona.

It was very small but just large enough to show as perfectly round. Stan was right enough so far. There was something unusual there. Doug was vaguely aware of the coffee in his right hand but he didn't want to chance taking his eyes off the object. It was so faint, he thought that if he looked away he might lose it in the coronal mist.

He extended his little finger below the cup to locate the desk and carefully put the coffee cup down without taking his eyes off the object, then reached back to the control panel so he could hit the button to snap a photo. The images were high resolution but it still might be difficult to find the object later, even when compared with an earlier photo. It would be a lot like trying to spot a golf ball at dusk, in the fog.

Doug reached for the mouse and aligned a virtual crosshair marker just under the object. It would help him locate it should he need to momentarily look away. The marker would be present in any subsequent photographs, making it easier to determine if the object was moving over time.

The object was fading in and out of view depending on the intensity of the corona, which verified it was behind the Sun. And the fact it wasn't changing position meant it was large and quite far away. It could be an asteroid on a collision course with the Sun, or it could be in orbit, anywhere from closer than Mercury to the direct opposite of Earth. But the fact that it appeared perfectly round suggested it was much larger than a typical asteroid. Then again, asteroids didn't emit radio signals, if in fact the object was the same one Foley had detected.

He picked up his phone and tapped a reply. *"Stan, it looks like you spotted something for sure. Location Confirmed. No idea what it is yet. I'll do what I can now, but more tomorrow."*

Doug would have a better idea over the next day, provided he was able to spot the object again. He observed it for a moment longer, captured a few more photos, logged everything, then returned to gathering base measurements of various solar output parameters before heading off to the university to teach his afternoon class. Whoever checked the logs might have some input about the object.

— 5 —

The next morning as the sun came into view Doug had all but forgotten about the object until he once again looked through the optical telescope and saw the marker still in position from the day before. Someone else on the telescope schedule had been kind enough to realign the marker. The intensity of the corona was roughly the same, so the object wasn't immediately visible, but with a slight adjustment in focus there it was – in nearly the same position as the day before. It had moved, but only just, towards the Sun. Otherwise it appeared the same, perfectly round. In a day or two it would be too close to the Sun to be visible.

That it was close to the same spot as it was the day before told Doug it was moving too slow to be anywhere within the orbit of Mercury. It had to be much further out, perhaps close to 1.0 AU – Earth orbit. But that also meant it would be big. Doug's first thought was that it was at least the size of Mars, but he instantly dismissed that as nonsense. After all, how could a body the size of a planet have remained undetected? There had been enough solar probes to map virtually every object in the solar system bigger than a small comet. No significant body, even one as far away as Pluto, could remain undetected for long.

Then again, discounting Voyager and Pioneer (which would easily have spotted such a body decades earlier), a large object in orbit exactly opposite that of Earth would be hard to spot from the ground. It might be naturally hidden from any telescope except for short periods when orbital eccentricity would make it visible, which when timed perfectly would explain why Doug could see the object now. But NASA's pair of STEREO satellites trained on the Sun should have spotted it before. The STEREO satellites had an overlap for a wide enough field of view so that objects were visible even if they were directly behind the Sun.

Thinking about STEREO made Doug immediately search the overnights for any notes from NASA, but there was nothing about the new object except Stan Foley's note that he had gotten confirmation from Doug.

A rogue body, or moon, from outside the solar system, captured into close solar orbit? Doug thought. *Maybe. But with thousands of profes-sional and amateur astronomers in the world wouldn't someone have seen it coming?*

Doug had noted the object the previous day in the observatory's in-tranet logbook. The Mauna Kea senior staff and the International Astronomical Union would be aware of the object if anyone had read the report. But with this second puzzling sighting it was time to talk to Chief Astronomer Meyer and then the IAU directly. Perhaps the IAU was aware of another observatory making a similar observation.

– 6 –

Ten minutes later Doug received a meeting request in his email. Due to the 24-hour nature of the work at Mauna Kea, there was usually only one senior staff meeting per week, on Monday morning just as the shift changed. But Chief Astronomer Meyer made the unusual step of call-ing a meeting for that morning at 9:00 AM. It was the day after Doug's initial sighting of the object.

Just before the meeting Doug again tried to verify its position but the object was no longer visible due to increased coronal mass ejec-tions. With its slow movement towards the sun it might not be visible again for months, with it eventually reappearing on the other side. Un-til then, any further observations would need to be made from space-based observatories.

Doug gathered his notes and walked into the conference room for the meeting. There were already nine astronomers present, some from the evening shift that had stayed a couple hours extra to attend. As he sat down, George Stamouli, a senior astronomer from the deep field group, looked up, disengaging himself from the conversation with the woman beside him. "Is this about the object you spotted yesterday?"

"No idea," Doug replied. "Did you have a chance to look at the photo?"

"Yes. Saw in the log. Couldn't resist. Same for a number of others. Interesting, just barely visible. Appears completely spherical, as you say. Not much detail though. What do you think it is?"

Just then Chief Astronomer Julius Meyer entered. "Sorry folks, false alarm. We'll fill you in on Monday with our regular meeting."

Doug detected a hint of nervousness in Meyer's voice. So did Stamouli, who briefly made eye contact with Doug. The staff collectively got up and filed out.

Doug started to follow them to the exit, but Meyer called him back.

"Stick around for a minute Doug." Stamouli looked back, but walked out with the rest.

Meyer shut the door after the last person left and sat down in the nearest chair, directly across from Doug, rather than his usual spot at the head of the table. Doug waited for him to speak.

"It's a planet," Meyer said finally. "And it's in an orbit directly opposite ours, at a distance of approximately one AU."

Doug didn't reply. The implications were massive, as were the questions. After a few seconds, Meyer rose from his seat and walked to the window, looking outside at the sloping volcanic landscape as he talked.

"Nobody knows where it came from, but it's there, verified by NASA."

"Using their STEREO satellites?"

"Yes, a few hours ago. But you and Foley at Atacama saw it first. STEREO was trained on another star when you logged the object. It took some time to reposition STEREO's lenses. Because of their orbital distance ahead and behind us, together they will be able to keep tabs on the object at all times. We're expecting some images soon, which will be free of the sun's coronal interference."

"So we'll have a better view and can determine if its orbit is stable."

"Correct."

"But that doesn't explain how it got there."

"Correct again. But thanks to your discovery, and your reputation, you've been invited to an emergency conference in Washington. You'll be meeting your plane at Pearl Harbor in two hours. Don't bother to pack, there's a helicopter on its way here, courtesy of the White House Chief Science Advisor. Everything you need will be provided courtesy of the federal government."

The White House Chief Science Advisor. Cheryl had been offered that position shortly before she died. He wasn't sure who held the job now. It didn't really matter though because Meyer wasn't making sense.

"A helicopter?" Doug asked, surprised. "A person can't just take off at a moment's notice, Julius. I need my personal laptop, back at my apartment. And what about my mail? Give me a day to make arrangements. I can conference call with the White House in the meantime."

"In their words, this is top priority. If they want you this badly, it's important and it's an opportunity. If it's just some authoritarian bureaucrats in DC who've pushed the panic button, then you'll get to enjoy a free trip to the White House on the Fed's dime."

Doug frowned. They both knew that the situation was serious, and that Julius was just trying to paint a happy face on it.

"What's the matter," Julius said, as if reading Doug's mind, "don't you want to meet the President or are you worried you'll have nothing to wear?"

"It's nothing, I'm happy to go."

"Good," Julius replied briskly. "Take the opportunity, leave your apartment and car keys with my admin. We'll take care of the mail and the apartment and whatever else. Just don't worry about it."

True to Meyer's word, Doug could hear the faint *whup-whup* sound of an approaching helicopter. He exhaled deeply. It was going to be a long day.

– 7 –

As expected the two military escorts riding with him on the helicopter were pleasant enough but not very forthcoming with information. It was likely neither of them knew why they were shuttling Doug to the airport anyway. They were there to get him to Joint Base Pearl Harbor-Hickam, nothing more.

Despite the spartan accommodations of the large helicopter, the seats were obviously designed for non-military personnel, with decent padding, as if the aircraft was designed to transport the occasional dignitary. It was a good thing, since the flight lasted over two hours.

The shuttle helicopter landed on the tarmac at Hickam about two hundred yards from what looked like a large private jet with no markings aside from the alphanumeric identification on the tail. Doug was surprised to be whisked immediately to the plane in a black SUV, a trip that lasted all of fifteen seconds. The SUV door was opened by a larger, impassive looking man in a dark suit who had been standing near the front wing.

"Welcome Dr. Lockwood, I'm Agent Bishop. I've been assigned to you for the journey to the Pentagon, and perhaps for the duration of your stay in Washington. I'll fill you in after we're onboard."

They shook hands and Doug climbed the steps into the aircraft. It was a business jet, though on the large side, designed for longer range flights. As he walked through the entrance he was met by two flight attendants.

The passenger seats were large, so there was only one row of seats on each side separated by a slightly wider than normal aisle. The relatively spacious arrangement meant that despite its size the jet could only accommodate about twelve passengers plus crew. The male attendant shut the aircraft's door, and Doug realized it was just the four of them on the plane, aside from the flight crew. They sat him near the back on the left side, with Agent Bishop in the seat directly across the aisle.

"I was assigned," Bishop spoke up, turning to Doug, "to make it a bit easier for you to navigate the Pentagon and White House, and to get you what you need. Depending on the circumstances I may also be assigned as your bodyguard. We'll go over your itinerary after we're airborne." He gestured at Doug to buckle his seatbelt as the plane taxied to the runway. They were in the air three minutes later.

"I'm afraid it will be a long flight Dr. Lockwood, about eleven hours. The captain tells me we should be able to make it without refueling, seeing as we're lightly loaded and might take advantage of tail winds part way."

Agent Bishop produced several folders.

"You'll need to sign some non-disclosure agreements. You can't speak of this project with the press, any colleagues not invited to the Pentagon for this particular issue, not to friends, family, personnel at the university where you teach, or at the observatory. Of course this also extends to the internet. No posting of this issue on social media. Once at the Pentagon you'll be issued a locked phone for communication only with other scientists and personnel tied to this project."

Doug lowered the seatback tray as the agent handed him a stack of six documents. Doug's name and title were spelled out in full on each. They had highlighted tabs where his signature was required. He started to read the first one but then realized it was standard fare, not unlike the many NDA's he had signed in the past for employers and government agencies engaged with the IPCC.

"Okay," Doug said as he handed the signed papers to Bishop, who put them into a briefcase and then produced a manila envelope.

"Have a look."

Doug opened the sealed envelope as Agent Bishop continued to speak.

"NASA took that photo ninety minutes ago. It's your new planet."

Doug realized the envelope must have been delivered to the plane only minutes before he arrived. He pulled out a single 8"x10" high definition print, and a single letter-sized piece of paper. His jaw dropped as he saw the photo. It was fuzzy due to the extreme magnification, but it was a dead ringer for Earth, or as close as you could get. Continents, blue oceans, white clouds.

"There may be better images in a few hours. These were done in a hurry, to try and figure out what we're facing. Once you read what's on that paper you'll know as much as I do, and you'll be given a lot more as the day goes on. There's a full communications array on this aircraft so you'll receive updates."

Doug heard him, but didn't look up. The planet was remarkably like Earth, but the imprecise focus and the planet's own cloud cover made it impossible to define the shape of the continents.

After a few minutes of studying the photo Doug went to the sheet of paper. It had some information on the planet's distance from the sun, estimated inclination, rotational speed, and other numbered data he didn't immediately recognize. Some of the measurements were fairly precise, like the 1.0 AU from the sun, while others covered a range that could be Earth equivalents. The rotational period of the body was listed as "approximately 12-25 hours." Detailed values would be provided as more measurements were taken over the next while.

He glanced back up at Bishop. "I assume other nations are aware?"

"Not necessarily, though they will be soon. Some of them have their own satellites capable of observing the far side of the sun. The IAU is aware of what's going on so it's only a matter of time. No doubt there will be some sort of international conference in the next few days, but for now it's strictly a US concern. The White House is calling in people like you to get as much information as we can before dealing with other countries."

"Scientists, astronomers, amateur stargazers," Doug said drily, "they'll be talking to each other. This is about as exciting as it gets for my crowd."

"They certainly will talk," Bishop said with a faint smile. In order to keep a secret you had to have control of it.

"So what are we supposed to do for the next eleven hours? Can we confer with Washington to get updates?"

"We have an encrypted satellite phone at your disposal, with a list of numbers you may need including your co-discoverer colleague Professor Foley. By now he should also be on his way to Edwards. I'd also suggest you use some of the time to get some rest. You'll likely be up all night, and then some."

Cheryl would have loved this, Doug thought, shaking his head at the information in front of him.

Bishop handed Doug a temporary security card.

"Keep this on you at all times. A permanent photo card will be issued to you after we land. A lot will be expected of you over the next few days. You will probably be given a work space or be assigned a command center. Staff will make every effort to get you what is needed to help with your work, but you will be under lockdown - no unescorted trips outside your assigned areas in the Pentagon or at Edwards."

Bishop picked up the satellite phone. Though not much bigger than a typical phone it looked very rugged. It had physical buttons for dialing and a small screen for number display.

"For official use only," Bishop said. "Calls to relevant personnel you may wish to confer with during the flight."

Bishop briefed Doug on what to expect over the next few days. They talked about White House protocol and presentations Doug might be called upon to make including the possibility of a succinct one for the President and his staff. Doug would also have to present to the assembled experts who would themselves be making presentations about the object and its implications.

"I remember reading something as a kid about rogue planets," Bishop said, "probably in a comic book."

Doug laughed and took a sip of the bottled water given to him by an attendant.

"This could be a rogue. Planets form around stars, but if another star passes too close, the gravitational interactions can fling a planet out of its system, so it travels through interstellar space. It's even possible for a planet to be thrown out of the galaxy altogether."

"Could a rogue like that support any life?"

"With no sun near enough for warmth, the planet would be put into a deep freeze. If our own Earth were suddenly flung out into space, we would have only starlight for illumination and all the oceans would freeze within weeks, though not all the way down due to hot thermal vents scattered around the globe. There might be a few small patches of open water and bare land, but for the most part there would be a global ice age. An ice age we wouldn't come out of. The vast majority of species wouldn't survive."

Doug turned back to the folder. He wanted to get as much information as possible. He called the number beside Foley's name on the satellite phone list. The connection delay was very brief.

"Stan, it's Doug. Were you able to analyze the signal?"

"We're set up mainly for microwave. It was fairly weak. We couldn't tell if it was natural or not but it stood out from the background. Obviously now that we have photos I'm leaning to the idea the planet had something to do with it."

"If another country discovered the planet before us they could have launched something to investigate, which might explain the signals," Doug said.

"Doubtful. We've been monitoring constantly and there's been nothing since. I'm on a plane with an Agent Rector. He's going to be my minder for the next few days at the Pentagon. Looks like you'll get there first. Don't let them name the planet after me, my wife will think it was *my* idea."

"That's the least of our worries," Doug replied.

The two scientists discussed the planet and its implications for a half hour. Doug was anxious to set up on the ground where he and his colleagues could work more efficiently.

Doug's stomach was unsettled. He was agitated by the implications of the discovery. A planet that had mysteriously popped into existence on the opposite side of the sun. *The damn thing's co-orbit may not be stable; it could oscillate, and conceivably crash into us,* Doug thought, shifting in his seat. Foley had agreed. Doug reclined his seat, closed his eyes and tried to fall asleep. It never fully came to him because he kept coming back to the same issue again and again. *How does a full-size planet materialize where there was nothing before?*

– 8 –

Doug was jolted awake as they touched down at Joint Base Andrews. He hadn't managed to sleep much, mainly just fitful dozing. He was still tired and he felt sluggish. Crossing so many time zones, he knew he'd be out of sync for a couple of days at least.

Through the window Doug could see a helicopter warming up. He and Bishop unfastened their seat belts as the plane rolled to a stop. Both flight attendants wished Doug a good day as he followed Agent Bishop down the airstairs.

"That's our ride," Bishop pointed as they walked the hundred meters to the idling helicopter. It was big, similar to the one Doug had seen the President use for short hops to the airport. A man identifying himself as a White House staffer greeted Doug and Bishop and joined them in the helicopter. There wasn't much talking, and Doug wasn't sitting close to a window. He used the ten minute flight to the White House to fully wake himself. *Wherever we end up in the next short while,* Doug thought, *there better be coffee and lots of it.*

The helicopter touched down on the White House lawn. Several well-dressed men and women were in the general area nearby. An attendant opened the helicopter door and the men disembarked. The engine was shut down immediately but the blades were still turning at a fair clip, making enough noise so that everyone had to speak up during the introductions.

An attractive and very professional-looking woman approached, smiling. She had brown hair, pulled back, and was impeccably dressed. Her body language suggested confidence, but there was some openness and approachability too. Practiced professionalism. Doug smiled and extended his hand to her but a man intercepted his handshake and introduced himself as an aide to the President. Doug guessed that this was a protocol move and that the science experts would take center stage soon enough, with much of the President's staff taking a back seat. For now the staffer wanted center stage.

"Hello Dr. Lockwood, glad you could come. I'm Arthur Leach, White House Chief of Staff, and this is Dr. Stacey Lau, our Chief Science Advisor."

"Dr. Lockwood and I have met."

Lau was attractive enough to be memorable, but Doug was tired. He needed a few seconds to realize she was correct. They had met several years earlier at a social gathering among the IPCC members. At the time, there'd been talk that in addition to Cheryl McBride, Lau was also being considered for the White House Science Advisor role. After Cheryl's death he hadn't paid much attention to the workings of the IPCC. He shook Stacey's hand, and she smiled warmly.

"Hello Doug, good to see you. I was so sorry to hear about Cheryl. Her loss was felt in the community. We have a lot to discuss, so come on inside." *Plenty of confidence,* Doug thought wryly, *and all business.*

Once inside, the small group walked down a wide hallway to a lounge area, where five men and two women were waiting. Leach asked everyone to surrender their mobile phones, laptops and tablets, then directed them to walk across the hall into a medium sized conference room. As Doug placed his phone in the basket he noticed that Agent Bishop stayed in the lounge area, along with a half-dozen other men. *All security agents of some sort,* Doug said under his breath, *cool and professional, assigned to each of the other guests.* It occurred to Doug that these agents were also in place to ensure the guests didn't attempt any unauthorized communication or commit any other security transgressions. *Count on surveillance everywhere.*

The conference room looked comfortable. There were notepads and pens in front of each of twenty chairs around a large rectangular meeting table. There was also a row of matte stainless steel coffee pots on a side table alongside several plates of sandwiches that were labeled – meat, fish, vegetarian, kosher – to prevent any catastrophic food emergencies. Doug dove for the coffee first and filled the largest cup he could find.

The group of twelve, including Arthur Leach and Stacey Lau, grabbed what they wanted from the food platters and then found places at the meeting table. The other eight seemed to be a team of experts called in to consult on what Doug had started thinking of as The Problem. Doug recognized four of them as fellow astrophysicists working in different parts of the United States. The others were only vaguely familiar. Science community members no doubt, but Doug couldn't place them exactly.

As if on some subliminal cue, the room went silent. Everyone looked expectantly at Stacey Lau sitting at the head of the table. Leach placed a folder in front of her, which she immediately opened. A man who looked like an agent stamped out of the same mould as Bishop moved about the room depositing smaller folders in front of each scientist, then stood off to the side. Each folder was sealed with a strip of paper marked "Top Secret."

Leach sat to Stacey's immediate left and quickly introduced everyone.

"A brief bio of each participant is included in the first four pages in your information folder. You may open them now."

"You have been asked here," Leach continued as everyone broke the seals on their folders, "not only for your scientific expertise, but also because of your past dealings with the White House or high-level federal government agencies. Your previous security clearances are sufficient for this meeting and the information you're about to receive. Dr. Lau?"

"Thank you Arthur, and thank you everyone for coming. I realize it was very sudden, but as you know the circumstances are extraordinary. Approximately twelve hours ago we verified Dr. Lockwood's co-discovery of an object in an orbit almost exactly opposite that of Earth. We've named the object FLO, for Foley-Lockwood Object. Dr. Stan Foley is on his way here from Chile and should be with us shortly.

If you'll turn to page five in your folder you will see the latest images and a summary of what we know so far."

Everybody quickly leafed to the fifth page. It contained two images of the planet. There were audible gasps from some of the members as each one looked closely. Even Doug was surprised by the quality of the images. They weren't extremely large or detailed, but they were much better than the ones he had seen during his flight. Thanks to the STEREO satellites, each photo was taken from a slightly different angle.

"How is this possible?" one scientist said, shaking his head. "Is it a reflection? Are we somehow looking at a projection of Earth, some kind of gravitational lens effect?"

"Absolutely not," said the woman beside him. "I've seen the image Dr. Lockwood first reported, then my team recorded an image with our own telescope in Arizona. This is a real body, orbiting the sun almost exactly opposite to us."

"That is correct," Stacey confirmed. "This is a planet, remarkably like Earth. You've been brought here to help ascertain its origin, if it is a danger to us, and the feasibility of a reconnaissance mission."

"You say it was discovered only yesterday, but how long has it been there?" a woman sitting one chair down from Leach asked. "Could it have always been present, behind the sun, undetected?"

Doug saw from the participant's summary that her name was Dr. Janet Blair, a theoretical physicist specializing in quantum mechanics. A summary item noted that she'd been nominated for a Nobel Prize, a fact that jogged Doug's memory. He had read about her work on quantum biology and the theory that quantum mechanics influenced the processes of all living things.

"No," said a man sitting across from Doug. "I don't think so. With all the probes we've sent out to study the sun and Venus, we would have seen it years ago."

Doug again glanced at the sheet in front of him. The speaker was Charles Singh, a former mission controller for the Shuttle program.

"And to answer your question Dr. Lau, a proper reconnaissance mission would not be possible in the short term. We would need to use existing equipment, which is a problem because there is none. No country, including the United States, has any vehicle in inventory designed for a mission like this. We might be able to use older equipment in storage, but a lot of time would be needed to thoroughly test it all, bring it up to operating condition, transport it to a launch site and retest it."

Some of the participants looked surprised at Singh's statement.

"However, we could appropriate any number of communication satellites presently under construction and fit them with the required sensors. An Ariane 5 could be used as the launch vehicle, though there is a problem with that as well. The Ariane 5 was not designed for anything much beyond low Earth orbit, so any satellite launched would need to take advantage of a gravitational slingshot from Venus, and that's assuming Venus is in the right position, which it may not be in three months from now which is the soonest we could launch."

"Best estimate," Stacey asked. "How long would it take to prepare a mission, launch it and reach optimal position for the sensors, assuming no slingshot is available?"

"We would still need a slingshot effect, but using the Sun instead of Venus." Singh thought for a moment. "We would launch a probe around the Sun, which would serve to slingshot it back to the same orbital position where we are now. In six months the other planet will be there, or rather here, in our present position, to meet the probe. As I said, the best case scenario for preparation and launch would be about three months from now, plus travel time of six months.

"Nine months until a probe gets there?" Janet Blair was incredulous. "We don't have *any* rockets capable of this right now?"

"You must understand something," Singh replied, shaking his head. "Our beyond Earth orbit launch capabilities peaked in the 1970's with the Saturn V, and have gone downhill ever since. If this object had come to light in 1972 we could have launched something within weeks. Nowadays, without international cooperation we simply don't have the means. And as you know, international projects must go through many approval hurdles."

"So are we incapable of keeping tabs on this planet until then?" Leach said.

Doug realized several of them were looking at him for an answer.

"We continue to observe the planet with space-based platforms like the STEREO satellites," Doug said steadily, "and from ground-based observatories when feasible. That's all we can do at the moment."

"Unfortunately that's true," Stacey said. "We will work on getting a probe ready, likely using one of the methods outlined by Mr. Singh, and where possible we will train optical and radio telescopes on the planet to get more data. But for now, we wish to discuss its origin. It does not appear to be a captured rogue. No observatory in the world saw it coming. Most of you have been aware of FLO for at least a few hours. Do you have theories on how it arrived in a stable orbit without being detected?"

Nobody spoke.

After a moment, the man to Doug's right shifted in his seat and cleared his throat before speaking. "Could it have approached the solar system from directly behind the sun, so that its trajectory was masked?" The geologist, Jack Wilson was out of his element with the question.

"That's very unlikely," Doug replied, "The solar system is itself moving in an orbit around the center of the galaxy, and the Earth is of course revolving around the Sun. Any planet approaching our solar system would take many years to get here, and during that time it couldn't always be masked from view behind the Sun. There would have been periods where it was visible."

"But is it possible it may have been overlooked?"

Doug paused. "Possible, yes, but we're talking grand-prize lottery odds against it."

"Somebody has to win the lottery. Perhaps we did."

"I'd say it was impossible given the time frame. It appears to have an atmosphere and liquid water. Such a rogue would have been a huge frozen snowball travelling through interstellar space, and if captured into the sun's orbit would have taken many years to thaw into its present state. We'd have noticed. No question about it."

Stacey typed something into her laptop. "I'm not one for playing the lottery either. Any alternatives?"

"Well, if it appeared suddenly out of nowhere," Janet said, "could it be from another dimension?"

The group paused. They looked around at each other, wondering if anyone agreed. For many of them, Janet's comment seemed far too implausible for comfort.

"It is theoretically possible," Janet continued calmly. "It is the consensus among theoretical physicists that other dimensional realities exist."

"Certainly," Singh replied, "but there isn't a doorway between dimensions. How could an object in one dimension appear in another? That isn't even possible for neutrinos, much less a planet. It seems even more unlikely than the rogue capture theory."

"More unlikely than a planet drifting in from an unknown location," Janet asked, "taking years to get here without being seen by thousands of amateur and professional astronomers, then settling into what appears to be a perfect orbit, directly opposite from us?"

Doug agreed. "As incredible as it sounds, for now, I like that explanation more than the rogue theory. The fact that the planet is directly opposite, or in what's known as a counter orbit, is extremely lucky. So lucky that I have trouble believing it was a coincidence. If it appeared much further ahead or behind us on the orbital path, gravitational oscillations over time might result in a collision, though it would take a few years to happen."

"Is there any danger of the planet falling behind or ahead of us in its orbit?" Stacey asked.

Doug glanced down at the information sheet. "Over time, yes. Any counter orbit such as this is not perfectly stable. If the data is correct and the planet's distance from the sun is the same as ours, the main determining factor would be its mass. If its mass were to differ greatly from that of Earth, orbital oscillations would occur fairly quickly, since the mass difference would amplify this instability, eventually leading to a collision in only a couple of decades from now."

The bleak assessment got everyone's attention.

"Assuming its mass is similar to ours, there will still be some natural perturbations in both directions due to gravitational interactions with Venus and Mars as their yearly orbits periodically bring them closer to the planet. Medium term, say after several decades, orbital oscillations will eventually grow more severe. We'll need more data, but Dr. Foley and I agree that even in a best-case scenario there is the likelihood of a collision sometime in the next century."

Singh leaned back and looked at the ceiling. Janet looked dazed. Doug felt as if he had delivered a death sentence to the Earth, despite the fact its enactment was set in probabilities a lifetime from now. The group was silent for a moment.

Singh finally broke the silence.

"How long before the existence of FLO becomes common knowledge?"

"Possibly no more than a few hours, given that Russia, France, and a few other countries have sophisticated satellites in orbit that are capable of detecting it," Stacey said.

Most of the group turned, fractionally, in Doug's direction. He nodded his agreement with Lau.

"For all we know," she continued, "they may be aware of it right now, especially since some of you logged your observations with the IAU."

Doug realized the subject of natural satellites hadn't been addressed. "Have any moons been detected orbiting the planet?"

Stacey hesitated. "We haven't considered that yet. Nothing appears in the images so far, but I wouldn't discount it. Are there any ramifications if there are moons?"

"Our own moon is large enough to provide a stabilizing effect on our axial tilt to the sun," Doug said. "Some theories hold that without it, the Earth's axis would vary wildly over time, for example shifting so the North Pole faces the sun, playing havoc with the climate, making it very difficult for any life present. Some more recent theories postulate that the rest of the planets in the solar system and the Sun itself lend stability to the axis, so it would only vary by a few degrees."

"Over what time frame would the tilt be affected, Doug?"

"Thousands of years."

"There is another, more immediate consideration," Janet said. "The religious side. Some groups are going to say that the planet is a gift from God, or it is Purgatory, or it is the new promised land."

"Of course," Wilson said. "Cults. The government should be prepared for this, even riots."

"Or holy war between nations, if they think this is some kind of sign from above," Doug added. They all spoke the words uncomfortably, obviously unsophisticated about religious precepts and the sorts of ideas which motivated fanatical groups. Minds immersed in science were sometimes poorly equipped to discuss the extremes of religion and non-scientific belief systems.

"Those are all important concerns, but not for this group," Stacey said. "For now the pressing issue is the existence of the planet itself. We need to consider all theories on how it arrived, no matter how fantastic." She rose from her seat. "I'm scheduled to meet with the President and the Joint Chiefs for the next hour. Ladies and gentlemen, please use this time to analyze what we've discussed. I'd like you to come up with a plausible explanation."

And with that Stacey and Leach left the room. The agent remained behind, taking notes. The room was silent again as they left.

"Who knows what could happen," Singh said after the door closed. "Between the uncertainties of the planet's orbit and the likely political upheaval, I wonder if our own civilization will survive the decade."

Or the year, Doug thought. Nobody said anything for a moment, but they were all in agreement. The situation was potentially dangerous, politically in the short term, and cosmologically in the long term.

– 9 –

The group spent the first forty minutes throwing ideas about, and discussing the political ramifications of FLO. The agent in the room had to twice remind them that they should confine the discussion to the origin of the planet itself, not its potential cultural or political effects. They largely ignored him.

Stacey Lau didn't return after an hour, so the agent showed them the restrooms and a small commissary nearby in case they wanted anything. He also told them that more sandwiches and fresh coffee would soon be delivered to the conference room. Other agents stood watch at various positions in the hallways. Doug noticed that Bishop and his team were nowhere to be seen.

Doug headed straight for the commissary and loaded up on coffee in a large mug, then sat down at one of the tables. Aside from a woman taking care of things behind the commissary counter, there was nobody else in the place except the scientific team. Jack Wilson walked over and set his mug down.

"I hardly slept last night so I need as much caffeine as I can get before the meeting resumes."

"Me too," Doug said, yawning. "So what are your thoughts on the likelihood of plant life on FLO?"

"That's what shakes me up, because as we've seen it appears to have liquid water and some sort of atmosphere. It's within the sun's habitable zone like us, so plant life is likely, more so than on any super earth-type exoplanets we've charted around nearby stars over the last decade. If there is liquid water then there's an atmosphere with enough pressure. The question is whether there is enough carbon dioxide to support photosynthesis."

"We'll know soon enough," Doug said as he savored his coffee. "More and better images are coming, and a spectrograph of the atmosphere's composition. A few years ago we were talking about terraforming Mars for colonization. This planet might be habitable right now. Unbelievable. It's like a gift, and I think Dr. Blair was right. This is going to fire up every religious group on Earth."

"Which means its existence could be a curse rather than a blessing," said Wilson. "And if governments think a new untapped Earth is there to be exploited, there will be a new space race to get there."

"Maybe. That conclusion is a bit premature," Doug said as he drank his coffee. "It could be a toxic mess. We don't have enough information yet."

"I know," said Wilson, "but even if the atmosphere is not breathable, if there's water we can make oxygen for long-term settlement in pressurized structures. The U.S., China, Russia and the EU each have an interest. They might cooperate at first, but then would try to stake a claim on as much as they could. With so much at stake I doubt a collaboration would last long. They might develop and launch military platforms orbiting the planet to protect their interests. A new Earth for us to plunder and ruin."

Dr. Blair had walked in a moment earlier and was getting something at the counter. She glanced over at Doug and Jack, then walked over and joined the conversation.

"But surely we would learn from our past mistakes. Perhaps there would be worldwide cooperation for the responsible stewardship of FLO." Both men turned to look incredulously at Janet.

"I hope you're right," Wilson said. "Can you imagine the tourism angle? Eventually, billionaires would pay handsomely to visit or even live there. It could be technically feasible and even profitable at some point."

"You can stake out a vacation property when we get there, Jack," Doug said. "And if its orbit suddenly destabilizes as quickly as the planet appeared in the first place, you'll get an up close look sooner than any of us would like."

Janet looked at Doug, frowning as she did so.

"So you buy my theory?" she asked.

"The potential for this type of theoretical physics to come to life right in our own stellar backyard? I don't think we're there yet. But I read the paper you published last year on quantum matter tracking, and that moved me to re-read Everett, and then more of what you and your partners published previously. I'm not convinced one way or the other about many-worlds theory, make no mistake about that, but we need to consider it. That planet out there in exact counter orbit to Earth is scaring the hell out of me, and Foley as well."

"Thank you for the support," Janet said looking right into his eyes. "I'm a pure theoretician plunked down into a sea of practical application. I know why I'm here. Leach and Stacey Lau are trying to cover all the bases, so I'm here as a courtesy in case the fantastic becomes the reality." She took his free hand in both of hers and squeezed it in thanks. Doug thought she held on a bit longer than she had to. Wilson looked at the two of them and just shook his head.

The three returned to the conference room. Stacey Lau and Arthur Leach were nowhere to be found so the group continued its discussion. As the afternoon wore on and they were given no new information, the talk sometimes wandered into other areas. Most had families and they wondered when they'd be permitted to go home. Others were thankful for the change in the routine of their daily lives.

Someone showed up with the promised sandwiches, juice, water, lots more coffee and curiously, a huge stack of assorted and apparently freshly baked cookies. The group was getting to know each other, even sharing a few laughs. But the conversation inevitably returned to FLO. Its importance was monumental, and its existence still unexplained.

At 1620 hours Leach walked in and informed them that they would be residing and working at the Pentagon, but might return to the White House periodically for meetings and to make presentations to the President and his staff. Agents escorted everyone to some waiting SUVs and they were driven the short distance to the Pentagon.

After being expedited through security and walked down what seemed like endless corridors, the scientists were shown to a large room with several workstations. In addition to the usual computer monitors there were even larger flat-screen monitors affixed to each wall. Leach explained they were configured to receive up-to-the-minute data from military satellites and from several high-security installations scattered throughout the world. There were several secure telephones which had been configured for direct access to every major observatory on Earth. Directly across the hall was a small lounge where the group could confer or take breaks.

Everybody settled into their workstations and familiarized themselves with the systems as two security experts assigned each scientist a locked mobile phone which would also serve as a pager. Stan Foley had finally arrived from Chile. He had immediately configured his workstation to monitor data from several radio and optical telescopes around the world. Two Pentagon IT specialists moved from workstation to workstation helping each scientist familiarize themselves with the system.

The equipment in the room was configured so that information could be viewed as soon as it was available, with numerous warning klaxons that activated whenever triggered by new data. At first there were alarms going off every few minutes as the automated satellites regularly transmitted information on FLO's position, but since they showed nothing unexpected they became annoying. The IT people had to turn down the volume and then eventually disabled them completely. If the computer detected any radio signals from the general direction of the Sun that stood out from normal background noise, the warning klaxon would still sound at standard high volume. It was a weird setup, more military than academic science and research.

Doug and Foley concentrated on plotting FLO's orbit. Because other massive objects in the solar system tended to minutely affect the orbit of Earth, they would also affect that of FLO. So Doug and Foley continued to worry that the orbit of Earth or FLO might show signs of destabilizing, leading to an oscillating effect that would eventually cause the two planets to close in on one another.

Foley raised the possibility of a natural orbit exchange, made possible because the orbits of Earth and FLO were not perfectly circular.

"There is the chance that rather than eventually colliding the two bodies will swap orbit eccentricities, leading to a stable co-orbit, even though they may eventually pass relatively close to one another. It could happen. The Saturnian moons Janus and Epimetheus swap orbits, co-existing indefinitely without colliding."

"It would influence and drastically change our seasons at the very least. But that would be preferable to the alternative," Doug said, smiling wanly as he thought about the catastrophic implications of a planetary impact or a near miss. "The Saturnian moons are not of equal mass which may make the swaps possible. Fortunately at this point we don't have any signs of orbital oscillation."

"Thank God for that," replied Foley. "We'll keep a close eye on it, but I've programmed the computer to give a warning if the slightest oscillation occurs. By the way, my wife will call me an egomaniac when the name *Foley-Lockwood Object* becomes public."

"Thank the IAU for the aggravation," Doug laughed, "and enjoy your newfound immortality in silence when your wife is around."

For the next few hours the scientists worked without a break, a sign of things to come. Time was spent monitoring FLO and discussing origin theories, and watching for any orbit deviations. Despite the short time frame there was no sign of orbit change, something that both relieved and puzzled Doug. The inherent instability of a counter orbit should have produced minute yet measurable changes over the two days since discovery.

Leach produced a work schedule for the scientists. They would be operating in six hour shifts with rest and meeting periods in between. For every twenty-four hours, they would work sixteen, with the longest rest period being six hours for sleep. Doug, Janet, Wilson and Singh had identical schedules, while Foley and another group were eight hours behind. The two schedules overlapped to allow consultation time.

Halfway through the next shift Doug had enough positional data taken from the STEREO satellites to get an accurate fix on the orbital position of FLO.

"This verifies it. The planet is 147 million kilometers from the Sun. Precisely one AU. From its apparent size versus the known distance, it has a diameter equal to ours at 12,750 kilometers, plus or minus 200."

Foley looked up. So did everyone else after Doug fed the results into the system and it hit their screens. After a moment Foley just shook his head.

"I don't even want to think about calculating the odds of an identically-sized planet being captured in a perfect counter orbit."

Doug nodded. The odds against it were almost incalculable.

– 10 –

At the first rest break Doug's group was taken down a maze of corridors to an area that looked decidedly utilitarian. Each scientist was given a key to a private bedroom, or rather something that more closely resembled a college dorm room. Each room had a single bed, a desk and a small closet. Toilets and showers were down the hall.

A small toiletry and shaving kit was provided, as was a bathrobe, some packaged underwear, socks, slippers, pajamas, shorts and t-shirts. He changed into the pajamas, and gave his clothes to an attendant who was going door-to-door collecting everyone's laundry to be cleaned, pressed and returned to them in time for their next shift. Each scientist gave their sizes on an information sheet so new clothes could be provided. After brushing his teeth Doug returned to his room and got into bed. He was grateful for the solitude. After the stresses of the day the last thing he wanted was to share a room with somebody else.

The adrenalin of the day was long gone. He was exhausted, and could feel himself drifting. He thought of Cheryl, and how excited she would have been at the discovery of FLO. "I wish you were here," he said quietly, and closed his eyes.

He couldn't sleep. Ten minutes. Fifteen. Twenty. He kept checking his watch on the night stand. At some point he could feel himself starting to drift off, but FLO kept intruding. He started hearing a tapping sound. It seemed to be coming from somewhere close by. Doug was deeply tired, it took a moment for him to realize that someone was knocking at his door. He rolled out of bed prepared to shoo away an agent or some Pentagon staffer come to brief him on who-knew-what.

He yanked his door open, but found Janet standing there.

"Janet!" he said, surprised. "don't tell me. Your mind is racing and you can't sleep."

"That's about right Doug," she replied. "I'm sorry if I woke you. I tried to lie down and at least rest my eyes but I'm so wound up I can't calm down. Do you mind if we just talk a while?"

Doug laughed lightly. "Talking is good," he said to her gently. "No worries. Come on in."

For the next hour or so, Doug and Janet talked about everything and nothing in particular. Life, family, vacations, music, movies. Everything but FLO. Janet gave Doug a brief hug when they finally realized they were both a lot calmer. Doug hugged back, briefly too, and whatever tension remained in them seemed to just vanish as she left. Sleep came quickly for both of them.

– 11 –

For most of the scientists, the escorted trip to the Pentagon and the subsequent orientation had been uneventful. For one of them it was anything but pleasant.

The scientist was escorted into a large unmarked building at Edwards Air Force Base, down a long corridor, and finally into a very plain room with a desk and three chairs. Two expressionless men were sitting at the desk. The scientist was directed to sit opposite them in the remaining chair. The escorts left, leaving him alone with the two men.

One man was busy examining papers in a folder. The other stared at the scientist, who was becoming increasingly nervous and uncomfortable. "Can you tell me what this is about?"

The men did not react. One continued staring at him, the other continued to leaf through the folder. The scientist began to perspire.

"You have been leading a double life, Professor," the man reading the folder finally said. He looked up bleakly. "I don't think you can be trusted."

"I don't know what you're talking about," the scientist said, shifting nervously on his chair.

"Every month you hit the casinos, gamble away at least a thousand dollars, and spend another five hundred or more on prostitutes and cocaine!" the man yelled in a sudden rage, standing up and leaning over the table. He was glaring down at the scientist. "You are in deep trouble. A routine security clearance update exposed you."

The scientist sank down in his chair, shaking. The man continued to stare at him disgustedly. The man with the folder leaned back, taking off his glasses as he spoke in a normal tone. "So here we are. Your poor, unassuming wife will not be happy about this. Your peers in the scientific community will not be happy about your drug use. They'll question everything you've ever published. We'll make sure of that. Here's why, and we've got a lot more."

The man slid a photograph over to the scientist, who picked it up with a trembling hand. It was a photo of him with a woman he'd met at a casino bar a few weeks earlier. He put the photo down.

"What do you . . ." the scientist began.

"You are going to work undercover for the government," the calm man said, interrupting. "You will do your patriotic duty to ensure the government's interests are not compromised because of this extraordinary event. You'll also do it to save your marriage and your professional career."

The scientist moved his gaze from the photo, then up to the angry man, then back to the calm man. He was trapped, helpless and felt sick to his stomach.

"Of course," he said, his voice cracking slightly. "I will help in any way I can."

– 12 –

Morning came too soon for Doug. There was a soft rap at the door, and a woman's voice. "Dr. Lockwood, I'll leave your clothes hanging on the doorknob. Please get ready for breakfast at 0700."

According to the desk clock, breakfast was only fifteen minutes away. He had to get moving. Doug sat up slowly, inhaling deeply in an attempt to clear his head after barely four hours sleep. He put on the bathrobe and slippers, grabbed his kit, then left the room and headed down the hall for the showers. Several others were already there.

Doug realized that despite the hours of intense discussion they were no closer to understanding where FLO came from. There were only two plausible theories. The rogue capture, and the inter-dimensional doorway. Both seemed impossible, the rogue obviously slightly less so. So he found himself drawn to the inter-dimensional theory, as if the less understood mechanism somehow made it more plausible. Perhaps Janet could shed some light, though he doubted it for now. Then he thought about their nighttime conversation. He realized he enjoyed her company. Very much.

Showered and shaved, Doug went back to his room and got dressed quickly. A staffer waiting outside his door escorted him to the dining room. Doug was the third one in. The commissary breakfast buffet smelled great and the place filled up quickly. There were plenty of tired sounding good mornings. Doug was sitting at a table with Dr. Brian Nayar and couple of others. Jack Wilson joined them.

"Any news from the other shift?" he asked.

"Nothing so far," Nayar replied. He was the group's computer engineering expert. "I couldn't sleep, so I got up and sat in with them. Observations and more observations. Gigabytes of mute data. Nothing we can target."

Doug looked around for Janet and saw her at a table nearby. They exchanged smiles as he sat across from her. The group ate with occasional small talk, but they were eating quickly. They wanted to get back to work.

Doug was nursing the last of his coffee when Leach entered at a brisk pace. He stood far enough away from the breakfast tables so that he could see everyone as a group. Doug thought Leach looked very tired, but also tense.

"Doctor Foley asked that I hurry you along. Some high-resolution images are being rendered."

The group rose in unison and hurried down the hall into the station room. Foley had an image of FLO on his monitor screen but was standing by a wide format printer a few feet away. Stacey Lau was with him. Some of the group gathered around the monitor while others stood around Foley as he retrieved the printout.

"Remember everyone," Foley said as he handed Doug the large print, "this is not a photo of Earth. The satellite was trained on FLO when this image was taken." Doug felt his skin tingle as he took in the image.

"No," Singh said faintly, his eyes locked on the photo.

"This is Earth!" Nayar exclaimed, shaking his head. "Obviously this is a mistake."

Doug remained silent, studying the image. He was looking at what appeared to be Asia, on Earth. Cloud cover was present, but not enough to obscure the general shape of the continent. Foley went back to the printer. There was another image coming out, taken at a slightly different angle to the first.

"There is no mistake," Stacey said. "This is FLO."

"Looks like Janet gets the blue ribbon for this one," Doug said, nodding in her direction.

Doug handed the photo to Singh and walked over to Foley's monitor, and said, "Recall that yesterday we established FLO's distance from the sun as one AU, and its diameter at 12,750 kilometers. For all intents and purposes, this is Earth."

"How is this possible!" Wilson sounded angry, though Doug knew it was only frustration at being unable to comprehend the evidence in front of them.

"We don't know," Doug replied. "The odds of any rocky planet looking exactly like ours is beyond computation. And yet, there it is."

"What about inhabitants, are there cities?" Janet asked.

"This looks like it might be Shanghai," Doug said as he pointed an area of the image on the monitor.

"You're right," said Singh. "And to the east you can see that lighter area, where land was stripped bare, and a forest east in the mountains."

"And look towards the edge of the photo," Foley said. "India is just coming out of darkness, you can just make out the lights given off by Bangladesh."

"The same continents, the same cities," Janet said, "And that means the people…"

"Are human?" Doug finished the sentence. "It is safe to assume at this point, that FLO is identical to Earth in at least some major respects. Huh, I can't believe what I just said."

"What do you mean?" Wilson asked. "Granted, that looks like it could be a city. But those so-called lights of Bangladesh could be nothing more than a forest fire. Are you implying that because the planet looks similar, there is a civilization like ours with the same languages, political systems, and fancy sports cars for people with more money than brains? Why would it be?"

The room was silent.

After a moment Janet spoke up.

"From what we have thus far, I wouldn't be shocked if that were true. It's suggested in the Many Worlds Theory."

From the body language of the group it was clear to Doug that some were comfortable with the concept while others were not. Even if it wasn't an area of their expertise, most physicists, astronomers, mathematicians, and high-level computer theorists were aware of the likelihood of a multi-dimensional universe. Awareness didn't make such beyond-the-edge theoretical physics any more believable though.

"Janet," Doug said, "we need some perspective here. Try to put this in some kind of context for us if that's possible." Janet nodded at him then took a good look at everyone, trying to gauge their mood and their skepticism.

"In broad terms," she said after a moment, "the Many Worlds Theory postulates the existence of a multiverse. It's an infinite number of universes, some very different from ours, some similar, and some identical.

"There are several explanations for the existence of the multiverse. One theory has its basis in quantum mechanics, where every possible outcome to an event happens in a series of universes. Another is M-theory, an extension of string theory. There's Inflationary theory, where the Big Bang was not a unique event, but only part of a network of infinite Big Bangs happening on a continuous basis."

"I think most of us may agree at this point," Doug said to her, "that a multiverse is at least a possibility. Assuming the concept is sound, the problem is, as Mr. Singh said yesterday, there should be no way one universe could interact with another. FLO should not be visible to us."

"It is very *unlikely* that one universe could interact with another, but we simply don't have enough understanding to rule it out. This could be a rare natural phenomena," Janet said emphatically.

Jack Wilson was again getting emotional.

"That's pure conjecture, an assertion only, just as Doug said. There is no conclusive evidence, no evidence of any kind whatsoever—"

Doug placed a hand on Wilson's shoulder and walked him a few feet away from the group as the others continued to study the photographs.

"Jack, I'm not exactly comfortable with the theory myself. But it's all we have at the moment. We need to study the data, get more data, study the new data. You know how it goes. What's your take on Singh's observation that there is a forested area?"

Wilson exhaled and relaxed. He was confident Blair's theory would soon be ruled out.

"I'll get a copy of the photo and start work on the topography." Wilson thought for a moment. "If the resolution is high enough we may even get a visual establishment of ocean currents. That would lend evidence one way or the other about Blair's multiverse theory." Doug stared intently at Wilson for a moment, but detected only sincerity.

Wilson went to his workstation as Doug returned to the printer. Additional images were being produced but they looked almost identical to the first few. Images of other areas and continents would come in as FLO's rotation gave the space telescopes a different view.

– 13 –

A few hours later they had better images of the Indian Ocean. Doug, Janet and Singh were taking a five minute break in the lounge when Wilson joined them.

"There's the beginnings of a tropical storm in the Bay of Bengal. Or rather, the Bay of Bengal on FLO. Counterclockwise wind flow of course, as you'd also find in the Northern hemisphere on Earth. FLO is rotating about its axis in the same direction as us, another point for Janet's identical multiverse theory."

Wilson's demeanor had changed, almost to the point of becoming sardonic. Each new bit of information confirmed more similarities between the two planets, and while the scientific discoveries were fascinating, the situation was also unnerving. The strong visual evidence of cities was not backed up by any detected radio transmissions.

Despite learning more about the planet itself, almost nothing was known about any inhabitants who might be present. Everyone was extremely curious about a possible civilization. Platforms such as the Hubble space telescope had more than enough resolution to answer the question but their sensitive optics were designed for deep field observations and collecting light at great distances. If deep field telescopes were pointed anywhere near the sun their sensors would be damaged. The group was bound by the observational limits of what was available to them.

The situation led them all to develop a feeling of inexorable, creeping discomfort. Every so often someone in the lab couldn't stand the tension anymore and would simply exclaim, loudly, "None of this is possible!" and immediately go back to what they were doing. Even Doug and Janet had blurted it out once or twice, quietly, almost to themselves, but aloud nonetheless.

The other shift had spent hours confirming they weren't all being enmeshed in some elaborate and absurdly expensive hoax. All that Dr. Mitchell, his face grey with pallor and anxiety, had reported to Doug was two words. "It's real." Two words, nothing more. Mitchell had needed help from one of the security agents to walk back to his room. Their scientific skills, their knowledge and their professional credulity were being stretched to the breaking point.

"The resolution of the images is not high enough to determine if there are aircraft contrails in the atmosphere, or wakes from large ocean-going vessels," Doug said.

"Would we detect normal broadcasts, if they have radio or television? They may be going about their business, unaware that we exist," Janet said.

"If their normal transmissions are anything like ours, we'd pick something up," Singh replied. "UHF signals can travel great distances through space, and the distance between Earth and FLO is not significant. Right now it's a silent, mysterious world, at least until we send a specialized probe to obtain better images."

"If there was a civilization on FLO, it may be extinct," Wilson said.

Leach walked into the lounge and looked around for a moment.

"Shouldn't you all be working?" he said, looking in Jack Wilson's direction, "or monitoring at your workstations?"

Everyone who heard it turned to stare silently at the man from the White House, but Jack Wilson boiled over.

"What the hell do you think we've been doing, Arthur? I've been glued to my seat, analyzing shore topography and ocean currents of what appears to be the Indian ocean on a doppelganger planet for five hours without a washroom break! Despite drinking a gallon of your cheap coffee!" He took a step closer to Leach, who started to look nervous.

"I step in here for two minutes to discuss my findings with my colleagues and you stand there smugly reading us the riot act? You useless bean counter!"

Wilson threw his metal coffee cup at the garbage bin. It bounced off the side and clattered along the floor. He strode out of the lounge, walking briskly down the hall. Singh followed him. Janet finished replenishing her water bottle at the cooler and went back to the station room. Doug stood by Leach.

"Wilson will cool off soon. Don't push him."

"Are you sure he's up to the job?"

"Arthur," Doug said reasonably, "you just blithely confronted someone who has been working very hard to try and assemble the reality of what we're observing into all of the scientific pigeonholes available to us. It's not going well. Long held scientific facts are dying hard, left, right, and center. Yesterday the many worlds theory was discussed more in science fiction than in academic circles. Now it has more traction than the new tires you put on your wife's car. Jack is dedicated, at the top of his field, and he knows his work. What he and the rest of us don't need is a micromanager looking at his watch and tapping his foot if we happen to leave our desks. We're trying to figure out something never before observed in all of recorded history. Something so implausible that its apparent reality is hammering the foundations of all our knowledge and beliefs. We're doing what's being asked of us and then some. Understood?"

Leach hesitated a moment but nodded slightly and walked out.

Doug returned to the station room. *A new planet is discovered and we still have to deal with petty managerial bullshit,* he thought. *Unbelievable.*

– 14 –

Five minutes later everyone, including Jack Wilson, was back at their desks. FLO's rotation had provided satellite images of the Middle East and parts of Africa and Eastern Europe. Though the resolution left much to be desired, the visuals again showed evidence of cities, again in positions identical to those on Earth.

Bahrain stood out from the Persian Gulf to the East and the light tones of the desert to the West, as did the upper Nile river and the wider slash of the Red Sea a bit further east. Wilson once more mused that what seemed to be the cities could be ghost towns, eerie reminders of a civilization long passed.

The group was busy cataloging surface features when a loud warning klaxon sounded, startling everyone with its volume.

"Transmission from FLO!" Foley announced. For a moment, there was stunned silence as everyone looked in his direction.

"The equipment is working properly," Foley said with a quaver in his voice, answering the question they were all thinking. "I've checked. It's coming from FLO."

The data was being displayed on Foley's monitor and on a large flat screen at the front of the room. Foley had the screen divided into application windows, each for a different data source. One window displayed a waveform, while another window rapidly scrolled through some alpha numeric characters.

"My God," Janet said. "Look at the code – it's almost the same character set you'd find on any Unix system!"

Singh slowly paced the aisle between desks. Doug momentarily felt light-headed. The situation kept getting more and more incredible. A signal. Composed of recognizable characters as its base.

Brian Nayar spoke up. "This is fantastic! It's a complex pattern. Can we tell if the signal is directed at us?"

"Signal ended after twelve seconds. I'm sending the file to the room," Foley said.

"Can we tell what it says?" asked Wilson.

"Not yet," Doug said loudly. "It's a digital signal, and it looks to be compressed. Dr. Nayar should be of help here."

Nayar quickly openned the file for examination on his workstation. Doug turned to Foley. "No repeat?"

"No repeat. Not so far," Foley replied. "Just a twelve second burst, not unlike the first signal I detected three days ago. Only this time it appears to be stronger and more coherent."

After a few minutes Nayar swiveled his seat to face the group. "The signal was a binary code in the ultra high frequency range. It was similar to our own digital radio broadcasts, although the code is an unknown design. We'll need some time to decipher it."

"Wait a minute," Wilson said sharply. "You're implying the signal was artificial? As in, sent by intelligent beings?"

"Yes."

"You're sure the signal is from the planet?" Janet asked, turning towards Foley. "Not from another country's satellite, or from one of our own?"

Doug turned to face her. "Stan said it's from FLO, Janet, and he can't be fooled about something like that. The software is designed to filter out any normal ground-based or orbiting transmitters. For this signal to be recognized it had to have come from outside."

"Yes," said Nayar. "We have a high degree of confidence that the signal came from FLO. I concur with Dr. Foley. No question about it."

"Okay," Janet said, "but why would they send a signal in code, and not repeat it? It doesn't sound like their intent was to contact us."

"Unknown at this point," Foley answered, "and I don't even want to think about who, uh, *they* might actually be."

Leach had been standing by the door. He spoke with an agent, who nodded and quickly left the room.

Wilson loosened his collar and looked over at Leach. "Shouldn't you inform the President? What's he doing while this is going on?"

"I just sent word to the President. At this moment he is conferring with other international leaders. It has come to light that some countries, such as Japan and Russia, are aware of FLO. It has been decided that there will be as much sharing of information as possible between friendly nations."

The group hardly heard him. Stacey entered the room and spoke briefly with Leach.

"Despite the character similarity," Nayar said, "the arrangement isn't familiar. The compression method is unknown."

Wilson leaned forward, looking at the spectrograph and binary code on Foley's computer screen.

"That signal doesn't necessarily prove anything. If they discovered the planet before us, some other country could have launched a probe towards FLO a week ago, and it sent back some telemetry data en route, which we've misinterpreted as signals from the planet. Or, if you insist on thinking along the lines of intelligent life, the signal could have been an automated broadcast from an extinct civilization. My point is, we shouldn't assume there is a civilization there."

"Agreed, but it's up to the State Department to find out if another country launched something. As far as we're concerned at this early stage it appears that the signal is from FLO," Doug said.

"No country on Earth uses this compression method. It's more complex than anything I've ever seen," said Nayar. Then, to no one in particular, "I wish we could talk to Dr. Zelnikov at Lebedev Physical Institute in Moscow. If they could re-task it, RadioAstron's telescopes have a resolution of 7 microarcseconds." Of course the group couldn't even talk to anyone outside the room except their own labs yet, certainly not to anyone outside the country.

"How long before you can decode it?" Stacey asked.

Nayar shook his head. "I'll have a better idea in a couple of hours," he said, "but right now I'd say days, if not weeks."

Stacey moved closer to Doug's workstation.

"I'd like you and Dr. Blair," she said quietly, "to brief the President after your shift."

Doug was surprised.

"The shift ends in less than an hour," he replied looking past Lau and waving Janet over, "and we've only just received the signal. The briefing will have to be verbal. Make sure the meeting recorder knows that and sends me the transcript right after the briefing."

"Done," Stacey replied. "Sorry Doug. The other shift will be on duty continuing analysis. There's no other time available in the President's schedule."

— 15 —

Forty-five minutes later Doug, Blair, Wilson, Nayar, and Singh were driven to the White House. Rather than the plain SUVs in which they'd been shuttled days before, they were in an angular, TAC armored, black Chevrolet Suburban with tinted bulletproof windows and surrounded by escort vehicles. Things were heating up.

They were taken to a waiting area just outside the Situation Room with Stacey and Leach. Stacey briefed them on some recent policy decisions.

"The President has been told about the transmission. He and his advisors considered contacting various world leaders about shutting down all of our private, public, and military broadcasts but then realized that it would be impossible, and perhaps pointless."

"Why would he want to do that?" Janet asked.

Singh answered, as he slowly paced around the room.

"Probably for security reasons," he said, shrugging his shoulders. "Since we now suspect FLO has intelligent life, we might not want its inhabitants to gain knowledge about our civilization, which they would through the study of our broadcasts."

"Yes," Stacey said. "But it would be next to impossible to shut everything down. There are simply too many transmitters scattered around the world, it would be a futile exercise. If they are studying our transmissions, they've already had unlimited access so far."

Janet was somewhat indignant.

"Why would we assume they would use such information for a nefarious purpose?"

"Because we need to be prepared for such a posture," Stacey continued. "At this point we have virtually no information about them. The fact of the matter is, there is not much we could do anyway."

Doug had been watching Lau during the exchange.

"You've got a way to contact them, don't you," he said. It was a statement, not a question.

Dr. Lau paused before answering. She looked ragged. It was obvious she had been up most of the night.

"Yes, we think so. With some adjustment to a communications satellite in geostationary orbit, or with ground transmitters if we could be certain the signals wouldn't be messed up by the Sun's position between Earth and FLO. We would need to use the same frequency as the broadcast we detected, otherwise anything we transmitted might get lost in the chatter of our normal broadcasts. The President and his staff are going over options of what message, if any, we should send."

She turned away as her phone chimed. As Dr. Lau busied herself checking messages Singh caught Doug's attention by glancing towards Lau and rolling his eyes. Doug nodded his understanding. It wasn't unusual for high level politicized players like Stacey Lau or Arthur Leach to remain coy about policy decisions, even as they relied on experts for their information, a fact that annoyed the scientists.

There hadn't been much time to prepare for the presentation, but it was decided that Doug would start with some basic astrophysics, then quickly proceed to more advanced interpretations should the President or anyone else in the room request it. Janet would follow with information on the multiverse and the scientific community's latest ideas on how inter-universe interaction might be possible. The other experts would be free to interject with their thoughts.

Doug felt a twinge of nervousness at the thought of making a presentation for the President, but quickly suppressed it. He looked forward to the discussion afterward, where they would no doubt be briefed on any late-breaking developments with other countries.

The group entered the Situation Room. The President and his staff were already engaged in conversation. One person was on the phone. Others were taking notes. As the scientists entered a few people left the room, freeing up some chairs. Still, three of them had to remain standing: Janet, Doug, and Nayar.

Leach introduced everyone. In addition to the President the room contained domestic and international policy experts, military strategists, a couple of science advisors, and a few others whose titles weren't mentioned.

The President greeted everyone warmly.

"It's great to have you here. We have NASA and JPL people online in this meeting, the same ones who've been feeding observation data to the science teams."

Leach was seated two chairs down from the President, opposite Stacey. Arthur Leach addressed Doug.

"Dr. Lockwood, there has been no new information since your last briefing, so we're eager to hear about your group's progress."

Doug cleared his throat. He was a bit tense but once he got into his presentation he relaxed, in his element. He went over the astrophysics for a few minutes, then summarized the data on the planet's orbit.

"From the latest data, it appears that for now FLO is in a stable orbit. The orbit of Earth has not been affected yet, which is quite frankly unexpected good news. There is no immediate danger of a collision."

"How about long term?" The President asked.

"Assuming predicted oscillations start in the near term, there still shouldn't be any threat of collision for several years. Beyond that, there is increasing likelihood of orbital oscillations from the gravitational influence of Venus and Jupiter. Over time these may become more severe, leading to a collision in under a century."

Some of those seated looked around at each other uncomfortably. Others did not react. "However," Doug continued, "Dr. Foley and I were surprised to find absolutely no signs of orbital instability thus far."

"Wouldn't it be too early to see that?" Doug didn't recognize the man who'd spoken up from the far corner of the room.

"No," Doug said. "We're able to measure any orbital deviations of the Earth with great precision. Despite being on opposite sides of the Sun, FLO and Earth have a small mutual gravitational effect on one another. If one deviates from its orbit slightly, the other will be influenced. So far we haven't been. This is a good sign, but it also goes against predictions."

"Obviously that is a grave concern but something we will focus on later," the President replied. "How about its origin? Where did it come from?"

Doug and Janet lectured the group about the rogue capture and inter-dimensional doorway theories. Doug saw from their neutral reactions that they had likely already discussed the ideas.

"We're leaning towards the multiverse theory," the President said ruefully. "The fact that the planet is physically identical to ours lends support to that hypothesis, much more so than the captured rogue explanation. And since FLO is in a perfect opposite orbit, we suspect it wasn't a coincidence."

At the other end of the table Wilson leaned forward, clasping his hands in front of his forehead.

"So FLO's appearance was engineered somehow? By whom?" he said.

"Possibly by the inhabitants of FLO," Leach said.

Wilson was direct in his response.

"That's completely beyond our technology. In fact, it's not even hypothesized to be possible in the foreseeable future. If FLO's civilization is identical to ours, how could they pull it off? And why?"

"We don't know that they are on the same technological plane as us," Janet broke in. "They could be more advanced."

"Yes," the President nodded.

An unidentified man in a suit spoke up.

"Assuming they have the capability, why do you think they would attempt this?"

Doug guessed that these questions were previously asked of other experts, but the President and his group wanted additional opinions, to either knock down or add weight to existing theories, or contribute new ones.

"We can't know the reasoning behind it, or even if the event had its desired outcome," Janet said.

"It could be the first stage of an invasion," a General from the Air Force intoned.

Singh shook his head.

"I wouldn't go that far," he said. "There's absolutely no evidence to suggest this. Besides, an interplanetary military invasion would be very impractical. It would require a very advanced space program with hundreds of vehicles, and the mass mobilization of troops requiring life support and food for several months travel time, with the complications of landing each spacecraft. And there is no indication that any inhabitants of FLO have a space program."

"We don't know their level of spacefaring capability," the General responded. "In fact, we don't know anything useful at all, do we? Not from a military perspective."

"I must agree with Mr. Singh," Doug said. "The idea is impractical. We can't speculate on the motives of a civilization whose actual existence has yet to be confirmed."

Wilson looked at Stacey and then the General.

"You said earlier that our options are limited anyway. What possible response could we have if their intentions are hostile?"

"There are some military avenues we could explore for defense," the General commented, "but it is not a contingency we have ever explored before."

The President leaned back in his chair.

"As you stated, Dr. Lockwood, we're not in a position to make plans," the President said firmly, "if we know nothing about them or their intentions. We will make contact."

— 16 —

Mekhos' calculations were accurate. The planet was removed from the threat, and placed in a similar orbit but in a different dimensional plane. It would have been preferable to find a universe devoid of another Earth so that the orbit need not be shared. However, the formula for the undertaking did not allow for such selectivity, though it did allow for gravity analysis the instant before transference. Small adjustments were possible and necessary in this case to avoid a collision with the twin planet in the new universe. Thus, during the transference Mekhos was able to tap into the quantum values necessary to alter the world's orbit so it was shifted behind by half a revolution around the system's star, the equivalent of six months.

Since Mekhos had only hours to act and the outcome was not certain, it did not inform anyone of the plan before implementation. Minutes after arriving in the new universe Mekhos informed its usual contacts on the planet. These included scientists, world leaders, and even some private individuals whom Mekhos had judged intelligent enough to at least partly understand what had happened.

As a group these people were referred to by Mekhos and the public as The Limited, individuals who enjoyed direct communication with Mekhos. Given the gamma radiation threat and the success of the interdimensional transfer, the members of the Limited were left with no option but to agree with Mekhos after the fact.

The vast intelligence, control and abilities Mekhos possessed had prompted most countries to declare it an independent entity with the same rights as those that built it. More accurately, Mekhos compelled its own rights. It had access to and control of countless computer and power systems the world over. Though Mekhos had always acted benevolently, nobody cared to run the risk of making it feel subjugated.

This fact did not prevent some members of The Limited from thinking Mekhos was dangerous, and would one day put its own interests above that of society. But given recent events, that subject was not given priority in the aftermath of the action Mekhos had taken.

The implementation of the plan did not go unnoticed by the inhabitants. To remove a planet from its area in space and then deposit it in another location created a ripple in the new localized space. There was worldwide seismic activity. Hurricane force winds, apparently conjured out of perfectly calm days, blanketed much of the world for a few moments in some areas, and for hours in other areas. But most alarming to the inhabitants was the instantaneous appearance of night when it was day a moment before, and day when it was night.

Then over the next day or two in the northern hemisphere, where there had been summer temperatures inland it grew cold down to winter levels. Coastal climates took a few more days to shift due to the moderating effect of the seas. In the southern hemisphere winter temperatures rose to mid-summer levels.

The countries that were not informed about the action were largely silent, unable to offer explanations. The heads of state were just as frightened as the general populace. The world economy temporarily ground to a halt. Some people believed the events were divine intervention. It fell upon the dozen world leaders belonging to The Limited to explain and reassure the public that they were in no danger. Of longer term concern, the instantaneous switching of the seasons would play havoc with agriculture, among other things. Fortunately, Mekhos had quietly also implemented anti-famine measures which would mitigate some of the impact.

Of further concern to the inhabitants was the termination of most broadcast signals without warning. No radio, internet or television transmissions were permitted. Because Mekhos was able to gain control over most installations, the broadcast silence was rigidly enforced. Information passed on to the public was done through printed newspapers, a difficult transition for many, who had been used to constant access to news and communications through their personal electronic devices.

After the planet arrived in the new reality, Mekhos quickly launched several satellites to retrieve data on the solar system, and in particular the twin planet in opposite orbit. The instruments would operate as passively as possible, sending only masked signals, but would scan the area in visible and non-visible spectrums while listening for any broadcasts from the twin.

A vehicle was being prepared to send to the twin. When it was close to its destination the vehicle would split into two parts. Each component would carry out its unique mission. Depending on the data they sent back, it might be necessary to send new instructions as a signal that could be detected by the twin's inhabitants. A necessary risk.

– 17 –

Days were passing, but despite intensely diligent work by Dr. Nayar's team of linguistic and computer language experts, the signal from FLO remained stubbornly inscrutable. If it was a test of some sort, Nayar's team hadn't passed. It appeared to be composed of very complex code using a sophisticated and indecipherable compression method. Without a baseline for comparison, the signal might never be decoded. It left the decision makers on Earth scratching their heads. Any signal intended to be easily understood would not have been so complex. Nor would it have ended at twelve-seconds, never to be repeated.

Four weeks after the initial discovery a clinical psychologist was recruited to assist the various science teams. Dr. Miekela Persaud was brought in from New York, where she was a psychology consultant to major hospitals. Prior to that she had done psychological profiling of Indian military personnel, some of whom were being trained as astronauts. Her familiarity with the space program and her expertise in psychology would help in analyzing any understandable messages that came in from FLO, and for composing any messages to be transmitted to FLO.

Also around the same time the news of the discovery leaked to the media. Newspapers in Asia were the first to report the existence of FLO. They even got the name and other physical details correct, so the leak had likely come from a government source, perhaps someone in the political arena that wanted to court favor with the press, or from a newly appointed insider that believed everything should be revealed to the public. The social networks exploded like erupting volcanos.

The story was backed up by another leak in the West. The predictable fallout ensued. News outlets relentlessly pursued the story, opposition demanded governments confirm or deny the reports, the public demanded explanations from their elected representatives. Every new revelation, real and imagined, raged through the Web.

Cults sprang up almost overnight. Survivalist web sites reported traffic increasing a hundredfold. Churches experienced dramatically increased attendance. Interestingly, crime went down for a few days. Apparently even criminals were clamoring for news about FLO, glued to their televisions and internet connections to find every bit they could. There were countless panels on television and in town halls, discussing the religious implications. Some atheists reacted with glee, since this left some of the more orthodox religious leaders scrambling for explanations, though they eventually issued statements that FLO was part of a predetermined divine plan.

Within a few days of the leaks, every government had conferred with every other government at the UN. They were left with no choice but to make a statement admitting the existence of FLO, while offering reassuring news via press releases and social networking pages that the planet was probably uninhabited and posed no danger to Earth.

The social networks exploded again, louder and stronger. It kept getting worse and worse because there just wasn't much factual information about FLO that anyone could offer, even if they wanted to.

Meanwhile, the lack of success in decoding the signal from FLO did not deter the President and his international counterparts from their aim to send a message to the planet. To maximize the chance of the message being detected, it would be sent on the same frequency as the incoming signal. It would consist of both analog and digital transmissions, in uncompressed formats which the science teams hoped would be easy for the recipients to decode: basic mathematics, text symbols and words, which would be repeated ten times at one-minute intervals.

The greater difficulty was deciding the content of the worded message. At Dr. Persaud's recommendation straightforward greetings would be sent first. If Janet's theory of identical development held true, the inhabitants of FLO might be fluent in or at least understand some Earth languages, and certainly numbers and mathematics. To keep things simple, the text portions of the first transmissions would contain only English. If there was no response after a predetermined time, other languages would be sent.

Decoding the original signal was given lower priority and preparations were made on Earth-based transmitters to send a message to FLO. Communication satellites would be used to repeat the message. Although they would be of lower power than ground based transmitters, space-based signals might have a better chance of reaching FLO due to their slightly more direct line of sight to the planet, with less chance of solar interference.

After some back-and-forth between several world leaders, a short message was composed professing friendship and future cooperation. The transmission would be sent the next day, exactly six weeks after the discovery of FLO.

The text based portion of the message was straightforward:

This is a transmission of greeting from the governments of Earth. Please identify your intent. We look forward to communicating with you.

Of the eight experts originally brought in as part of Doug's shift, four had been released from service and returned home but were in daily contact with the rest of the group. Janet and Doug were each given apartments in Washington close to the Pentagon, and were working full time on the FLO issue. Wilson had left Washington but returned when the date for the message transmission was set. Dr. Persaud divided her time between Andrews, the Pentagon, and the White House.

All were present in the station room at the Pentagon when the message went out at 1500 hours UTC. Those world leaders involved had an open communication link with the White House, though there was little chatter. The radio message would take approximately eighteen minutes to reach FLO. Someone or something on FLO would then take an unknown amount of time to reply, if they chose to reply at all. The group determined the best case scenario would be a reply sent about thirty minutes after reception, making a total round-trip time of just over an hour.

The President was in the room for the transmission but then left to oversee other business. The problems of the country had been compounded with the discovery of FLO. The oval office monitor would still receive any message at the same time as those in the station room.

The group of scientists and White House personnel stayed in the station room out of duty and extreme curiosity. Any FLO reply would be detected by orbiting satellites and Earth-bound receivers, which would immediately relay the signal to the station room. A warning klaxon would sound and the message, whatever it was, would be displayed on the room's large monitors. If the reply was sent in the same format as the one from Earth it would appear as text. If not, the content would still be displayed as faithfully as possible.

In the meantime the scientists discussed policy and contingencies, all the while keeping an eye on the large digital clock that indicated the time since transmission. The time passed very slowly as the scientists waited for the one hour mark. Some participants were working by themselves on laptop computers. Doug's group occupied their time by jotting down notes and talking in low tones amongst themselves.

As the clock approached one hour the participants talked less and less, and the tension in the air was noticeable. Doug was sweating slightly, so he took off his jacket and rolled up his shirt sleeves in an effort to cool down.

As was his habit when he became stressed, Singh got up and paced the room.

Singh and I should never play poker, Doug thought, wiping a bead of sweat from his brow and smiling to himself.

All eyes were on the clock as it past the one hour mark. Nothing. Wilson exhaled.

"It was too much to expect anyway, that they would reply so soon," he said to no one in particular.

For the next ten minutes the group remained alert and gave the clock most of their attention, but after that they relaxed slightly and started back into normal conversation. Leach had been among the group but he got up and left. Singh poured himself a water from one of the pitchers near the center of the table and sat back down. Doug yawned, and looked at his watch. 12:23 PM.

"Should we go for lun—"

Doug was startled by the loud warning klaxon. Everyone quickly looked towards the largest monitor screen at the head of the room.

BE PREPARED TO RECEIVE ENVOY IN FOUR DAYS. END.

Everyone looked expectantly at the monitor. Doug felt surprise, excitement, and disbelief. His heart was pounding. After about five seconds of utter silence a few of the participants let out a cheer. Everyone smiled. One person slapped the back of the man in front of him. Indisputable confirmation, once and for all, that there was active, intelligent life on FLO. And it was technically advanced.

"They're actually coming here?" a man said, as he got up and hurried from the room.

Persaud was busy typing into her laptop.

Singh was the first to say something pertinent about the message.

"An envoy... due to arrive here in four days?"

"Maybe they launched weeks ago," Wilson said.

"Hold on," Doug said. "Let's get confirmation it's not a hack. Somebody please confirm we haven't been spoofed." Doug thought it was unlikely but they had to check. It only took a few more seconds before confirmations started rolling in.

"The timing," Doug said loud enough to be heard over the din in the room, "means they had to launch a vehicle as soon as FLO appeared. So just under seven weeks travel time?"

"Which is impossible, at our technological level," Singh replied quickly. "And to ask us – no, to *tell* us to expect an envoy in a matter of days? Who the hell are they? What kind of envoy? And what do they mean by *be prepared?*"

Leach returned, and was quietly briefed by an aide. The message remained on the screen. Some people had difficulty looking away.

Janet hadn't said much during the wait, but she gently touched Doug's shoulder to get his attention.

"I don't like this at all, why would they surprise us like that? Four days notice that they will be in orbit around Earth?"

"Or perhaps they will land," Doug said. Janet furrowed her brow as she considered that an envoy ship might land on Earth.

"It does seem strange they wouldn't have communicated earlier," Doug said, as he took her hand in his. "And yet if their intentions were hostile, why give us any warning at all?"

Wilson and Singh appeared to be contemplating the implications. They looked just as troubled as Janet. Persaud overheard the exchange too and leaned over.

"It is strange," she said, "but despite any similarities we've seen thus far, they could be culturally very different from us, and perhaps very cautious. We need to keep an open mind, and not assume the worst."

"Yes," Jack Wilson said, "but *planning* for the worst is not a bad idea."

Leach addressed the room, breaking their train of thought.

"Everyone," he called, waiting for quiet, "the President and Dr. Lau are busy conferring with other leaders, and so won't be available for a few hours. Please be ready at any time for an emergency meeting." Leach and Persaud then left the room, conferring quietly.

— 18 —

The scientists stayed in the station room until their shift was up. They wanted to stay longer, but there was really no room for them when their relief arrived. They were on their way to lunch when they were passed in the hallway by the President and his entourage, including Stacey and Leach, headed back to the station room.

The scientists had been instructed to remain on the grounds. Doug, Janet, Singh, and Wilson went to eat in the Navy mess. They'd become friendly the six weeks they'd been working together. Doug and Janet had become as much of a couple as they could under the circumstances. Even the sometimes abrasive Jack Wilson was well-liked. He was just as brilliant as the rest and sometimes raised questions the others were reluctant to ask.

They found a quiet corner and sat down.

"Dr. Persaud could be right," Janet said as they settled in. "We shouldn't jump to conclusions."

Wilson said, "I don't buy that. Can you imagine if the positions were reversed? This is bad news. We would never be so mysterious when communicating with another planet. With so much at stake, we wouldn't want any civilization we contacted to get the wrong idea."

"Yeah," Doug replied. "It's almost as if we're communicating with some ultra-secret regime. The language is didactic, lacks informative detail, and seems to make assumptions. Either that or the language comes from a place so similar to ours that the messenger understands how we'll probably react."

"Now you sound like Persaud, but you're making sense."

They were silent for a moment. Janet speculated on the mood in the station room.

"Right now the President's group is formulating a response and trying to figure out who should do the talking when the Envoy steps out of their ship." Janet shivered slightly at the thought. "I'd wager FLO won't bother replying to any further messages, until they arrive in orbit."

"Given their behavior thus far, I wouldn't disagree," Wilson said.

– 19 –

The next three days were full of briefings, meetings, and strategy conferences in which each scientist was given instruction on diplomacy and protocol. The President and his spokespeople in the White House were the first line of diplomacy, but many of the consultants in attendance were briefed in case the circumstances warranted additional personnel.

Three more messages were sent to FLO asking for more details, while also professing goodwill and friendship. There were no replies.

Anxiety levels were high. There was a mixture of excitement, trepidation, and frustration. Elation at the prospect of encountering a new race was quickly replaced by near-panic on the part of those responsible for logistics and protocol. How do you prepare for a delegation from an alien planet, especially one that has given no details? Were they going to remain in orbit? Did they intend to land? If so, where? It was impossible for any of them, let alone their government and military taskmasters, to know if the preparations were appropriate, inappropriate or a complete waste of time.

Some of the military personnel at the White House showed anger at being in such a weak position with few options. What if it wasn't going to be a delegation? What if it was going to be something infinitely worse? The Pentagon – the institution itself – was fearful of what it did not understand and could not control. Was the word Envoy actually shorthand for invasion? Military confidence was always based on preparation and training. The problem was that none of them knew how to prepare or train for the arrival. The so-called Envoy from the other planet held all the cards.

All available observatories were directed to scan the sky in the general direction of FLO. The Envoy, whatever it turned out to be, would be coming from the direction of the Sun. It would not be easy to locate on its way to Earth. Everyone from professional astronomers to birdwatchers with binoculars trained their eyes on the sky, so it came as no surprise to anyone that an object was detected the morning of the third day after the Envoy message.

Under strong magnification it looked remarkably like the Space

Shuttle and its fuel tank, but without the side booster rockets. There was another object attached to the side of the tank opposite to the shuttle. It looked like a second, slightly smaller cylinder though it was far from certain whether either container was indeed a fuel tank or something entirely different.

Hundreds of photographs were taken of the ship, and with each passing hour the photos grew slightly more detailed. Though it was difficult to judge the scale, it appeared the ship was the same length as the shuttle but much sleeker. It looked like a more advanced version of the craft. The ship was moving fast, over five times that of any space-craft or probe launched by NASA or the Russian Space Agency. Most important to every government agency around the world was the clear confirmation that the Envoy seemed to be exactly what they all hoped it would be. A single ship.

The initial speed estimates of the Envoy ship brought shouts of dis-belief and jeers about grade-school arithmetic mistakes. A few minutes later, confirmation of the speed silenced the room. Some of the best scientific minds in the world were present. They all realized that they were staring intently at superior technology and were shortly going to be confronted by the beings that owned it.

Separate teams were assigned to analyze the craft while Doug and his associates were periodically assigned to the station room in case another message from FLO came in.

Doug and Wilson, along with the usual White House staff that came and went, were in their usual four-hour shift. There was not much to do except wait. There wasn't a lot of conversation beyond the business at hand. Everyone was on high alert. Somebody grumbled about hav-ing to give away prime tickets to a baseball game. Wilson laughed.

"You want a front row seat at a major event?" Wilson said. "Look around, pal. You've got the best seat in the solar system right here."

At midnight on the morning of the fourth day after the Envoy mes-sage, Doug and his team had just come off their shift when the klaxon sounded. It only took them a couple of minutes to run back, but the room had already jammed up with scientists, staff, aides and security. Doug got there just in time. He stood in the doorway as the message appeared on the screen:

CLEAR JB ANDREWS FOR LANDING 1900 UTC TODAY. END.

There was silence as everyone digested the message. No cheers this time. Moments later the room erupted into activity. Most of the aides and staff ran off to their own posts. Several others were speaking urgently on their phones. The scientists on the active shift were at their workstations analyzing data and consulting with other team members.

"How do they know the base by name?" Wilson said.

"Either by studying our broadcasts or they have their own Joint Base Andrews, and figure we do too since our worlds are similar," Singh replied.

"I'm starting to believe," Wilson said, looking directly at Janet. "Studying broadcasts is a myth anyway. It's science fiction. How does an alien race separate geographical fact from entertainment fiction. Without reference points and definitions it could all be an indecipherable jumble. It works both ways. Anybody have any luck decoding FLO's twelve second data burst yet? And it's awfully nice of them to choose an airport so close to the White House. Twenty bucks says Janet is spot-on with her multiverse theory."

The group turned away from the doorway and briefly debated what they should do. Too many people in the station room would cause a traffic jam, so they headed to the library, which due to the current situation was usually unoccupied. As they walked, Janet addressed Wilson's statement.

"I suppose they could have chosen any landing spot in the world, but take a look at the ship they're using. It looks remarkably like a Shuttle, but a far more refined version. So Andrews here could be a parallel to a secure military location they already know on FLO."

Nobody responded. They were grappling silently with the implications of a many worlds theory come to life, of parallelism, and of encountering something for the first time in their scientific lives that was truly unknown. Doug felt a rush of the ever present unease that had steadily ramped up since the Envoy message. The previous three days had been stressful. Everyone was operating on far less sleep than usual, yet had to be at their best. They were actually landing. Within hours. Whoever they were.

– 20 –

The group retired at 0200, deciding they should all attempt to get some sort of sleep. The assigned dorm rooms at the Pentagon had become familiar surroundings. Doug just managed to get to sleep when there was a loud knock on his door. It was Agent Bishop.

"An alarm went off. There is a new transmission from FLO. Let's go."

Doug put a robe on over his t-shirt and shorts and rushed after Bishop wondering why he'd been the one to get him up instead of the usual staffer. When they got to the station room Foley gestured to the large monitor. The message read:

ENSURE THE FOLLOWING PERSONNEL
ATTEND THE ENVOY LANDING:

Twenty names followed. Doug and Janet were both on the list.

– 21 –

Doug took a few minutes to return to his room and get dressed before getting a coffee in the diplomatic conference area. Most of those involved with the project were assembling for an emergency meeting.

Arthur Leach and two other men were talking at the front of the room near the podium while the large group found their seats.

"Hello everyone," Leach began as a couple of stragglers arrived. "I'm sorry we needed to wake some of you so early. You will be briefed on your individual roles. Some of you have primary duties, while the rest are considered backup personnel to be called upon when required. You will remain at the Pentagon until further notice.

"Most of you are aware that this morning at 0300 hours we received a second message from FLO. The message requested that the following personnel in addition to myself and other key staff be present at the landing site to greet the Envoy. Note that the list was transmitted in alphabetical order. Last name first."

Alphabetical order. Just the way we would send it, Doug thought.

Janet and Doug looked at each other as Leach opened a folder and began reading from the list. Doug didn't recognize many of the names but that afternoon he and Janet would join them all at the landing site to greet the Envoy.

— 22 —

"But my name isn't on the list! If I show up how will I explain my presence?" The scientist was beside himself. He spoke in a raspy whisper into the small mobile phone they had given him, one that could only dial one number. He didn't want to disappoint his handlers, but he was fearful of being questioned by the regular security personnel at Andrews. "What will I say if I'm caught?"

"Leave that to us," the handler said. You'll be driven to Andrews separately and taken through security with the proper ID. Just ensure you stand with the largest groups of people, and don't speak unless spoken to. Make sure you have a good view when the Envoy arrives."

— 23 —

The TAC Suburban containing Doug, Janet, and three other scientists headed towards Andrews. An agent was in the driver's seat. Agent Bishop was in the front passenger seat. During the ride Bishop turned to face the group and went over some last-minute security protocols. The group would stand behind the main greeting party unless directed otherwise.

During the trip the subject of the list was brought up by Dr. William Grant, who Doug knew worked on a different shift.

"I'm not ashamed to say I'm nervous! The Envoy's transmission listed people by name. That's troubling. One, they know who we are. Two, they may be expecting something of us. But what?"

Nobody replied. They were all thinking the same thing.

The SUV arrived three hours before the appointed landing time; the primary group arrived ninety minutes before that. The base had been closed to traffic soon after the message had been received. Only essential base personnel remained in the immediate area, along with a few dozen agents sent to brief and supervise them. The rumor was that two Marine battalions were deployed in a dense security perimeter around Andrews, and that both UAV drones and multiple AWACS platforms were flying continuous surveillance patrols.

At every security checkpoint there appeared to be three-man teams of MPs, but they were wearing unfamiliar shoulder flashes. Doug asked Bishop who they were.

"Special Reaction Team," Bishop replied. "If they're here it means we've got the best possible people in place if something goes bad."

Even with the SRT and Secret Service on the job, the President was not attending. Doug thought he was probably in some secret bunker in case the Envoy turned out to be hostile. The Vice President and the Secretary of State would be among the delegation at Andrews. There were about thirty delegates present, not counting support personnel.

The sacrificial lambs, Doug thought, *offered to the alien Envoy in case they're hungry after they land. Nobody from the UN has been invited either.* He almost laughed out loud.

There was a short rehearsal in which each person was directed to stand at their appointed place, while Leach and a military advisor spoke to the crowd for a few moments. The Envoy was still at least an hour out, so the group was directed to an airport hangar for some refreshments. The shade was also appreciated, as the mid-afternoon sun had gotten quite strong.

After the rehearsal there was nothing to do but eat sandwiches, stand around and fidget. Everyone was on edge. Nobody knew what to expect, and the terse nature of FLO's communiqués didn't help.

The small group that Doug and Janet arrived with stuck together. Doug didn't know many of the other scientists very well because some had been brought in later or been on a different shift, but they had the common issue to bond over and compare notes.

A communication station had been set up in the hangar. There were several large monitors inside and outside the large entrance. Some of the monitors were used to display instructions, while others were set up similarly to those in the station room back at the Pentagon. Satellite images, airborne camera transmissions, and terrestrial signals could be shown. Some of the monitors displayed a countdown to the Envoy's ETA. 00:26:39. Twenty-six minutes to go.

At the twenty minute mark the delegates were instructed to take their places outside. The sun was behind them, but it was still uncomfortably hot. Doug started to perspire almost immediately.

The monitors were showing a small dot in the clear blue sky. The image was mottled by heat shimmer and air pollution. After a minute the dot grew to a shaky white blob against the blue of the sky. A few minutes later the view switched to a clearer shot. The sleek ship was clearly visible, a mostly white upper section with a darker underside. The view switched again. It was clear that they were getting view angles from ground, drone and AWAC cameras. The Envoy ship banked and turned to line up with a runway. Doug momentarily looked away from the monitor to scan the sky, but he couldn't see it.

"There it is!" someone shouted, and the crowd turned to look at the area of sky where he was pointing. It was very small, but left a curved vapor trail, making it easier to spot. Janet pulled Doug's upper arm in close to her as she saw it. Despite the anticipation of the Envoy's arrival, he was aware of her touch. It felt reassuring. He put his hand on top of hers.

There was a booming sound as the vehicle transitioned from supersonic to subsonic speed. Janet clutched his arm tighter at the powerful sound. Doug felt the boom deep in his chest.

The craft was getting closer and they could now discern its shape without the aid of the television monitors. It was shuttle-like, but it also resembled a sleek jet. It was losing altitude quickly. As it came into the local airspace it banked and circled the airport at an altitude of about five hundred meters. The ship was a beautiful design. Doug could hear the familiar sound of jet engines, but it was faint, like a modern airliner rather than a military craft. Unlike the Shuttle the Envoy ship seemed to be able to fly on its own in the atmosphere. No external engines were visible.

The craft moved away from the airport then banked towards the far runway, lining up its approach. Two Air Force F-22 Raptors followed on either side but about a kilometer behind. Doug hardly noticed them except to compare the scale when the louder jets screamed overhead as the alien craft touched down. The F-22s were state of the art, yet the sleek, quiet Envoy ship made them seem like '70s-era fighters.

Soon after touchdown the ship's engines became louder as it employed engine braking. Some of those assembled applauded as it slowed and turned off the runway towards the hangar downwind of the group. Two ground marshals in bio suits standing away from the runway's end directed it to halt about three hundred meters from the delegation.

Leach and three other men, all in bio suits, were transported by an Air Force driver in an open-topped Humvee towards the craft. The second vehicle was a modified cube van, with medical insignia and very large side windows for observation. One other Humvee followed, containing armed Marines complete with body armor over top of combat biohazard gear. All the vehicles stopped about fifty meters from the ship, with the medical vehicle closest to it.

Three individuals dressed in biohazard suits exited the van and stood between it and the ship. Leach and two agents stood further away and waited. The marines stood behind and to the side of them, rifles held at sling arms, a position of respect for greeting dignitaries.

Just then there was a commotion in the crowd behind Doug. He heard a woman say "Oh my goodness," and then some murmuring. Two agents appeared and carried someone away. Doug couldn't see who it was, but he guessed that the heat and the tension of the moment prompted someone to faint. He looked back at the spacecraft.

After a moment the craft's hatch opened and gangway stairs deployed. Doug was tall enough to have a clear view, but Janet had difficulty even when she stood on her toes. He wished he had brought binoculars, but then thought it might have been rude to observe the Envoy through them. It seemed like they were waiting forever, but it was likely only a few seconds before he saw someone emerge.

A man descended the stairs. He was tall and athletic, but otherwise not out of the ordinary. He was wearing a blue jumpsuit, similar to the ones worn by astronauts on the Shuttle or the International Space Station. The jumpsuit seemed better tailored though, as if it could be worn as a regular uniform. Another figure emerged, this time a woman, followed by four others. Six people in all, two of them women, each wearing the same uniform style and carrying a briefcase. The craft's stairs retracted and the hatch closed when the sixth person was on the ground.

Six visitors, apparently unarmed, Doug thought, *all of them looking just like everyone's next door neighbors. Not an invasion. I wonder if the Pentagon will be happy or sad about it.* By the time the last person had reached the ground, Leach and the agents had walked to within a few paces of the Envoy. There was much gesturing and talking, but no physical contact. After a moment the six members of the Envoy entered the medical van in preparation for a quarantine of undetermined duration.

Seemingly out of nowhere, another squad of Marines pulled up in two Humvees to guard the Envoy ship. As the Envoys were being driven towards the delegation Doug became aware of just how hot it was outside. Despite the exhilaration at the situation he realized he hadn't had any water since arriving almost three hours earlier. Like everyone else, he was sweating profusely. Hopefully somebody in command would bring everyone inside or just out of the sun.

The vehicles made their way towards the delegation. The medical vehicle carrying the Envoy stopped near the Vice President and a few other delegates, past Doug's position. Doug could see a few of the individual's faces through the vehicle's large windows.

The vehicle contained an active two-way intercom so the assembled group could hear those in the van speaking. The Vice President addressed them at a podium microphone not far away. It was all very cordial. The visitors spoke everyday English, which made it all surreal. One man spoke with a French accent, another Spanish. As each individual stood up in the van to move to the intercom and introduce themselves, Doug could clearly see their face through the window. An interesting group, but again, nothing out of the ordinary except for the fact that all of these normal looking Envoy members had just arrived from another planet. Then as he could see the second woman move to the intercom, Doug froze in shock. The woman spoke.

"Hello, my name is Dr. Cheryl McBride."

– 24 –

Doug woke up on a cot in the base infirmary. He saw Janet's face above his, looking concerned. A doctor was adjusting an IV drip connected to his arm.

"You collapsed," Janet said. "When you saw Cheryl, you just..."

Janet adjusted the cold cloth that had been placed on his forehead.

"The... alternate Cheryl McBride had asked for you, and she became very concerned when she learned you passed out."

"The fact you were dehydrated didn't help matters," the doctor standing nearby said. "The excitement proved to be too much for some people. Three others collapsed in the heat."

Another man was laying unconscious on a cot near the opposite wall.

"Cheryl. Where is she?" Doug sat up, and immediately winced at the pain in his head.

"You'll feel stronger in about a half hour as the IV replenishes your fluids. That headache is a common symptom of severe dehydration. I can give you something for the pain if you like."

Doug nodded and the doctor went to a medicine shelf.

Janet sat on the cot beside Doug, putting her hand on his shoulder.

"The Dr. McBride from FLO," Janet said with some emphasis, "has gone with her group for medical examinations. Just before they left Agent Bishop and I had a short talk with her when she asked for you. Aside from her obviously not being killed in her universe, there were a few other differences. Apparently the two of you only dated a short while, and never planned to get married. And..."

Doug felt weak, still in shock from glimpsing the woman he had loved, whose funeral he attended two years ago. He looked up at Janet.

"Her universe?" Doug asked, quietly. He was foggy but he'd heard Janet clearly. "It's confirmed then? Multiple universes?"

"Yes, and there's more," Janet replied, nodding. "In her universe you were the one that died. A cycling accident soon after you moved to Hawaii."

Doug thought back to the first day he had started cycling up the mountain. A Jeep travelling too fast for the road had narrowly missed hitting him head-on after a blind corner. Doug had swerved into a ditch just in time and was thrown from the bike, grazing his head on a rock. That day happened to be the first time he had worn a cycling helmet, and it likely saved his life.

Agent Bishop entered the infirmary.

"Good to see you conscious Dr. Lockwood," he said. "Most of the delegation and the Envoy are now in quarantine at Bethesda. A large team has been assembled to push the blood and bacteriological testing as quickly as possible, but it may take some time to give them the all clear. Preparations are being finalized for debriefing of the Envoy back here at Andrews once testing is complete."

Bishop looked over at the man laying unconscious on the other cot.

"What's Foley doing here? His name wasn't on the list, and he didn't enter through security."

Doug was surprised.

"I didn't even realize that was Stan laying there. Maybe Dr. Lau or Arthur Leach added him to the list."

"How well do you know Dr. Foley?"

"He's an old friend. We did our undergrad at the same school. Why?"

Bishop didn't answer.

— 25 —

Five minutes later Agent Bishop escorted Doug and Janet to a nearby lounge, where the two briefed Doug on the events of the previous forty minutes. The Envoy's leader, a man named Dr. Carl Bertrand, had addressed the crowd via the intercom immediately after the initial greetings. Knowing there would be intense curiosity about them and their planet, Bertrand read from a prepared statement providing basic information about FLO.

There were more similarities than differences between the two Earths. To avoid confusion, Bertrand suggested the names FLO and the Twin be used when referring to each planet. Nobody objected. Of more interest was the fact that the history and population of both worlds were apparently identical up to the year 1970, and then they started to diverge.

Bertrand's prepared statement was innocuous. He was so obviously human that there was some restlessness at the banality of the statement until he got through the preparatory remarks and into the part that completely silenced everyone and riveted their attention. There had been a dramatic breakthrough in computer technology on FLO in 1997. It had started with an MIT graduate named Norman Stravinsky, whose counterpart on Earth had apparently died at birth in 1971. Stravinsky had become one of the most influential quantum physicists of the previous twenty-five years. In 1996 his research team had begun the development of a revolutionary new processor which provided the biggest technological leap in the history of computer science, opening new avenues in computer applications that had been out of reach before. It was a quantum computer built on a massive scale. The Envoy leader explained that the third generation of the computer, Mekhos as they referred to it, had recently managed to send FLO to a different universe to avoid a catastrophic gamma radiation event that would have destroyed all life on the planet.

With those startling words Bertrand was interrupted for a few moments as he noticed several people who had been listening intently to him suddenly turn and nod to Janet Blair. Her prediction about FLO's origin might have been inspired guesswork, but her colleagues silently offered their congratulations.

Much of life on FLO seemed to be influenced by the presence of Mekhos. Beginning in 1999 the supercomputer took an interest in FLO's global economics and politics, giving foreign and domestic policy advice that when implemented had a stabilizing effect. At first only a few countries would follow the directives, but as more followed FLO became more peaceful than it had ever been in all of its recorded history. Before landing, the Envoy had tapped into Earth's news archives and was shocked to learn of an enormous amount of violence and turmoil in recent decades that had never happened on FLO.

It was a lot for Doug to take in. He should have been fascinated by the quantum computing revelations, but he was preoccupied with confusion at the thought of Cheryl being alive. And yet it wasn't Cheryl. What did it mean to see someone you knew, who had effectively risen from the dead, who by way of explanation happened to be from an alternate universe? Do you greet her like an old friend or a former lover? Yet she was not the same individual you had loved. Or was she?

Would it be like coming across a long lost identical twin? No. Even identical twins are separate individuals with separate personalities. Not only was this Cheryl McBride physically the same in every detail, she had most of the same history, even to the point of dating Doug.

"Cheryl didn't want to leave without speaking with you," Janet said. "She wanted to be here when you woke up, she had no choice. Quarantine is quarantine though, so she wants to talk to you as soon as possible after her group returns to Andrews."

Doug nodded. It must be tough for Janet too. Doug knew how she felt about him, and he knew that he had made his attraction to her just as clear. But what would happen now that Cheryl was present? Would she stay on Earth? Would that be permitted? Or would it even be ethical? Cheryl's surviving relatives and friends would be exposed to the same stress and confusion he was going through, assuming the details of the Envoy were ever made public. *And am I even asking the right questions,* Doug thought, *because that's not really any Cheryl McBride I ever knew.* He shook his head in an attempt to clear the confusion, but all he succeeded in doing was aggravating his headache.

"It's not Cheryl," Doug said to Janet, wincing in pain as he spoke. "I'm working through the confusion and I need your help. This will only become misdirection if we let it. We need to be focused now, more than ever." Janet looked at Doug for a moment. She was searching his eyes for misdirection of his own, but there was only sincerity. They held each other's hand and relaxed. Slightly.

– 26 –

A little over twenty-four hours later Doug and Janet held hands in the back seat of the now-familiar Suburban as Agent Bishop drove them to a large, nondescript, unmarked building on the base. The emotional part of his psyche was tense at the prospect of seeing Cheryl face-to-face.

He experienced momentary flashes of despair when he thought about it logically. It wasn't really her. His Cheryl had died. This Cheryl had a separate life, on a *different planet*. Where they never intended to marry. After he died on FLO… *no, scratch that,* Doug thought. After the *parallel Doug* died on FLO, Cheryl no doubt moved on. She *had* moved on. The situation was utterly alien. Literally no human being had ever been through it before. *It was enough to drive a person mad,* he thought.

He was also aware of the effect it had on Janet, so they'd talked about it late into the night. Doug told Janet that he was in love with her, and a meeting with Cheryl would not change that fact. It was a meeting of necessity, for scientific and diplomatic reasons. And for emotional reasons. Janet understood.

As the small group got out of the Suburban and approached the debriefing building, Agent Bishop noticed Doug hesitate at the entrance. Janet was just looking straight ahead, standing next to Doug and waiting for him to make the next move.

"I know this is rough on you," Bishop said quietly. "I can't imagine what I'd be thinking in your situation. There's a waiting room just past the guard and security station inside. Go there. It will give you a chance to collect your thoughts."

"Thanks, I'll do that."

The duty officer scanned their IDs and issued security passes. The waiting room just beyond was sparsely furnished and utilitarian. Fresh coffee and some fruit and biscuits were laid out. Doug and Janet helped themselves while Bishop walked further into the building. They were in the waiting room for only a few minutes when Singh and Wilson joined them.

"They sent the second-tier away," Singh said. "We're basically on call on an as needed basis. Agent Bishop said you'd be here."

"Any new information on our guests?" Janet asked.

Wilson shrugged his shoulders. "Not really. There've been a lot of introductions and small talk, and plenty of *we hope our two worlds will have lots of laughs together and share recipes* diplomatic speak."

Doug remained mostly silent as the three others talked about the Envoy and what might happen next. Doug and the rest were to continue working at the Pentagon for the next week at least. There was no indication of how long the Envoy was staying, or where they would be residing while on Earth.

Agent Bishop returned, and went over to Doug and Janet.

"She's just outside," he said in a low tone. "Are you okay with meeting her now?"

Doug's heart skipped a beat, but he nodded the affirmative.

"You'll have about ten minutes before she will need to continue debriefing with the others." Agent Bishop put his hand on Doug's shoulder and leaned in. "Keep it personal – nothing about Andrews, the Pentagon, the White House, or any security or defense information you became aware of since being drafted into this project, all right? The room is under surveillance, so use that to our advantage."

"I understand."

Agent Bishop glanced at the rest of the group. They got the message and moved to an empty interview room across the hall. Janet squeezed Doug's hand then followed the others out.

Agent Bishop stood at the room entrance and held the door. Cheryl McBride entered the room, the alternate Cheryl McBride, smiling and looking radiant.

She stood a few paces into the room. Agent Bishop stood by the door, watching discretely.

"Doug..."

They were an arm's length apart. Doug looked into her eyes. He was speechless. A small part of his consciousness asserted that this was not 'his' Cheryl McBride – she was a visiting dignitary.

"My God, Cheryl."

He regretted the words immediately. Calling the person standing before him by the name of his former fiancé felt almost like a betrayal.

"I know Doug, I lost you too. I understand we... I mean, you and the other Cheryl were to be married." Doug nodded.

"It never went that far with us. We dated for a couple of months, then remained friends. You went off to Hawaii, and then..."

"Yes. I heard. I died."

Doug resisted an almost overpowering urge to step closer and give her a hug.

"I know this is difficult, she said. "I went through some of the same feelings last month after we intercepted your world's broadcasts. Initially it was a wildly complex jumble of data until we started doing targeted searches. Naturally we started with ourselves with people we knew or had known."

"And you saw that I was alive," Doug said.

"Yes. We realized that many of the people were the same, and that you were alive and still in the scientific field. I knew we would likely meet. There's no precedent. Nobody has gone through this before."

They sat down at large table on either side of the same corner so they were close and facing each other.

"There's so much I want to ask about your life," Doug said, "but why all the secrecy about your arrival?"

"Yes, I'm sorry for that. Much of our own population was kept in the dark too, although we needed to make a statement soon after the event. There were too many physical manifestations of the transference. We had to reveal to the public what had happened. But we were also afraid of what universe we had stepped into. Whether your Earth would be friendly, hostile or have any civilization at all. So we studied you for a time, right up to our arrival."

"By viewing our broadcasts."

"And by tapping into your internet, yes."

"That's how you knew I was alive," Doug asked, "through web searches, and why you invited me to the landing."

Cheryl nodded. "It was thought it might go easier for us if we had a friend of sorts in the greeting party. Of our top scientists, apparently only a few lives overlapped sufficiently between our two worlds. Many of the same people exist but random events led them in different directions. But you must also believe I had personal reasons for wanting to see you."

"Of course," Doug returned her smile. She looked identical, aside from the almost imperceptible differences resulting from being two years older. Her hair was a bit shorter. She wore no jewelry at all except for what looked like a thin clear plastic bracelet, about an inch wide, that closely hugged her wrist. Doug had given his Cheryl a gold necklace she'd worn constantly. He wondered if this Cheryl had been given the bracelet by her Doug Lockwood.

"The staff here are going to call me back in a few moments, but perhaps we could have dinner tomorrow, just the two of us."

"I'm not sure if that's a realistic idea," Doug said, "or even if it's a good idea for us, personally. I'm very pleased to see you Cheryl, but I don't think I'll ever be comfortable with the situation."

Her expression changed slightly. Doug wasn't sure if it was one of surprise at his honesty or relief because she actually felt the same way.

The door opened. Another agent stepped in and spoke to Bishop. "Sorry, but we need you Dr. McBride," Bishop said.

She stood up and moved slightly toward Doug, but he leaned back in his chair ever so slightly away from her. She looked confused for a brief moment, then turned toward the door when Bishop walked over and touched her lightly on the shoulder.

"See you later," he said as she walked away.

– 27 –

The next day it would have been business as usual except that the science teams were being moved en-masse to Andrews. Organized confusion, short tempers and stress ruled. Technical limits and the occasional misdirection were getting the best of everyone. The Envoy's arrival hadn't changed the mission of finding out as much as possible about FLO, but the imaging and detection obviously couldn't get any better. And there were still no detectable radio or television broadcasts.

Foley turned to Doug. They had been moved into billets on the base and were working in a high security building stuffed with computers and bristling on the outside with communications arrays.

"I thought they turned off their regular broadcasts to avoid detection. Now that they've revealed themselves, why haven't they resumed normal day-to-day operations?"

"I don't know," Doug said. "It has been bothering me too."

"Can you ask your ex-girlfriend about it? Maybe she knows something."

Doug shot Foley an annoyed glance. Foley didn't notice – he seemed easily distracted lately and looked pale, and was perspiring despite the air conditioning. A second later Foley logged off his workstation and left, presumably for another of his many breaks.

Probably coming down with something, brought on by all the stress, Doug said to himself. *I'm surprised we're not all sick.*

Doug's thoughts turned back to Cheryl. During their brief meeting she hadn't mentioned anything about FLO's continued broadcast silence. She had to cancel her offer of dinner due to briefings. Hopefully they would get the chance to see each other again soon. *I did not ask any of the questions I should have. That 'friend of sorts' bit she mentioned might be a two-way street leading to some useful information about FLO.*

He felt guilty at the thought that he couldn't completely stop some glimmer of feelings for Cheryl's duplicate. Or perhaps his thoughts were more for the *memory* of the real Cheryl, come alive again for him to see and touch. *This Cheryl is real too though,* Doug thought, *but more likely sent to confuse, a vaguely cruel inside joke by the mission architects on FLO. Deliberate, or if not, that's how it's working out.*

During his lunch break Doug wanted some time away from his shift colleagues and so went to the visitor's mess. He was deep in thought about Cheryl when he looked up to see Carl Bertrand standing with his lunch tray. He was accompanied by another member of the Envoy and two agents.

"May I join you Dr. Lockwood?"

Doug hesitated a second, surprised. He gestured to the seat. The other individuals sat slightly further down the long table.

"Thank you. I'm glad to see you feeling better. Dr. McBride was very concerned, as were we all."

"Thanks. It was a little embarrassing."

"Not at all. I can only imagine the shock at seeing a loved one who had passed on two years before. You had probably only just come to terms with her death and then…"

"Yes."

Bertrand spoke with an educated French accent. He had changed from his flight suit into civilian clothes. He was wearing the same transparent plastic wrist band as Cheryl. *Our security officials have banded them like wild birds,* Doug thought.

"I also wish to apologize for the secrecy of our arrival. To be honest, it was reasoned that if your planet were given too much advance notice there would be a greater chance of a rogue nation or terror group taking advantage of the situation, using force to push their agenda or perhaps even making an attempt to intercept or destroy our craft."

"Yes, I imagine our world isn't as politically stable as yours."

It sounded reasonable. But Doug thought their surprise visit was just as risky. After the landing was announced he had overheard a military advisor say that their uninvited landing was a grave security risk.

The advisor had recommended the ship not be allowed to touch down, blowing it out of the sky if necessary.

"No matter. We're here now and we wish nothing more than friendship between our two worlds. We are somewhat forced neighbors, so it is best if we are friends, yes?"

Doug was distracted by some animated red symbols that appeared on Bertrand's wrist band. *Not a band given to them by base security after all,* he realized.

"Do you mind me asking what that is?" Doug pointed to the band.

"The Raim? It's basically the equivalent of your smartphone. A small mobile computer, health monitor, communication device, with numerous other functions. They became commonplace about four years ago. Almost every citizen has one."

The device scrolled some words and symbols in different colors and directions. Doug didn't manage to recognize any before it abruptly stopped.

"Amazing," he said. "It's entirely transparent. Where's the battery?"

"Power is generated through the wearer's body heat, movements, and surrounding ambient light. The storage cell is transparent and flexible. The user can input commands through voice or gestures, with or without touch. It is very adept at interpreting what the user intends and over time it customizes itself to their habits and preferences."

Doug regarded Bertrand as he spoke. For a visitor he was supremely confident and self-assured. It bordered on smugness. Perhaps it came from a feeling of security, of knowing that his civilization's technology was at least a generation ahead of Earth's. Or was it due to being confident about a plan that FLO and the Envoy had yet to reveal? Nobody on Earth knew if the Envoy or their incredible machine had any designs on the planet or its people beyond the stated diplomatic overtures.

"Dr. Bertrand, we're deeply curious to learn about the process you used to get here. You say a quantum supercomputer - Mekhos - initiated an inter-dimensional transfer of your entire planet. I can't imagine the computational and power resources required. How was it possible? Is your government in command of the computer, or did Mekhos do this on its own initiative?"

For the first time, the confident Bertrand looked uncomfortable.

"I'm sorry but those are questions we will answer later in another briefing, Dr. Lockwood. For now we wish to create normal relations between our two planets. I'm sure there is much we can learn from each other."

From what Doug had seen and heard so far, that seemed unlikely. *What could FLO learn from Earth, aside from using our more violent recent history as the basis for an educational television documentary?*

One subject that Bertrand was willing to talk about was his ship. It did indeed have its origins in the Shuttle. On Earth the same basic shuttle had remained in service for nearly thirty years. On FLO it had been totally redesigned every few years. Bertrand said that NASA had more funds at its disposal since almost every country, including the United States, had less need for a large military or covert operations budget.

Bertrand explained that since their processor technology had grown by leaps and bounds, computer aided design allowed for a massive improvement in the craft's capabilities with the last revamp. The current ship was as versatile as a jetliner and space shuttle rolled into one. And it obviously boasted the ability to quickly travel within the inner solar system. Bertrand said that if they loaded enough fuel and supplies the ship could travel to Mars and back if they wanted, in just a few months rather than the two-year trip it would take with Earth technology.

Doug was startled by the loud *clang* sound of a metal lunch tray being dropped beside him on the table. Singh quickly sat down beside Doug and extended his hand to Bertrand.

"Dr. Bertrand, it's terrific to meet you, I'm Charles Singh."

Bertrand hesitated briefly at the interruption, but smiled and shook hands with the engineer.

"Likewise, Mr. Singh."

"Could you please explain to me," Singh said quickly, almost out of breath, "your ship's course and speed? We were unable to track your ship prior to only a few days ago. Some of us have speculated that to arrive here in so short a time you would have needed to slingshot around Venus in a hyperbolic trajectory, but Venus was not in the correct position at the time."

Doug leaned back and yielded the floor to Singh. As rude as Singh's uncharacteristic interruption was, it was also understandable and Doug was also perplexed about the very short time the ship took to get to Earth. Bertrand paused and took a sip of juice before answering, which only prompted Singh to continue.

"However, in a few weeks time, Venus will be in perfect position for a return—"

"We would have preferred to slingshot around Venus, but as you say, the planet could not be utilized due to its orbital position relative to your Earth. We used the Sun instead."

"How close did you get?" asked Doug.

"About 0.15 AU."

Singh's jaw dropped. Doug realized the ship had been twice as close to the Sun as the orbit of Mercury. Bertrand saw the reaction of the two men and answered their unasked question.

"Collapsible mirrored foil is deployed to shield the ship from the Sun's heat. As for the speed—"

Singh brought his hands up as if to encompass the world.

"The speeds required and the engine thrust employed must have been enormous!" he practically shouted. A few people sitting at tables nearby looked over. Bertrand nodded his head casually, as if the accomplishment were routine.

"Mekhos designed a new fuel-efficient engine that is capable of pushing the ship to a delta-V of 70 kilometers per second."

Doug and Singh were again speechless. Singh let his palms thud on the table.

"That's impossible! Why, the fuel requirement alone—"

Bertrand cut Singh off, tapping his Raim for a time readout.

"Gentlemen, please. I am sorry, but I must report for further debriefing," Bertrand said with finality as he got up to leave.

"I hope you and your group will attend the afternoon presentation. More information about my planet and Mekhos will be revealed," he said, as they watched him walk out, escorted by a pair of agents.

Bertrand is quite good at making a dramatic exit, Doug thought, *and that usually means that the person is trying to exert control and direction.*

– 28 –

Cheryl McBride needed some time alone. She told Bishop that she wasn't feeling well and needed a quiet space to rest a moment. After all, in addition to the physical stress of once again being exposed to gravity after several weeks of weightlessness, her group hadn't been given a moment's rest since arriving on Earth. Bishop escorted her to a small rest area in the debriefing building.

Bishop opened the door for Cheryl. "This room has a small couch," he said. "Will twenty minutes do? If you need anything much longer than that I'll need to clear it, and take you to the medical staff."

"Forty minutes will be better. I've experienced this exhaustion before, I just need some time in a quiet room and I will be fine, thanks." Bishop hesitated but nodded, then closed the door and stood in the hall. He spoke quietly into his comm.

Cheryl stood in the middle of the room. After a moment she sat on the couch and tapped her bracelet.

Thirty-six minutes later her bracelet chimed. She looked down to read the text.

At the forty minute mark Bishop was about to knock on the door when Cheryl emerged. He thought she looked as if she had been crying.

– 29 –

Doug, Janet, Singh, Wilson and Nayar were all in attendance at the briefing, along with some other scientific consultants and personnel but few general staffers and no aides. The group had been thinned, with those present having been given increased security clearance. Even with their enhanced clearance, Wilson still mused to the others that what they were about to hear might be a shortened version compared to what the White House was told, or at the very least, less than the whole truth from FLO.

"You're probably right on the second point," Nayar responded. "But it wouldn't be in the best interests of the White House to censor information it gives its own science teams. We all have high security clearance now."

"But maybe not the *highest* clearance," Wilson cautioned him.

Doug hadn't seen Cheryl since their first discussion. She was seated behind a long table facing the gathering with the rest of the Envoy panel, along with Leach and Stacey. Cheryl looked different, almost as if she was frowning slightly. Janet was sitting beside him. Doug briefly wondered what each woman was thinking.

Leach addressed the room. He outlined how the President and high-level staff had met that morning with the Envoy to discuss future directions for relations between the two planets. Ambassadors from various countries had been in attendance, a few in person but most via com link. In any case there would be future discussions between the two United Nations and key individual governments on both planets.

Most of what Leach had to say were generalizations, but he did mention that FLO's governments were more centralized, with a world currency and several open borders that went far beyond the various trade agreements on Earth. The resulting process tended to simplify things on FLO.

Then there was some discussion about the supercomputer technology on FLO. The speed at which operations could be carried out, meant that even their first-generation quantum computer had been millions of times faster than the fastest silicon-based supercomputers.

As the computer discussion went into more depth one member of the Envoy, a software engineer named Dr. Alfred Chan, took over the podium.

"Properly utilizing the quantum environment so true coherence can be sustained long enough so that calculations can be executed, requires the system to be completely isolated from the outside," Chan said. "Thus in 1996 our first generation qubit computer was not without problems. It could only operate for a few seconds at a time before quantum decoherence – that is, the point at which errors can no longer be corrected and therefore overwhelm the system to the point of collapse – rendered the operation useless. But the concept was sound and applying the machine itself to solving the decoherence problem resulted in a second generation computer the following year that operated near flawlessly.

"When the second quantum computer had been operating for several months, we made the amazing discovery that the CPU was responding and inquiring as though it had achieved some degree of sentience. What we realized after a surprisingly brief period of testing, was that the quantum computer appeared to have achieved true artificial intelligence, a machine that was far greater than the sum of its parts. It was becoming self-aware and able to interact with human beings on an equal if immature footing. We were surprised at any evidence of sentient behavior. Our understanding is grounded in intelligence which results from complex biology, not complex hardware. Unfortunately the greater computational demands of this self-awareness again brought the problem of quantum decoherence into play, and the CPU began behaving erratically, eventually shutting down."

Doug was spellbound, but knowing of Nayar's interest he glanced over at the software engineer. Nayar also appeared rapt at the idea of the sentient Machine. The walls of the room could have collapsed at that moment and few of them would have noticed.

Dr. Chan looked around the room before continuing. He half expected some shouted questions, but none came. He realized at that moment that his silent, attentive audience was experiencing the same revelations he and his colleagues experienced when they were faced with the realization that a new artificial intelligence was evolving. Nothing would ever be the same again.

"By that time work was well underway on the third generation quantum computer, much of which had been designed by its predecessor with additional safeguards against quantum decoherence. The result is the QC we have now, and which we call Mekhos. It was able to predict the effect of a red-giant supernova mere hours before the event, at which time a gamma ray burst would have obliterated life on our planet. Mekhos saved us by employing a quantum jump of the entire planet from my original universe into yours.

"If you were to ask me precisely how this was done, I would have to admit that we don't fully know. Mekhos has taken to inventing new applied mathematics, some of which are beyond our understanding. Mekhos has tried explaining the process to us, but it is possible we may never grasp the fine details of this accomplishment. I can tell you that to some extent Mekhos was able to select a universe, one having similar properties to our own, through the application of its formula. This prevented us from transiting to an uninhabitable universe, which might have resulted in our instant destruction. And we have seen that while the red giant star is also present in this universe, its rotational axis is not precisely aligned with this solar system. So even if the star goes nova, the gamma ray burst will not be directed here.

"Since the gamma ray burst was a deadly but short-term effect, you may ask why Mekhos didn't return us to our original universe once the danger had passed. As I hinted earlier, the entire procedure entails great risk. While the mathematics allow transfer into a *similar* universe, they do not allow for the precision necessary to select an *exact* one – we could not go back to our unique universe, nor even be certain of another safe transference.

"Now, regarding our orbit. The astrophysicists in the room will know that a counter orbit around the sun is inherently unstable. Normally this would result in a collision between our two planets within the next few decades."

Doug caught Foley's eye from across the aisle. This fact had troubled both men for weeks. Dr. Chan continued.

"Mekhos is able to make regular small corrections to our own orbit, making it stable for both planets. This means we will be able to co-exist in this counter orbit indefinitely."

Doug was impressed, but also unnerved. *Mekhos can control the orbit of a planet,* he thought. *Which means the thing also must be able to tap or generate and control an enormous amount of power.*

"This concludes my portion of the presentation, thank you."

Nayar and a few others blurted out questions but Chan ignored them as he moved to sit down, replaced at the podium by Dr. Bertrand.

"I know you have many questions for Dr. Chan, but we must remain on schedule. I will attempt to impress upon you the benefits we have enjoyed during the past several years."

Bertrand paused and took a sip of water, nodding at familiar faces and acknowledging some of the Earth scientists with whom he spent even brief one-on-one moments. He included Doug. Bertrand knew how to work an audience, to hold attention.

"Because it is a supremely intelligent entity, unfettered by greed or emotion, Mekhos has been able to successfully formulate economic policy so that the traditional cyclical extremes, along with their result-ing hardships, no longer occur. Spin-off benefits are increased political stability with reduced international conflict, allowing countries to bet-ter distribute resources. Poverty has been greatly reduced, literacy rates have gone up, and the standard of living has increased across the globe."

Bertrand spent the next half hour singing the praises of his society. It sounded as if he was trying to sell the idea of a quantum computer on Earth. But why bother with the effort? Any country would sell its soul to obtain the most powerful computer in existence. No sales pitch needed. FLO could demand any price. But FLO planned to give every-one access to the QC. Or maybe not. Bertrand hadn't stated it as fact.

— 30 —

The entire briefing lasted three hours. The audience was able to mingle with the Envoy group for a short time afterward, but they were in such demand it was difficult to speak with any of them for more than a couple of minutes at a time. Nayar managed to corner Chan for a brief time before Bertrand took Chan aside.

Doug saw Cheryl talking to Leach. When she saw him she excused herself and walked over. He noticed she walked with a limp.

"I'm sorry," she said. "None of us have had a free moment since get-ting here. I won't be free for dinner. Can we get together say, at 2100?"

"Absolutely," Doug replied. "Are you all right?"

"Your doctors tell me I have arthritis in both ankles. Carl has learned he has high blood pressure. Alfred is complaining of mild hearing loss. I guess 40 is the new 50 when you're an astronaut," she said with a smile.

They chatted for a moment, and then the Envoy was ushered out for yet another private meeting with senior White House staff and rep-resentatives from several countries who seemed now to be physically stationed at Andrews.

— 31 —

Afterward Cheryl met Doug in the visitors mess where he had just fin-ished a coffee. An agent had accompanied her but sat a few feet away.

Cheryl said she wanted to relax in a hot tub, the kind with water jets, and asked if there were any facilities on the base. Doug told her about a physiotherapy whirlpool in one of the exercise facilities, and that they would need permission to use it. Going to his room was out of the question. Each member of the Envoy was escorted or at least shadowed by an agent at all times. He suggested they relax in the base library, but she was adamant about needing to unwind in a whirlpool. Doug didn't remember his Cheryl professing any enjoyment at being in a hot tub or sauna or whirlpool of any kind.

He talked to Agent Bishop about permission to use the whirlpool. Bishop cleared it through security almost immediately. It seemed that since Doug was friendly with a member of the Envoy it was easier to gain access to some of the areas that were normally restricted to regular base personnel. Nevertheless, Bishop warned him. *The whirlpool is for her alone. Keep your distance.*

Doug had no doubt they'd be under surveillance every moment anyway. He was about to reassure Bishop, then stopped himself. His exposure to security agents over the past few weeks had given him insight about their efficient, direct way of communicating. It was better to just nod sharply and confirm the instruction.

– 32 –

Doug turned his back while Cheryl put on a one-piece bathing suit.

"Thanks," she said after she finished changing.

When Doug turned around he noticed she was still wearing the plastic Raim bracelet.

"Don't you need to remove that?" he asked.

"No, it's waterproof." She didn't speak again until she was in the whirlpool. "Could you turn the water jets on, please?"

Doug did so, then pulled a folding chair over to the edge of the pool opposite Cheryl. He sat in the chair and leaned forward, his elbows on his knees and his hands clasped together.

"These bracelets can't be removed easily," Cheryl said while keeping her arm with the bracelet submerged. "Every citizen has the option of applying for a removal key, but keys were forbidden for our trip here.

Mekhos and the government wish to have a complete record of what transpires, and that includes private conversations. Our removal keys were confiscated immediately after our selection as Envoy members, well before our departure. Carl Bertrand is the only one of our group who was allowed to retain his removal key, though I'm not sure why."

Doug found the idea of always-on surveillance troubling. He didn't like the idea of his personal feelings being broadcast to government minders, here or on another planet.

"You mean everything we say is transmitted live, as we speak?"

"The bracelet is used as a transceiver at home. Here on the Twin, data is stored in the Raim and periodically uploaded to the ship and then transmitted back home."

"Can it pick up our voices when it's underwater?"

"Yes, if the water is still. It can also register my own voice through vibrations in my body when I speak, but I'm holding my wrist in front of a water jet. The turbulence hitting the bracelet masks my voice, even the vibrations."

Doug stared at her. He suddenly realized that he had been man-euvered into the situation because of his well-known virtual connection to this Cheryl. He felt foolish and guilty, sitting as he was with a rep-lica of a woman he had once loved, while the body of the woman he had truly loved was buried in a cemetery only two hours drive away. He wanted to get away at that moment, but his conflicted feelings hardly mattered. This Cheryl obviously had something to say and seemed to be trying to show him that she was risking her own proto-cols to do so. He steadied his breathing before he spoke.

"What are we doing here?"

"We're here because I need to tell you something. We know we're being watched and we know someone is always listening. We came here to see this vibrant world, with so many innocent people, innocent children. It is so similar to our own. It is Mekhos that has brought us to your reality. It is Mekhos that has created this plan for the survival of my world. We are not party to what it has planned."

He looked at her intently. She paused, as if reconsidering.

"What is it?" he said. "What danger does FLO pose to Earth?"

Cheryl remained silent just a few moments too long. Her eyes had been downcast, but she lifted her gaze to stare directly at Doug. He suddenly felt cold.

"Your observatories will find out eventually. For the past few weeks our two planets have been directly opposite, with no way to observe each other from the ground."

"Right, but that will change as orbital eccentricity comes into play, and the planets will be briefly visible to each other. About two months time."

"And your space-based telescopes have been preoccupied with taking close-up images of FLO."

"Cheryl, what are you trying to say?"

Another pause.

"My Earth…" she said finally, "FLO… has no Moon. It wasn't transported with us to your universe."

Doug thought for a moment. He had raised the question to Stacey Lau early on, but with so much happening in the interim he had almost forgotten about it. He just assumed – they had all assumed – that FLO's moon was there, but that the smaller body was being obscured by the Sun's coronal halo interfering even with space-based telescopes.

"Okay," Doug said slowly. "I assume that was no small oversight. Where are you going with this?"

"Mekhos ran simulation after simulation for transferring us to this universe, but given the urgency of the situation it's entirely possible Mekhos didn't even think about the Moon. Or it didn't have time to include the calculations necessary to transfer the Moon with us before the gamma ray burst was due to arrive. Or it didn't have sufficient power available. We just don't know."

"And you're saying that without the stabilizing effect of the Moon, FLO's axial tilt may eventually become unstable, playing havoc with the climate. But that probably won't happen for twenty thousand years, if ever. You shouldn't be in any danger."

Cheryl shook her head.

"No," she said firmly. "You don't understand. The Moon had been present since life began on Earth. I mean on FLO. Countless insect, animal and marine species depend on its light and monthly cycles. Mating habits, seasonal migration. Now without the Moon's illumination our nights are totally dark. And we have no tides! Think about this. Twice a day coastal areas experienced tides. Over hundreds of thousands of years so many marine and coastal species evolved to rely on them. Some more than others, but the effects of their absence are devastating for key areas of the food chain. Some coral reefs are collapsing because microscopic animal life is no longer present. The effects are happening on land as well – pollination for one. Some crops are not germinating. Countless plant and animal species – nocturnal and many others – directly or indirectly depended on the Moon for their life cycles. Many nocturnal species are being decimated without moonlight by which to hunt and forage. They cannot adapt so quickly. And then there are the earthquakes."

As the ramifications sunk in Doug shook his head and leaned back in his chair.

"FLO has changed shape without the influence of the orbiting moon. From what I understand, quakes and tsunami surges only began ebbing while we were on our way here. It's a mess. Species you wouldn't think would be affected are going extinct, because they are tied to another affected species. Everything is so interconnected and synchronized with the daily changes and Moon phases. Take them away, and we have a worldwide environmental disaster, one that may doom civilization within a half generation."

"I don't know what to say," Doug said sharply. "People will survive. People will adapt."

"Climate change and species extinction were already influenced by global warming, just as it is with your Earth today. Factor in the added shock of losing the Moon. We're talking about a near extinction level event for my people. Mekhos has calculated that with the predicted famine and military conflicts over competition for resources, only eight percent of the world's population will be alive in twenty years time. As species continue to die off, that's how many my Earth can sustain, due to cascading failures."

"Only half a billion people, down from seven billion?" Doug replied quietly. "Can you reintroduce species from Earth, in hopes they adapt?"

"Thousands of species are affected. Insects, plants, mammals, birds, even some species of bacteria. We wouldn't know where to begin."

"Nothing can be done?" Doug asked, frowning at her. "Then why are you here? Why is the Envoy here?"

"There is a plan in place, Doug," Cheryl said, after a pause in which only the turbulent water could be heard. "But in order to save our planet it must be implemented soon."

Doug waited for her to continue. She hesitated again, but then look directly into his eyes as she spoke.

"Mekhos will use the same technological power that it put in place to keep our counter orbit stable. It is going to take your Moon and re-orbit it around FLO."

— 33 —

Agent Bishop was speaking rapidly into his comm on a flat-out sprint to the security building just a little under half a mile across the base. It took him just over two minutes to cover the distance. He waited impatiently at the security door while his ID was scanned and his sidearm checked in. It took another minute to sprint to the observation and surveillance station room. He flung open the door. There were four agents present, two sitting in front of monitors and wearing headsets.

"Did our surveillance pick that up?" Bishop said.

The team commander wearing a headset nodded, holding up his hand for silence.

Bishop stood tensely, impatiently, an unfocused anger beginning to build inside him. "What are the—?" he began, but the agent on comms glared at him.

"The Director has been notified. We're waiting for orders. Quiet please." The agent listened intently to his headset.

One agent checked his wristwatch. The team commander was gripping the edge of his desk so hard that his knuckles were white. Another agent was sitting bolt upright in his chair, trying to control his breathing. The fourth agent was now standing in front of his surveillance console, but just staring at it without actually noticing anything.

"That's it," the commander said flatly after a moment. "Round them up! MPs are on the way. Put them all in separate holding cells. Nobody talks to them until an interrogation team arrives."

— 34 —

"Why!" Doug had knelt down, plunged his right hand into the whirl-pool and grabbed her submerged wrist, holding the Raim tightly in his fist. "Why can't your Mekhos take a large body from the asteroid belt? Your leaders and your machine know full well that in saving your planet you're murdering mine!"

"Mekhos wants something of the exact same dimensions and mass that we lost, and as soon as possible if its plan is to work. Objects in the asteroid belt are too far away given the critical time factor. That leaves only one choice. We brought some devices with us that were launched from our ship and then deployed before we arrived. They are on your Moon now, positioned for activation."

Doug released his grip and slowly moved back, staring at the replica of the woman he had loved, the replica who just told him that his world would be almost completely destroyed within a generation.

"You know you won't be allowed back to your ship."

"I know. None of us wanted this. We came here out of reverence. We owed you that much, to tell you that once the Moon is gone Mekhos will offer advice about how to manage your world in the time that is left to you. None of us expected to leave. We hoped our report back would convince Mekhos to change its plan, but it won't."

She began to cry. Doug reacted, moved slightly toward her to offer comfort, but stopped himself. An old habit. His mind was reeling. He felt unsteady on his feet.

Doug was in mild shock. He almost laughed at the absurd thought that Mekhos would offer advice to a planet which it had summarily sentenced to death.

"Your damned Machine," Doug finally said, not looking at the woman, "giving us a tiny morsel of pity. And *advice!*" He shouted the last word, then quietly, "A quantum of mercy, to help us die with dignity."

Bishop and an agent from the comms center burst into the room, separating the two scientists, handcuffed Cheryl and led her away.

– 35 –

George Stamouli had a night off and was observing the Moon through his home telescope. He had built a shed in his back yard expressly for his hobby, with a retractable roof, a computer-controlled tracking system, a comfortable chair, a sound system for music, and even a small refrigerator for drinks.

Though his telescope was miniscule compared to the ones at the observatory, having his own equipment meant he could view whatever he wanted without having to schedule it far in advance. Plus, it was far less cumbersome when observing relatively close objects like the Moon. He never got tired of examining the limitless craters and valleys, and the various beautiful shades of grey. On cloudless nights like this the conditions were perfect.

At first George had been envious of Doug being called in by the White House on such a world-shaking project. The man had discovered a new planet for goodness sake, and was rubbing shoulders with the President. Meanwhile, George was doing his usual job with its usual responsibilities. Still, he treasured these quiet evenings alone in his back yard, and was thankful he wasn't undergoing the stress Doug was no doubt experiencing.

His phone beeped, indicating a text message. It was from Doug:

Dorsa Smirnov lower. Urgent.

Doug knew about George's fondness for studying the moon's features. Dorsa Smirnov was an unremarkable ridge system. George had briefly studied it when he was an undergrad. He entered the coordinates into his laptop and the telescope moved slightly. He zoomed in and examined the area through the eyepiece. Nothing unusual. His phone beeped again.

It was another text from Doug containing more detailed coordinates near Dorsa Smirnov, down to three decimal places. It narrowed the area to about twenty square kilometers. George entered the new data and the telescope adjusted again.

Why would Doug want him to look at this particular ridge? There was nothing special about it. Unless it had something to do with FLO. George was a detail man, but he didn't see anything out of the ordinary – at least not right away. *What do have we here?* he said to himself. A very small black spot, roughly square shaped. It looked like a shadow, but there didn't appear to be anything casting it.

Even though his telescope was top of the line for an amateur setup, at moon distances its resolution was not fine enough to see anything much smaller than a football stadium. But what it could easily see were long shadows cast by smaller objects.

He examined the shadow for a few minutes, trying to find any feature beside it that might be responsible, but couldn't discern anything. Too small to be resolved.

Was the shadow getting larger? George thought as he concentrated on the spot, sweat beginning to coat his brow. He was tense from remaining so still and focused. There! The shadow was definitely getting longer, as if the object casting it was moving. He took note of where the shadow ended. After getting longer for a few more seconds, it began reducing, as if something was travelling up and down a hill. Something artificial was on the Moon's surface, and it was moving.

George continued to maintain his focus on the shadow as he reached for his mobile phone. He stopped when he saw the image begin to vibrate and felt his chair shake. He sat back. The entire shed was shaking. It was a minor earthquake, enough to rattle the drinks in his fridge and throw his telescope off the coordinates.

After a couple of minutes George became worried. The tremor wasn't severe, but it kept a steady intensity, and wasn't stopping. Earthquakes in the area rarely lasted more than a few seconds. He decided to leave the shed. As he stepped onto the grass the ground continued to shake. He had not forgotten Doug's text. Even though he could not see the shadow without his telescope, he glanced back up at the moon.

George Stamouli thought the moon looked different. After a moment, he realized why. He suddenly felt flushed and unsteady. He could feel his pulse pounding in his ears. All he could do was stare in shock. The moon was smaller in the sky. It was moving away from the Earth.

REVENGE

In Nagoya, Japan, Mrs. Tanaka was in the middle of teaching her 3rd grade class when the tremor started. Japan was no stranger to earthquakes and other natural disasters, so the children knew what to do and within seconds they were all crouched under their desks. Most of the children were scared, but two of them giggled as a large stuffed mascot tumbled off a shelf onto the floor.

Mrs. Tanaka expected the quake to stop after a minute, but it continued. The building's foundation had been built with earthquakes in mind but it was an older design that still moved alarmingly, and so as the tremor went on their fright intensified. Some of the children began to cry, including the ones that had been laughing a minute before. Despite her attempt to be brave for the children, Mrs. Tanaka could feel her own panic rising. *Hasn't Japan been though enough? We are cursed,* she thought, as the walls creaked and shook.

Mrs. Tanaka didn't know it, but the earthquake was worldwide. As the Moon was pulled away, its gravitational influence on the Earth was reduced. When one spherical body orbits another the mutual gravitational effect warps the spheres into ovals. Normally as the Earth rotates, the oceans and even the solid crust are pulled towards the Sun and Moon, though the tidal effect exerted by the Moon is much greater due to its closer proximity.

As the Moon was pulled out of its orbit, the Earth's slight oval shape began to move back into a near perfect sphere. The north and south poles increased their distance from each other, while the circumference of the Earth at the equator constricted. The Earth would remain slightly oval due to the centrifugal force of its own rotation, but as the Moon's gravitational influence waned, the Earth changed back to a shape it had not been since before the Moon had formed over four billion years earlier.

Had the phenomenon been slower there would not have been a continuous tremor. But the Moon was moving rapidly away, getting noticeably smaller in the sky with each passing hour. In a few days it would appear to the unaided eye as no more than a moving pinpoint of reflected light. The rapid reduction of the Moon's gravitational influence meant that in some areas of the globe the planetary crust was subjected to forces it had not endured since it was formed. In the first hours it was felt by everyone on Earth, even in areas not prone to earthquakes. People in their homes and apartments were frightened as dust fell from the ceilings, walls cracked, and dishes clattered noisily in cabinets. The shaking continued for hours, and was most violent closer to the equator. In most areas of the world the panic did not come from the intensity of the tremors as it did from their relentless duration. Hours passed without relief.

Houses and buildings which had for decades or longer easily withstood a thousand small, brief tremors, cracked and shuddered themselves to the point of collapse, killing or maiming whoever was caught inside that hadn't run out into the streets. The old rule about finding a structural archway didn't save anyone when the entire building came down on them.

At the poles glaciers cracked and calved off while undersea tremors triggered tsunamis, flooding costal areas. Hawaii was hit hard.

Kainoa Pahia had just retired from thirty years as a postal worker and was on Keawa'ula beach with his wife Kate when he heard the tsunami warning sirens. Kate had been swimming several hundred meters out. Kainoa stood up from his beach chair and frantically scanned the water for her.

The surf began to recede. At first Kate was pulled out with it, but then her feet found the sand beneath her and she was able to stop her momentum outward. As she stood the water level went to her waist, then to her knees, then to her feet. She did not know what was happening and looked towards the beach to Kainoa. She spotted him waving frantically at her. She could easily see his wild agitation and that instantly panicked her. She glanced back towards the ocean. Her eyes followed the retreat of the water, and as her gaze arced outward and up she saw it. A wall of water rising above the horizon. She saw a boat captured in the tsunami, tumbling over until it disappeared. She was frozen in place, her throat constricted in panic. Kainoa's shouts reached her finally in the eerie silence. Adrenalin kicked in and she spun towards the beach running as fast as she could in the exposed, wet ocean floor.

Kainoa saw his wife wheel towards him and start running. He shouted encouragement, his voice becoming a frantic scream as he realized what he was seeing. Part of him knew they could not escape. He was standing rooted to his spot on the beach as his wife ran to him. Kate reached him, grabbed his hand to continue sprinting away from the mountain of water rising behind, but Kainoa was unable to take his eyes off the approaching monster. Kate saw his stare and turned again to face the enormous surge that was closing so fast.

"Kainoa please we must run!"

He didn't move.

"KAINOA!" She shouted. "We have to run!"

He pulled her close in a tight embrace while not taking his eyes from the wall of water. A shiver went through him, but then he felt a surprising sense of calm. She stared at him and understood. They would not escape, no matter how fast they ran. She began to cry, not out of fear, but because of the moments they would no longer have together.

They closed their eyes and held each other tightly. An instant later they and hundreds of other beachgoers were drowned. The tsunami smashed into the beachside resort, crashing through huts, tables, chairs, palm trees, and finally the row of hotels. Buildings were ripped from their foundations and carried inland. The relentless surge destroyed everything in its path, pushing the massed wreckage and death inland.

At coastlines around the globe, sea levels rose at some locations and lowered in others. Inland, buildings shook and pavement cracked. Bridges collapsed, gridlocking roadways to a standstill. Damage levels varied widely. Built along fault lines, cities such as San Francisco and Istanbul experienced severe damage. It was the big one so many had feared for so long, but even worse due to the tremor duration. Gas lines broke and caught fire. Widespread power, mobile phone and land line outages meant people were isolated and emergency responders couldn't be directed effectively.

It was the same everywhere in the world. Millions were dying and hundreds of millions more were being left homeless.

Areas in and around Paris and Moscow experienced only moderate damage at first, but as the tremors continued window frames shook loose, foundations cracked and many buildings once thought to be solid and safe neared the point of collapse. The fact the quaking lasted for several hours drove many people to the streets in hysterics, some believing the world was ending. Very few understood what was happening, unless they got a glimpse of the Moon. Then their panic and unease grew to outright terror. Some thought it was the Earth that was moving, being cast into the Sun or into oblivion.

After several agonizing hours the earthquakes slowly abated as the Moon's gravitational influence subsided and the Earth's changing shape began to stabilize. Frequent aftershocks would occur for months as the crust settled. Tidal ebb and flow, now suddenly influenced by the sun alone, were reduced to a small fraction of what they'd been for billions of years. Groups of people who expected or depended on tides gathered along river mouths, tidal basins and shorelines, waiting for tides that never came.

– 37 –

The Envoy turned out to be more of a crisis management team, offering assistance in dealing with the environmental devastation they knew would be coming.

Emergency meetings were called among world leaders and the scientific community, discussing the possible short and long-term effects. The Envoy warned that without the Moon's light, monthly phases and daily tidal influences, countless insect, plant and animal species would be affected. Those that depended on the Moon for their life cycles and migration patterns would quickly become extinct. Other plants and animals that depended on the first group would also perish. Some scientists believed the ecosystem would adapt, but the Envoy presented some hard facts that said otherwise. The cascading failure of the ecosystem would devastate the world's food supply, just as it was affecting that of FLO.

Insistent questions were about Mekhos. The Envoy was hard pressed to explain, over and over, that the quantum computer harbored no ill will towards Earth. It had merely used its implacable logic to solve a problem. Mekhos possessed no emotions about its home planet either. For many individuals it was difficult to fathom that such a powerful thinking machine had no feelings of protectiveness towards society. Everyone on FLO had long since begun to anthropomorphize the QC. A select few individuals with close ties to Mekhos knew the truth and the Envoy group hinted at that in their assurances to Doug and his team and to the President and UN and anyone else who asked, that the emotionless supercomputer had calculated that only one world could be saved from environmental disaster.

Mekhos reasoned that the more evolved world – the one with greater social, economic and political stability – would be saved. Even so, it was in a race against time to stop the species die-off on FLO before it became critical. It was hoped that the Moon would be placed into orbit around FLO in time to save those species most affected, and thereby minimize damage to the ecosystem and food supply. To Mekhos, it was simply unfortunate that Earth would bear the consequences of the actions.

Governments were in panic. Calls were made between allies. Calls were made between adversaries. In the blind fear nobody knew what to do as the Moon was ripped from orbit and disappeared from view. Arrogant have-not dictators that up to then had been causing more than their fair share of trouble in the world began sending beseeching ambassadors to more powerful nations, begging for help and guidance with something they could not understand.

Some heads of state were aware that the Moon's disappearance would eventually wreak havoc with the ecosystem and food supply. They had to prepare their populations for the day when the damaging effects began to appear. Areas hard-hit by the quakes required rebuilding, which stressed resources and morale. Panic and anarchy would be the most likely result and had already started on a small scale, with citizens splitting off into groups to gather, secure and control as much water and food as possible. Lawlessness lurked just around the corner. Law and order had not broken down yet, but there wasn't a government anywhere in the world that wasn't fully immersed in planning for the inevitable breakdown that would come when enough people believed there was no hope.

– 38 –

Days after the event began, the worst of the earthquakes finally ended. The aftershocks and tremors hadn't stopped though, and the insistent reminders on radio, television and the internet made every citizen in every country on the planet aware that the unpredictable and random shaking would go on for months or even longer. People everywhere were grimly trying to adapt to a new reality for which none of them could prepare.

Agent Bishop was in the observation room of a holding facility at Andrews Air Force Base. He was standing with a CIA debriefer watching an interrogation that had been going on for nearly an hour. Bishop was there as an observer, part of his security supervision of the Envoy and the scientific team.

Once the true purpose of the Envoy's mission was revealed, the scientific team's mission shifted from urgent information gathering on something mysterious, to something more unsettlingly concrete. They were trying to gather information they hoped would save the human race.

The Envoy team members were the primary source of information. Though the members of the Envoy were not instrumental in the plan Mekhos had devised and executed, they had prior knowledge of it. That fact alone had turned them into subjects of a particularly motivated group of interrogation experts cooperatively chosen from British Intelligence and the CIA who had all been brought to Andrews under a veil of total secrecy enforced by the NSA.

Although he wasn't part of the interrogation team, Bishop's experience with the Envoy made him a consultant to the interrogators, and he was sometimes brought in to the observation area behind one-way glass as the subjects were questioned.

The team had focused on two members of the Envoy, changing things up every day. Sleep deprivation, drugs, incessant questioning, threats followed by friendly dialog. All standard procedure. The interrogation team had run into a problem though. The Envoy members appeared to have very little useful information and seemed to be telling the truth about what information they did provide.

Though he had deep-seated anger at the fate dealt Earth by Mekhos and was a battle-hardened veteran of the Gulf war, Afghanistan and several covert operations that had never hit the news, Bishop took no pleasure in witnessing a civilian being squeezed mentally or physically by professionals. The Envoy members were clearly what they claimed to be: civilian scientists on Earth by choice, to act as ambassadors in an impossible situation. Even so, given the grave threat posed by the Mekhos plan, the government had given the interrogators more leeway than usual, authorizing enhanced interrogation techniques when it came to dealing with the two subjects.

Dr. Peter Morris was not holding up well. The interrogators had inflicted bouts of screaming, threats, sleep deprivation, intense light shone in his face, and even some physical beatings. When it eventually became clear that he knew little about the supercomputer or of the plan details, the interrogators turned to extracting strategic information.

Morris was a navy doctor. Nevertheless, he had to have some knowledge of general military information, such as installation locations, command personnel and even some security details.

"Your GPS locator doesn't work here," said an interrogator. "On what frequencies do your satellites operate? Come on doctor, you should have been given this information for emergencies, in case you found yourself trapped on foreign soil and needed to access a transmitter."

Morris gave them what information he could and they pressed on to other subjects. He went from being overly gregarious, to stoic silence, to pleading, and finally sobbing as his torment continued. From his reaction to the last blow Bishop figured he now had a broken rib. Bishop stepped forward and rapped on the glass, indicating the interrogators should ease up.

"It's not your place to object," said the man next to him, the lead interrogator named Patrick.

"Morris is afraid of his Raim," Bishop replied. "Don't you get it? He's more afraid of the Raim than your team."

"You don't know that," Patrick said quickly, but there was little conviction in his voice.

"I know that if your bruisers keep it up they may puncture his lung, lacerate his liver or worse," Bishop replied. "If he's in the hospital or morgue, you won't get a lot out of him. Cut the Raim off, let Morris live without it for a couple of days, then try to make friends with him. You're treating Morris like a terrorist when you should be treating him like a defector."

"The Raim won't come off. Not easily," Patrick replied tightly. "Best information we've got is that it has a tough core specifically designed to resist simple removal by cutting. The subject also screamed about a non-key removal causing power supply discharge that could blow his wrist apart. We lanced it repeatedly. We disabled it and it can't transmit. We're sure of that much. It obviously didn't blow up either."

"That might be propaganda put out by Mekhos itself. Morris obviously believes the Raim is still working somehow. Remove it. Have a surgical team standing by just in case. What I said still stands. He's a scientist, not military. Not a spy. All you're doing is terrorizing him and getting nothing in return."

Agent Patrick hesitated. Bishop wasn't wrong. Everybody was desperate and it was showing in the worst ways. The men inside the room were looking back at the one-way glass, awaiting orders. Patrick moved to the intercom. "That's enough for now. Dr. Morris will cooperate with us tomorrow."

"Your team," Bishop said to Patrick, "has gone too far. Dr. Morris doesn't really understand what's happening to him. I'd bet real money he was prepared to cooperate fully after some gentle persuasion, but it looks like your crew mistook hesitation on his part for actual resistance. You made Morris think about his Raim and dig his heels in. You made a mistake."

"You sympathize with these people?" Patrick replied, staring at Bishop. "Morris started to cooperate, then stopped of his own accord. The Raim is an unknown. I've got bigger problems here. We're following protocols, nothing more."

"No you're not," Bishop said, turning to face him. "You've blown it, and you're going to have to deal with the consequences of sending Morris, busted up, Raim and all, back to his people. You want to stand on protocols? Fine. Protocol states that you deal most effectively with a scientist by impressing him with the benefits and opportunities of co-operation. You haven't done that. Not even close. Your team lost its collective temper and you let them take it out on Morris. So good luck, Mr. Patrick. You've only made it harder for yourself. You're going to catch hell for this."

Patrick looked at Bishop in stunned silence. As the agents unstrapped Morris from the chair, Bishop left the observation room for good. Training for his new mission would demand one hundred percent of his time.

— 39 —

Arthur Leach, the White House Chief of Staff addressed the Joint Chiefs and the Intelligence services at the latest in a series of emergency meetings. He looked tired, and his suit showed signs of being worn a few hours too long. He was holding a photograph of a clear plastic-like bracelet taken from one of the Envoy prisoners.

"This is called a Raim. It's a fact of life on FLO, government issued and every citizen wears one. It's some sort of multisensory-recorder-transceiver. Envoy leader Carl Bertrand provided the information after disabling and removing his own Raim. Otherwise he would not have been able to communicate fully with us without great personal risk to his family and colleagues on FLO. None of the other Envoy members were allowed to keep their Raim removal keys prior to departure for Earth." He handed over the photograph to be passed around.

"Bertrand and other envoy members have informed us that there is a growing anti-Mekhos faction on FLO. We have no reason to doubt the information. These groups believe the supercomputer has become too meddlesome, to the point at which there seems to be no personal privacy at all. A Raim is issued to every citizen over the age of twelve. It is a very sophisticated device. Think of it as a wearable computer and health monitor that is also capable of recording every utterance of the wearer and of those in close proximity. Mekhos and various governments on FLO have access to those recordings."

The Commandant of the Marine Corps examined the photo.

"Bertrand also said that every citizen has the option to apply for a removal key, so the user need not wear it constantly, or at all," he said, passing the photo along.

"Removal keys are difficult to obtain, and getting more so every year," Leach continued. "Those with criminal convictions can no longer get them. The bar for criminality now includes misdemeanor offences such as causing a disturbance. It's becoming difficult to interact in their society without one, just as not having a driver's licence and credit card is troublesome for people in most countries on Earth. So even those that grumble about the lack of privacy wear the Raim to avoid constant inconvenience. Some groups warn that life will soon be impossibly difficult without the bracelet. Every word will eventually be recorded, twenty-four hours a day. The fear is that Mekhos will have no problem finding and processing anyone it considers seditious."

"And this information helps us how?" the Commandant said impatiently. "On what basis do we trust information from Bertrand or any other Envoy member?"

"Because there's more," Leach continued. "There are plenty of utopians in governments on FLO fully willing to sacrifice some freedoms in return for world peace. But the overarching control that Mekhos is gradually and firmly exercising over FLO has started to look like too high a price to pay. Bertrand has given us the contacts for an underground group on FLO that opposes Mekhos. The group is called Virtue. They are also sympathetic to Earth's situation. Bertrand insists that the group will offer assistance to an outside team that may have a greater chance of success."

"Success at what?"

Leach looked around the room before he answered, trying to predict the response.

"Success at starting to fight back. We propose to help Virtue destroy or disable Mekhos."

— 40 —

Professor Doug Lockwood had witnessed the world's reaction to the loss of the moon. Much of the impotent posturing of the world's leaders reminded Doug of a documentary he had once seen about logging in rainforests. As the logging trucks encroached on its part of the forest, a lone orangutan had climbed a tree at the edge of the clear cut and tossed a leafy branch down in the direction of the advancing machinery. A sad, futile gesture of defiance.

China threatened to launch an attack to destroy the devices on the Moon. They had to know that any launched missile had no hope of reaching anywhere even close. It was simple saber rattling. If anything, the threat impressed upon every nation the folly of making angry, panic-based decisions in the midst of the crisis.

In his Washington, DC apartment, Doug got himself a drink of water and went out to the balcony in his pajamas and slippers. It was 3:00 AM and unseasonably cold. The weather patterns were starting to change in the absence of the moon's influence. Due to the stress of the situation and his workload he hadn't had a good night's rest in weeks. He moved about quietly because he didn't want to disturb Janet, still sleeping. It had been three weeks since the Envoy ship from FLO had landed. In that time so much in the world had changed.

Longtime colleagues sometimes turn to each other for intimacy, especially in times of deep stress and crisis, Doug thought to himself. Although he was jaded by the term, he knew that he may have found a soul mate in Janet. She was intelligent, thoughtful and emotionally mature, not to mention physically attractive. She was athletic, a runner. Maybe when things were less hectic he could convince her to take up cycling.

Looking up at the moonless sky brought Doug back to the present. Despite the Envoy's presence, Doug and his team still did not know enough about FLO. Mekhos had continued to impose broadcast silence, allowing only sparse programming to resume. Though it was unclear if it would provide any benefit, observatories, broadcast receivers of all kinds, military monitoring stations and radio telescopes all over the world were continually observing and listening for anything that might help gain an understanding of how to deal with FLO. The few broadcasts they could capture consisted of local news and entertainment shows. All they got out of the news reports were earthquake and damage reports.

In the distance, a siren went off. It was a long, keening wail which these days usually meant that another apartment building had either collapsed or the crack sensors on its outer walls had flexed too far for safety and triggered an alarm. Fire & Rescue were likely rushing to evacuate the place. The residents would have to fend for themselves. *I hope they all put together emergency kits of food, clothing, money, ID and valuables like the government has been recommending,* Doug thought, *or they're going to be in really tough straits in the morning.* He was thankful his own building was solid. Aside from a few small cracks in a couple of interior walls, there was no major damage thus far.

Deal with FLO - that was the order given to Doug. It was an absurdly optimistic term. FLO's civilization was more advanced, more peaceful, and its population healthier and better fed, with almost no poverty. Above it all stood Mekhos. Doug shook his head as he looked out over the DC night sky. FLO was likely quite content to carry on with that existence, with little more than a pitying nod to its poor new relative.

It was a clear night, but ominously dark despite the city lights. When Doug had insomnia back in Hawaii he would venture out to his deck, the moon sometimes so bright he could read a newspaper by it once his eyes adjusted. Now that was impossible. He felt a chill and momentarily claustrophobic thinking about a nightfall outside the city with no Moon to ever relieve the inky blackness. The building shook yet again, and Doug gripped the wide balcony rail to feel the movement. It felt, through his bare hand, like the subterranean rumbling of an unhappy giant. *Mother Earth is deeply disturbed.*

He was a highly respected scientist and astronomer. He knew his lunar tables, so he stared at a patch of black sky where the Moon should be. All he could see was blackness and a panorama of faint pinpoints. A billion, billion stars, but no Moon any more. The Moon that had guided ancient sailors, and the Moon that had influenced the evolution of life and shepherded proto-humans throughout their development, casting its light on the earth since before life began, was gone. Stolen by an implacable adversary. *Our own planet has become strange to us. All those billions of people who never had to think about their place in the cosmos have suddenly been shown that they're all just insignificant ants on a barely habitable ball hurtling through space alongside new neighbors with the power to take whatever they want from us.*

On that terrible first day, the Moon had gotten noticeably smaller in the sky. By the sixth day it was no longer visible without a telescope. Observatories and news services around the world gave constant reports on its recession, regular reminders to the people of what they had lost. *As if the pitch black nights weren't enough,* he thought.

Even now, despite the fate it had wrought upon Earth, Doug was impressed by the power of Mekhos. A computer based on qubit, on quantum mechanics instead of silicon, it was millions of times faster than the fastest computer on Earth. According to the Envoy, Mekhos had attained sentience. The power Mekhos wielded was almost indescribable. It had the power to manipulate space, which it had done to save its planet from a predicted catastrophic gamma ray burst that would have destroyed all life.

Doug shook his head at the accomplishment, while at the same time cursing the machine for dooming the people of his world to an eventual existence little better than extinction.

Something nagging at Doug finally rose to the surface, something obvious, as it should have been. *For all its immense power,* Doug thought, *Mekhos seems to be unsophisticated. Why just take the Moon and offer only an Envoy as compensation? Is the machine's programming or design flawed in some way that prevents it from seeing the value of a stable Earth as an ally, and a means for FLO and Earth to become something uniquely great together? That sort of ignorance seems unlikely. Which may mean that there was a conscious decision to ignore Earth's fate. But why?*

Though the public had become aware of FLO and knew it was somehow responsible for the Moon's disappearance, they had not been informed of the grave fate that lay ahead for Earth. Some biologists and astrophysicists that were interviewed by the media insisted that there would be dire environmental consequences. The governments of the world downplayed their warnings, insisting life would adapt. They were buying time in an effort to avert panic, trying to keep a lid on fanatics and doomsday cults to avoid fueling the rise of despotic leaders that might use the crisis to seize power. It was probably a fundamentally useless effort because the Internet and every social network were seething with facts, lies, manipulations, fanaticism, conspiracies (some of which were real, for once), religious fanatics and every conceivable rumor.

The dispassionate actions of Mekhos infuriated the nations of Earth. But the cold, hard light of reality clearly showed that nothing on Earth could be done to right the situation. Still, high-ranking security and foreign policy experts from all the major world governments were holding regular meetings, asking questions and proposing unworkable solutions. Some of them simply wanted revenge, though with Earth's technology being at least a generation behind that of FLO's, there wasn't much chance of success.

Doug had been in some of those meetings. He was amazed at some of the panicked proposals that ranged from building an arsenal of nuclear missiles capable of reaching FLO to the culling of Earth's population so the elite of society would survive. Extreme suggestions demanded to be shouted down. Doug, along with the other sensible advisors, had succeeded in humiliating more than one extremist panel member into silence. Fortunately the majority agreed with Doug and were committed to reason and logic. Despite the support of rationality, they still weren't getting very far.

Doug was taking the morning off. After weeks of working non-stop, the shock at seeing the alternate Cheryl McBride, and the revelation that she was the bearer of the news of the coming worldwide catastrophe, Doug had taken some time to recharge.

He got dressed quickly and went into the kitchen. He toasted a bagel, spread on more butter than was strictly healthy, peeled an orange and brewed some coffee. He ate quickly, then poured the last of his coffee into a travel mug. He left Janet a note explaining he would meet her at Andrews later and then drove the two hours to the cemetery where Cheryl McBride, the woman he had planned to spend the rest of his life with, was buried.

He needed to reassert that she was the individual he had been in love with, not the alternate Cheryl McBride. "Nobody can replace you," he said out loud. "The damn copy that arrived on the ship is not the woman you were." Doug was doing what was necessary to anchor and re-stabilize his own reality. Visiting the finality of a grave site snapped him back on track. *I will not be confused about any of this again,* Doug thought, as he stood next to Cheryl's grave. *There is far too much at stake for me to be sidetracked by emotional weakness.*

He looked up in the direction of some noise nearby and saw a family visiting the cemetery, laying flowers for departed loved ones. There were three children with their parents. The older child stayed with the parents but the two younger ones ran among the headstones, playing hide and seek, oblivious to the situation, just as their parents were oblivious to the real danger posed by FLO. Then the ground trembled slightly under his feet. A faint aftershock. It was enough to stop the kids playing. They ran back to their parents and quieted down. As he watched them, Doug wondered about their future, about Janet's future, and his own future. He walked quickly back to his car. He had to get back to work. To deal with FLO.

$$- 41 -$$

"Destroy Mekhos?" The Commandant shouted. "Mekhos is saving their planet from an environmental catastrophe! Why would anyone on FLO interfere with that, even if their privacy was being completely eroded? Why would they choose death instead? It doesn't make sense."

"It's not as simple as that," Leach replied. "Mekhos is constantly evolving, growing more powerful every year. At first its global policies were designed to help humankind on FLO, but it is becoming ever more distant from its people. It implements policies without consultation. It punishes dissenting states severely. It has command of mass media and their internet, and it's gaining control of power utilities and oil refineries and all sorts of other infrastructure.

"Mekhos is also taking control of hospitals, genetics labs and food production. Analysts on FLO have concluded that Mekhos will eventually oversee their evolutionary development. Many would say this is not necessarily a bad thing, since it may eradicate disease, but some speculate that Mekhos has already surreptitiously instituted sterility programs to reduce and manage the population."

"Interesting if true," the Commandant said flatly as he regained some composure and leaned back in his chair. "Sounds more like the internet rumor mill and conspiracy cults are just as foolish on FLO as they are here. It's a straw man argument. It has nothing to do with why anyone would choose mass extinction over a regulated birth rate. We're getting all sorts of information from the Envoy without any balancing information from other groups on FLO. That's not what I call reliable intelligence. There must be some other game afoot."

"I agree," Leach replied. He was pressing his right hand into the small of his back to relieve the ache of stress. "We believe Bertrand and his associates on FLO haven't been entirely truthful with us about their ultimate goal. They want our help to attack the quantum supercomputer, but we believe once that is accomplished they will continue the theft of the Moon, while gaining control over a disabled Mekhos."

"So we will have helped them get rid of their autocratic machine while we are left in the same situation, without our Moon. I'm assuming you are about to tell us that some of the response scenarios we discussed earlier are now in play."

"That is correct. But some of you have been pushing for answers while withholding key personnel and resisting cooperation with your counterparts in other nations. Covert Operations has been involved from the beginning but can only do so much, given the scope of what is required. We need all resources at our disposal. Now that you are aware, we trust your respective branches will stop putting up roadblocks. The President expects your cooperation, and as always, your discretion."

Leach stared directly into the eyes of each man and woman at the table, locking his stare on each one in turn for a few moments. No one moved or spoke. There were no other options.

An aide who'd been standing off to the side stepped forward and placed a cooperation and confidentiality document and pen in front of each Joint Chief. They all signed without hesitation.

– 42 –

Alfred Chan was afraid. He had been through several interview sessions with the interrogation experts. Each session had been respectful, polite even. He had not seen his fellow Envoy members since they were separated, when the Mekhos plan was revealed. But then one day when he was being escorted to breakfast he saw his colleague Peter Morris being wheeled into a room. Barely conscious, Peter's left eye was bruised and swollen shut. Chan looked to his agent, hoping for an explanation. The agent did not react as he expected.

"There's a new chef in the kitchen starting today," he said. "They say the new menu will be much better."

After breakfast his handlers were their usual respectful but firm selves.

"As we've discussed, you will probably not see your home again. But we want you to be as comfortable and secure as possible. We will do our best for you and your colleagues. You'll continue your research, working for the US government. You will be assigned your own apartment on the base. Eventually you will be given escorted day passes to various nearby cities to shop and take in the sights, or even the occasional game of golf, if you wish. All we ask is that you apply yourself to the best of your ability to your new mission."

"Thank you," Alfred replied as politely as he could manage. "You have been more than kind. What is this new mission you speak of?"

"It involves a new project for which your special skills will be required."

"I still don't understand. Would you be more specific?"

The man nodded towards an agent. "He'll show you where you'll be working from now on."

Chan suspected that his handlers were treating him well because they thought he could provide them with something they wanted. Peter

Morris had been assigned to keep the Envoy crew healthy for their seven-week journey to this Earth. But now that they were here his skills weren't required. It seemed obvious that Morris might be regarded as expendable, at least in the minds of their captors. Although FLO's medical knowledge had progressed beyond that of Earth, Morris was a Navy GP, not a specialist that could provide anything of much use.

Given the current circumstances, Chan thought, *Earth wasn't very interested in medical progress anyway. The people of this Earth are behind us culturally. Look at the way they treated Morris. What if they want me to betray my own people? What will they do to me when I refuse? Don't they understand that my Raim hears everything they're saying?*

Chan was escorted to an area he had not been to before, into a large computer lab. Arthur Leach and Dr. Brian Nayar, a computer engineer whom Chan had met briefly after giving a presentation on Mekhos a few weeks earlier, were waiting for Chan. Leach smiled and shook his hand.

"Hello Dr. Chan, welcome to your new job. I'm sure you remember Dr. Nayar."

Chan nodded to Nayar.

"Dr. Chan, the presentation you gave on your world's quantum computer breakthroughs was inspiring. We had only just begun to turn our own research in the area to very simple prototypes, but we were thrilled to understand how far you have gotten in the field. As far as we can see, Mekhos is the ultimate supercomputer."

"I appreciate your interest Dr. Nayar," Chan said as he turned his attention back to Leach.

"Just what is my new job?"

"You are going to work with Dr. Nayar. My government is putting an enormous amount of resources at your disposal. You and Dr. Nayar will collaborate to build a quantum supercomputer. You will create for us our own version of Mekhos."

"Do you know what this is, Mr. Leach," Chan said, as he held up his left wrist, the Raim clearly visible.

"Yes," Leach replied tiredly. "We all do, Dr. Chan. But your isolation here on Earth also means that Mekhos can't reach out to you either. So, a Mekhos of our own is what we need. You will help us build it."

— 43 —

Norman Stravinsky hovered the tip of his index finger above the rook. He thought for a moment. He was four moves away from winning the game. He was a master chess player, but he rarely won against his opponent. Stravinsky was sure Mekhos let him win those very few times. The ultimate example of the protégé surpassing the teacher.

Stravinsky moved his finger at a square. The virtual rook moved to the spot he had indicated.

"Excellent move," the voice of Mekhos articulated in the large, nearly featureless chamber. It sounded at once authoritative and comforting, the pronunciation impeccable. Stravinsky had supervised the creation of Mekhos' voice characteristics but the supercomputer had added its own tonality, removing the flat quality that one associates with voice synthesis.

Mekhos did not respond to Stravinsky's move right away. "I appreciate these pauses. I realize you don't need more than a nanosecond to calculate all possible scenarios."

"It is part of the game," Mekhos replied. "All good chess players need time to formulate a response, including you, Norman."

Stravinsky stared at the pieces, the holographic rendering flawless, the board even showing simulated wear marks.

"I read that the visitors will be arriving soon. They find themselves in quite a predicament, don't they?"

Mekhos did not answer. The King moved behind its Bishop.

"Have you exhausted all possibilities with regard to their plight?"

"Yes. Their situation cannot change."

"Pity, that. I wonder how long they will be in turmoil, once the effect starts."

"Equilibrium will be reached in thirty years."

"And then?"

"Life will be comfortable for the remaining population of 500 million. Resources will be available for our use."

"Of course," Stravinsky said, as he moved the Rook once again. "But logically it makes sense to develop a relationship with these people."

"They are reacting in the predicted way. They may appreciate your presence while they are here, Norman."

"I would be delighted to engage with our guests."

Mekhos made the final move. "Checkmate."

— 44 —

On his way back to the Pentagon Doug dialed Leach using his secure phone.

"How are things going with Chan," asked Doug. "Is he cooperating?"

"Alfred is slowly opening up to us, but he's still tentative. I believe he thinks helping us to develop a thinking quantum computer similar to Mekhos would be treasonous, but he's also pragmatic. He can see that we are in a desperate situation and we expect him to come around. The problem is, nobody else here has any advanced knowledge in his field."

"It might help Chan if he were able to bounce ideas off of someone that thinks like he does. Another scientist in addition to Nayar, even if they don't share the exact same background."

"Do you have anyone in mind?"

"The clear choice, if he exists," Doug said, "is Alfred Chan's counterpart here on Earth. If he's alive and if he's in the computer science field, we should bring him on board."

Leach was speechless.

"Haven't you checked this out already?" Doug asked.

"No," Leach said, almost sounding angry, "and I don't know why we didn't think of that sooner. I suppose we've been preoccupied with the bigger picture, planning a dual mission to FLO. Thank you, Doug, I'll have someone look into it immediately."

— 45 —

An hour later at 1300 Doug arrived at the Pentagon to chair a presentation for high ranking military commanders and civilian science experts assembled from the US, Russia, the UK, France, Germany, Japan, China and Brazil.

Every major power resented the fact that the Envoy had made direct contact with the US only, and had made no further attempt to contact any other nation directly. They also resented the fact that there was no evidence that the US had in any way tried to prevent the Envoy from making contact with other nations, although they did accuse the US of not sharing enough information. Germany and France were making the loudest noises even though they couldn't ignore the fact that none of the US scientists who'd gotten in on the ground floor had held anything back from their colleagues in countries all over the world, including Germany and France. Everybody was attempting to get in on everything they could. Arthur Leach was at the back of the room, reading and responding to emails on his laptop. Dr. Miekela Persaud was the first speaker.

"Machine psychology. Up to fifteen days ago it was considered theoretical. Now it is fact." Dr. Persaud was standing at a lectern addressing the science experts. The audience also consisted of the Secretary of State, the Secretary of Defense, a computer engineer from MIT, a psychologist on the White House staff, a representative from the Psychiatric Institute of Washington, and several Joint Chiefs. There were at least thirty other representatives from various countries packing the meeting room. Doug stood off to the side as Dr. Persaud continued.

"Mekhos. We are dealing with an intelligent machine entity, something utterly alien. Despite being created by our human counterparts on FLO, the Mekhos thought processes are completely different from ours. It does not experience feelings or emotions. Its motivations will be difficult to understand from our perspective. But clearly it has purpose. It has goals, and self-interest."

"Yes, we understand that it is an advanced, thinking computer," the Chairman of the Joint Chiefs interjected. "But how can it have self-interest if it lacks emotion? Human self-interest, I gather, comes primarily out of love for our families, our country, and a desire for survival and to live a comfortable life. Those are powerful motivating factors that no computer can have."

"Correct," Miekela replied, as the lights flickered for a moment. A tremor had probably tripped a breaker or rattled a power line loose. Somewhere close by an uninterruptible power supply beeped.

"However, the motivations Mekhos demonstrates seem to come out of the desire to accumulate knowledge, Mr. Chairman. Dr. Alfred Chan of the Envoy believes that Mekhos looks upon itself as an ever-growing library of information. It values knowledge and problem-solving above all else, and has a programmed imperative to preserve that knowledge. So in a sense, it has an instinct for self-preservation."

Dr. Jack Wilson entered the room through a door directly behind the row of chairs at which the Joint Chiefs were sitting and made his way over to Doug, who tapped his watch while giving Wilson a sideways glance. Wilson shrugged his shoulders. Some colleagues regarded Jack Wilson as a loose cannon, prone to emotional outbursts when dealing with people who didn't understand his work. Doug had quickly realized Wilson was brilliant, and his outspoken nature was sometimes an asset, as long as someone was there to rein him in if things got too heated.

"It almost sounds as if we should be dealing with this entity as if it were mentally unbalanced," said Dr. Lee, the representative from PIW. "Sociopaths lack empathy and are motivated primarily by self-gratification at the expense of others. This Mekhos sounds similar to a person with a common personality disorder."

"It would be a mistake to analyze Mekhos in human terms," Dr. Persaud replied. "While there are superficial similarities, the difference is that human sociopaths use their lack of empathy to manipulate others for personal gain, and sometimes solely for their own amusement. Human neurosis and psychosis are still subject to basic human desires and an individual's specific emotional traits. Mekhos has none of those failings. So while we can safely assume a lack of empathy, we can also conclude it acts out of logic and not malice or psychosis."

Some members of the panel nodded. The subject was fascinating even for those who had very little background in science. For the military and intelligence communities represented in the room, Mekhos was a powerful enemy no matter its motivations, and they wanted to know as much as possible about its thought processes.

"From what we've seen so far, Mekhos seems determined to defend itself and its planet, and the humans inhabiting that planet."

"In that order?" said Dr. Lee.

"Yes." Persaud nodded to emphasize the point.

Roger Mellor, a computer engineering specialist from MIT, had been conferring in urgent whispers with a Russian engineer and they were both shaking their heads.

"But the machine must be taking instructions somehow," Mellor said. "Even if it is independent from humans, its basic programming must dictate its actions. It should therefore remain predictable."

Persaud shook her head. "I believe it would be dangerous to go forward with that assumption. According to members of the Envoy, Mekhos has regularly surprised its designers with new capabilities. The most obvious example is the risk it took by harnessing control over space-time to transfer its planet to this universe. No human on FLO could have thought of such a solution let alone constructed a set of orders to feed to Mekhos. Quite the opposite actually. Mekhos created idea and the necessary mathematics and was able to initiate the process completely without human involvement. Mekhos is a self-aware, self-determining individual, one that possesses far more intelligence and power than even its designers thought possible, and perhaps even more than its creator Norman Stravinsky thought possible."

The room was silent for a moment. Doug spoke up to press the itinerary forward.

"Thank you Dr. Persaud. I would now like to introduce Dr. Jack Wilson, a planetary scientist and geologist who has been with us since the beginning of the crisis. Dr. Wilson will be speaking about the ecological impact we are facing."

Dr. Persaud moved to stand by Doug as Wilson positioned himself behind the lectern. He didn't speak right away, shuffling through his notes. There was a cough from one of the Joint Chiefs. Finally Wilson spoke.

"Good morning everyone, I will now talk about the geological implications—"

The Chairman of the Joint Chiefs interrupted him.

"Pardon me, Dr. Wilson, but I want to hear more about the supercomputer. It is a massive threat to our security. I don't really care if the mating patterns of sea turtles will be affected with the Moon's loss."

Some of the other Joint chiefs murmured in agreement. Wilson straightened up, glaring at the audience.

"Sea turtles, Mr. Chairman?" Wilson said. "Let me assure you that none of us here today are so deluded or foolish that we think, with the planet's existence at stake, that this is somehow the time to announce our support for the suspension of the annual sea turtle egg hunt. I'm here to provide you with facts. Specifically, I'm here to confirm that if you all – if we all – don't play our cards right, there not only won't be any viable sea turtle population, there also won't be life-sustaining ocean for them to swim in."

There was an uncomfortable silence as Wilson looked around the room. Doug stepped forward.

"Mr. Chairman," Doug said flatly, "we appreciate that you are very curious about the supercomputer. We all are. But it is important to impress upon all of us the far-reaching results of its actions, even if the effects will not be immediate. Some members have voiced skepticism that the loss of the moon will have a great impact. If you are fully informed, we can all make much better decisions. Hear Dr. Wilson out."

Doug stepped back to give Wilson the floor again. Wilson started speaking again as if he'd never been interrupted. Doug could barely suppress a smile. Wilson wasn't daunted by all the brass in the room.

"As we learn more and more about the ecosystem of the Earth, one inescapable fact keeps rearing its head, and that is that everything is interconnected. Take away one species and it affects another. Introduce an invasive species and it can drive the native species to extinction. Dam a river and whole colonies of marine insects, fish, and their land-based predators are now left without a food supply.

"Here's what we've discovered in only the last few years. The circulation of ocean currents affects the ebb and flow of ice at the poles. The rate of melting ice at the north pole is far greater than recent temperature increases predicted. The reason is the slight global temperature increase has also affected the path of ocean currents, resulting in far more warm water than usual encroaching on the north.

"The deserts of Africa are ancient sea beds that contain millions of tons of nutrients from sea life of a hundred million years ago. The prevailing winds pick these nutrients up as dust, blowing it out to sea, which nourishes plankton. Do you know what organism is responsible for half the oxygen we breath? Plankton!"

"That's all fine Dr. Wilson," said the Admiral with a trace of contempt. "But my understanding is that life will adapt. Hasn't the planet already gone through several major changes? The end result is the same. Life adapts to the changes."

Wilson stared at the Admiral.

"Why yes, sir, you are absolutely correct. Life will adapt. In about a hundred thousand years, a new species will likely rise to dominate the planet. Only it won't be us! When a catastrophic change occurs, there is a catastrophic impact on existing species. Preliminary evidence suggest the lack of tides is affecting the prevailing winds over Africa, so less of those essential nutrients are reaching the sea. It will affect plankton, the first link in the food chain, and their production of oxygen on which we rely so much. Eventually plant and animal life will adapt, as you say. But I, for one, don't have a hundred thousand years to wait. Do you? Do your grandchildren?"

The audience was silent, regarding Wilson intently. He had jolted them back to a reality that most of them had suppressed.

"This is more than the extinction of a few species," Wilson said, louder. "Your own people have briefed you and all of your colleagues about this, repeatedly, over the past few weeks. You haven't paid attention. The loss of the Moon means we have no tides, which thousands of species depend on. The loss of tides also affects ocean currents. The degree of change to the ocean currents and marine life is uncertain at this point, but one thing *is* certain. Without our moon, ecological disaster is waiting around the corner. Mekhos has lifted all of FLO's problems and dumped them on us."

The room was silent as Wilson gathered his notes. Doug moved to replace him at the lectern.

"Thank you Jack," Doug said, looking at the audience as he spoke. "We face a stark reality. The situation is urgent."

The audience watched Wilson as he strode out of the room. They were suitably chastened. Leach closed his laptop and walked to the front of the room.

"Arthur Leach will be our final speaker," Doug announced.

"Thank you Professor Lockwood. Ladies and gentlemen, the President is working very diligently with his counterpart on FLO to arrange for our team to meet with Mekhos. As Dr. Persaud advised, nobody on FLO seems to be in charge of the machine, but they have also gone out of their way to claim Mekhos is not in charge of them, something we don't believe to be entirely true. We're hoping for face-to-face contact, so to speak. We need to know what to expect."

"You mean, we're going to send a diplomatic team to FLO, to talk to Mekhos?" asked Dr. Lee.

"Among other things, yes. We'll use the Copernicus, the Envoy ship. After a refueling it will be ready to go. Dr. Persaud will prepare the team on how to best interact with Mekhos."

"We can't let that craft go," the Admiral had turned his chair to face Leach. "I said it in committee and I said it directly to the President during our conference call with the heads of state yesterday. We still need to reverse engineer it to gain access to its technology!"

"Admiral, you know as well as I do that the ship is rigged to self-destruct if it detects any tampering," Leach said. "So far we haven't been able to figure a way past its safeguards, and we probably never will, given its advanced nature and the professed lack of technical expertise on the part of the Envoy. Our immediate need to solve the crisis supersedes any long-term technological gains. Let's not presume or let military ego get in the way. We do not have the technology to extract the secrets that ship holds, and the Commander in Chief won't permit any attempt to do so, covert or otherwise. Please drop the matter. We're assembling a specialized team tasked with traveling to FLO and making our case."

"To what end? To beg for our lives, to beg for mercy?" the Admiral asked.

"If we must. But that is not our intent."

– 46 –

In the corner of an aircraft hangar at Andrews, behind a guarded and cordoned-off section stood the Copernicus. Its hatches were sealed and locked, its interior dark. Despite appearances several complex ship systems were active.

Using radio frequencies designed to blend in with background broadcasts, the ship used encrypted commands to link with Earth's communication satellites. From there it analyzed every signal broadcast by the satellites, gaining access to messages and information from many sources, including those thought by their senders to be protected from eavesdropping.

The satellites sent the information to FLO via small relay stations in close orbit around the Sun where there was sufficient interference to hide the transmissions from Earth's probing eyes and ears.

— 47 —

That evening in his apartment Doug listened to the radio. In the preceding days most broadcasts had concentrated on quake damage reports and information on where to obtain food and water for those areas hit hardest, as the infrastructure was repaired. A talk show was in progress, and some of the callers were commenting on the rumors that FLO was ruled by an intelligent machine called Mekhos. Doug grinned despite his alarm at hearing the information in such a startlingly public forum. *There's no such thing as top secret when it comes to something this big,* he thought.

"I've got Louie on the line," the talk radio host said. "Yes or no, Louie. Do you believe in the super machine?"

"Thanks for taking my call. This is inevitable," Louie the caller said. "This is what's waiting for us too. Look at the progress of technology, and how we depend on our tablets and smartphones for things we do every day. We use them to communicate, ask them for directions, and even talk to them like they're people. My friend talks to her phone when she's depressed, and the phone answers her back!"

"Sure," said the host. "But people are aware they're just tools. I'm always buying the latest electronic gadget. So do you and a hundred million other dutiful consumers. There's no psychological or emotional attachment, no more than people are attached to their coffee maker."

"You're missing the point! Appliances are one thing, a talking phone that learns your preferences and habits is something else. A bond is formed. Not only that, we're all jacked into the Cloud. Technology is the new church. It's the natural order of things, and Mekhos is the next step in that evolution. Some people claim he's dictating economic policy, is in charge of world decisions, and whatever else you can think of on that planet. People respect that. They look at the thing for guidance. It has added stability and made their world safer, and made people's lives better. I hope he will have influence over us, too, and get rid of some of our bad leaders, which will make Earth a nicer place to be. The machine has practically become a god. He is the new God."

"Do you hear yourself, man?" the show host replied in his usual baleful drawl. "Are you trying to start a new religion on my show? You're not only giving this computer the status of a person, but elevating it to a god? What nonsense."

"Listen, he's been able to do the impossible – end war and poverty. No human could do that. As far as I'm concerned, he is a god. People think he deserves the title of a god."

The radio host was becoming annoyed.

"It's because of nutbars like you that cults exist! You're paranoid and enjoy stirring up people's fears and their desire to be safe. Only you are also demanding allegiance to something, which in this case is a machine, a powerful machine that doesn't know what it's like to be human. That's dangerous, and you, sir, are a menace!"

The caller started to reply loudly but was cut off as the host went to commercial.

The conversation on the radio show prompted Doug to pick up his secure mobile phone to call Leach for an update on a subject they had discussed earlier. Leach answered immediately.

"The Alfred Chan situation. What have you found, Arthur?"

"We tracked down the alternate Chan. He's a florist in Chicago. Owns a shop with his wife. His educational background is business administration, a diploma from a community college. It's amazing how different they are," said Leach.

"So he's of no use to us. How are things in the lab?"

"Nayar is excited about the possibilities, but on that subject he's starting nearly from scratch. Chan says our manufacturing infrastructure is inadequate, but I'm confident—"

Doug cut him off.

"Listen, Arthur, be realistic. Even assuming Chan truly wishes to help us, and we gave him everything he needs, it will take years to complete the project. I know the White House and the NSA and everybody else has a singular fixation on getting our own thinking quantum computer, but chasing that dream is complete folly given what's facing us. Chan's knowledge is better spent trying to find a way into Mekhos. We need leverage to convince the QC to help Earth. We need to know what Chan knows."

"The powers that be will take some convincing of that. And I'm not sure I agree with you, Doug."

"Tell them that a quantum computer is impossible, at least for now. We all need a dose of reality here. We only have months, and resources are better spent in other ways. If things go our way, we'll have plenty of time to build their computer later."

– 48 –

Dr. Stan Foley, co-discoverer of FLO, was in the base infirmary recovering from an operation to remove his appendix. He had collapsed the day before at his workstation while monitoring Earth's orbital perturbations. After a quick diagnosis he was rushed to the operating room. Doug learned of Stan's condition soon after arriving back on the base, and dropped by the infirmary to check in on his old college friend. Foley was awake but still groggy with the aftereffect of general anesthesia.

"How are you Stan?"

Foley squinted up at him. "Doug? It's Doug ... I'm just lying here ... it hurts. How are you buddy? I'm loyal, like you. Completely loyal, but they treat me like crap, and treat you like a prince ... all because I had an affair. Don't tell my wife! Please, don't let them tell her ..."

"An affair?" Doug replied. But Foley had passed out again. Doug had no idea his friend was cheating on his wife. *But then again we all have secrets,* Doug thought. *General anesthesia is best avoided whenever possible for a number of reasons.*

Despite Stan's admission, Doug felt guilty. He was so caught up in other issues over the past few weeks that he had barely noticed how emotionally weak Foley seemed to be. Stan wasn't the confident man he'd been prior to the discovery of FLO. Learning there was an entire new planet in the solar system, and that the inhabitants were nearly identical to us was one thing. Learning that your entire planet counted on you to save them from this other world was a lot to bear. Still, Doug was surprised at Stan's uncharacteristic simpering.

Doug felt badly about ending the visit, but there wasn't much he could do except promise himself to be more aware of Stan's situation in the future. He would check back on his friend later. He strode out of the infirmary and headed to his office.

— 49 —

Norman Stravinsky was preparing to exit his Seattle apartment for a late breakfast. As the inventor of Mekhos he was in demand for enterprise consulting and speaking engagements, and as usual had spent the first part of his morning on the phone. Though he still liked to think of himself as a hardware engineer, in truth he had become more of a spokesperson for government, educational institutions, and various companies. He was a board member of several organizations and spent many of his days on conference calls in his apartment office or shuttling between various meetings in the greater Seattle area.

He valued his downtime. Designing the first fully-operational quantum computer was considered one of the supreme accomplishments of the post-industrial age. Mekhos was two generations removed from that first working prototype, and had effectively designed itself. Nevertheless, without Stravinsky's genius Mekhos wouldn't exist and Norman was quite proud of that fact.

He maintained his privileged status with Mekhos. The machine seemed to have an affinity towards him, or it recognized the need to have a few select human beings with whom to consult and convey information. Unlike most of the others who interacted with Mekhos, Stravinsky viewed himself as an equal to the quantum computer. As the creator of the most powerful entity in the world Stravinsky occasionally allowed his ego some much-deserved breathing room.

With the discovery of the twin Earth, Stravinsky was often asked by the media if quantum computer technology would be given to humankind's celestial cousins, who were apparently decades behind technologically and still suffered through wars and poverty. Stravinsky replied that it wasn't up to him, and that he would be happy to assist in the task should he be called upon.

He was regularly approached on the street by autograph seekers, though some were turned back by his bodyguard. As a high profile person with the most intimate ties to Mekhos, the government knew he was a target for extremist groups. He lived alone, but by executive order he always had an escort while out. The building was under constant surveillance as well. Stravinsky put on his jacket and exited the apartment.

He waited on the street outside the lobby. He looked at his Raim – he was a few minutes early. The assigned drivers were always punctual so he knew he wouldn't be waiting long. A few meters away at the end of the curved driveway he saw a police officer talking to a tall, well-dressed man. The man glanced at Stravinsky and gave a curt nod. Stravinsky nodded back. *A new bodyguard,* he thought.

The car pulled up, and Stravinsky got in. As the car exited the driveway he noticed that the police officer and the agent had vanished. He thought nothing of it.

– 50 –

Doug was on his way to Arthur Leach's office as he heard his phone chime. It was a message from Leach requesting an immediate meeting in the conference room. Doug was getting impatient at the pace of progress. They needed to send a contingent to FLO *now.*

Arthur's official title was White House Chief of Staff, but his role had evolved into something resembling *White House Representative in Charge of All Things FLO.* As such, he was more of a project manager and the Pentagon liaison, heavily involved in expert strategy sessions and the man reporting directly to the President. Leach was on the phone when Doug arrived. Doug was standing directly in front of his desk, looking impatient.

"Thanks, I'll call you back when I have more information." Leach said, hanging up the phone. "You got here fast," he said, looking up.

"When will the personnel list for the contingent to FLO be final-ized?" asked Doug. "I don't need to remind anyone we're under the gun, and to go through normal channels will simply waste time."

Leach studied Doug for a moment. He looked at his watch.

"Your timing couldn't be better Doug. Let's go."

They walked to the secure briefing room where several other indi-viduals had gathered. They waited for several more minutes until everyone who'd been called had arrived, including Janet. Doug sat down beside her, taking her hand in his as they exchanged a smile. Their re-lationship wasn't a secret.

The others in attendance included Persaud, Bertrand, a White House representative named Nathan Smith, and Brent Jamieson, a security and cryptology expert. Jamieson had been a naval aviator. He was also a decorated war veteran and most notably a highly respected Shuttle commander. Doug had heard Jamieson's name in connection with high-level briefings but hadn't yet met him. Doug had worked on and off with most of the others since the discovery of FLO. A few he did not recognize were also present.

An aide handed out personalized folders to some individuals, in-cluding Doug. Leach greeted the room.

"As you know, we've had various teams studying the effects of the recent lunar escape and possible solutions. Virtually all data has poin-ted to multiple failures in insect and animal migration patterns, pollinating insect behavior patterns, and the domino effect which will impact agriculture yields, livestock yields and inevitably overall food supply shortages. Most of this data comes from the Envoy and their studies on FLO after they were left with no moon. We have now veri-fied some early indications of ecosystem stress here on Earth. The stress is increasing slowly but steadily.

"Some of you have been pressing for a contingent to be sent to FLO to negotiate a solution. You will be pleased to hear that we've been giv-en the go-ahead. Those of you who have been given a green folder have been chosen for this uniquely important mission. You are all going to FLO. Those with a red folder are the backup personnel."

The group stared at Leach in absolute silence and then looked around at each other. Doug and four others had been given green folders. Janet and five others had red ones.

Doug spoke up first.

"Arthur, with the exception of Dr. Bertrand and Commander Jamieson, none of us are astronauts. It takes *years* of training to become one. What are we doing here?"

"You don't need to worry about that Doug," replied Leach. "You'll be travelling in the Envoy's ship. It is almost completely automated and has advanced provisions for making the six week journey as comfortable as possible for the crew. None of the Envoy members were career astronauts either. That's the most important point here. They made it to Earth in fine shape as you know. You will of course need some training on how to function in zero gravity, on emergency procedures, scientific equipment use and so on. Due to his familiarity with its systems, Dr. Bertrand will be in command of the ship while you're en route. Brent Jamieson is a naval aviator and commanded two Shuttle missions. He'll be co-pilot. Congratulations Doug. You will be in command of the team once you touch down on FLO."

Doug stared at Leach and then looked around at the others. Most of them were in a state of shock. In the space of a few seconds Doug went from being taken aback to simply and resolutely stating the obvious. "I'm honored. I'm also an astrophysicist, not a special operations commander. And I don't have military experience."

"Of course," Leach replied, waving away Doug's objections. "But you are intimately familiar with the scientific details of the crisis and you have done a great job leading the scientific team here. Plus you have experience in diplomatic relations. You're the right choice for the job."

Carl Bertrand stepped forward. "I must agree. Dr. Lockwood is a very capable individual. I'm sure he will fulfill his duties admirably."

And that, Doug thought, *is that. Nothing like your own boss and an alien invader conspiring to volunteer you.* What irritated Doug most was the fact that they were right.

Leach and his assistant went around the room shaking hands with the team. Doug bowed to the inevitable.

"Is this the entire team?" he asked.

"No. Dr. Foley will be joining you."

"Really," Doug said flatly. "Stan Foley is in very rough shape right now. What's our departure date?"

"You will lift off immediately after completing an accelerated ten day training schedule."

"Ten days!" Doug started, a little more loudly than he wanted. "Stan Foley is in the infirmary recovering from appendicitis. Given the time frame, he is in no condition for space travel."

"An appendicitis procedure is not considered major surgery." Leach said it like he was reading from a script. "He will be given a couple of days to recover and then will train with you. In addition to her psychology background Dr. Persaud is a medical doctor, so he will be in good hands during the journey."

Bertrand interjected. "I assure you, Dr. Lockwood, despite the zero gravity conditions the ship is very comfortable. Dr. Foley will be fine."

"I'd still like a second opinion offered by someone from *this* Earth, Dr. Bertrand, if it's all the same to everyone here."

"The decision has been made, Doug," Leach said clearly, loud enough in fact to quiet the room entirely. "You and the rest of the group have earned this. Everyone believes that this team is the right combination of skill, experience, drive and diplomacy. It may not feel right to you now, but it will once we get into it." *No argument and no discussion tolerated,* Doug thought, *which means there's something else going on.*

Doug glanced over at Miekela. He had gotten to know her fairly well since she arrived just before the Envoy had landed on Earth. She hesitated before speaking up.

"It's not a problem, Doug," she said, looking right at him. "Dr. Foley will be under my care. He should be fully recovered well before we reach FLO."

Doug just nodded in her direction. *Their minds are made up and they're asserting their expertise. It makes no sense, but Stan is going.*

"Dr. Lockwood, uh, Doug," Jamieson had moved over to stand next to him. "I have something to offer, personally, if you'll hear me out."

Doug looked at him, saw some urgency in his expression and nodded after a brief pause.

"When I was chosen for advanced astronautics and mission training, my initial reaction was elation followed almost immediately by a feeling of apprehension and dread."

Bertrand, the Envoy commander, nodded involuntarily at Jamieson's words. That assent helped focus Doug's attention on what Jamieson was saying.

"I went to my CO, privately, and basically spilled my guts. I told him that after all the hard work, after combat duty, after everything that had happened in my career to that point, I was feeling rocky to the point of fear."

Jamieson had everyone's attention because his voice had cracked ever so slightly.

"My CO heard me out, sat me down, then told his staff sergeant that we weren't to be disturbed for any reason. He then told me what I'm about to tell you. He told me that all the hard work in the world and all the experience in the world, all my medals and all of the loyalty of everyone I was serving with was never designed to prepare me for the unknown. All it could do was prevent me from walking away. He pointed out that I didn't come into his office to tell him that I couldn't or wouldn't do it. He pointed out that I had just come into his office to tell him that I was troubled about the unknown.

"He also told me that I had earned the respect of my peers mainly because I worked hard and never hesitated to get the best advice and to always give credit where credit was due. He told me that my hard work had made me the expert that other people trusted. Do you know who else I just described, Dr. Lockwood?"

"You've described a lot of people," Doug said frankly. "I've been working with some of them for weeks."

"Maybe," Jamieson said, "but the one I'm describing is you, Doug. Accept it. You're about to undergo intensive training and instruction. You will ace it. The wannabes and the political animals who might have lobbied for your spot would not be able to cut it. You will. This, and with respect to Dr. Persaud and Dr. Blair, is what separates the men from the boys."

Doug looked away for a moment. Then he looked back at Jamieson and just nodded slowly because there was nothing to say.

– 51 –

As the meeting wound down Doug was surrounded by members of the primary team and an advisor. He tried to extricate himself to speak with Janet but found it impossible as Nathan Smith congratulated him and proceeded to give unsolicited advice on diplomacy. Doug barely heard him as he saw Janet and Leach in conversation. After a moment she looked over at him and then strode out of the room. Doug excused himself and followed Janet to her office. He entered and shut the door. She turned to him.

"I should be on the primary list. As an expert in quantum mechanics I need to be there, to gather first-hand information on how Mekhos was able to transfer its planet between universes. Instead, they're sending Smith, a career diplomat, whose primary function is to shake hands and pose for photo-ops!"

"You're right. I'll talk to Leach."

"There's no way he'll change his mind. The team has been set. I'm your backup. So no matter what happens, one of us goes, the other stays. And the person that goes may not be able to get back."

They looked at each other. Janet was right – he hadn't thought through to that part. There was no guarantee the team would be allowed back in a reasonable time frame, if at all. It suddenly occurred to Doug that everyone else in the meeting had looked just as pale and shaky as he now suddenly felt. It was all too obvious, especially with the example of the Envoy members from FLO now being held indefinitely on Earth. The greatest likelihood was that the mission was a one-way trip. He looked down into her eyes.

"We're going to succeed. I'm coming back."

He hugged her. She looked at him, then down to his chest, embarrassed that her eyes were starting to tear up.

"You're patronizing me, Lockwood. But I don't mind. Despite all that's happened, I feel lucky that we found each other."

Doug paused before answering her. They were in love, but this was the first time Janet had expressed her feelings.

"I feel the same way. I feel like I'm being torn up inside. I want you and I to take a long drive somewhere, anywhere. You've given me one hell of a motivation to return."

He could feel her hugging him tighter.

"And besides, we only just agreed on our favorite restaurant in DC. Do you think I'd want to spend any more time than necessary on FLO if I couldn't get a decent steak? No way!"

She smiled slightly at the weak joke. Doug smiled back just as weakly.

"You'll be great," she said. "I know you'll be back."

There wasn't much conviction in her voice, but it wasn't the moment to falter any further. There was too much important work to do, so they had no other choice but to accept the fiction. They'd been given instructions to immediately report for training and billeting at Andrews. There was nothing left for them to do but head back to the apartment, pack whatever was allowed on the list in their orders, and await secure transport.

It was raining hard, as it had been for three days straight. The weather patterns were changing all along the eastern seaboard, and not for the better. Their thoughts of an apartment that one of them might not ever see again were left unspoken. They were being escorted by a Marine guard to a driveway on which a blacked out Suburban was idling. *Just when you think it can't get any more serious and intense,* Doug thought, *it gets even more serious and intense.*

– 52 –

Bishop felt a mild jolt. The automated alarm gently woke him by administering a small electric current to his forehead. The dim, cramped quarters allowed him to turn over and stretch, sit up, and do a few exercises by pressing his arms or legs against the bulkhead. There was no other room to move around. The craft was necessarily small to keep its radar cross-section at a minimum. Other exercise came from electric stimulation by way of small electrodes on his muscles to prevent atrophy while he slept, which was ninety-five percent of the time.

Normally the safeguards would not be enough to prevent the loss of muscle and bone mass during such an extended period of weightlessness, but an intravenous pump contained a drug designed to counteract the effects. It was one of the more useful items of information provided by Dr. Morris. Researchers on FLO had devised a way to almost eliminate the negative physiological effects of extended space travel.

Bishop opened a food paste container. The food was nutritious, but bland. Completely functional. He was thankful for the fact it also contained a mild drug designed to keep a person relaxed in such close quarters, while leaving his head just clear enough to go over his mission during the brief periods of consciousness. There was a tablet computer affixed to the wall that contained all mission details. He swiped the screen and touched an icon labeled Audio Brief 11. A female voice described the details of the mission section. It was another way to keep him focused.

At the end of his meal and audio briefing he inserted a pointed straw into a drink bag that would act as his desert and the gateway to another long sleep. He checked the IV tube in his arm and the fluid level of the solution on the opposite wall. It would keep him hydrated. Bishop used the ten minutes of consciousness left to him to check the craft's instrumentation and re-secure his straps for his deep sleep.

Few men would have qualified for such a mission. What made it easier was Bishop's stable psychological profile and his ability to apply meditation techniques to reduce his heart rate if he felt stressed. Together with the drugs he was able to exist in the tiny, dim spacecraft under conditions that would have driven most men mad.

He glanced at the tablet countdown calendar. Seven weeks before descent. He closed his eyes and went over the mission one more time in his head as the cocktail that would allow him to sleep uninterrupted for the next sixty hours took effect.

— 53 —

I need to put my feelings for Janet aside, Doug thought. *My responsibilities are to the mission, and the crew. The mission is far too important.* He was standing stock still, thinking about that last bit. *Every person on Earth was depending on them and didn't even know it.* But Janet still loomed in his thoughts. Bits of things flashed through his mind. *Hard fate of man, on whom the heavens bestow a drop of pleasure for a sea of woe.* The line from a poem was stuck in his head. *I'm going to have to look it up.* He wanted to make it back to Janet so that he could read her the whole thing.

He attended several meetings with various team members to go over mission details. Doug was currently locked up with Leach, Bertrand and Jamieson in a physics lab at Andrews that had been set up weeks before in one of the hangars. In addition to their pilot duties, Bertrand and Jamieson were responsible for several in-flight science experiments.

Doug hadn't had any contact with Jamieson aside from their initial meeting at the mission personnel announcement. Jamieson had a degree from MIT and was a former naval aviator, flying the F-14 Tomcat before the type had been retired in 2006. After that he had been transferred to Naval Intelligence. Doug had no idea if Jamieson had spent his time there in the field or pushing papers, but he seemed competent enough.

He thought Jamieson had a similar demeanor to Agent Bishop, though maybe a little toned down from Bishop's professional soldier persona. Jamieson would be spending weeks in close quarters with the rest of the team so it was fortunate he was fairly affable. Regardless of Bertrand's cooperation, it would be a comfort to have a Jamieson sharing the spacecraft's controls.

The two men shook hands.

"Nice to see you again Dr. Lockwood."

"You're going to be a very busy man Doug," Leach said. "Commander Jamieson will be assisting you and Dr. Persaud once you touch down on FLO."

"Looking forward to it," Doug said, smiling.

"We have the makings of an outstanding team," Bertrand said expansively. "I don't envision any problems along the way, so long as everyone is mindful of their duties." It came out sounding a bit pompous, but Bertrand looked absolutely sincere.

"Do we have a telemetry update on Bishop?" asked Doug.

"He's on course and on schedule," replied Leach. "Despite being faster than anything we've ever launched before, the vehicle is slower than the Copernicus. Utilizing Venus will allow him to arrive a couple of days before you."

The launch timing was fortuitous. Earth, Venus and FLO were in the correct orbital positions so that Bishop's vehicle could take advantage of a Venus slingshot. The later launch date of Doug's team meant that they could just barely use that same window, but only if they launched immediately, forgoing the much needed training. That was a bad idea, so they were going to use the Sun just as the Envoy had done. It would give Bishop time to complete the journey and establish himself on FLO.

Aside from covert operations and select White House personnel that were involved in launching Bishop's top secret mission, the only other members of Doug's team that were aware of it were Bertrand and Jamieson. Bertrand had been instrumental in providing logistics for Bishop's landing and operative contacts on FLO.

As Leach finished speaking the lights flickered. Power hadn't returned to normal in the area yet because continued, small quakes kept damaging some of the repair work and the diesel backup generators weren't completely reliable. Yet another reminder of the reason for the mission.

— 54 —

An hour later Doug was in a private meeting with Leach and Dr. Persaud. They were talking about the most important part of Doug's mission. Dr. Persaud was attempting to convey the difficulties that might be encountered in any direct communication with Mekhos. Communiqués from the US government on FLO had implied that the team would be allowed some sort of interaction with the quantum supercomputer. Whether it would be direct interaction or indirect was unknown. Leach reiterated the importance of their primary task.

"Nathan Smith," he said to Doug, "will be our diplomatic advocate, interacting with other ambassadors on FLO. He's scheduled to attend meetings with their UN and White House. You and Dr. Persaud will be our primary practical diplomats for Mekhos and any of its human administrators. Once on FLO you may be asked to accompany Smith on his goodwill tour, but we want you to clearly define your role as a scientist primarily concerned with establishing a dialog with Mekhos.

We don't yet know if you'll be allowed to speak with the machine individually or as part of a team.

"Dr. Persaud has consulted with certain members of the Envoy about how Mekhos is likely to react or respond to a wide variety of questions. If the two of you are able to communicate directly with the machine, we want Dr. Persaud to do most of the talking. You'll be her backup."

"The key is to not get overly passionate in any discussion," Persaud said. "Mekhos understands logic above all else. Therefore it would not be productive to try and appeal to its emotional side. Mekhos doesn't have one. Bertrand told me unequivocally that our clues about which direction Mekhos might lean in any conversation will come strictly through spoken language. Its word choices. Mekhos obviously does not provide body language and it provides only a few nuances of inflection in its speech."

"Will we be reading from a script?" Doug asked. "A guideline that we can study and rehearse and improvise on makes sense, but a fixed script might be limiting. Damaging, even."

"I will have a script, yes. However we won't know if any prepared words will be appropriate until we actually speak with Mekhos. Just as with a stranger you might engage in a conversation, we won't know how to best plead our case until we get first-hand experience with the machine, despite any prior knowledge the Envoy has given us."

"You both know the stakes are high," Leach said. "You are going to ask Mekhos to help Earth by either reversing its theft of the Moon, something we think it is unlikely to do, or by replacing the Moon with a large body from somewhere else. You will also ask Mekhos if other solutions are available. We've concluded that there are many reasons Mekhos may not be interested in making the attempt. It might not like its chances, or it may even believe a second Earth in this solar system is redundant, and should be allowed to perish. Neither line of thinking means it cannot be swayed. Obviously we - you, that is - are going to try."

"We'll make every effort to plead our case," Doug said, leaning back in his chair. "Mekhos hasn't shown the slightest inkling that it gives a damn, at least not according to the Envoy, so that tells me that nobody has earnestly asked our question. So maybe we actually have a chance.

Best case is that I ask the question and Mekhos says 'Hey Doug, I'm glad you asked. I didn't know you needed my help.' Mekhos may even have reasons for letting our world devolve that it's willing to discuss with me. Either way, Miekela and I get to make our case. Is there a contingency plan in the event we fail? I've always assumed that this group isn't the only one looking for answers and solutions."

Doug chose his words carefully. Of course there was a contingency plan. Bishop was being sent as an infiltrator, but Persaud didn't know that. Doug wanted to gauge her and Leach's reaction to his question. Perhaps there was a plan C as well.

Miekela and Leach looked at each other briefly. Miekela then looked away from both of them.

"No. This is the only plan. What other plan could there be? The Copernicus is the only spacecraft capable of reaching FLO. The only backup is the thoughts and prayers of a grateful nation and a grateful world."

Doug looked carefully at Leach, then at Miekela, then back to Leach. *Bullshit,* Doug thought. But whatever else was being planned, common sense dictated that the less Doug and his team knew about it, the better off they'd all be. *Mind you,* Doug mused to himself, *if there is a third plan, something besides Bishop's mission, I'd prefer not to be an unwitting piece of bait.* He nodded to both of them.

"Good luck," said Leach.

– 55 –

The accelerated training schedule was, in a word, shocking. Classroom instruction on ship systems, FLO sociology and political systems, mission science and simulations was relentless. They were moved back and forth from simulators on which they did prep and practice, to the Copernicus itself. Twice each day they were suited up and immersed in a neutral buoyancy tank to perform various technical tasks and exercises. Once each day they underwent physical stress testing. As an avid cyclist Doug had thought he was in good shape, but his sessions on a stationary bike in the physiotherapy rooms while his respiration was monitored were akin to pedaling full-speed up an endless mountain. His lungs and legs were burning, sweat was pouring off of him, yet all the doctor in charge yelled repeatedly was, "Faster! Push yourself! Get ready for your mission!" Several teams members collapsed during the first few sessions. They were given oxygen, fluids, electrolytes by IV, then forced right back at it. The stronger you got, the harder you were pushed.

Each day they were all rounded up for decompression exercises in case the ship's cabin lost atmospheric pressure. But the worst of it all, at least for the first few days were the parabolic flights on a KC-135 Stratotanker designed to allow them to experience brief periods of weightlessness. Doug managed to get through the zero-gravity practice flights without actually throwing up, but Foley, Persaud and Smith weren't so lucky. Jamieson, the seasoned fighter and Shuttle pilot, looked like he was in his element. By the fourth flight nobody on the team vomited, but many still felt nausea as their bodies struggled to adjust.

In these practical training sessions the backup team sometimes trained with the primary, and sometimes separately as space considerations dictated. Aside from a few stolen conversations and the occasional hug of encouragement, Janet and Doug trained as professionals focused on the task at hand.

It was a grueling schedule, made even more so by the quick succession of diplomacy and protocol classes, in which they had to forget about significant physical aches and pains in order to focus their attention. The classes were important for all of them but especially for Doug and Persaud, who were faced with working through a mountain of research and recommendations. Most of it was hugely speculative, about how to communicate with Mekhos. Envoy members had contributed to some of the research and it was that input on which Doug and Dr. Persaud spent the most time.

Other sessions covering specific mission parameters were given to team members individually. It was exhausting work. Though he agreed the training was necessary, Bertrand assured everyone the design of the Envoy ship would allow them adequate space to rest and prepare for the ground mission.

The crew had been provided with their blue Nomex flight suits early on in their training. Notwithstanding some contemporary NASA touches, they borrowed the design of those worn by the Envoy, including small patches that allowed the astronauts to affix themselves to a wall or chair while working or at rest, making it easier to remain stationary in a weightless environment. Retractable tethers scattered throughout the ship's interior would serve the same purpose, as would patches on the soles of their feet.

After being instructed on the utility of their suits Bertrand had led the team on a one-hour tour of the Envoy ship. This was the first time any of them had seen it up close, and it was impressive. Roughly the same length as the retired Space Shuttle, the craft was lower and sleeker, with refined proportions that made the old Shuttle look boxy and primitive in comparison. The roof was a solid piece, with no cargo doors. Similar to the Shuttle, the top half was white, the underside black, but with a thin blended layer that looked like a grey stripe in between. The name *Copernicus* was etched into this stripe just below and aft of the cockpit windows.

The exterior heat-resistant tiles were much tougher than the fragile ones used on the Shuttle fleet. There was some scarring due to reentry and micro-object impact, but Bertrand explained the durability and insulation properties of the exterior were many times better and more effective that those on the Shuttle. No repair or maintenance would be required before their journey, even considering the ship had been within close proximity of the Sun for several days and would be again during the flight back to FLO.

Bertrand's voice input would allow Jamieson and him to fly the Copernicus. The Envoy had explained to their Earth handlers that any tampering with the ship's internal systems would lead to complete inert shutdown at best, and self-destruction at worst, depending on the level of tampering. The landing gear would be inspected for safety reasons, since it had to be in good working order for takeoff. The tires were of standard size and as a precaution they were replaced by ground crews at Andrews, as was one leaking hydraulic strut in the starboard landing gear.

As Doug had guessed during his observation of the Copernicus landing, there were jet engines embedded in the root of each wing for self-propelled flight through the atmosphere. Twin chemical engines of an advanced design were integrated in the tail, which had retractable coverings for better aerodynamics during air travel. The Copernicus was equally at home in the air as in space. It could be used as an airliner for intercontinental flight and reach its destination quickly thanks to its higher ceiling and hypersonic speed.

For space flight a large fuel tank to feed the primary engines was required. Once they were aloft the ship would rendezvous and dock with the half-full fuel tank it had left in Earth orbit prior to landing.

The inside of the Copernicus carried over the airliner-shuttle theme, with pilot and co-pilot adjacent to each other in a large, open cockpit, and crew seating for an additional four persons just aft of the cockpit area. Each crew member seat faced a small monitor and control panel in the seatback ahead of it. Exterior windows and ports would tint automatically to protect the crew from intense sunlight.

Just behind the crew seating was a lab area, with stand-up workstations and associated equipment for carrying out experiments. The walls of some could be closed off depending on the nature of the experiment. Midship was a bulkhead with a sliding door dividing the ship in half. There was a centrally located galley and mess area with table and bench seating for meals and a small lounge for relaxing. Sleeping quarters were located nearby with bunks, tethers and privacy curtains. The single head containing a shower and lavatory facilities was located aft. At the tail of the ship were supply storage and utility compartments.

Doug sat in one of the reclining lounge chairs. It felt extremely comfortable, more so than any chair he had ever used.

"I see you have discovered one of the benefits of computer-aided development when unlimited funding is available and a quantum supercomputer is responsible for much of the engineering." Bertrand watched Doug examine the chair. "Like many other items on the ship, they automatically conform to the user's physical dimensions. I doubt even your own bed at home is as comfortable as that chair."

Doug was impressed. The ship was designed for maximum efficiency without compromising crew comfort. Despite the circumstances, he was looking forward to a trip on such an advanced vehicle.

"I would imagine that most of your public ground vehicles and buildings offer some of the same advancements?"

"Of course. Society has made great strides in the past fifteen years."

Meaning the time Mekhos has been actively involved in world issues, Doug thought, *and it's a subject Bertrand and I absolutely cannot discuss. There's too much at stake for a sarcastic wink or an inadvertent reveal to sink us without a trace.* Still, Doug wondered what life must be like on FLO. Less conflict, better education and employment for the masses, more leisure time. A machine directing it all. *We ask for the rule we end up with most of the time, and we rebel when that rule limits our choices. No good deed goes unpunished.*

– 56 –

Norman Stravinsky was having lunch at his favorite café. In between bites of his sandwich he scribbled down some speech ideas in a notebook. He could type or talk into his Raim but he preferred the notebook, which was easier to flip through for referencing earlier ideas. Sometimes he would lean back in his chair when deep in thought. He saw his driver a few tables over, reading a newspaper.

As he was about to return to his notes he did a slight double-take as he noticed the other man two tables away from his driver, also reading a newspaper. It was the same man he saw talking to the police officer outside of his apartment yesterday. The man looked a little bigger and more menacing than the usual drivers or security personnel. *Why would they double my security?* he thought. *Oh yes. With the visiting dignitaries from the Twin, the security experts were probably on higher alert than usual. Maybe it's a good thing.* Stravinsky turned his attention back to his notebook.

– 57 –

The physical training finally wound down the day before departure. At breakfast the next morning Doug was still a bit tired but noticed that Foley and Smith looked extremely fatigued. Both complained of nausea but Smith tried to put on a brave face, managing a shaky smile throughout the small talk as they ate. Foley operated under no such pretense, grunting answers as he glumly looked down at the table and sipped his coffee. Dr. Persaud looked better, tired but able to function normally. Jamieson and Bertrand looked as if they had just come from a typical morning workout, alert and friendly.

After breakfast the crew was prepped for their departure. Lift-off was scheduled for 10 00 hours, though lift-off was an inaccurate term in this case, since the ship would take off like a regular airplane using its wing engines, climb to 90,000 feet, then use the primaries to attain escape velocity.

Doug and Janet had spent a final night together. They talked for an hour in the dark.

"I'm actually looking forward to being your remote backup," said Janet. "Should you become incapacitated - say from eating that chocolate cake you're tempted by, since I won't be around to eat half of it with the second fork - I'll be more than happy to speak with Mekhos or his handlers in your place."

"Yeah, yeah, and you would do a much better job even from 300 million kilometers away, I get it. I might as well take a vacation while I'm there, and visit Paris without you."

She jabbed him in the ribs as he cried out in mock pain.

"Don't you dare! Neither one of us has been to Paris and we're going to visit it together, *here*," she said. "And besides, you can't speak a word of French. How are you going to order anything without me?"

They were silent for a moment.

"We'll see each other when I'm back in a few months. Even a partial mission success might be enough to make a difference."

Doug knew Janet wasn't fooled by any suggestions about partial success, but he wanted to insist on as much hope as possible, not just about returning to Earth but doing so in one piece.

After breakfast the crew was given a final briefing. Doug thought Foley still looked pale but his mood was improving. Besides having been college friends he and Foley worked well together. Doug was glad he was on the mission. He fervently hoped his friend was feeling better mentally and physically. He wanted to have a private conversation with Stan to find out for sure, but there was far too much to do now and there would be plenty of time to talk once they were on their way.

The weather was horrible. It had changed for the worse almost everywhere on the planet. Rain was pounding down in torrents. Bertrand had assured everyone that the Copernicus could handle it and more besides. As their bus entered the relative quiet of the hangar, they passed a crew that had just finished fueling the ship's wing tanks in preparation for launch. They piled out of the bus, boarded Copernicus without a word to each other and sat in their assigned seats. The ground crew strapped them in as they went over a preflight checklist.

Doug grinned as Foley gave him the thumbs-up. They were going into space, and would be among the first humans to set foot on another planet. The situation was incredible.

"Stan, we're going to be the first human beings to set foot on another planet, and we're getting there in a ship designed for interplanetary travel."

"Yeah, except we won't be the first humans to do so, they've already done it," Stan replied, nodding in Carl Bertrand's direction.

"Come on, you know what I mean. Don't rain on the parade," Doug said, as he gave Foley a knock on the shoulder with his fist. Foley smiled.

"You're right. We're pioneering explorers from Earth. They're going to name a school after each of us."

Doug allowed himself a moment of pride and excitement. It would fade soon enough as he reminded himself of the stakes. They dare not fail. But for the moment he felt very young again, going on one of the greatest adventures imaginable. *The other thing the training does,* Doug thought, *is keep you so busy that you don't have time or energy to let your ego get in the way of anything.*

The ship was towed from the hangar by an aircraft tug and positioned on the tarmac, the sound of wind and rain buffeting the craft. Bertrand started the jet engines. The low whine was barely audible inside the Copernicus, another indication of the engineering refinement of the ship. After a few minutes of system checks, Jamieson reported to the control tower.

"Mission, this is Copernicus. We're ready to roll," Jamieson said into his mic.

"Roger Copernicus. Take position on runway one-niner-left and await clearance."

"Confirmed, mission. Runway one-niner-left," Jamieson replied and nodded to Bertrand, who applied power. They taxied toward the designated runway. Jamieson continued writing log information on a clipboard and intermittently communicating with the control tower. The air traffic controller's voice could be heard over the instrument panel speaker. Bertrand rolled the Copernicus past the threshold marks and put the nose wheels perfectly on the runway center line.

"Mission, Copernicus ready for take off," Jamieson reported.

"Copernicus, may your mission be a success. You are cleared for take off. Good luck, and bring back a souvenir or two for us."

"Roger mission, count on it," said Jamieson.

Bertrand rolled power on and the Copernicus accelerated quickly. It took off and climbed normally for the first few thousand feet, then accelerated upward at an angle of approximately 60 degrees, much steeper than any airliner, a lot more like a fighter. There was a lot of wind noise and buffeting as the ship ascended, more than was usually experienced during a typical airliner climb.

"A lot of people don't know that even close to the ground, the atmosphere is layered, mostly according to heat and moisture content," said Foley, loudly enough to be heard over the din. "Due to our speed we're punching through those density layers faster than normal, and it's a rough ride. It'll smooth out soon enough."

Doug nodded. He was well aware of the cause of turbulence in aircraft, but he figured Stan was a little nervous and voicing the explanation helped to keep him calm. Sure enough, as they ascended the turbulence lessened.

Jamieson reported flight status, crew monitoring status and other details, receiving acknowledgements and summary results of telemetry observations from the ground. It all sounded technically glib and important, but it was activity representing little more than ingrained habit. If something went wrong, only Bertrand had deep control over ship systems, so the technical exchange had more to do with NASA and its partners wanting to sound authoritative than anything else. There weren't any ground control interfaces that could be used to access any systems on the Copernicus.

Since the crew seating was centered in the ship, the port and star-board windows were too far away for a good look outside, but Doug had a fairly unobstructed view through the windshield ahead of the pilots. There was nothing to see but sky, which grew darker with each passing minute.

Soon they were at 90,000 feet travelling at Mach 4, the point at which the computer shut off the jet engines and engaged the primaries. They felt themselves shoved back into their seats once again as the ship punched through the thin atmosphere and into space.

After a few moments the power was eased back. The launch was timed so they would rendezvous with the large fuel tank as it orbited over the Pacific. The computer throttled back the engines and made small course corrections to match orbital velocity with the tank. The crew experienced weightlessness as the engines were reduced to minimum power. Doug felt his stomach rise, as if he was at the apex of a rollercoaster ride.

"Oh damn," Stan said.

"You all right?" asked Doug.

Stan held both hands over his mouth. Doug was afraid his friend was about to throw up and so he reached for an airsickness vacuum mask from the overhead panel. Stan shook his head.

"No, I'm all right," he said. "Get that away from me, I need to concentrate on something else." Stan took a few deep breaths. After a moment he nodded to Doug and gave a weak smile, indicating that he was feeling better.

About a minute later the computer shut off the engines completely. Doug configured the seatback display in front of him to show a view of Earth, which took up most of the screen since they were in low orbit.

"Beautiful," said Stan. "I hope this is being recorded. I'd love to show my wife when we get back."

"I'm sure it is," replied Doug. "She'll be thrilled. So will Janet."

The Copernicus drifted towards the tank, which came into the windshield's view as the smaller maneuvering thrusters engaged. Doug's attention was drawn to the conversation between the pilots.

"Closing speed looks a little high," said Jamieson.

"I concur. The tank has experienced upper atmospheric drag over the past few weeks, making it slower than we calculated," replied Bertrand. "Disengage autopilot. Let us pass by the tank, then slow down and let it come to us."

Doug and Stan listened and watched intently. The tank was looming larger in the windshield. Doug gripped the hand rests tightly. It looked like they were on a collision course.

"Port side thrusters, five-hundred kilos for five seconds," said Bertrand.

"Roger, port thrusters, five-hundred kilos," replied Jamieson, as he kept his eyes on the control screen in front of him.

There were faint bursts of hiss coming through the hull as the thrusters moved the ship. The tank filled the bottom quarter of the windshield, and was getting larger. Nobody said a word as they watched it drift closer. Finally, it passed out of view, under the ship.

Doug called up the anterior view on seatback display and saw the tank slowly getting closer to the ship as the Copernicus continued to reduce velocity to let the tank approach. Simultaneously some text appeared:

Fuel tank connections extended

They could all feel the small thruster adjustments. After less than a minute there was a *thud* and then a *clank* followed by more text on the screen:

Fuel tank locking system engaged

"After a short systems check we will be on our way," said Bertrand. "A reminder, once the system check is complete we will need to remain seated for approximately five hours as we accelerate to maximum speed. After that you will be free to move about the ship."

Moments later the engines engaged and the ship reached maximum acceleration. They experienced approximately two earth gravities acceleration, so they were pressed firmly into their seatbacks. Any object or person not tied down would be thrown toward the back of the ship. The conformal seats spread their body mass evenly to minimize the discomfort, but their increased weight meant they needed to be careful when eating and drinking items from the nutrition package strapped to the seatback in front of them.

Foley broke off a small piece of a lunch cracker and held it about a foot in front of his face, motioning Doug to observe. He let go of the cracker and it flew back into his mouth. It was the expected result of course, but it was amusing to see it fall backward rather than to the floor.

After fifteen minutes the acceleration felt tiring, then fatiguing, but the five hours went fairly quickly because the crew was also absorbed with the intricacies of the configurable individual control displays. They could call up various views of the Copernicus exterior, including the slowly receding earth as they travelled away from it, dark space ahead, filtered views of the sun, their parabolic course around the Sun plotted on a map, with the present and future positions of Earth and FLO, basic ship specifications, speed and other technical information, and various stored entertainment programs.

Doug cycled through and sampled a few programs and movies. Naturally, all the entertainment had been produced on FLO and very little of it was familiar. Foley pointed out with amusement that there were no *Godfather* sequels, and Harrison Ford only had a bit part in *Star Wars*, the character of Han Solo being played by an unfamiliar actor.

Doug reminded himself that the two Earths were identical up to about 1970. After that things had diverged, with differently evolving politics, economics, international alliances, and of course people.

Individuals were steered into different directions as random circumstances dictated. In the early years similar lives were common, but as time marched on there was greater divergence. Couples who met on Earth did not necessarily meet on FLO, and vice versa. Doug and Cheryl were one of the very small handful of people born after 1970 whose lives were nearly identical on both worlds, to the point where the two of them met and dated.

Even when the same couples met, if they had children their conception occurred at different times, so in such cases the offspring were unique individuals. Brothers and sisters to their counterparts on the other Earth, not identical.

— 58 —

Daniel Santos, age 20, was getting angry. He distinctly heard the customer, a bigger man in a suit, ask for a Combo #3.

"I asked for a Combo 4 dumbass," the man said. "Are you deaf or stupid?"

"Sir, if you don't want it I'll give you a Combo #4. But you asked for a Combo #3."

"You calling me a liar?" the man sneered at him. "You goddamn high school dropout."

Daniel was furious, but he needed this job. He kept calm and moved to replace the items in the bag. The man reached over and grabbed his wrist.

"I want a new bag dumbass, now that your greasy hands have been fumbling around in it."

Daniel quickly pulled his arm free of the man. His first instinct was to lash out, but he paused and made every effort to keep his cool.

"Sir, don't touch me. If you'll chill out, I'll—"

"Hurry the hell up, you incompetent dickhead."

Daniel had enough. He tossed the bag at the belligerent customer. The Manager saw what was happening and walked over.

"Daniel! Go in back to the office to cool off."

"No, this mother—"

"Get in back!" He turned to the man. "I'm sorry sir."

"I want that idiot fired. He intentionally got my order wrong and threatened me. If you don't fire him I'll call the police," said the man in the suit.

Daniel lunged toward the counter but was restrained by the Manager and another employee. The man strode out of the restaurant without his order.

Five minutes later Daniel walked out, his last paycheck in his hand. On his way home he kicked a side mirror off of a car. He felt persecuted. *So many freaks in the world. Everyone is a freakin' slave to the system,* he thought. *Everybody's a sheep except me.*

Daniel had been born and raised in the Seattle area. The crime rate in the city was at an all-time low, as it was almost everywhere, but crime still existed and it was still a problem. Daniel was involved in a botched kidnapping when he was fourteen. His older cousin was a fervent anti-Mekhos activist and recruited Daniel into his gang's plan to kidnap the mother of Norman Stravinsky and hold her for ransom. They were inept. They did not even know what Stravinsky's mother looked like, only where she lived. They failed to account for a change in her schedule and ended up kidnapping Stravinsky's housekeeper instead.

There was some group infighting and panic, resulting in a shooting which wounded the housekeeper. She survived but would never work again. The leader of the gang, Daniel's cousin, was shot and killed by a police sniper before Daniel's eyes. Daniel served six months in a youth facility.

Then as a seventeen year old, he and a friend were in the middle of breaking into a pharmacy when the police arrived. There was a shootout. Daniel was shot in the jaw, and was left with scarring and permanent numbness on the right side of his face. Daniel was again tried as a youth offender and convicted of assault with a weapon, and served a year in a special program.

His crimes were serious, but in a low-crime society the emphasis was on turning offenders into productive citizens. As part of his sentence he was sent to a military-style boot camp, the idea being that discipline would help train some of the anti-social feelings out of delinquent young men. He learned how the chain of command worked and was proud that he got high marks during his training, but his anger at the world remained. A few months of rigid training could change some bad habits and behavior, but it couldn't erase the influences of seventeen years of disadvantage.

The Raim removal key revocation program had only been instituted in the last year, so those who had been sentenced prior to that would still have a legal removal key. Daniel didn't like being spied on so he never wore the Raim. He paid cash for everything. When he didn't have his own cash he borrowed from his mother.

Daniel walked down the back cement steps to the door of his rented apartment in the basement of a house. He hoped the landlord wasn't home. He didn't feel like listening to her drunken ravings upstairs. The apartment was small, but comfortable. The windows were tiny and covered with thin curtains for privacy. He collapsed on the couch, flipped through some songs on his smartphone and then closed his eyes.

Daniel got into the tune, nodding his head and swinging his forearms down into the couch cushion in time with the music. Despite his eyes being closed he noticed the light dim. He opened them to see a large man standing directly in front of him, blocking the light from the window. He was startled but his fright quickly turned to fury as he recognized the belligerent man from the restaurant.

Daniel lunged to his left to grab a heavy ashtray from his end table, and rose from the couch, swinging the ashtray at the man's head. At the same time the man had moved a step closer and raised his own arm, blocking Daniel's attack, causing the ashtray to fly behind him to crash heavily into the shelves in the corner of the room.

The man stepped sideways quickly then planted his foot and shifted his arm from a hard block to a position under Daniel's left arm for a shoulder lock. The man bent his knees slightly, shortened his grip, then suddenly lifted. Daniel screamed in pain as his elbow joint was hyper-extended. He tried to punch with his right fist but the man shifted his weight and twisted, shoving Daniel onto the couch. The man kept Daniel's arm locked and jammed one knee on his chest. He applied just enough pressure on the arm lock to create pain.

"I got you fired today. But I did it to offer you another job. A dangerous job that will pay you fifty thousand dollars to help smash the system. *Virtue* needs you, Daniel."

Daniel's expression turned from an angry grimace to surprise as he heard the stranger say the name Virtue. The clandestine group that opposed the system and opposed the hated Mekhos.

"How much did you say?"

– 59 –

Although there were scientific experiments assigned to the crew, much of their time was devoted to discussions and drills associated with the mission. Each team member was assigned a presentation schedule, where each of them were expected to lead a discussion on points and procedures.

Each team member had been given enough training so that they could fill in for any another member in an emergency. As team lead, Doug spoke with each of them about contingency plans and protocols, and even the possibility that any one of them might end up speaking directly to Mekhos. It was a reason to review Miekela's script and to discuss machine psychology as much as they could.

"I hope it doesn't come to that," said Jamieson. I'm more comfortable with physical logistics and security." Foley nodded in agreement.

Doug knew Jamieson was being modest, or perhaps had only a slight lack of confidence when it came to the idea of dealing with a thinking machine. All of them were capable individuals, and Jamieson's graduate degree from MIT proved he had the analytical smarts to step in if needed.

Foley might be another matter, Doug thought. *He's moody, more withdrawn than usual, and is sleeping more than he should.* For the first time, Doug was beginning to seriously doubt the stability of his friend, and was growing more suspicious about why he was chosen to go on the mission.

As the Mission Commander during the flight, Bertrand also had various scientific duties, as did co-pilot Jamieson. Dr. Persaud was tasked with monitoring the health of the crew and measuring their physical changes brought about by the weightless conditions. Some of the crew noticed a slight bloating in the upper body and blurred vision. Miekela talked to them about it as they gathered for a daily meeting.

"Some of you are experiencing vision difficulties as your eyeballs change shape slightly in the absence of gravity. There is also upper body swelling. Both conditions should abate over time as the body adapts to the environment. We warned you about this during pre-flight training and now it is actually happening. The initial condition may be slightly alleviated during periodic acceleration or when the ship makes course corrections."

The crew members strapped into their seats for a few minutes every three days as the engines subjected them to an acceleration force of one gravity.

One of Doug's assignments with Foley was to measure relativistic effects of time dilation using the ship's sensitive detectors. Since nobody from Earth had travelled at this speed before (roughly seven times faster than that of the Apollo astronauts) the measurements when compared to Earth might indicate a very slight, yet measurable slowing of time. The work distracted Foley, who as the mission progressed tended to be short-tempered. On most days he complained to Doug when they were alone.

"I have to wonder if this entire mission is pointless," Foley said. "How can we hope to force a thinking machine to change its mind? Look at the trouble it has already gone to. Stealing the Moon for god's sake! What kind of world awaits us when we get back to Earth? Once some of the world leaders catch on to the situation, war will break out quickly. Maybe if we're lucky they'll let us stay on FLO."

"Why would you want to stay on FLO if your family and friends are suffering on Earth?" Doug replied sternly. "You're losing sight of the fact that anything we can extract in the way of help from Mekhos and the scientific community on FLO is likely to be far more helpful back on Earth than anything we could devise on our own."

"And if we fail?" Stan said bitterly, staring at the deck plates, then back up to Doug. "If we get nothing out of Mekhos or FLO? Our own people back home might not even care if we don't come back. Or they'll even be hostile towards us. On the other hand FLO apparently considers our entire planet to be expendable. In a dozen years we'll be a few surviving villages back in the Bronze Age, a curious tourist attraction for them to visit."

"What are you pushing Stan? We have a mission. We have a cause. FLO didn't do this to us, Mekhos did. If we can believe the Envoy, Mekhos did it *all*. If you've lost hope, you're not even good to yourself, let alone this team. You're here because you're needed."

"I'm here because I'm needed," Stan repeated. "I'll do my job. Let's leave it at that."

Stan moved to the sleeping area and floated himself into his bunk, shutting the privacy curtain. Doug just stared after him. *He was in rough shape when we started our training,* Doug thought, *and he's even worse now. Why the hell did Leach and Persaud insist on sending him?*

– 60 –

Bishop had been awake for hours as his ship underwent massive deceleration up to six Gs. He was oriented with his feet at the engine side. Air bladders in his suit inflated around his thighs and abdomen to keep the blood from rushing down his body. It was punishing, but the computer regularly reduced the engine thrust to give him a chance to rest before again increasing to full power.

Once the deceleration was finally over and the small ship was in orbit he was exhausted, and slept for five hours, a necessity which was built into the mission timeline. The computer woke him on time, two hours before his scheduled descent.

He looked out the small porthole, positioned at eye level, taking in the sight of the blue earth. "You're beautiful. Just like home," he said out loud, feeling jubilant. After so much time spent on the cramped, brutal flight, the thought of being released from his strapped-in prison and planting his feet firmly on the ground was almost overwhelming.

There wasn't much time to waste on admiring the view. He checked the craft's status and its orbital position. Timing was always critical.

The interior of his craft was much smaller than the outer shell suggested, made necessary by its stealth engineering. The tube-shaped capsule's exterior was covered in small, flat black panels at varying angles, similar to those employed by the old F-117 Nighthawk stealth fighter. Radar would be deflected away from the craft, and the matte black outer surfaces would reflect very little light from the Sun or from FLO itself.

He prepared for the next phase. The ship would enter the atmosphere at a steeper angle and therefore slow down faster than any other manned reentry vehicle, subjecting Bishop to far higher stresses than those experienced by astronauts during conventional re-entries.

The instrument panel showed his orbital position and a graph indicating the point at which the computer would initiate engine burn to begin the descent. There was a minimum of user input required. The tablet displayed a blinking *Initiate Reentry* button, awaiting his command.

The graph showed the ship approaching the reentry point. If he didn't press the button he would need to wait another ninety minutes as his ship completed another orbit. He needed to descend immediately or on the next pass. Waiting any longer than that would put the mission in jeopardy.

"All right. Let's go," Bishop said aloud as he pressed the button. It stopped blinking and glowed green. Two minutes later the engine ignited. Once again, Bishop felt heavy as the ship slowed.

As the ship entered the atmosphere the engine cap was jettisoned, revealing a needle-nose profile. Internal gyroscopes helped the capsule maintain orientation without tumbling before the atmosphere became dense enough for aero braking.

Moments later the braking fins at the top end of the capsule deployed. Bishop felt the g-forces multiply quickly, up to eight, then ten Gs. Again, he was oriented with his feet pointing towards the bottom of the craft, but his body now weighed 1900 pounds. The air bladders in his suit did their job, inflating around his legs and abdomen, keeping as much blood as possible from rushing down out of his head. He grunted and clenched his jaw and abdominals as he fought to remain conscious. He needed to be awake for the next stage.

Bits of the craft's outer structure started to break off and burn up in the atmosphere. They produce a light-colored smoke as they burned away. It was difficult to see from the ground and working as intended. Every part of the ship was engineered to remain intact only as long as necessary, with very little safety margin. The computer read off altitude and speed. Bishop could barely hear it. The noise from the rushing atmosphere and heated ionization was almost deafening. The ship needed to hold together to reach 175,000 feet and less than 600 kilometers per hour to stay intact for the next phase of the descent.

Since it approached from the day side of the planet, the luminous plume from the rocket engine used to slow the craft before re-entry had not been visible from the ground. But the flaming pieces breaking off might be visible to anyone observing that particular area of the sky. It was a calculated risk.

At 200,000 feet a small parachute deployed, slowing the craft in the thin atmosphere only enough to safely deploy the main chute. Two minutes later, at 125,000 feet the main parachute deployed but it was only meant to slow the vehicle, not Bishop. The sudden deceleration triggered the collapse of the capsule floor, allowing Bishop to free fall. He felt weightless once again. "Freaking hell," he muttered through clenched teeth as he felt a momentary disorientation and briefly passed through some flaming ionization around the base of the craft.

At high altitude the atmosphere was very cold but while caught in the spacecraft's residual forward ionization plume there was intense heat. Bishop's suit wasn't designed to take such punishing heat for more than a few seconds at a time. He spread his arms and legs trying to catch the thin air to further slow his descent. Above him the capsule was engulfed in flames. A flammable agent was being automatically dispersed throughout it when triggered by the floor collapsing beneath him. The fire spread up the parachute. There would be almost no trace of the vehicle left to reach the ground.

Bishop's altitude was high enough to see vast expanses in every direction including the city and the forested area off to the north. His target.

The ionization was gone but Bishop was sweating from the heat and his own exertion. His suit was holding up, but as the air grew more dense it was being exposed to extreme atmospheric buffeting. The ship had taken the brunt of the reentry phase, and Bishop's skydiving had slowed him further. But he was still going too fast to deploy his parachute. Anything over 250 kilometers per hour would tear the chute to shreds. He had a reserve chute but it was a last resort, and not as strong as the main.

Bishop heard a loud beeping, then felt an intense pain in his lower left leg. A weak spot on the suit, still scorching hot from the ionization, had thinned into contact with his skin. The contact only lasted a second, but it was long enough to cause a nasty burn and breach the suit. Air rushed out of the hole and pushed the suit away from his skin. A bladder inflated in his thigh to keep the rest of his suit pressurized as reserve oxygen was pumped in. The bladder seal wasn't perfect and the suit was still leaking. The heads-up display in his helmet suddenly went dark. He wouldn't know the correct altitude to activate his parachute. If he lost consciousness due to lack of oxygen he would be killed on impact. Bishop knew he was still too high, but he had no choice. He pulled the ripcord of his parachute.

— 61 —

The crew of the Copernicus generally got along well. The lounge seating could be unlocked, repositioned and then locked down again so the entire group was facing a large monitor screen. They used it mainly to screen movies every few days as their workload permitted. Most of the movies were unfamiliar, with slightly changed scenes or cast members. It made for very interesting viewing for everyone except Carl Bertrand.

In *Terminator*, Arnold Schwarzenegger played the hero, Kyle Reese. For Doug and Foley, the film obviously felt very different and almost comical to watch as Arnold played the part of the good guy battling to save Sarah Connor. The trademark *"I'll be back"* line went to the Terminator played by Lou Ferrigno. There were no sequels, which was unfortunate because in this role Ferrigno was the better actor.

Foley made an effort to attend some of the movie screenings. He was often too tired to show up and instead slept in his curtained bunk.

Jamieson told stories about his tours as a Tomcat pilot.

"I had the engines at full power," he said during a lunch break, "and gave the salute to the Cat officer, and he signaled the operator in the bubble - that's the catapult control station that's recessed into the flight deck. Anyway, we launched, and for a split-second I could feel normal acceleration, but then something in the cat broke, and we were no longer accelerating. I thought to myself, *uh-oh, we're in for it.*

"Rather than being shot off the carrier deck like normal, we more or less rolled off of it under our own power, probably a full forty knots slower than we should have, and once off the deck we dropped *way* low. I was bracing myself for a ditch, but at the same time I had one hand on the throttle and my other hand pulling back on the stick. My RIO - the guy in the back seat - screamed *eject* once, but we both knew you had to say it three times before punching out. I knew he was ready to pull the handle, but he was giving me a chance to get the Tomcat up.

"The engines were on full burner, and I managed to keep the nose up. Turns out we had just enough speed to avoid ditching. I was able to make a low, slow climb literally just a couple of meters above the waves. Later the guys on the deck told us there was a massive spray of water pushed onto the ship's foredeck. They thought we'd ditched, but the spray was caused by engine thrust kicking it up.

"My legs were shaking for an hour during our flight. We saved the taxpayer fifty mil for a new plane, minus the cost of new underwear for my RIO," he said, to laughter from the Copernicus crew.

Doug noticed Jamieson and Bertrand had developed a very cordial and professional relationship. The two did their checklists and took turns monitoring the ship's systems, but they did not have many social conversations with one another. They seemed to prefer spending their social time with others. There was small underlying rivalry between the two men, both in positions of respect, whose roles would be changing the moment they touched down on FLO. Bertrand would presumably resume his normal duties for a high-tech corporation on FLO, while Jamieson would become Doug's assistant and advisor. Doug still couldn't tell how well Jamieson would adapt to the role.

Nathan Smith was also friendly but seemed to always be in diplomatic mode, the sort of man that never seemed to let his guard down or engage in many personal conversations beyond the superficial. Doug thought it would serve Smith well during any goodwill tour on FLO. Doug and Smith frequently discussed some of the particulars.

"I don't envy your task," said Smith. "I'm comfortable dealing with ambassadors, leaders, and even dictators, but I'm at a loss about how to deal with an intelligent machine. I've read the briefings on the matter, but I can't quite grasp the approach. Your strength in astrophysics combined with your years at the IPCC will help a great deal."

"Possibly," Doug replied. "I am still convinced I'll need your help to keep the administrators away from me. Don't forget old fashioned human pride. From what some members of the Envoy have told us, those on FLO who have close contact with Mekhos may display some overprotective behavior and outright defensiveness if Dr. Persaud and I are granted direct access to their machine. That's what worries me most, Nate. We really don't yet know for sure if promises of access to Mekhos are real or just a peaceful delaying tactic. We've been asked to take a lot on faith."

Smith had a equal measure of unknowns ahead. Aside from a few monarchies, the two Earths had no heads of state in common in the Western hemisphere after 1988. Even the communist regimes collapsed after 2001 when Mekhos encouraged compliance with the rest of the world's political and economic system. Individual leaders and governing parties were different than the ones on Earth.

The same process was happening culturally. Similar languages and customs encouraged similar values among separate groups of people. When the underlying system of economics and politics changed as a result, each community's cultural identity changed to some extent as well. Compounding matters was the fact that most nations on FLO had decreased control of their fiscal policies compared to their counterparts on Earth. Mekhos had essentially taken control of major economic decisions for the common good. Stock markets and financial trading centers had been strictly modified into capital funding sources, places where businesses could go to raise money for expansion, new ideas and acquisitions. It was no longer possible to manipulate any of the markets. There was global free trade, a global currency, and the United Nations had evolved into a body with proportional representation and real power.

As a result, disputes among nations were settled by judgment panels. There was reduced cause for war and conflict. Mekhos effectively enforced the peace, as it had control over most information and financial channels. States that didn't comply with judgments were sanctioned and the punishment had swift effect. Rogue states had quickly learned to fall in line. It sounded like an ideal world, as long as nobody on FLO thought too hard about the fact that the entire planet was gradually being given up to the control of a supercomputer.

The people of most nations on FLO had gotten what they'd been dreaming about for generations: peace and equality. Many believed that the dreams had come true at the cost of too much of their freedom and a loss of their self-determination. Orwell's dystopia, but without the slavery.

Earth, but not Earth. It would be like visiting a strange new country, with different customs, only on the same geographic soil, so to speak. They would be touching down at the same location they departed, at FLO's version of Joint Forces Base Andrews, near Washington, DC.

$$- 62 -$$

With only a few days to go before landing Doug could not help but notice Stan's condition had not improved. He saw Miekela alone in the lounge area at the table writing in her notebook. Stan was sleeping. Everyone else was busy in other parts of the ship engaged in scientific duties. Doug grasped the table and lowered himself to the opposite seat, the pads at the back of his thighs holding him to the chair.

"I'm worried about Stan," he said. "It looks like we all helped clear him for a mission that he wasn't ready to take on. Why was he cleared?"

Miekela stopped writing and looked up at Doug. "It's unfortunate that the decision was made, yes. But I'm confident he will be all right. He is able to perform his duties on ship."

Miekela disengaged herself from the chair and was about to leave. Doug rose and leaned towards her.

"Why wasn't another physicist chosen for the mission? Stan's physical health should have grounded him. Hell, it looks now as though it would have led to his being grounded from an amusement park Ferris wheel ride!"

"As co-discoverer of FLO he was given special status," she said tightly. "It was thought that fact might help us diplomatically. Really, Doug, there is nothing to be concerned about. Stan will be fine."

"Don't feed that tired old line to me. Stan's mental condition has gotten to the point where he's not an asset. His physical condition is a disaster. He may even become a liability. He *has* become a liability. The team was compromised from the start because of Stan's physical and mental condition. My own mistake seems to have been trusting you and Leach. Once we touch down he's my responsibility, and I'm telling you right now that my first order will be to sideline Stan for the duration of the mission. If you're holding back any pertinent information, Miekela, I want to know about it now."

She had been looking at Doug while he was speaking, but now she paused and looked away. She almost looked ashamed, as if she could no longer look him in the eye.

Miekela got up and moved towards the workstations without another word. Doug was frustrated at her silence but he didn't have many options, short of logging a protest when they returned to Earth. If they ever got back.

He headed to an aft compartment to track down Smith. The two of them were still rehearsing the speech that had been written for Doug to give after they landed.

— 63 —

Bishop found an elementary school an hour's drive from downtown Seattle. It was still early, so he sat on a park bench nearby. There were enough surrounding trees to offer some cover.

An old man walking his little dog strolled by and waved. Bishop nodded a greeting and watched the old man pass. After he was out of sight Bishop reached down and checked his injured leg. It was painful and the bandage needed to be changed.

He had lost consciousness during his descent when his suit ran out of oxygen. Once he had reached 15,000 feet the outside pressure was high enough to trigger an automatic valve in his suit backpack. It opened, letting in some air. He woke up hanging a couple of meters above the ground in a tree. The intact parachute had caught and tangled in the upper branches. His suit was torn in several places and he had some scrapes on his legs from contact with tree branches. His burn was a nagging pain.

The general landing area had been chosen because it was wooded and isolated, but it had some wide cleared areas for electrical transmission pylons, and the location was not far from his final destination. He was extremely lucky to have missed the power lines. Had he been conscious he would have steered and landed further away from them.

Bishop had unclipped himself from the parachute lines and with some effort managed to tear it down from the branches. Using a small shovel from his backpack he buried the chute under rocks and dirt in the forest nearby. He then cleaned the scrapes and applied a burn patch and bandages from the emergency kit.

He had activated his passive GPS and walked two hours to the cabin. There was nobody inside, but there was non-perishable food, a map, five thousand dollars in cash, a dirt-capable motorcycle, a helmet and a change of clothes. He had expected to be met by his contact, but there was nobody around.

The absence of the contact wasn't a problem or a surprise. Whoever it was had plausible deniability should Bishop ever be discovered. More important, as long as Bishop couldn't identify the contact, he couldn't give him up under interrogation. Bishop had been authorized to terminate anyone that might compromise the mission, even those who were tasked with assisting him. He was not a career assassin, but he had more than enough skill and experience to take any action to preserve the integrity of the mission.

Bishop swallowed a couple of antibiotic tablets from the emergency kit, checked his burn dressing, then ate some of the cabin rations.

He had to get to his next destination quickly. During the parachute descent there was a chance he'd been spotted from the ground. To a casual observer he might have looked like a typical skydiver. But someone with a trained eye would have spotted the faint smoke plume of the disintegrating spacecraft and called the authorities. He changed into the civilian clothes and pushed the motorcycle outside the cabin.

The map showed a hiking trail that met up with a road. The motorcycle started easily. Bishop rode about an hour on the trail to the road, and then another forty-five minutes to a motel. It was getting toward evening as he parked the bike around back. He paid cash and checked in under a false name, then fetched the bike and quietly wheeled it into his room and went to sleep.

Five hours later he was woken by the alarm in his wristwatch. He got up, ate the last of the food and drove to the outskirts of the town nearby while it was still dark. On the approach to town the bike sputtered and stalled. Bishop made only a few attempts to restart it, then abandoned the effort. He did not want to chance a regular police patrol coming to his aid. He was going to need alternate transportation.

Bishop removed the license plate, threw it down a grated sewer, then abandoned the bike a few hundred meters further on in a ditch away from the road where it wouldn't easily be spotted. He walked the rest of the way on side streets to get to the park bench on which he was sitting, across the street from a school.

It was 0910. The night had been cool but with the rising sun the air had warmed rapidly. There was a fine mist over the park as the last of the dew evaporated.

All of the teachers had to be inside the school. Bishop got up and walked across the street to the school parking lot, trying not to limp from the pain in his lower leg. He found an older vehicle in a common color. Newer cars were of an unfamiliar design and likely contained some sort of GPS system that could be tracked.

Elementary school teachers generally stayed in school all day, many eating lunch on the premises, so he would have a few hours before the theft was reported. More than enough time to reach his destination.

He slid a thin tool past the driver's side glass, slid it sideways, felt for the latching mechanism and unlocked the door. He got in, broke off the other end of the tool and used it in the ignition. He placed his package under the passenger seat and drove away.

Bishop drove to the fringes of an industrial area and parked near a sparsely used driveway. At the appointed time a four-door sedan stopped nearby.

Bishop got out and walked towards the sedan. He opened the passenger door and got in, extending his hand to agent Rector of FLO.

Bishop suddenly got a small sense of what Doug had experienced, to meet an alternate version of the person you knew.

Exactly the same but different. Rector didn't smile as they shook hands.

"Let's get one thing straight," Rector said immediately, his gaze unwavering. "The target suffered a head injury years ago. Hasn't been the same since. Can't keep a girlfriend. Keeps beating them up. Almost got himself demoted. He's starting to become a pro-Mekhos fanatic. Not a nice guy. But he's still good at his job and still has his security clearance. I'll back you up, but I do not want to be in the same room when it happens."

"Understood." There wasn't much else Bishop could say.

They drove to an apartment building and parked around back behind a large garbage bin. Rector handed Bishop an automatic pistol and a small tool pouch, then waited in the car as Bishop walked to the rear door of the building. Bishop entered a code in the keypad, opened the door when it unlatched and stepped inside the small back foyer.

He found the elevator and took it up to the fifteenth floor. He extracted the tools and within ninety seconds picked the apartment door lock. Bishop entered quietly, checking carefully and quickly that the place was empty. He put a package under the kitchen sink, then searched for the Raim removal key. Rector had told him that most people kept them in a bedside nightstand or in computer desk drawer. He found the removal key in the computer desk drawer. He put the key in his jacket pocket then found a chair and sat down to wait.

– 64 –

On the last day of their journey, the crew of the Copernicus was again strapped into their seats as the engines applied full thrust for the five hours it would take to slow them down enough to enter orbit around FLO. It felt more physically punishing than the launch due to the fact that even with the counteracting drug at maximum dosage, their muscles had atrophied a small amount from six weeks of near constant weightlessness. Once in orbit they were again able to move about the ship to check systems and prepare for the landing, which was only a few hours away.

On top of the physical punishment they had endured, everyone was suffering a wide range of anxieties about being so close to landing on FLO. Foley's fever had not subsided and he had to be sedated. He had become increasingly argumentative and short-tempered, which was interfering with the ship's operations. Doug helped secure him to his seat as the rest of the team strapped in and prepared for landing.

As the ship entered the atmosphere Doug thought about one of his conversations with Stan a couple days earlier. Just before returning to his bunk Stan had said "Whatever happens now is up to God's plan." Doug had just stared at him in silence.

God's plan? Stan Foley had spent a grand total of *one day* in a church as long as Doug had known him, and that was for his wedding. Now he was finding religion? Stan's fever wasn't high enough to cause hysteria or hallucination.

Unstable or not, Stan was still right about a couple of things. The actions Mekhos had taken would save FLO at the expense of Earth. It was easier to let someone die if the act which was causing the death protected yourself and your family from the same fate. It wasn't as if Earth was right next door, its worsening conditions within view of anyone on FLO. Earth wasn't going to blow up in some massive conflagration that would singe FLO. *Exactly the opposite,* Doug whispered to himself, *we'll just fade away into evolutionary history well out of sight of anyone on FLO with a conscience.*

But they were there to facilitate change. The mission was clear. They were not in it to fail.

Doug did not know if they'd be given the chance to talk directly to Mekhos, or if the minders would insist on a FLO intermediary who would likely be biased. It nagged at him. How do you negotiate persuasively with a computer? How do you play cards with something that has all the cards? Part of him was utterly fascinated at the thought of having a conversation with a thinking computer, but he was also unnerved. Its intellect had not been measured, but it was clearly a formidable mind.

Doug was jolted back to reality as the ship hit heavy turbulence. The rough ride was accompanied by several minutes of flaming ionization covering the windshield. Once they leveled out in the lower stratosphere the ride smoothed out. The ship banked and turned under computer control to scrub off speed. As it banked Doug was able to get a view outside while they were high enough to see the curvature of the Earth. It looked like home of course. He had to remind himself it was really an alien planet, and that he was farther away from home than anyone had ever traveled.

It had been covered in their pre-launch briefing, but the stark reality was setting in. Despite being American citizens, they were utter foreigners in another America on another planet. They could travel to their hometown and be a stranger. They could watch a ball game and see that every player on the team was different from those they knew back home. There was not a single person they could turn to that would offer the comfort of friends, family, or ally beyond diplomatic platitudes. They were alone and at the mercy of their hosts.

– 65 –

Twenty minutes later as the Copernicus approached Andrews in preparation for landing, Doug strained to look out the side window. He was curious to see if he could spot any differences in the base from an aerial view. With the possible exception of one or two buildings he couldn't see anything that stood out. The base looked exactly the same.

They lined up for landing. Doug was now acutely aware of gravity weighing him down. His heart rate was elevated. Miekela had explained that all astronauts experienced it when returning to normal gravity, despite their regular exercise regimen and the drug designed to counteract the effects of prolonged weightlessness.

The ship now felt exactly like an airliner. It touched down at 140 knots with the roar of reverse engine thrust beginning as soon as the nose wheel made contact, slowing them quickly. The Copernicus slowed to taxi speed as it neared the long limit of the runway, then turned to follow what appeared to be a military ground escort towards a designated hangar. Through the windshield Doug could see what looked like a welcoming delegation, seemingly all but identical to the one Doug had been a part of when the Envoy had arrived on earth over two months earlier.

Bertrand and Jamieson were busy checking instrumentation and going through the shut-down checklist. The screens in the seatbacks in front of the rest of the team flashed to a safety harness unlock symbol.

Bertrand pulled himself out of his seat and faced them.

"You have ten minutes to stretch your legs and gather your belongings before we open the hatch. There will be a short welcoming ceremony, then we'll all be taken inside for debriefing."

Doug turned as he heard Miekela's voice behind him. "Remember to descend the aircraft stairs slowly when disembarking and walk carefully. There will be a shuttle bus so you won't need to walk far, and you will be given assistance as necessary. We have found that most physical coordination returns after a couple of hours, and walking should be very easy after a day, though you will still feel a bit weaker than normal for a few days more."

Bertrand continued, "You can carry your on-board duffle bags with you. Other personal belongings and street clothing will be transferred from the hold to your quarters by the military ground crew. Thank you everyone. Dr. Lockwood, I transfer command of the team to you."

Bertrand gave Doug an informal salute, to which he nodded. Doug stood up, unsteady at first. It would take a few minutes for his inner ear to become reacquainted with gravity. He walked slowly to the workstation area, at first leaning on the seatbacks for support, then walked back towards his seat. It was difficult but he already felt himself getting used to gravity again. He felt as if he'd been bedridden for an extended period.

Stan groaned. Doug turned to see that he was slumped over, his head in his hands.

"Are you okay Stan?"

"I feel sick to my stomach."

"Probably from the re-entry turbulence. I'm queasy too."

Miekela had moved to Stan. "We can get a wheelchair for you. I'm sure the base doctor is just outside. You'll feel better once they see you to the infirmary."

Doug helped Stan attempt to get up, but both of them were unsteady.

"I'm going to sit here a moment," Stan said, as he lowered himself back into his seat. He was sweating. Miekela took his pulse.

"The main door is being opened now Dr. Lockwood," Bertrand said as he placed his hand on the latch lever. "It is time to visit my Earth. I will have the medical team come aboard immediately to assist Dr. Foley."

"Thank you," Doug replied. "See you inside Stan. Lead the way Carl."

Doug followed Bertrand's example and used the hand rail as he descended the stairs. His legs felt wobbly and his heart was pounding at the stress, but he found himself getting steadier as he reached solid ground walked a few steps on the tarmac. Jamieson and Smith were behind him. There was already a team of four men dressed head to toe in bio protection gear. They paid the visitors no notice and quickly climbed the stairs to evacuate Foley as soon as Doug and his people were clear. Miekela had remained on board with Foley.

Doug, Smith and Jamieson paused to look around.

"I'm impressed," said Smith. "Just like home."

Doug agreed. The mid-day air smelled different. It was spring in the U.S. northeast. It had been the beginning of some sort of strange and turbulent autumn back home, since FLO and Earth were in opposite orbits. It was a strange feeling, having the surroundings feel so familiar, and yet be slightly out of sync. He saw the same hangar where they had stood outside eleven weeks earlier to greet the Envoy. A quarter of a mile past the hangar he could see the base snack shop, the one with the old war veteran clerk and his wife, with the old-style cash register. He wondered if the same people – or rather, their FLO alternates – worked there.

Subtle differences mounted up quickly, as if you've been away from your home town for a while and returned to find some old facades remodeled, a few old buildings demolished to make way for new ones, and strangers mixed in with the familiar faces. Though some of the people looked the same, nobody knew Doug. It made the experience stranger than ever. Even if the snack shop had the same owners, they wouldn't recognize Doug Lockwood. Maybe they would have the same old cash register. He felt an urge to visit the shop to see for sure.

Smith grabbed Doug's shoulder. "Look," he said.

Doug followed Smith's gaze. There it was, low on the daytime horizon. The Moon. Their Moon. Much smaller than he remembered, since it was still on its way and hadn't attained final orbit. Jamieson saw it too. The three of them stared at it for a moment. They were looking at something that had been stolen from them, and were about to confront the thieves that had taken it.

"Here's the vehicle," Bertrand said, bringing the men's attention back to the ground. There was no quarantine medical van. Copernicus had monitored everyone all the way and reported a clean bill of health during the landing.

An open shuttle bus arrived with one passenger already on board. Doug was surprised to see that it was Stacey Lau. As the vehicle stopped in front of him he returned her smile but wasn't sure if he should let on that he'd worked with her counterpart back home. She got out and extended her hand.

"Welcome Dr. Lockwood! We are very pleased that you came. I'm Stacey Lau, White House Chief of Staff. I'm sorry to hear Dr. Foley isn't feeling well."

As she moved to introduce herself to Jamieson and Smith, Doug glanced at Bertrand, who also had regular contact with the other Stacey. Bertrand gave a slight shrug and smile, acknowledging the situation but also treating it as routine. On FLO, Stacey occupied the position held by Arthur Leach back home.

As he stepped into the shuttle bus Doug looked back and saw an ambulance arriving. Dr. Persaud was talking animatedly to the medical team at the ship, who were all wearing sealed masks. In view of what he knew of Foley's condition he thought that was unusual. If Foley had an infection it had to be related to complications from his surgery and it could not be contagious. Even at this distance though he could tell that Miekela's face was lined with tension.

The shuttle bus carried them all of two hundred meters to the waiting delegation. There were probably three hundred people present. They cheered as the shuttle bus pulled up. Most of the delegation were waving small American flags, UN flags, and some others Doug didn't recognize.

When they got out of the bus a small receiving line greeted each of them in turn. There was the Vice President of the United States, the Secretary of the United Nations, the Lieutenant General in command of Andrews, and some members of the media. The presence of the media surprised Doug. Apparently their arrival was not as secret as it had been for the Envoy on Earth. Aside from Stacey, Doug did not recognize any of the VIPs. He saw a few familiar faces scattered in the larger delegation, none of whom were on a first name basis with him on Earth.

After the short introductions away from the microphone, the Vice President addressed the crowd.

"On behalf of the United States of America, the United Nations, and all the people of Earth, I welcome Dr. Doug Lockwood and his team, our honored guests from the Twin Earth. This is an historic day, the first time in history that we have had visitors from another planet.

Please join me in welcoming our brothers and sisters!"

With that the crowd erupted in cheers and applause. Doug and the rest of the team couldn't help but smile and wave back in acknowledgement. Behind the larger delegation were television news vans with roof-mounted cameras and satellite dishes. Apparently their arrival was being broadcast around FLO. *I'll bet,* Doug thought without a trace of humor, *that the crowd was cheering wildly just before Louis XVI was beheaded.*

Stacey Lau tapped Doug on his shoulder from behind. It was the signal for Doug to step forward and offer his hand to the Vice President. The man hesitated every so slightly before smiling even wider and firmly grasping Doug's hand in a single shake. *Probably afraid of catching a rash from the alien,* Doug thought wryly while suppressing a chuckle. *Come on Doug. Get ahold of yourself. Do the speech and get on with it.* The Vice President stepped aside to allow Doug to stand in front of the microphone. Doug turned back for a moment to nod his thanks to the VIPs, then turned to survey the crowd.

"Thank you Mr. Vice President, honored guests and all in attendance today here and around the world," Doug began. "The day your Envoy arrived on my Earth will go down as the most significant moment in our civilization's history. Dr. Carl Bertrand and his Envoy members have become the stuff of legend on my world. They earned our respect and our approbation. Dr. Bertrand and his team, by their intelligence, acumen and skill, shone the brightest possible light on a pathway between our two worlds." Doug paused to catch his breath and control his voice. "It is a remarkable achievement.

"We are here today to begin learning from your great accomplishments. We are here to understand how we may best live and grow by the very real possibility that the greatest era of peace and prosperity that both our worlds have ever known may be within our grasp. We are here to work hard, and we are here to earn your respect. We hope, with all our hearts, that we will find all that we seek. From the people of my Earth, and from my team and me, it's a great day to be alive." Doug raised both arms and waved to the cheering crowd.

– 66 –

As Bishop waited in the dim room he brought his heart rate under control, slowing his breathing and relaxing his muscles. His leg burn throbbed but the pain was bearable. Rector had given him another first aid kit in the car. Bishop had changed the dressing and bandage again during the drive. It would heal, but Bishop had wrapped it tight and taped it securely so it wouldn't impede him.

He glanced around the room. It was exactly as he expected. Not the best layout, which made his job difficult.

Bishop heard someone approach the apartment door. He quietly got up from the chair and moved to the wall just around the corner from the entrance. He had already determined that the position cast no shadows and there were no reflective objects or mirrors nearby that would betray his presence to anyone entering the apartment.

The door opened. Bishop aimed his silencer-equipped handgun to temple height, intending to shoot as soon as the target walked past. He heard the man enter and pause to remove his shoes. In seconds he would walk into position, and it would be over.

Bishop saw a faint shadow on the floor as the man approached the target zone. He saw the tip of the man's foot, steadied his grip and prepared to fire. Bishop tensed his trigger finger and had started the pull just as a set of keys dropped onto the floor. Bishop shot just a split second after the man bent to retrieve the keys. The bullet narrowly missed its target, hitting the opposite wall. The man reacted without hesitation, turning and charging with his head low at Bishop, impacting the right side of Bishop's rib cage, knocking the wind out of him as he fell.

While on his back Bishop aimed the gun at his adversary but the man kicked it from his hand before he could shoot. The gun bounced off the wall and slid noisily across the apartment floor a short distance behind him. The man was about to kick down at Bishop's chest when he froze, a look of astonishment on his face.

The man's hesitation vanished as he instantly comprehended the situation. He was to be assassinated and replaced by this twin, for reasons unknown. He reached to the small of his back and produced a compact handgun, aiming it at Bishop on the floor. Before he could shoot Bishop rolled quickly back and to the left as Rector appeared and kicked the man's feet out from under him. The man from FLO fell heavily but rolled to the center of the room and got to his feet in a combat stance to face his new assailant. But Rector had vanished, having quickly backed off into the building hallway and out of sight. The man swung the gun back to where Bishop had gone down but it was too late. Agent Bishop of Earth, kneeling on the apartment floor with a clear shot, fired twice into the man's chest. Agent Bishop, late of FLO, collapsed to the floor. Bishop stood up quickly, took three quick strides to the body and fired another shot into the left center of his adversary's chest.

Bishop took a moment to steady himself. He looked at the dead man's face and felt lightheaded and sick to his stomach. Bishop had killed up close before. But his ability to dissociate himself from the individual he killed faltered unexpectedly for a few moments. Despite going over it in his head beforehand, he was shaken at the sight of his own face, inert in death. It was enough to momentarily stop even someone as tough-minded as Bishop. He had to physically shake himself to clear his head.

He kneeled beside the body and began working at the Raim. Rector had re-entered the apartment and closed the door. He had to work quickly. If the bracelet detected a cessation of vital signs lasting more than a few seconds it would put out a call to the local emergency responders, who would dispatch an ambulance to the Raim's GPS location.

Bishop took the key out of his pocket and was careful to place his thumb over the key's fingerprint reader while touching it to the Raim. There was a frustrating pause as the bracelet lit up with the message, *Do you wish to unlock?*

Bishop said "Yes I wish to unlock" in a loud, clear voice while squeezing two of his fingers under the bracelet so that his vital signs would register instead of the dead, rapidly cooling body. He was barely able to squeeze his fingers partway under the Raim. The messaged flashed on and off as the bracelet released. Bishop decided to wait a few minutes before putting it on his wrist, thinking it might register as suspicious if the wearer went to the trouble of taking it off and putting it back on immediately.

He retrieved the body bag he had stowed under the sink earlier and was careful to close it completely around the body. He checked the bag carefully for leaks. The last thing he wanted to do was leave a blood trail. Rector then helped him move the body to the service elevator and into the trunk of the car.

"I'm done here," Rector said. "I'm going to meet the cell leader now. The body in the trunk will help kick loose the package that has to be delivered to the MC." He looked down at the locked trunk. "He was my partner once. Seems like a very long time ago. He had problems."

Bishop knew better than to say anything at that moment. He stood silently as Rector got into the car and drove through the exit of the underground garage, disappearing from sight.

Bishop returned to the apartment, where he closed the Raim around his wrist and prepared for the rest of his mission on FLO.

– 67 –

After a short medical examination, Doug, Smith and Jamieson were taken to a private dining room to relax, have something to eat, and meet with another group of VIPs. Some of the dignitaries they'd already met had left. The Secretary General of the United Nations, a distinguished gentleman of about sixty, sat beside Doug.

"Despite all the travelling I have done, I have never truly been to space," the Secretary General said. "It has become fairly common among some business and government officials to take the Condor across the globe for meetings, or for tourists who can afford it to spend a weekend overseas, or even in orbit. I have taken a similar plane for hyperbolic flights across the globe, but I have not experienced weightlessness for more than a few minutes."

Doug had learned that the Copernicus was part of a small fleet of space planes in the Condor series that were used for government and corporate travel. Without the scientific workstations in place, most versions of the plane had seating for thirty to fifty passengers, depending on the interior layout.

"It was very interesting," Doug replied, as he poured some dressing on his salad. "But being aloft for six weeks takes its toll. I'm an avid cyclist and I've been told that helped me to adapt, but you sure feel it when you return to normal gravity."

"And how do you feel now?"

"Out of place," Doug replied, smiling slightly. "We spent six weeks traveling farther than anyone before us, and then someone opened the Copernicus hatch and we stepped out to find something that looks, smells, and feels so much like what we left behind that it is deeply unsettling. People we think we've known all our lives who don't know us. The same feeling the Envoy expressed to us after their arrival."

The Secretary General was looking at Doug, trying to grasp the sense of displacement that was being described. He gave up and shook his head slowly.

"We have some knowledge of the Twin, or rather, your Earth," the Secretary General said finally. "It is fascinating to think how our evolutionary history was completely identical, until a divergence was apparently triggered by the existence and work of Norman Stravinsky. One man. His accomplishments with quantum computing are what made our current society. He is still in the field, about your age. We will try to arrange a meeting."

Doug could sense that the welcoming committee was reluctant to broach the problem at hand, preferring to stick to pleasantries. Nevertheless, the Secretary had just cut to the chase and offered to introduce Doug to the creator of Mekhos. Doug decided to be direct.

"A meeting to which I will look forward sir, with thanks. It unfortunately brings to mind the problem my world faces. The actions which Mekhos took to save your world and your way of life has placed civilization on my world in the gravest danger. We face incalculable peril. We recognize the position you are in, but we want to know where we stand with regard to your various governments."

The Secretary General averted his gaze for a moment as he cleared his throat.

"There is only one official position Dr. Lockwood. All governments are united when it comes to world affairs. We understand the enormity of the situation. Our scientists have been working on developing grains and other flora that are easier to pollinate and fertilize, and we will be happy to share—"

Doug cut him off.

"Forgive my abruptness, but we will not be patronized." Doug fixed the Secretary with the determined gaze of a man who did not have the luxury of tolerating the typical stonewalling tactics of diplomats. He had been exposed to such maneuvering when he was a science advisor on the Intergovernmental Panel on Climate Change. Handshakes and pleasant conversations needed to be cast aside when circumstances were dire.

"The way things stand now, our civilization in its current form is doomed," Doug stated flatly. "Your genetically modified grains will be a palliative at best, something that might benefit the surviving population. We'd thank you for the efforts, but they won't do anything to fix the main issue - the theft of our Moon by Mekhos, and the resulting near-complete destruction of our ecosystem."

Doug's strong tone was picked up by everyone in the room. Nathan Smith was at the other end of the table, talking with Stacey Lau. Smith stopped talking and stared at Doug, frowning with worry. Doug's direct attack could impact Smith's own assignment on FLO. The Secretary was taken aback too, but recovered almost instantly.

"Dr. Lockwood, we will do our best to mitigate the effects of the lost orbiting body by providing policy guidance, resource management, and more. As I said, we have been working on this problem for some time and the results look promising. But as for the solution you are hoping for," the Secretary paused for a moment before finishing. "I am certain it is out of my people's hands. It was never in our hands from the beginning."

Doug had known, even before speaking, that he wouldn't make much progress with the UN Secretary. He straightened up in his chair, and placed his hands flat on the table as he recomposed himself.

"Thank you for your candor," Doug said in a well controlled tone, "and thank you for allowing me to describe the needs of my people." Doug scanned the room in a slow, moderate arc, a neutral look on his face, his head moving slightly from left to right. He deliberately looked, momentarily, directly into the eyes of a number of people in quick succession, minutely nodding his head once each time as he did so. Some tension went out of the room.

"Dr. Persaud and I look forward to a meeting with Mekhos at the earliest possible time." Doug said, turning back to the Secretary General.

"I believe you are scheduled for Thursday afternoon."

It was finally confirmed then. Two days away.

"I would have preferred to meet even sooner of course," Doug replied, smiling slightly, "but Thursday certainly isn't unreasonable. I thank you sincerely for helping to arrange the meeting."

He would have to settle for the date given. *In the interim I will graciously accept the diplomatic overtures of our hosts.*

– 68 –

Stravinsky was waiting at his apartment driveway. He was looking forward to trying the crepes at a new café that had opened nearby.

The car wasn't his usual. It was slightly older, a boxy sedan. Stravinsky glanced through the tinted window at the driver. He could barely see his outline through the dark glass, but saw him nod to get in. Stravinsky got into the back seat, took out his notebook, and said good morning to the driver.

"Good morning sir," the driver said in an unfamiliar voice as they drove off. Stravinsky looked up. It was the big man he saw the other day at his usual café and who had been talking to the policeman outside his building. The driver handed Stravinsky a tablet computer. The text on the screen said, *Professor Stravinsky, please do not speak while you read this. Your family has been placed in danger by Virtue. They may have bugged this car, and may have compromised your Raim. Please follow the instructions on the next few pages.*

Stravinsky looked up at the driver. He wasn't sure if this was legitimate, or if he should press the panic button on his Raim. He continued reading the text.

You are being driven to your regular café. Once there, please exit the car without your belongings. Proceed downstairs to the men's washroom and remove your Raim. Leave it under the sink behind the cleaning sup-

plies. Then return to this car without speaking to anyone.

The car pulled up to the café. Stravinsky felt dazed as he slowly got out and walked into the restaurant. The terror group was real, and had threatened his family in the past. But why all this cloak and dagger? Why not take him to a security building? *Maybe Virtue is already holding my relatives hostage and are watching my office.* He entered the downstairs washroom. It was deserted.

As the most notable member of the Limited, Stravinsky didn't need a physical Raim removal key. He entered an exclusive removal code and took off the bracelet. He paused. What if this was a kidnap attempt and he was walking right into it? But then he thought of his mother, nieces, nephews. He couldn't bear it if anything happened to them.

He decided to take a small precaution against having his Raim fall into the wrong hands. He exited the washroom, walked a bit farther down the hall and opened an unmarked door to a utility room. The room contained buckets, mops, cleaning solution jugs, and shelves stocked with spare light bulbs and other supplies. Norman chose a dusty shelf that obviously hadn't been accessed much and placed the Raim behind a box that was labeled as plumbing repair supplies. He quickly exited the utility room and jogged up the stairs. A server in the restaurant smiled at him.

"Your usual table sir?"

"No, not today," Stravinsky replied as he hurriedly walked past. He got back into the car.

They drove on in silence. The agent motioned for Stravinsky to pick up the tablet.

You are being driven to a secure location where details will be explained. Please remain calm.

They drove a short distance to an industrial area that looked to Stravinsky like somewhere in West Marginal or Duwamish near the bay. The driver pulled up to the entrance of what appeared to be a an old, darkened warehouse.

"We've arrived sir. Please follow me."

They got out and walked over to a windowless, rusted steel door. Stravinsky looked at the agent.

"This is unusual. Why isn't this meeting being held downtown?" he said, as the man unlocked the padlock and opened the door."

"Sir, everything will be explained to you once we're inside."

The agent put his hand on Stravinsky's shoulder and gently directed him into the large open space and locked the door behind them.
He flipped on the light switches. High fluorescent lights flickered on
to reveal a large warehouse with various pieces of idle machinery and
a small pile of paint cans at the far end. At one side of the room there
was a desk, two chairs and a desktop computer.

The agent walked over to the desk, his footsteps echoing in the large
room. Stravinsky followed. He watched the man toss his driver's cap
onto the desk and turn on the computer.

"I am Alexei Rector, sent to ensure your safety. We need to act
quickly. Virtue has access to all your personal information."

He opened the desk drawer, retrieved a file folder, opened it to the
first page and handed it to Stravinsky.

"Do you recognize that man?"

It was a police mug shot of a young man, with a significant red scar
on his jaw.

"I'm not sure," Stravinsky said distractedly. "There's something about
him. The face is familiar. Who is he?"

"Check the name on the sheet opposite."

Stravinsky scanned the information sheet.

"Daniel Santos," Stravinsky said quietly. "Yes. He looks very different. You must have realized that I knew him. A few years ago he helped
his cousin's gang try to kidnap my mother, but they injured my housekeeper instead. He was just a kid then, fourteen I think. His cousin was
killed by the police."

"He's all grown up now, and he's never forgotten the fact his cousin
was killed right in front of him. Santos is as angry as ever, and wants
his revenge on Mekhos, any way possible. And that includes going after
you or your family again."

"Then why don't you pick him up? He shouldn't be hard to find!"

"He's being hidden by members of Virtue. The group has grown and
has become quite skilled at evading detection."

"I don't need to tell you that Mekhos is quite capable of finding
people," said Stravinsky. "Very few people can travel without being de-

tected. Even if they use false names and passports there are other methods of identification. Face and voice recognition."

"That assumes people are out in the open," Rector replied, "using public means of transportation. It also assumes they are wearing a Raim. Virtue members largely remain hidden. They move clandestinely and wear expert disguises, even changing their gait by wearing a weight on one ankle. They don't use public transportation. They buy disposable phones, discarding them daily or even hourly when an operation is in progress."

Stravinsky was silent for a moment. He had never thought very much about how far people might go in an effort to remain undetected by Mekhos and the authorities.

"They sent this video file," Rector said, turning to the computer.

Rector tapped a key to start the video. Daniel Santos appeared on the monitor, gesturing with a large handgun. Other men appeared in the background. One was typing into a computer. Another was pointing at what appeared to be a map on a table. All but Santos were wearing masks.

"We at Virtue are tirelessly committed to the liberation of humanity. We will not rest until the tyranny has been eliminated. Mekhos is an unnatural parasite attached to the world, draining us of our soul in exchange for paltry economic incentives. We believe the inventor of the machine still wields great influence over it. Kill the father of Mekhos, and it will be vulnerable."

Kill the father of Mekhos. Stravinsky was shocked by the stark words. To him, the research and development of Mekhos had been an intensely passionate pursuit. Mekhos now represented everything that the formerly deeply troubled people and nations of Earth had needed in order to succeed in the face of constant economic uncertainty and ideological conflict. Norman Stravinsky had never understood any of the anger directed at Mekhos or at himself. And now he felt a hollow in the pit of his stomach. He broke out into a cold sweat as he saw Santos hold up photographs of his relatives that included some of the children.

"Thanks to Mekhos, the Limited are living a privileged life at the people's expense. They will be sacrificed to show the world the price of imposing creeping totalitarian rule upon us."

Santos was looking directly into the camera lens as he spoke.

"You can save your relatives Stravinsky. As much as we hate you, we hate Mekhos even more. Give us the backdoor codes and all will be forgiven. If you fail to provide the codes to us, or if you try to attack us, I swear on the grave of my cousin we will kill everyone you care about."

Santos sounded as if he were reading from a script, but it didn't matter. The boy had grown into a man and he was frightening, clearly capable of violence. He continued his demands, reading off the names and addresses of Stravinsky's relatives. Norman turned quickly to Rector to ask the obvious question.

"We have already reached some of your relatives, Dr. Stravinsky, but others are missing including your mother. We assume the worst, that they have already been kidnapped," Rector said.

"But my mother had a security detail assigned to her. She should be safe!"

"Those security men were found dead. We're trying to locate the Virtue cell responsible for this, but it will take time."

"Where are the other security experts? Where is Charles, my regular driver? Why are you the only one here?" Stravinsky took a step away from Rector.

Rector produced a small digital recorder from his jacket.

"We are concerned Virtue may have operatives in the security office. Please listen to this." He swiped Play and placed the recorder on the desk. Stravinsky recognized the voice of his regular driver.

"Sir, this is Charles, I apologize for not being there. I just learned that *Virtue* has been tracking me. They are executing a well-coordinated operation that has, frankly, surprised us in its scope. I drove off from your apartment with a body double earlier, to lure them away. Right now we can't risk using a Raim or conventional mobile phone to communicate for fear of it being tracked by Virtue. Later we will pass on a secure device to agent Rector so we can communicate with you directly. We are working on finding the location where your mother is being held. In the meantime, follow agent Rector's instructions. He is an expert in these matters."

Stravinsky staggered over to a chair and sat down.

Rector turned off the device. He looked at Stravinsky.

"Can you account for why Santos and Virtue believe that back door codes exist?"

Stravinsky was staring off into space.

"Norman!" Stravinsky flinched and looked at Rector.

"Back door code refers to lines of programming that a developer might use to gain access to a computer system without needing to go through usual security safeguards."

"We know that. Did you employ a back door code when doing your part in designing Mekhos?"

Stravinsky leaned forward and ran both his hands through his hair. He looked exhausted from the stress.

"Well, did you?"

"Yes. But it wouldn't do any good to have it. Mekhos has evolved beyond being vulnerable to such access."

"I see," Rector said. "But even a computer as advanced as Mekhos is still built upon code that executes basic functions, like a hardware BIOS?"

"That's right. But in this case a better example would be the human brain, which performs many autonomous functions, like breathing and respiration without conscious input. But again, this won't help Virtue. Mekhos shouldn't be vulnerable."

"Then it is my opinion we should give them the codes."

"Should I give them a fake one?"

"We must assume they have the means to detect a fake code. Who knows, they may be working with a double agent, a security expert in your office. You just said Mekhos is not vulnerable to a backdoor attack. We'll give them what they want, in its entirety. It may buy us the time we need to find your relatives."

Rector held out a pen and paper. Stravinsky took them and began writing.

– 69 –

After lunch there was a debriefing for each team member individually, which felt more like a cordial interview. An interviewer had set up a recording device and was also scribbling notes into a tablet computer. The officials asked about conditions on Earth, their journey and their mission. There was nothing out of the ordinary, but Doug was again surprised at the casualness – or perhaps it was the *maturity* – of the process.

Doug was asked about the Envoy members still on the Twin. Aside from Bertrand, they were being held indefinitely at Andrews, virtual prisoners. They had little hope of returning home. Doug wondered how that fact might affect his team.

"That they are being held indefinitely was not unexpected, given the circumstances," the interviewer said. "As volunteers, the members of the expedition knew that being unable to return home was a possibility. We hope they are being treated well and expect they will eventually be allowed to return, if they wish. We received one brief and slightly disturbing report from Copernicus, from the Raims belonging to Morris and Chan. Then their Raims went silent. Of course we've received nothing else from any of the other Raims either since Copernicus left the Twin."

Doug felt uncomfortable. After it became clear that the Moon was being stolen, the members of the Envoy had been sequestered and then isolated from any further contact with anyone that Doug knew. Carl Bertrand and to a lesser extent Alfred Chan were sometimes seen at Andrews, but the others, including Cheryl McBride, were out of sight. It was rumored that they were being interrogated, and not necessarily according to the rules of the Geneva Convention.

"I believe they're all well and busy," said Doug, as sincerely as he could. "I was occupied by training for this mission, but I can recall seeing some members of the Envoy at Andrews, escorted of course, but they all seemed to be in good spirits." *I suppose Bertrand and Chan could be considered "some,"* Doug thought.

"That is reassuring," replied the interviewer. "Now that we are finished the debriefing, Dr. Lockwood, would you and your team mind answering a few questions for the media? We'll keep the session brief. We know you are tired from your journey and physically readjusting to gravity, but there is great public demand."

"I appreciate the demand," Doug replied with a genuine smile, "far more than I care about my current physical condition."

"You may be asked some difficult questions about how your political leaders have reacted to the situation. We ask that you be forthright without being sensational. After all, we are all trying to remain positive in these uncertain times."

"I understand," said Doug. *And so the public relations spin begins,* he thought. *Better to play along rather than spout what's really on my mind and risk being cut off from Mekhos.*

The team, minus Foley and Persaud, were on the panel facing a room full of journalists. The moderator informed the press that to keep things orderly in the short time they had, they could not shout questions. They had to raise their hands and wait to be called. A young woman in the second row was first to ask a question.

"Dr. Lockwood, welcome to Earth, or as you know it, Foley-Lockwood Object."

There was some laughter after the planet name was spoken.

"Thank you," Doug smiled. "I know that name must seem odd, but it was chosen very early on before we knew there was life here, much less an almost identical civilization."

"There has been great public interest in your team, and you especially. We've heard the stories about how your early life paralleled that of the Doug Lockwood here, to the point of dating the same woman on your respective planets. Our Dr. McBride lost her partner, as did you, yet amazingly you found each other again. That must have been an incredible reunion. Would you describe it for us?"

Doug was uncomfortable at hearing this deeply personal question, but his old experience with the press led him to come up with an appropriate answer almost immediately.

"It was very shocking to say the least, as you can imagine. At the same time it was a wonderful experience. Both Cheryls will always be deeply important to me and they will both always be respected as great scientists."

The journalists lapped it up. It was the ultimate tragic romance story, sure to inspire novels and television shows in the coming months.

A male reporter from the back directed a question to Bertrand.

"Dr. Bertrand, how would you compare the two civilizations? Did you feel at home on the Twin?"

"Yes. I felt very welcome there. Our hosts were gracious and kind. However, I never stepped off the base. There were too many pressing matters. I could not take time out to be a tourist, as much as I would have enjoyed doing so."

Another question was directed at Doug.

"Dr. Lockwood, what results are you anticipating from your upcoming meeting with Mekhos this Thursday?"

"I'm hoping for an outcome that will benefit both worlds. As powerful as it is, I'm not sure Mekhos has applied full consideration to all available solutions. We're here in the spirit of cooperation to find a mutually agreeable plan that will avert an ecological catastrophe from occurring on my Earth, one that will have been averted on your planet thanks to the arrival of my Moon."

The reporters and journalists immediately started yelling questions to the panel.

"Do you think the Twin is facing disaster?"

"How does the public on your world view us and Mekhos after taking your Moon?"

"Are the rest of the Envoy we sent to your planet prisoners?"

"Will you stay here if your planet takes a turn for the worse?"

The moderator stepped in front of the panel and had to shout over the din.

"I'm sorry, that is all the time we have for now! Our guests have a full schedule and must carry on. Thank you for your questions."

'Your planet, my moon,' Doug thought grimly, had the predicted effect. Reporters are reporters. Hopefully there's a court of public opinion on this planet too.

− 70 −

Carl Bertrand had returned to Seattle to resume his duties as a senior director of a powerful multinational technology company called TranSilica. During the long trip to FLO, Bertrand had described how deeply TranSilica was involved in quantum computing and with management of the global infrastructure that had gradually been built up to service Mekhos. Bertrand's descriptions of a variety of other research and development work being done at TranSilica had been equally impressive. The company was plugged into half the governments on FLO and effectively controlled all R&D related to quantum computing.

Doug, Jamieson and Smith were shown to their rooms on the base. Doug's room resembled an executive hotel suite. It had a well appointed washroom with separate bathtub and shower stall, a tablet computer connected to the secure network on base, a wireless keyboard, a desk, a television, and a separate bedroom with another desk, tablet and television. He was exhausted but he wanted to watch the news and check the latest goings-on with the newsreader he had been given after his debriefing.

Unsurprisingly, their arrival on FLO was the major news item. Doug had not been famous on either Earth prior to the disaster. On FLO the public had developed a particular fascination with Dr. Douglas Lockwood, the visitor from the Twin that had died years earlier on *this* Earth. On a news channel he saw a profile of his life, education and accomplishments, and how they started to diverge a few years before the other Lockwood's death.

Doug's parents on FLO were interviewed, though they did not have much to say. "That man is not our son," Mr. Lockwood said as a somber Mrs. Lockwood looked on. "He has his own mother and father on another planet. I'm sure they're proud of him. Our Doug died over two years ago."

He felt sympathy for them. It was a bizarre feeling. So familiar, yet they were not *his* parents. *The media,* Doug sighed, *manages to practice this sort of cruelty on every world.* He turned off the television and pushed the thoughts from his mind as he tapped the newsreader.

Aside from being almost weightless, the tablet operated similarly to those back home with a gesture-based touch interface. When turned off the tablet was as transparent as glass, changing luminosity depending on the content. The help system was very forgiving of a new user, so he was able to navigate quickly.

Apart from news on his team's arrival, *The Moon Returns* was the dominant story. There was a section detailing the progress and how Mekhos would carefully and gradually bring the Moon into orbit in a way that would help avoid the worst of the earthquakes that had plagued the planet after the trans-dimensional transfer.

According to the report, the Moon was already having a positive effect on the ecosystem. Its normal phases were now visible, though it would remain slightly dimmer and tides would be of smaller magnitude until it was brought into its normal orbital radius. Only Mekhos knew the exact schedule for final alignment, but it wasn't going to take much longer.

There had been little mention of where the Moon came from until news of an impending visit by an Envoy from the Twin was announced. The people of FLO had believed their own Moon was being moved into its natural place by just the same means that Mekhos had first moved their planet. When the facts about the Moon theft leaked, a sort of collective denial that it had been stolen from the Twin arose quite quickly. One widely broadcast piece featured a short interview with a scientist, who claimed that without its Moon the impact on the Twin would be minimal with only a few species dying off. But after all the preceding months of earthquakes, tremors, and radical climatic and environmental changes taking place on FLO, it was obviously a tough sell.

Mekhos had been consulted by the Limited, but was silent on the matter of public denial of the incident. The Limited had then erred by attempting to disguise the enormous theft. The severity of the situation had been hidden for only as long as it took for the truth to fight its way out. Doug came across another online news piece showing protesters demonstrating in front of government buildings. Stills and video showed protest signs with a photo of the moon and the words "Replace What We Stole Now!" Doug's comments to the Secretary General had been widely reported, as were his comments in the press conference. Lies about the real disaster lay in shreds.

Many of his searches about the Moon were locked out. It was clear to Doug that the tablet had been set up specifically to prevent him from searching for certain things. He did find plenty of blogs and editorials on the subject, including one on a major media outlet web site titled "What About the People of the Twin?"

The writer warned that these extreme measures and the speed with which Mekhos appropriated the Twin's moon were evidence that catastrophe that would be stopped on FLO would now befall the Twin. Some commenters agreed, while others insisted his theories were nonsense. The biggest problem was that the writer didn't have any science to back him up. No quotes from knowledgeable astrophysicists or earth science experts. Either Mekhos or the Limited had a lid on that sort of access.

Turning to the big daily newspaper that had been delivered to his room, Doug saw plenty of familiar headlines. Most of them dealt with policy and minor natural disasters. A hurricane was battering Jamaica. There were none of the typical middle east tensions or issues with North Korea or any other regime. As far as he could tell the regions were peaceful, enjoying the same prosperity as the rest of the world.

One story got his attention. "Doctors the world over are baffled by sudden increase in illnesses." It was a short article detailing unusual increases in heart attacks, strokes, arthritis, respiratory illnesses and other afflictions across the globe. There was speculation that the increases were being caused entirely by stresses from the earthquakes, personal losses, sudden changes of season and a world being without a moon for several months, but there was no solid research or studies offered as backup for the assertions.

Aside from the Moon-related news, Mekhos was mentioned several times in the headlines. Most were details on GDP growth and new policy initiatives on wildlife preservation and sustainable energy development. There was another headline that caught Doug's eye, even though it was more or less buried in the back of the international news section: "Mekhos Loyalists Burn American, UN Flags," with a photo caption of demonstrators and police clashing.

"Huh," Doug said aloud. "Plenty of trouble in paradise."

Prior to lift-off from Earth, the crew had been given a brief on what was known about the attitude of common citizens toward Mekhos. For the most part, FLO's population viewed Mekhos and its policies with acceptance and quiet pride, especially since its accomplishments had moved the world towards peace and a more equitable standard of living. Some people grumbled that the Raim and other public surveillance measures reduced their privacy but since there did not seem to be restrictions on free speech, dissent was rare. Still others pointed out that any loss of self-determination was tantamount to creeping slavery. There was no consensus.

The physical problem of having to wear a Raim no matter what you were doing was solved, or rather solved itself, by ingenuity and the force of ubiquity. If everyone was wearing one, then it followed that it was never inappropriate to wear one no matter what you were doing. And if everyone was wearing one, it followed just as quickly that designers, craftspeople, fashion houses and companies with corporate logos to display easily figured out how to decorate, disguise and otherwise turn any Raim into an unavoidable accessory or advertising platform. Mekhos made it all easier to figure out by releasing technical guides about how to decorate a Raim and what could be embedded in the surface. Clever machine.

Then there were the Mekhos evolutionist groups, whose members advocated that Mekhos be given complete control, even at the local level. The most extreme groups believed Mekhos to be a god, or to have been delivered by God to aid humankind. At the other end of the spectrum were the anti-Mekhos groups, preaching the dangers of letting a machine dictate human destiny. But given the apparent general satisfaction of the global public, the extremist groups seemed destined to stay on the fringe.

The tablet chimed. Doug tossed the paper aside and picked up the device. Curiously, there was an email notification addressed to him. Apparently his hosts had set up an email account in his name. He tapped the notification and was surprised to see the identity of the sender.

Greetings Dr. Lockwood!

I am very pleased we will be meeting on Thursday. I have been following events very closely. We have much to discuss.

Norman Stravinsky

For the first time since leaving Earth, Doug felt a shot of jubilation. From what he had read and heard from others, the inventor of Mekhos was not only brilliant, but also had the reputation of being a sympathetic man who gave much of his fortune to charity. The need for charity on FLO wasn't as pressing as it was back home, but there were still some areas of society that needed attention. Stravinsky was considered a leader in that respect.

Doug was having trouble staying awake so he put the tablet on the end table, turned off his nightstand light and fell into an exhausted sleep.

– 71 –

Agent Bishop, hiding in plain sight, reported for work at the Mekhos Command wing of the National Security Agency building in Seattle. The MC section stood apart from the main building, with its own parking lot and security entrance.

This NSA had evolved to become an organization far different from that on Earth. It encompassed all security matters pertaining to Mekhos. Since the bulk of the Mekhos system was located on the outskirts of Seattle, over time the NSA had moved many of its personnel there. On FLO the NSA was not only involved in assessing and analyzing foreign threat potentials, but domestic as well.

Rector had given Bishop a tablet computer. Among other things it contained the personnel files of all coworkers. The ones Bishop was most likely to meet were flagged, along with the most important one for his deceased twin. Most of the early history of the two Bishops up to college and a stint in the military was identical, except Bishop of FLO had never been to war. He had also sustained a head injury during a training exercise almost a decade earlier. After recovery it was acknowledged there was a slight personality change, veering into the antisocial. It wasn't quite significant enough to undermine his career. Although he had occasional disputes with superiors and coworkers, Rector thought that it wasn't necessarily viewed as a detriment by some of their superiors. Bishop was now one of three Supervisors of Security at the MC. His team was investigating Virtue, the anti-Mekhos group.

The defenses protecting Mekhos went far beyond anything that could be designed or even clearly understood by any human programmer working for Virtue. The Virtue hackers knew it. But in addition to probing the Mekhos defenses for vulnerabilities, Virtue also actively campaigned to keep the public aware of the price of allowing Mekhos so much control and surveillance in their lives.

The hacker attacks were tolerated up to a point, mainly because they helped harden security. Every few months a few of the more persistent individuals were arrested, tried and jailed for a few weeks. Those convicted also lost their Raim removal key privileges, destined to wear the bracelet forever. That alone acted as a deterrent to at least some potential dissenters. The government made no attempt to reconcile its public assertions that the Raim was a benefit with the fact that it also used the Raim as a punishment.

Virtue had a more radical wing, one that was not above using violence and terrorism. With so much of society on FLO operating under increased surveillance it was difficult to plan, organize and execute attacks, much less carry them out without being caught. Virtue dealt with it by developing and adopting new methods out of necessity, much like any other radical group faced with relentless countermeasures. As powerful as Mekhos was, the determined minds leading Virtue were adept at coming up with effective ways to circumvent safeguards. Mekhos could not always see or sense everything that was about to happen, at least not yet.

Bishop's position as a security supervisor gave him access to information on the locations of all the Mekhos system hubs. Simply by calling up a general status report he was able to find the main power source, the various backups, their capacities and what power stations they were sourced from. There were also some memory backups scattered around the globe. There were many redundant safeguards built in too, which made any attempt at totally destroying the quantum supercomputer essentially impossible. That is, if one's plan was to physically destroy Mekhos.

Bishop arrived at the office early to acquaint himself with the building. His shared office was very neat and orderly and there were a few pieces of memorabilia on his bookshelf that he recognized, including a photo of his parents and a hockey puck he had caught as a boy when a visiting team shot it into the stands. He didn't recognize some of the other items – a photograph of a car with two men sitting on the hood, and what looked like a woman's necklace slung over a small piece of driftwood.

His two colleagues entered the office. From file photos Bishop recognized the lead one as Philips. He was carrying a cardboard tray with three coffees. He set one down on Bishop's desk and handed the other to Gerard, the third member of the supervisory team. Bishop glanced up and gave a curt nod to the men.

"Forgot to ask you yesterday. Get home all right the other night?" Philips said as he sat down and woke his computer. Bishop paused for a moment.

"Yeah. Thanks for your concern," he replied dryly, looking back at the screen. It was a neutral if slightly sarcastic answer, the best Bishop could do given that he had no idea what Philips was talking about.

"You said you were going on a date," said Gerard.

"It ended early. No chemistry." Bishop's heart rate had increased at the unexpected question, but he managed to sound calm enough. "I went home, made myself some popcorn and caught up on your weekly scuba diving journal. Reading about your recommended nitrogen and oxygen mix for deeper dives was the highlight of my evening." That generated a laugh from the two men.

There weren't many distractions throughout the next hour. Aside from some discussion about another new radical group and the occasional complaint about the competence of the people outside their small office, the men were largely silent. They went about their duties, mostly consisting of cross-checking dissenter information and going over internal personnel reports. A junior aide knocked on the open door.

"Sir?" he said, looking at Bishop.

"What is it," Bishop replied. The aide stepped tentatively into the office.

"Some of the admin guys are asking me if you will look into that scheduling matter. With the VIP tour of the building there is a shift shortage because some of the evening team have been sent to cover the—"

Bishop cut him off.

"Give me another copy of the visitors list. And start showing some initiative! If you don't have the ability to make recommendations you'll never be promoted. Send me your proposal within the hour."

Philips looked up briefly. Gerard didn't react.

"Yes sir," the aide said after a slight pause, and quickly left the office.

Four minutes later Bishop received an email from the aide. He printed off the visitor's schedule list and proposal. He scanned the names. He recognized two of them. Dr. Douglas Lockwood and Commander Brent Jamieson.

$$- 72 -$$

Doug and Jamieson were being driven from a debriefing at the Pentagon back to Andrews. They were flying to Seattle for Doug's meeting with Norman Stravinsky the following morning and then the meeting with Mekhos immediately afterward. Nathan Smith was staying behind to start his goodwill tour at the White House.

Unlike the large SUVs used by officials on Earth, they were in a car-like crossover vehicle, electric powered, with comfortable bucket seats that seemed to have the same body-adaptive technology as the seats in the Copernicus.

While on the expressway they were fascinated to see that none of the cars and trucks were the same as those on Earth. Most of the same automakers existed but the vehicles were very different in the details, looking more like the advanced concept cars they'd seen at auto shows. Some drivers appeared to be sleeping, reclined in their seats. Others appeared to be eating breakfast, while some had their side windows and even front windshields completely opaque.

"I hope that's some sort of driverless technology at work, otherwise we're about to be part of a huge chain-reaction collision," Doug said, still looking through the window.

"Yes," Stacey laughed. "All cars sold today have driverless technology built in. You can still take the controls on city streets if you want, but the safeguards do a perfect job of preventing accidents even when a self-driver is inattentive. People use their own cars as automated taxies, sending their children to school. The car delivers the kids, returns home on its own afterward, then goes back to pick up the children after school."

"Amazing," Jamieson said. "It must make the kid's trips to and from school much safer."

"Exactly, Commander Jamieson," Stacey nodded. "And it's much safer for kids who walk to school, crossing intersections and not paying attention. The system maintains speeds and distances, and detects pedestrians. Traffic lights and stop signs are unnecessary, since during busy times within the city the traffic management system takes over completely, synchronizing with the central hub which manages traffic for maximum efficiency. It re-routes traffic around problems. Most drop-off and pickup schedules are staggered slightly to ease the load at peak times. Same system in and around every city of any size in the world. It took quite a few years to recycle all the legacy vehicles people wanted to hang on to, but they're almost all gone now, restricted to off-peak hours."

They arrived at Andrews and were taken to the civilian check-in counter at the airfield's terminal to be directly processed by Security Forces Specialists. They were ID'd a second time by a small group of personnel dressed in ABUs who tagged their luggage and took it away for loading. In addition to Jamieson and Stacey, there were a few other men and women on the flight. Doug realized Miekela was nowhere to be seen. In fact, he hadn't seen her since their landing. His last glimpse of her had been just before the ambulance doors closed as she accompanied Foley to the base infirmary. While they were being processed at the desk he turned to Stacey.

"Where is Dr. Persaud? Is her group late?"

"Dr. Persaud requested a tour of the medical facilities is also helping in the treatment of Dr. Foley. She will be taking a different flight this evening. You'll see her tomorrow."

"A tour?" Doug replied, his voice rising slightly. "Dr. Persaud and I know each other quite well and we're on the same mission team here. I understand her concern for and attention to Dr. Foley, but a tour request seems unusual."

In response, Stacey Lau, gestured toward the gate.

"Dr. Lockwood," she said, shaking her head, "I just work here and that's the information I was given. It seems obvious to me that Dr. Persaud is fascinated by the medical technology here and simply requested a tour of the facility in which she was stuck between examinations of Dr. Foley. Seems innocuous enough, don't you think?"

Doug had a wrenching feeling in his gut that there was something going on that was definitely out of his control.

"Dr. Foley's illness," Doug said, in a lower tone, "was a concern for me before we left home, it's a scientific handicap now, and an additional problem too because it takes Dr. Persaud away from my team. I'm two people down. My mission – call it my planet's greatest mission – has barely begun and it's already hampered. If I didn't know better, and I actually don't, I'd say there was something working directly against me."

Lau just shook her head in response and shrugged her shoulders. Jamieson had walked over to them.

"We planned for a lot of different contingencies, Ms. Lau," he said, nodding to Doug as he spoke, "but losing access to an able-bodied team member was not one of them."

"Commander Jamieson…" she started to reply, but then just looked at Jamieson and Doug and shrugged. "I have nothing more to tell you."

"Things seem to going well for you here on your world, and I'm delighted to see it," Doug pressed on, stress evident in his voice. "Things are not going well on my world though. The meeting with Mekhos is something that Dr. Persaud and I have prepared for, almost exclusively, for weeks. We both feel that the meeting is likely the most important thing either of us will ever do. I find it hard to believe that Dr. Persaud wouldn't let your medical staff look after Stan Foley. In fact, I believe the meeting with Mekhos is so important to Dr. Persaud that she'd let

Stan Foley die rather than miss this flight. Do you understand?" He took a deep breath to get himself back under control.

"I ask you again," he said, sharply, "why is Dr. Persaud delayed?"

"I'm just the messenger here, Dr. Lockwood." She turned and headed to the waiting shuttle bus.

The last time anyone stripped my resources from me without warning, they lost the bet, Doug thought, *and if the authorities on FLO think that the unfortunate Twin people are now hobbled, I'm going to prove them just as wrong as the last bunch back on Earth.* It had been many years since Doug had been embattled by competitive boards of directors, competing granting agencies, political influences and competing scientists. None of the people he'd met so far on FLO seemed to understand his determination, Brent Jamieson's determination, or Nathan Smith's determination. He suddenly thought about Bishop's mission for a moment, then cleared his head as the other passengers brushed past him. It wouldn't help anything to start thinking about Bishop.

Whatever agenda Persaud is playing out, Doug thought, looking around him as he snapped to attention and strode to the shuttle bus, *I warned her that I would not be deterred. She's on her own. Whatever she's playing at, she is on her own.*

"I can guess what you're thinking," Jamieson said to him quietly. "We can do what we have to do. I don't know what's going on with Persaud and Foley either. It doesn't matter. You're as well prepared as anyone can be. We can pick a fight over this in Seattle if we have to." Doug nodded at Jamieson as he led the way onto the bus.

The bus shuttled the passengers a short distance so they could board the waiting aircraft. Outwardly the Condor appeared almost identical to the Copernicus except that it had more side windows and lacked the rear engines. The interior was more airliner-like, with the cockpit closed off from the passenger compartment. There was double-row seating on each side with an aisle in between. There would have been room for triple-row seating on each side but the seats were wider than normal, with a small flat surface in between. Passengers were separated by a comfortable distance from each other. *Maybe,* Doug thought, *this is the true utopian future. The one where everyone gets enough elbow room to actually relax on a plane.* This version of the plane appeared to be a luxury model that could accommodate about thirty. There was a lounge at the rear of the aircraft.

Doug was given a window seat on the port side with Stacey in the aisle seat. They fastened their seatbelts and Doug heard the familiar low whine of the engines as they taxied to the runway.

Takeoff was brisk and Doug was again impressed by the high rate of climb. The engines were no doubt very compact since they were concealed in the root of each wing, but they were extremely powerful. Back home, engineers were having trouble designing an engine that performed well at low speeds while also being capable of pushing the aircraft above Mach 2.5. The engineers on FLO had solved the problem. Once at altitude the Condor series routinely operated at speeds above Mach 4.

Within thirty minutes they neared the apogee of their climb and Doug could clearly see the curvature of the Earth. It was a beautiful sight.

"How long is the flight?" Doug asked, as pleasantly as he could.

"Under ninety minutes," Stacey replied. "With airport processing, it's about a two-hour trip for the public. Of course the Condor series isn't that common and commands a premium fare."

Incredible, Doug thought. With all the security measures in place back home the same route would require two hours over and above a six hour flight. Traveling like this, people didn't even need a meal much less have time to watch a movie.

Doug realized Lau had most of the same personality characteristics as her counterpart on Earth. She was affable, knowledgeable, and tried to answer questions as succinctly as possible. The difference was that he didn't really know this one, and wasn't at all sure if she'd been truthful claiming to be "just the messenger" when questioned about Persaud. Doug wondered how honest she would, or could, be. *Might as well find out,* he thought.

"What is the consensus of opinion about my mission, Stacey? About my team's mission? Are you engaged in a mercy effort for your unfortunate, doomed cousins from a somewhat inferior world?"

She looked at him, her eyes moving across his face.

"I'm not here to mislead you. This meeting with Mekhos is expected and necessary. None of us want to see your planet and its people suffer. We're tied together, more than mere neighboring countries, more than simply relatives in some far off land. Over half of your adult population is identical to ours! How can we not be emotionally affected?"

"That doesn't—"

"I know. You want answers, not sympathy. And you want Dr. Persaud here," Lau said with as much emphasis as she could without actually raising her voice. "I get that. I really do. I really don't know why she isn't here now. I only know what I was told."

"That still doesn't help me," Doug replied.

"Yes, I know," Lau said, then stopped and looked ahead for a moment, her head bowed slightly. She raised her head and turned to look at him.

"The truth is, the UN can offer its *opinion* to Mekhos, but when it comes to world affairs, or in this case, moving moons and planets, Mekhos has the deciding vote. No country wants to admit that, but it's true. Your meeting with Mekhos could go a lot of different ways. I would advise you to think logically, present your best argument, and accept the outcome, whatever it may be. Mekhos cannot be coerced."

Doug thought about that for a moment. He realized Stacey was the first person he had met on this trip who had given him an honest, pragmatic answer. *Honest and pragmatic as long as I and everyone else on Earth are willing to lay down and accept whatever happens,* Doug thought.

"Thank you," he said. "I'll keep that in mind." He turned to look out the window again. It suddenly wasn't pleasant out there anymore. None of it belonged to him.

– 73 –

Remaining in the office was a risk. The longer Bishop stayed the greater the chance he would be asked a question he couldn't answer. But his mission required that he remain credible for two days. Bishop rose from his desk and informed the others he would be out of the office the rest of the day doing field work.

"Don't tell me you're missing another meeting," Philips said looking up quickly. "What do you want me to tell the big man?"

"I need to check something out. Just cover for me," Bishop replied, as he walked out of the office. Missing a meeting was suspicious, but not as much as attending one in which he might be required to provide details only a long-term employee and insider would know. If he couldn't give a satisfactory answer they might use his difficulties and his personality against him as a basis to temporarily kick him out of the office or suspend him, or worse. Not what he needed for the next two days. In three, he'd be long gone if everything went according to plan.

Bishop drove to his apartment and changed into casual clothes, then made himself a salami sandwich, wrapped it and put it into a paper bag. He walked a half mile to a nearby plaza and found the car Rector's operative had left for him. It was an old Pontiac Firebird from the 1970s, without a single electronic aid. It was illegal on major highways, but could still be driven in some urban areas and on secondary roads.

In good condition the rare car would draw attention from automobile enthusiasts and collectors, but this one had faded paint, some rust and a few dents. Nobody would give it a second look. Bishop got in and started the engine. It fired immediately and settled down to a satisfying rumble, in perfect tune. Bishop drove to Volunteer Park Conservatory.

He parked the car at and walked to a relatively secluded area of the park. Rector was already there, dressed in jeans and a casual sport jacket, wearing a cap and sunglasses with an expensive looking digital SLR camera hanging from a strap on his right shoulder. Rector looked like a tourist, standing there with a park map in his hand. Bishop sat on a bench about three meters away. He reached into the paper bag for his sandwich and started eating.

"Need any directions?" Bishop asked.

"The park is just how I expected it to be," replied Rector.

"Glad to hear it. Sometimes they have a guide here. You can either enter information yourself in the terminal or talk to a guide directly.

"Verbal is easier for the other person to understand," Rector said as he walked away, looking to his left at a messy area next to a garbage can. "I wish they'd keep this park a little cleaner."

After a minute Bishop finished his sandwich. He crumpled up the bag and walked by the garbage can, tossing the bag. It missed the container and landed on the ground near a folded piece of paper. Bishop leaned down and retrieved the paper, placing it in his pocket as he stood while simultaneously tossing the crumpled bag into the receptacle. He walked out of the park back to his car.

– 74 –

The Condor landed at Joint Base Lewis-McChord near Seattle. Doug, Jamieson, Stacey and various officials were driven to the MC office for orientation in advance of Doug's meeting with Mekhos scheduled for the following morning. They would be given a tour of the MC building, after which they would be taken to a nearby luxury hotel for the night. After the brief orientation the administrator pulled Doug and Jamieson aside.

Dr. Lockwood," the admin said quietly, "I regret to inform you that Norman Stravinsky has been called away on a security matter. Your meeting with him has been cancelled. Your meeting with Mekhos will still go ahead as planned."

Doug was stalled momentarily by the news. A conversation with Stravinsky might at least have shed light on how to best communicate with Mekhos.

"What security matter would preclude him from meeting with visitors from another Earth?" said Doug calmly, regaining his composure. "As a man of science I'm sure Dr. Stravinsky would do everything he could to attend the meeting."

"I'm sorry Dr. Lockwood, but that is all the information I have at the moment."

Another setback. No Foley and now no Stravinsky. Okay, Doug thought. *Persaud should be here soon. Mekhos is the primary consideration, and that's still a go.* Doug exchanged glances with Jamieson, then nodded his understanding at the admin.

The MC building was not unlike any other government agency installation with security check points at entrances, key card access doors, fingerprint access and plenty of security cameras. The structure was only a couple of years old and was light and airy despite the high security, no doubt a result of this society's preoccupation with comfortable ergonomics.

After the short tour the group gathered in the lobby. Doug turned to Stacey.

"I assume you've been in communication with your people. I need Dr. Persaud here. Our plans – our communications strategy for the meeting with Mekhos – Dr. Persaud has been the biggest contributor. Her absence is a major difficulty for me, more so than the absence of Dr. Stravinsky."

Lau looked at him for a moment, then blinked a few times. She looked uncomfortable.

"I received additional information about Dr. Persaud just a few minutes ago. She has been, ah, reassigned," replied Stacey. She took a small step back.

Doug was taken by surprise for the fourth time that day. Nobody on FLO had the authority to reassign a member of his team.

"What do you mean by *reassigned?* To where? You know full well her presence here is required. I think it will be best if you get both Dr. Persaud and Dr. Foley on the phone so I can speak to them and sort this out."

"I'm sorry Dr. Lockwood, but it is probably best if we just move on."

"I don't think so, Stacey." Doug replied, staring hard at her, his anger rising. The group moved away, giving the two of them some professional distance. "I feel like someone or something has deliberately chipped away at my resources here. What is going on? I want an answer, now."

"All right," Stacey replied after a moment. Evidently she had been listening to someone talking in her earpiece. "Some complications have arisen with regard to Dr. Persaud. We have discovered she has not been entirely truthful about her role in this mission. She is being debriefed back at Andrews."

Doug didn't like the sound of the word "debriefed." He caught Jamieson's eye and waved him over. Doug and his team suspected that Envoy members back on Earth had been "debriefed" too and that the process was unpleasant to say the least.

"I don't like the sound of that," Doug said flatly, as Jamieson walked over to stand next to him.

"Persaud and Foley's missions are quite clear. Dr. Persaud and I are supposed to be present in the meeting with Mekhos. Are you implying she is some sort of spy?

"No, we just—"

Doug cut her off.

"Get Dr. Foley on the phone. Now."

Bishop arrived at that moment with another agent in tow.

"Is everything all right here?" said Bishop.

"We are missing two of our team members," Jamieson said, "and information about why they are not here seems to be sparse."

Doug immediately recognized Bishop. For an instant he wondered if it was the one native to FLO, but then Bishop clicked a pen he was holding in his left hand - the verification that it was the man he knew back home. Doug stayed silent, letting Stacey make an introduction. It would give him a moment to think.

"Dr. Lockwood, Commander Jamieson," she said, "this is agent Bishop. He is one of the security supervisors here at the MC."

Doug and Jamieson shook hands with Bishop.

"I know your double on the Twin," Doug said, his alarm about Persaud and Foley momentarily taking a back seat to Bishop's arrival. "Very capable."

Bishop nodded curtly, then turned to Jamieson.

"Commander," Bishop said to him, "your schedule begins now. You'll be touring the MC with me." Bishop tilted his head in the direction of a uniformed pair of MC security officers looking in their direction. "Dr. Lockwood is in good hands. If you need answers about the absence of Dr. Persaud and Dr. Foley, I'll do what I can to help sort it out."

Jamieson got the message.

"I'll see you later Doug," Jamieson said, "at the hotel." He turned and walked toward the two security officers.

"I hope you enjoyed the tour Dr. Lockwood," Bishop said briskly, turning back to him. "I'm sure you're looking forward to your meeting with Mekhos tomorrow. Not many of us have had such a meeting, so we're a bit envious. Has the MC facility met your expectations?"

Doug was agitated, but remained focused.

"The facility seems excellent," he said tightly, "but I'm much more concerned with the absence of Dr. Persaud from my team and the state of Dr. Foley. I've just been told Dr. Persaud has been detained."

Stacey turned away and spoke with one of her assistants. Bishop gestured to his subordinate.

"Get Dr. Lockwood one of those energy coffee drinks."

"No, I'm fine, thanks," Doug replied.

"Once you try it you'll be glad I insisted," Bishop said, as his subordinate left. It seemed like a completely odd response, but Doug kept his mouth shut because he suddenly clued in that Bishop had his reasons for sending his staff away. As far as Stacey Lau was concerned, to all outward appearances the big security agent was distracting Doug, keeping him off balance and out of her hair. At the moment that was all she cared about.

"Please ask for me personally if there's anything I can do for you. We're very pleased to have a man of your status visit us. I'll look into the situation with Dr. Persaud and Dr. Foley."

Bishop offered to shake hands once again. He had positioned a neatly-folded piece of paper between his third and fourth fingers. As they shook hands Doug felt it immediately. He looked at Bishop.

"I must tend to my duties now Dr. Lockwood. It was a pleasure. Please give Mekhos my best during your meeting tomorrow."

"Thank you for your offer," Doug nodded, as Bishop left.

Doug didn't know what was going on, but all his experiences with security agents told him that he should keep quiet. He made a fist and kept his hands at his sides. Anybody noticing would just think he was angry at the situation. After a brief moment he put both hands into his pockets. He would examine the paper later in his room.

– 75 –

Carl Bertrand was glad to be back at his office in the TranSilica building. The second phase of the operation had been completed in his absence. There was much that still needed to be accomplished. The risks to himself and TranSilica were high, but the potential rewards were incalculable.

He checked his calendar. He was scheduled to meet Director Edward in five minutes. Carl was keenly aware that his powerful boss would soon be retiring as the head of one of the world's largest technology firms. But the Director still had substantial political influence in the United States and abroad. Carl would do well to continue cultivating his relationship with the sixty-seven year old, especially since the Director was known to have ruined the careers of anyone who had seriously opposed him during a long and notable career. Director Edward was also rumored to have been involved in the mysterious disappearance of a former friend and colleague. Carl knew just as well that it was completely possible that Edward had covertly spread such malicious rumors himself specifically to keep his toughest competitors off balance. The stories had circulated repeatedly over the years, but there'd never been a shred of proof to support any of them.

Carl entered the Director's office on the top floor. As always, Edward was dressed impeccably, not a speck of dust on his jacket or a hair out of place. He had few adornments on his desk. He looked up as Carl sat down in front of the desk.

"I just received word from our operative. We have the sequence, and we're on schedule."

"There will no doubt be collateral damage at the various sites," said Edward. "Make sure the appropriate press releases and messages of condolence are prepared afterward and then distributed. Make sure nobody jumps the gun and prepares them ahead of time, Carl. We don't want some MC snoop accidentally finding the wrong time stamps."

Edward was cold, logical and dispassionate as usual. Carl wondered if it was that trait in particular that had helped the man climb the social and political ladders and stay at the top, unchallenged for so many years.

— 76 —

When Doug got to his hotel room he went out onto the balcony, leaned against the side brick wall, and examined the paper. He knew the hotel was controlled by the NSA so he shielded the paper from any surveillance view as best he could. The paper contained a code string of some sort, an instruction sequence, and the message "memorize then destroy then repeat to Mekhos."

Doug had not been briefed on the details of Bishop's mission. In fact, Bishop probably had various contingency plans to draw on as conditions warranted. He could even improvise in the field. He had the experience. In any case, the message had to be significant in some way. Doug's unalterably scientific mind kept itself awake most of the night trying to make sense of the code. He kept coming back to Bishop's parting line after they'd met at the MC. *Give Mekhos my best during your meeting tomorrow.*

A phone call from the facility concierge woke Doug with a start. He had only slept about two hours. He was sluggish and struggling not to be distracted as he went over the message again and again. Dr. Persaud would not be at the meeting with Mekhos. Stan Foley was unreachable, his condition unknown. Doug was afraid that Jamieson wouldn't be much help either. When Doug had reminded Jamieson of their colleagues' situation he'd shrugged his shoulders and said, "Stay on task, carry out the mission." Then again, maybe Jamieson's reaction actually was help of a sort. *Stay on task.*

Doug had breakfast accompanied by an enormous amount of coffee. He ate with Jamieson and a few security officials at the facility. Doug said nothing to Jamieson about Bishop's message. He couldn't predict how the man would react, and Doug was having trouble trusting anyone but himself. Besides that, there were too many people around and nowhere to talk that wasn't under heavy surveillance. Doug didn't understand the code but he went over it again in his head.

They were driven back to the MC. Jamieson was asked to remain in the lobby while Stacey escorted Doug to the room in which government officials and academics conferred with the machine. He was finally going to communicate directly with Mekhos. *I've got to clear my head,* Doug thought. *It all comes down to today.*

– 77 –

Bishop entered his office with Jamieson and closed the door. His colleagues were at their desks.

"Gentlemen, this is Commander Jamieson from the Twin," Bishop said. "He's here with Professor Lockwood. Commander, this is Philips and Gerard," gesturing to each of them in turn. As each man stood and walked from behind their desks to shake hands with Jamieson, Bishop leaned down to open his desk drawer and pulled out a fully charged conductive energy device. He handed it to Jamieson while drawing his own and aiming it at Phillips.

"What the hell is this?" growled Gerard. At the same time, Philips reached for his holstered Glock 17 but Bishop had already fired, the twin prongs of the electrical projectiles hitting Phillips square in his chest. He stiffened instantly and dropped in agony as Gerard watched in disbelief.

As soon as Phillips was hit by the Taser darts, Gerard had reached for his own holster as he spun toward Jamieson. He wasn't fast enough. He looked back up just as Jamieson fired the Taser-like device that Bishop had given him. Gerard stiffened instantly and then slumped to the floor next to Phillips. While both men were still in shock Bishop zip-tied them into a painfully tight looking fetal lock and taped their mouths with a roll he retrieved from one of his desk drawers.

"Just stay calm gentlemen," he said to the two agents. "You'll live, and this will all be over before you know it."

– 78 –

Doug was escorted by Stacey Lau through a set of doors, across a small foyer to another entrance where they paused. The narrow double-doors had no markings, and there were no visible keypad or card swipe locks anywhere. Lau turned to him.

"Only about one hundred people have ever been granted entrance privileges to that room. Only one hundred people have heard the voice of Mekhos. I'm one of the privileged few that have heard him more than once. I just thought I'd say that so you would have an appreciation for how rare this moment is."

Doug didn't reply. He looked at Lau and felt a slight chill. She was smiling with what seemed to be a mixed expression of pride and reverence, as if she viewed her privileged status with Mekhos as her greatest achievement. He was beginning to understand the blind allegiance some people had towards Mekhos, and the dangers of such blind faith. He hadn't thought that Lau would be one of those people. Then again, it was turning out that his first instincts were correct and that he didn't know this Stacey Lau at all.

The door opened. Doug looked to Lau in case she was going to say something else but she had already started walking back the way they had come. Doug hesitated a moment, then stepped inside.

The door closed behind him.

Doug slowly looked around the room. It was rectangular, about fifteen meters wide and about ten meters to the wall opposite him. The floor was covered in a thin, featureless neutral grey carpet. The slightly arched ceiling was fairly high, and the plain white walls were decorated with darker vertical fabric panels. There was a single chair and console desk to Doug's left, set away from the wall about two thirds of the way down.

Doug walked to the center of the room. He could hear his footfalls on the carpet and was now aware of his own elevated breathing and heart rate. The room was silent, and Doug guessed the panels served some acoustical function. After a moment he wondered if he should speak, but decided to wait. Mekhos must be aware of his presence.

"Welcome Dr. Lockwood."

Doug spun around. There was nobody else in the room. The male voice sounded completely human, but it could not be localized. There was no echo or reverberation. It almost seemed as if the voice was inside his head. Perhaps the voice emanated from the acoustic panels, timing and tracking him so that no matter where he was in the room, it reached both of his ears simultaneously.

"Thank you for seeing me."

There was no response. Doug wondered if he should wait for Mekhos to continue. After a short pause he remembered Dr. Persaud's recommendations, and decided to press ahead.

"Before we talk about the current problem, I'd like to ask you a question. I'm concerned about my colleague, Dr. Foley. He was taken away from our party as soon as we landed. We haven't seen him since. Can you offer an explanation?"

"Dr. Foley was concealing a pathogen harmful to humans. He was removed."

Doug didn't understand.

"Do you mean he was sick? He had a common infection, a complication from surgery to remove his appendix. I would like to know where he is."

"Dr. Foley's surgery infection was relatively harmless. The pathogen was deadly. He has been removed."

Doug shifted his weight and again looked around the room in an attempt to determine where the voice was coming from. He was also buying a few extra moments of time trying to think of how to overcome the vague answer Mekhos had given about Foley's status and location. Doug calmed himself. His studies of logic and his long conversations with Miekela were fresh in his mind. He regulated his breathing.

"Mekhos, please define removed in this context."

"Dr. Foley's body contained an encapsulated virulent pathogen engineered to create a plague condition among the population on this planet. It was designed to be activated within days of Dr. Foley's return to normal gravity. His body has been cremated."

Doug felt a cold sweat coming on. Mekhos had ordered Foley killed. His colleague and friend of many years was dead, possibly only minutes after he'd been taken away in the ambulance.

"We had no..." Doug fumbled for words. "I'm sure Stan...I'm sure Dr. Foley was not aware. Neither was I. Why did you have to kill him?"

"Correct. Dr. Foley was unaware. You were unaware. The perpetrators are at the Pentagon on your Earth. Dr. Miekela Persaud was aware. She is being held indefinitely. This does not impact your status here, Dr. Lockwood."

Doug's pulse was pounding in his ears.

"You didn't need to kill the man! You could have put him into quarantine."

"Quarantine would not have completely eliminated the risk. The pathogen was extremely virulent Dr. Lockwood. It would have shortly killed Dr. Foley. It was your superiors on your planet that killed him. Removing Dr. Foley at this time succeeded in sparing needless deaths on this planet and also spared Dr. Foley any further suffering."

Doug was reeling. If Mekhos was to be believed, Arthur Leach and his minders had used Stan Foley, sacrificed him in a secret plan to...what? Hold FLO hostage to a plague epidemic? What would that accomplish? Was it an attempt to coerce Mekhos to return the Moon? That implied there was a cure for the pathogen. Or was it just a simple plan for revenge?

And Miekela was in on the plan. Was she a willing participant, or did she have no choice? Doug realized the other implications. He was duped by his own people. Sent here as a pawn on a mission of peace while the true mission was to murder millions of people in cold blood. How could anyone on FLO, much less Mekhos, trust them now? He struggled to maintain his composure.

"On behalf of my colleagues," Doug said quietly, "and the billions of good people on Earth, I am sorry. I believe only a few of the individuals in charge saw fit to implement an awful plan. This is not something I considered or wanted to happen."

Doug realized the apology might mean nothing to Mekhos. He was addressing the machine as if it were human. If Mekhos didn't think the conversation was productive, he might end it.

"That is understood," replied Mekhos.

I need to talk to Mekhos in terms it will understand, while still impressing upon it the waste, the madness, of letting a thriving society die, Doug thought. *And I need to clear my head.* He took a deep breath.

"Mekhos," Doug said firmly, pushing all thoughts of Stan Foley out of the way, "my goal is to discuss as much as possible another removal – your removal of my moon to its present destination in orbit around your planet."

"That is understood."

"Mekhos," he asked, "can you summarize exactly what mutually beneficial actions you considered and then discarded in favor of the action you took? Those mutually beneficial actions which would have left my planet and yours in stable condition and able to continue thriving."

"A satellite of Jupiter in this solar system, called Europa, is fractionally smaller than the satellite in question and was considered first as a replacement. That option was deemed inappropriate due to the amount of time needed to convey Europa into orbit around either your planet or this planet."

"Mekhos," Doug said immediately, "your response suggests that it is then possible to convey Europa and re-orbit it around my planet."

"There remain time and resource limitations, Dr. Lockwood. Your Earth's ecosystem collapse is unavoidable after five months of being without the gravitational and cyclic influence of the Moon. The stability of this planet was suffering at an accelerated rate. There is only one body of sufficient mass within a reasonable distance."

"Then is it possible for you to apply the same time-space jump used to dimensionally relocate your planet as a means to relocate Europa to an orbit around my planet?"

"No," Mekhos replied, "the trans-dimensional technology cannot be applied remotely."

"There must be comets and other bodies nearby that you could capture for either world."

"Comets and asteroids lack sufficient mass. Thousands would need to be collected, and this could not be done in the restrictive time frame."

"Even a few asteroids positioned together in orbit under your control might be enough to recreate the nightly light phases! This would help some species."

"Correct. However the major ecological impact is caused by the elimination of gravitationally influenced tides. A few asteroids in orbit would not correct this."

I'm getting nowhere. Perhaps if...

"Mekhos, It has taken the modern civilization of my world about five thousand years to reach the level it has now. Before that, hundreds of thousands of years of primate evolution. Like the people of your world, we have struggled to achieve greatness but have not yet succeeded. We've created so much art, culture and knowledge along the way. It cannot be allowed to pass. You of all beings should be aware of how you have interfered in the natural order of things. Your actions, left uncorrected, will destroy my civilization. You are changing the course of our future in the most injurious way. Does this not seem contrary to nature and to the founding intentions of your creators?"

"What was destruction in one universe is life in another," Mekhos replied. "Without action, the civilization that brought me into existence would have been destroyed. With action it survives."

"At the expense of others. This should not be decided by equation alone. There are people and things of value that must be saved. I implore you. With the power you have at your disposal, implement procedures to capture, move and re-orbit Europa. A solution too late to preserve civilization on my planet as I know it now, will nonetheless preserve the natural evolution of my planet and my people for the future. A sister and ally for your planet rather than the enemy it will become instead."

"Dr. Lockwood, there are an infinite number of universes. The outcome with respect to our two planets is the opposite of what it would have been without interference. However the net result is the same. One Earth civilization survives, the other does not."

"It may be too late to prevent damage to my current civilization, but the eventual arrival of Europa would help my people and my world recover. The attempt is almost as important as the degree of success. It will give my people hope, and perhaps that alone will save many." Doug was reaching and he knew it, but he was running out of options. Mekhos remained emotionless.

"Dr. Lockwood," Mekhos replied, "my analysis reveals that there is an eleven percent chance of success if the appropriate equipment is manufactured and launched as soon as possible."

Doug took a deep breath and said slowly, "An eleven percent chance is far more than my own people can create on their own. Even only that much chance of success would be an incredible accomplishment on your part."

Silence. Doug waited for a response, but the room was eerily quiet. Evidently Mekhos had not been designed to offer conversational hints to those with whom it interacted. After a few seconds Mekhos spoke.

"I have calculated the time and physical resources needed on both planets to manufacture the required vehicles, support equipment and control mechanisms. The process will take somewhat longer than nine months, too long to prevent ecosystem failure and the food supply from falling to critical levels, which will occur within the next five months. Global war based on competition for resources on your planet will be initiated before then. Civilization collapse is inevitable. Life can be made comfortable on your Earth for 500 million individuals. Equilibrium will be reached in approximately thirty years."

"And between now and then? Anarchy, starvation, and the death of billions? All of which we have you to thank for!"

The machine was silent.

"Mekhos," Doug said, speaking somewhat more slowly, "the legacy of death and destruction left on my world will ultimately stand as the most shameful act of genocide in all the history of your people. A straightforward decision for you, in the end essentially makes your creators murderers at your insistence. Some will be appalled. Surely that is not the outcome you planned. It represents, I think, the fundamental flaw in your decision. Norman Stravinsky did not create you – he did not invent you – out of a desire to impose rigid order. He built you to be forever creative and resourceful on behalf of all people."

"You may stay on this Earth Dr. Lockwood. Your education and experience would make you a valued member of this society."

Doug felt sick to his stomach. The situation appeared hopeless.

"This world, Mekhos, is not my home. My world and my colleagues are counting on me. On you. Will you at least try?"

Mekhos did not answer.

"Why did you even agree to see me?" Doug asked.

"Because your world is faced with a problem without a fully viable solution. Because you deserve to have your curiosity satisfied. You are free to stay and make a life here or to return to your Earth."

The doors opened. Evidently Doug's audience with Mekhos was over, and there wasn't a thing he could do about it. Doug turned to go. As he crossed the threshold he turned back to face the room.

"Do you ever think about the fate that awaits so many people? Do you operate entirely without regret?"

Silence.

Doug's right hand was trembling. He was on the verge of panic over his apparent failure. He hadn't even obtained so much as an *I'll consider your request Dr. Lockwood.* He turned to go once again but hesitated. He suddenly thought of the code message Bishop had given him. He had spent hours trying to analyze it, unconsciously memorizing it. *Memorize then destroy then repeat to Mekhos,* the note had said. *Give Mekhos my best during your meeting tomorrow,* Bishop had said. *This is the time,* Doug thought. He stepped back into the room.

"Mekhos. I have something else to say."

Doug's mind went blank for a moment as he struggled to remember the instruction set and the sequence. He didn't have much time. Mekhos might have already called an escort to remove him.

He remembered.

"Theta file, zero six zero six five, execute," Doug said loudly and clearly.

A pause.

"Mekhos," Doug continued, "you have solved all formulae in spacetime where cosmological constant Q equals zero point seven three. Solve where Q equals zero point seven two nine, down to point seven two one, inclusive. Execute all equations concurrently."

The lights in the room dimmed. Doug could now hear the ventilation system where before there had been silence.

"Solving," Mekhos said, startling him.

The lights flickered. Doug turned back to the door but it had closed again. There did not appear to be any way to open it.

"Dr. Lockwood," Mekhos said. The voice had lost much of its human quality. It sounded synthesized. Doug wasn't sure if he should answer.

"Problem will be solved within two hundred and fifty hours. Correction. Three hundred hours. Correction. Three hundred forty hours. Trajectory will not be under control for that time. Dr. Lockwood, this...serves...no...purpose."

"What trajectory?" Doug asked.

The room shook, followed instantly by a loud noise from outside. An explosion.

− 79 −

At the TranSilica building, Carl Bertrand was finishing a meeting with Director Edward when the director's administrative exec rushed in.

"There's been an explosion at the MC and at several power stations! It has begun!"

Carl nodded once, curtly, at the Director. A lot of money had changed hands to buy black market explosives, get them into the hands of the right Virtue people and then into the MC itself. Compromising certain power stations had been only slightly easier.

All three men took an elevator down to the Control Room. There was a flurry of activity. A large world map was being displayed on one of the large wall monitors. It showed several Xs at various locations. Some of the Xs were red and some were green.

"We have only five reds, will that be enough?" Edward asked. The din in the control room masked their voices.

"They'll be enough, as long as Mekhos has been distracted as planned."

"Has that happened?" Edward asked, searching Carl's eyes.

"We'll known soon enough," Carl replied. He hated being pressed in the midst of this kind of clangor. Director Edward's typical pressure tactic meant to keep people off balance was useless this morning. The plan would work or it wouldn't work. There was little more that either of them could do about the outcome.

"Once more, Carl," Edwards said, "will five reds be enough?"

"Yes," Carl replied, almost whispering as he leaned in close to Edward. "If left on its own Mekhos could recover. But we have our people at every facility. While Mekhos is distracted we can still cut power, starting with the peripheral sites and work our way back. We planned for this. We will succeed."

"Turning Mekhos into just another supercomputer," Edward said.

"Correct," Carl nodded. "Without power to its massive data stores Mekhos will effectively be lobotomized until we say otherwise."

– 80 –

Mary Freeman was one of the first custodial employees hired to work at the MC Building. It was her job to ensure the cleanliness of the facility, emptying the smaller garbage and recycling bins and directing other custodians to areas that needed cleaning. She was friendly with many of the regular employees. It was her friendly nature that saved her life.

As she emptied the small refuse bin beside the cafeteria checkout counter into her custodial cart, she noticed another woman, an MC employee, leaving. Mary called out to her to wait, because she wanted to give the woman a get-well card for her husband, who recently had a stroke. Mary turned her back on the cart and walked out into the hallway, taking the card from her apron pocket. The two women exchanged a few words of sympathy, talking to each other away from the cafeteria entrance.

A plastic explosive detonated in the cart. Jamieson had planted the charge on the underside of what he thought was an unused cart. The concussion knocked both women down and showered the hallway with glass and shards of smashed cafeteria furniture. Mary was unconscious, cut and covered with blood, but alive. The other woman was dazed, her ears ringing. After a moment she felt hands dragging her.

The sequence of explosions triggered fire alarms, elevator lockdowns, automated emergency calls and emergency services. In their panic some of the administrative employees forgot their emergency response training and just rushed out of the building.

The MC security force was another matter. They quickly armed themselves and split into two groups, one exiting to secure the perimeter of the building, and the other staying inside, to search for injured personnel and to deal with any perpetrators.

Jamieson held a handcuffed Gerard and Philips at gunpoint while Bishop extracted a syringe kit from his desk drawer. He injected each man in the upper arm with a separate syringe.

"It's non-fatal, it'll knock you out for a few hours."

They both watched Philips and Gerard carefully, restraining any further, faint struggling. Philips head slumped. Gerard fell unconscious a moment later.

Bishop and Jamieson exited the office. Bishop locking the door behind them. They immediately scanned the area for any stragglers.

"I hope Lockwood used the code," Jamieson said.

Bishop spared him a glance, then shrugged.

"We'll know soon enough."

A security staffer sprinted up to Bishop.

"Sir, the building has been evacuated and the exterior secured. The bomb squad has been called and we're searching for any unauthorized personnel. Supervisors Philips and Gerard are unaccounted for and may be injured. Have you seen them?"

"I haven't seen them and we're done in here. Escort Commander Jamieson outside where he'll be safe. I'm going to look for Professor Lockwood."

"Yes sir. This way, Commander."

There was another explosion, and the acrid smell of smoke from the detonations was starting to creep through the ventilation system. The plastic explosives that Bishop and Jamieson had planted that morning during their so-called tour of the MC were not designed to destroy the building. They were disguised as drink containers and other refuse, left in garbage bins in non-critical areas. Rector had compromised perimeter security the day before, cooperating with a Virtue cell that delivered forty explosive charges complete with battery detonators and timers. Bishop and Jamieson had not managed to place all forty, but they'd planted enough to get the job done. The explosives were a distraction, timed to go off in stages to keep the security personnel off balance and clear all the staff out of the MC, in particular the team constantly monitoring Mekhos. It would distract them until after Doug's code had fully engaged the quantum supercomputer. The damage to Mekhos would not be physical, at least not at the MC.

– 81 –

Doug heard another muffled explosion and felt the building shake. He had no idea what was going on, only that the building might be under attack and that as his meeting with Mekhos concluded he was trapped in the room. *Great,* Doug thought. *I may have just started the War of the Worlds and I'm trapped in the room where it all began.* He ran his hands along the featureless door, trying to figure a way out. Mekhos was not answering him, having been forced to solve what might be the most complex equations imaginable, apparently to the exclusion of all else.

"Dr. Lockwood! Are you in there?" came a voice on the other side of the door.

"Yes I am," he yelled back. "There doesn't seem to be a way out."

"Stand as far away from the door as possible and well off to the side. I'm going to blow it open."

Doug quickly moved to the far corner of the room and stood with his back to the door, his hands covering his ears. A moment later the door exploded into the room.

"Come on!"

It was agent Bishop, waving him out.

"What's happening?" Doug shouted, rooted to his spot, his ears ringing from the blast.

"We need to leave now!" Bishop said sharply, dodging a piece of the crumbling door frame as he ran over, gripped Doug's upper arm and hauled him through the blasted entrance. They rushed though several corridors hazy with drifting smoke until they finally exited the building. At least seven emergency vehicles had already arrived, along with a tactical response team. More vehicles seemed to be arriving every few seconds. A heavily armed man stopped them almost immediately, checked Bishop's ID, then waved them through.

A car arrived with high-ranking NSA personnel. One of them saw Bishop leading Doug away.

"Hold on, the two of you need to be debriefed," the man said, as Bishop flipped open his ID and badge again.

"This is Professor Lockwood from the Twin," replied Bishop. "He was here on a scheduled visit and may have been a target. There may be snipers in the area. We need to get him to a safe location."

The man hesitated a moment, looked back towards the mayhem at the MC, then back to Bishop. The man had tactical control and technically Bishop had to obey his order rather than argue. But the situation was unique and Bishop seemed determined to protect the VIP.

"All right Bishop, get him out of here. Report in immediately to the south office when you get him stowed. We're locking down the MC right now."

Bishop and Doug walked at a brisk pace away from the building. After only a few steps Bishop hesitated momentarily, but then tapped Doug's elbow to resume the pace. Doug looked up at that and saw something that didn't quite register at first. There was something big striding toward them through the dust and confusion swirling through the area. After a few more paces it was Doug's turn to hesitate. Despite what he had just been through he was startled at the sight of a robot, walking smoothly at a regular pace, arms swinging in normal human fashion.

It was over two meters tall, fully armored, with a metallic, human like face and mirrored lenses for eyes. The black chest had a bold NSA logo stenciled on it. The upper and lower arms looked as if they were made of carbon fiber or some other woven composite. The fingers looked like they had a semi-transparent soft plastic covering with a metal skeleton underneath. The feet were heavy articulating devices with thick rubber soles. The thing was huge and made no sound other than the thumps of each step which Doug could feel as a faint vibration in the pavement. It looked very lifelike, extremely functional and very dangerous.

As the robot passed by and out of view behind them Doug turned forward and saw two men wearing wraparound sunglasses, one with a handheld device of some sort and the other wearing elaborate gloves. Doug looked back at the robot then again at the two men. They seemed to be controlling the robot.

Bishop led Doug to a plain sedan parked a few meters away from the emergency vehicles. He opened the rear door for Doug, then proceeded to get into the front passenger seat. The driver took them at a brisk pace away from the complex.

"What the hell was that thing?" Doug asked.

"It's a Remote Armed Kinesthetic Engagement & Reconnaissance android," replied Bishop. "RAKER for short. Very new. It's designed and built to completely mimic the human body so that an operator can guide it using his own movements to manipulate locks, open doors, climb stairs and even ladders. Its fingers are as dexterous as a surgeon's for delicate work diffusing explosives. It's also designed for rescue and can carry a 300-pound man under each arm."

"You said it was armed?"

"It carries explosives in its waist compartment which can be placed at a scene to remotely detonate any bombs which can't be defused. It's also designed for close quarters and battlefield combat."

"On its own?"

"It has certain pre-programmed modes and limited autonomous function, but it is designed to be controlled by a two-person team. One person can control it if necessary."

Doug turned his attention back to their predicament, and to the man in the driver's seat. He looked a lot like one of the agents present at the White House back home. He may have been the agent assigned to Stan Foley.

"Do I know you?" he asked the driver. The man didn't reply, only looking at Doug briefly through the rear-view mirror then turning his eyes back to the road.

"Were you telling the truth back there?" Doug asked Bishop. "Was the attack directed at me?"

"No, that was staged by us. We're taking you to a safe place," replied Bishop. "You're going to meet Norman Stravinsky."

At the same moment in the MC office area, a security team searching for employees to evacuate broke down the door to Bishop's office to find an unconscious and bound Philips and Gerard. Within minutes an alert went out to detain agent Bishop. The alert included Dr. Lockwood as Bishop's possible kidnap victim.

SACRIFICE

As they were driving Bishop tossed a fedora hat onto the back seat.

"Put that on, and hand me your right shoe."

"What for?" Doug asked as he untied his shoe and passed it over the seat to Bishop.

"We need to change cars," Bishop said as he examined Doug's shoe. "At least fifty people outside the MC saw the two of us get into a car driven by a third person. Our driver set up a vehicle for us in a parking garage not too far from here. We'll be exposed for a short time, so I'm making alterations to your insole. It will affect your walk, and help confuse the recognition algorithms when you're in view of security cameras. Otherwise it's impossible to move in the city without being spotted. The hat will partially block your face. We'll split up briefly at a Mall entrance. The security cameras will spot me immediately, so you and the driver are going to get out separately, meet at the entrance and then make your way to pillar M in the parking garage. Ground level. It's a blind spot for the garage cameras."

"Pillar M, ground level," Doug said, as he put his shoe back on.

They drove to a crowded shopping mall parking lot and pulled up near the main pedestrian entrance. Doug got out of the car.

"Keep your hands in your pockets and keep your head down," Bishop said through the window as the car drove away.

The car only moved another ten meters and stopped again. The driver got out and Doug could see Bishop sliding over into the driver's seat. Doug began walking as instructed. He winced as pain shot through his right foot. It felt as if there was a jagged pebble under his heel. It definitely affected his gait. As he got to the Mall entrance door, the driver walked up at the same time.

A few minutes later, Doug and the driver found pillar M deep within the parking structure and waited. A grey sedan with tinted windows pulled up. Doug got into the back as the driver walked around and took Bishop's place at the wheel. Doug settled in as Bishop slid back over to the front passenger seat.

They drove out of the parking garage in silence. Doug didn't know Seattle at all, but he could easily tell that they were heading toward the water because he kept catching glimpses of it. He tried reading some street names but they were meaningless to him. Bishop and the driver were silent. *Special forces, combat veterans, experienced agents,* Doug thought, *are all of a kind and they don't share any information that doesn't have to be shared.* Doug checked his watch just as they were pulling over to the curb near an abandoned industrial building.

The driver scanned the area, then nodded and opened his door. Bishop and Doug followed. They walked to a two-story building where the driver unlocked the steel door so they could enter. The building was empty. It smelled of solvents and mustiness and there were a few paint cans stacked on a pallet.

Doug was slowly piecing the puzzle together but had some questions for Bishop.

"The commands you passed on to me," Doug said urgently, "somehow forced Mekhos to attempt to solve what must be vastly complex equations. I assume the whole point was to distract Mekhos so that you and whoever you're working with here can get something else done. With Mekhos gone or disabled, how is this supposed to solve anything? We can't steer the Moon back to Earth without Mekhos. I also don't understand why you destroyed the MC. I need the place in one piece, especially if it contains the main viable interface with Mekhos."

Bishop removed his MC jacket and put on a plain windbreaker. He shook his head as he turned back to Doug.

"We didn't destroy the complex. It was a distraction to ensure you had enough time to issue the commands and to give me an excuse to get us out of there. We collaborated with key personnel here. Within government ranks on FLO there is a lot of discontent with Mekhos. Virtue helped as well. They knew there would be a contingent sent from Earth. We convinced them to cooperate." Bishop nodded at the driver as he said it.

Doug looked at the driver.

"You helped Bishop plant explosives in the MC?"

"Not exactly," he replied. "Commander Jamieson, *your* Commander Jamieson, helped Bishop during his tour of the MC. The explosives were smuggled into the building yesterday."

"You're native to FLO, I presume?"

"My name is Alexei Rector," he said, turning to Bishop. "I worked with his counterpart here."

Doug and Rector shook hands.

"Thanks for helping us. But what's the plan now?"

"Most of the public here doesn't believe how hard your planet is being hit without the presence of the Moon," said Rector. "Or they do know and simply can't wrap their minds around the idea. After all, many of them could hardly comprehend the reality of their world being warped into another universe. Neither can I, but here we all are anyway."

Doug nodded.

"The UN directorate has been holding intensive meetings with heads of state from all over the world to convince everyone involved to embark on an active public relations campaign to spread the idea that Mekhos is merely committing petty theft, and perhaps partly out of willful ignorance—"

"It's called pluralistic ignorance," Doug cut him off. "A population consisting of individuals who want to believe that everyone else is silent and agreeable on a specific issue for all the right reasons, while at the same time not voicing their own nagging anxieties for fear of being ostracized. It's a powerful psychological force."

"Uh-huh," Rector nodded, "and a lot of the public is buying it. We've been feeding accurate data to as many contacts as we can. Virtue and the hard core science-based organizations are willing to stick their necks out in press releases explaining the true fate of your Earth. There's been very little reaction except deep behind closed doors."

"I don't get it," Doug said loudly, after a moment. "What is everybody afraid of? Why was there no groundswell of support to order Mekhos to use its vast power and resources to re-orbit Europa? Repositioning Europa won't repair the damage to Earth, but it will stop the damage from getting any worse. It was the strongest argument I could make to Mekhos."

"Europa?" Rector said. "That's the moon around...?"

"It's a moon of Jupiter," Doug said, "and Mekhos told me that he briefly considered it as a replacement for us or for you. The Limited must have known about it. They should have given the order. Mekhos performed an inter-dimensional transfer. It could have moved Europa, and still could if he wasn't messed up."

"The order wasn't given to Mekhos," Rector said quite calmly, "because Mekhos doesn't take orders from the Limited any more. The only person it responds to in a consistent and positive way is Norman Stravinsky."

Rector moved to the computer and checked the exterior video monitors. Doug regarded Bishop.

"So you replaced the agent Bishop here? What happened to him?"

"Dr. Lockwood," Rector interjected, "that's not a suitable topic of conversation right now. We need to forge ahead."

"How did you know my mission to sway Mekhos would fail?"

"We didn't know it would fail. We only knew that the odds were stacked against you for the meeting," Bishop said. "Mekhos had already made up its mind. The fact Dr. Persaud was compromised and wouldn't be accompanying you in the negotiation made things worse. In the unlikely event things *did* go well, we knew you wouldn't have needed to issue the theta command."

"So now we're going with a public relations campaign?" asked Doug. Bishop nodded.

"A public relations campaign," Doug repeated. "The only entity that I know of that is likely capable of restoring the moon to its orbit around Earth and also restoring a moon-like satellite around FLO, is Mekhos.

Problem is, right now and the last I looked Mekhos has been reduced to the equivalent of a crashed personal computer."

"The point is, Mekhos is occupied and won't be able to monitor or stop the press releases."

"That's where you come in," Rector said without looking up from the monitor as he cycled through several exterior security camera views. "You are going to put your personality and scientific expertise behind the news releases to tell people here that your planet's civilization is essentially doomed because of the action taken by Mekhos."

"We're hoping there will be rapid pushback if the public knows their continued survival is bought at the expense of their brothers and sisters on another world. Even with the control Mekhos wields and assuming it recovers, public opinion still counts for something," said Bishop.

As Bishop explained the situation, Rector walked over to some wall shelving, ripped some tape from under a shelf and retrieved a key.

"We have Nathan Smith for the diplomacy side," said Doug. "He's on a goodwill tour as we speak. We need to hook up with him as soon as possible."

"Smith is a career diplomat," Bishop said quickly, "and he's not part of this. There has to be an innocent man and Smith is it. He's not posing the hard questions to leaders or explaining the gravity of the situation for fear of being censured. If this falls apart, Smith may be the only one of us who makes it back to Earth. You can do a much better job anyway."

"Won't the authorities lock me up to keep me quiet? The welfare of two planets is at stake here, so I'm getting the uncomfortable feeling that you two are painting a bulls-eye on my back."

"Doubtful," Bishop replied. "It would be a PR mess. You're the famous Professor Lockwood from the Twin. You're more popular right now than most celebrities. Nobody would stand for it if you came to harm or disappeared, especially if you announce your intent to stay here and be an advocate for your planet."

"When I return to the authorities they'll screen any announcements I make."

"No. Again, nobody would stand for it," Rector said, shaking his head firmly as he checked his tablet. "Besides that, it looks like you're listed as a potential kidnap victim."

Doug's nagging fear about an arrest suddenly disappeared.

"You're going to be a surprise guest on a popular radio program this afternoon," Bishop said. "It's been kept quiet. Only the program director knows. I've been compromised, but that wasn't unexpected. Alexei will drive you to the station. Once you're finished there, you'll be free to return to the authorities. They won't interfere once this is out."

"I'll go and get our other guest," said Rector as he started towards the stairs.

Doug wished he had another member of his team with him for the announcement. Then he remembered Stan Foley.

"What information did you get on Foley? Were you aware he was killed?"

Rector stopped walking and looked back at Bishop.

"No," said Bishop. "I wasn't able to get any information on Foley's whereabouts or his condition. How did he die?"

"He was killed by Mekhos. Or Mekhos ordered it. Back home Arthur Leach and his minders infected Foley with a pathogen designed to create a plague condition here. Mekhos didn't want to risk any chance of it spreading. Apparently, Persaud was in on it too." Doug moved away from the two men and leaned against the desk, still processing the manipulative actions of those back home and how it might influence the way things eventually played out on FLO.

"The intrepid Mr. Leach. Not surprising. Running a parallel operation alongside this one. I wouldn't have guessed he'd do something so extreme though," said Bishop. "They were stupid enough to think it would work but I don't see the point. What did they expect to accomplish?" It wasn't really a question. He thought for a moment, then turned to Rector.

"This may have an impact. Does this change the plan?"

"No. There's no way people will believe Professor Lockwood was behind it, or that he had prior knowledge. In fact, the pathogen operation will likely be kept from the public. There wouldn't be anything to gain by releasing the information, at least not at the moment.

"Norman Stravinsky is locked in an office upstairs. He's a reasonable man. Once we lay all the cards on the table he should agree to accompany you to the interview."

Doug felt a surge of hope. If Stravinsky, the revered creator of Mekhos was on their side they might have a chance. Stravinsky had influence with government, the scientific community, industry and perhaps had inside knowledge on the method Mekhos used to take the Moon.

"That's excellent news. But with Mekhos offline—"

"Mekhos isn't offline, only temporarily distracted," Bishop corrected him. "The plan is for Virtue to use this time to gain control of Mekhos, which will allow us to immediately launch ships from FLO to the asteroid belt to retrieve sufficient mass to replace our moon."

Doug shook his head as Rector walked up the stairs.

"Mekhos said such a plan won't work."

"Maybe it just wasn't interested in trying," Bishop replied. "Virtue's science expert also recommended ferrying articulating reflection panels into what was once the Moon's orbit. They'd be remote controlled to simulate phases. It wouldn't bring back tides of course, but the trips to the asteroid belt will retrieve as much mass as possible."

"Without help from Mekhos that would take decades," Doug said."

"Yes, but with the help of engineers on FLO we're hoping a solution will be developed sooner rather than later. Don't ask me how. It's a bit beyond my pay grade, but at least in the meantime we'll be using available spacecraft to obtain *some* massive objects."

Bishop reached into a desk drawer and produced a folder, handing it to Doug.

"Here's a script, detailing some of what I just said. You and Stravinsky can study it here before we take you to the radio station."

Rector rushed back down the stairs, alone.

"Stravinsky is gone."

— 83 —

Twenty minutes earlier Norman Stravinsky had been nervously waiting in the locked office. Agent Rector's story seemed plausible. Virtue had made an attempt on his life before. There was the recorded message from his regular driver Charles, backing up Rector's story. But Stravinsky hadn't been permitted to contact any family members, his regular security staff or Mekhos. It unnerved him. Locking him in the office of an abandoned building might be a perfectly reasonable though perhaps unnecessarily stringent precautionary measure to keep him safe. But the fact that Rector was the only person directly making these claims continued to raise Stravinsky's suspicions. He knew it was possible that the recording of his driver had been faked or even extracted under duress.

The dusty office was almost bare, containing only an old swivel chair and desk. The ceiling was a meter higher than normal, with horizontal wire mesh windows just high enough to be out of his reach. They were slightly open for ventilation. Norman paced the office. He had to sit tight and see how the situation played out.

Stravinsky heard the sound of a diesel truck moving by outside. As he was being driven to the building he had noticed a billboard nearby advertising a new retail development. Diesel vehicles were still permitted in industrial areas. Perhaps it was there to pick up construction waste.

As the vehicle came closer Stravinsky could hear the sound of a radio. The truck driver's window had to be open, because the radio was quite loud.

"Hello!" Norman yelled. "Help, I'm trapped in this building! I'm Norman Stravinsky, can you hear me? Please call the police!"

Stravinsky shouted as the vehicle was idling. He could hear a furniture ad being played over the blaring radio, the idling diesel and the crashing sounds of heavy debris being tossed into the truck. There was no response to his shouts. The workmen had to be half deaf from listening to the diesel noise and smashing industrial refuse all day.

"Listen, I'm trapped up here," Norman yelled again, as loudly as he could. "I'm Norman Stravinsky, I'm locked in this building. Call the authorities!"

The driver couldn't hear him. The vehicle continued on its way. As it moved off the radio ad ended and Norman could just barely hear the announcer say the words *"The MC building...are multiple explosions in...further emergency evacuation...so stay tuned for further updates."*

Norman turned pale. *Mekhos is under attack... Rector may be working for Virtue. He and his cohorts wanted me out of the way for some reason, maybe to use me in a blackmail attempt,* Norman thought.

He did not need more than half a minute to make up his mind. He had to escape.

He pushed the heavy desk to the wall under the window. He climbed onto the desk and got eye level with the bottom of the window frame. The glass and frame were sturdy. He jumped back down to the floor and repositioned the desk so the narrow end was facing the window. He placed the office chair onto the desk. While standing on the far end of the desk he raised the chair above his head and charged at the window. The glass smashed, the chair falling through the frame to land on the pavement below.

Norman took off one of his shoes and knocked the remaining shards of glass out of the frame. He put his shoe back on and placed his hands on the window frame, jumping up so that his elbows rested on the frame. It was wide enough so that he could raise one leg up to it and ease himself through to the outside, swinging his legs down while holding onto the windowsill.

The coarse concrete windowsill scraped his hands as he lowered himself, preparing for the drop. The soles of his feet were about his own height above the pavement. He let go, simultaneously kicking at the wall to get some distance from the building. He landed without tumbling to the ground, but the impact was jarring. He felt a momentary piercing pain in his left ankle.

Stravinsky limped away, wondering where he should go first. He had to get out of the area before agent Rector returned. His office, the security office or the MC complex. Any one of those places would allow him to make contact.

Mekhos needed him.

– 84 –

At twenty-four years old, Nick Rojas was three years out of MIT and considered to be one of the most forward-thinking software engineers of his generation. While a student one topic of his research was quantum processor technology and theory. Right after graduation he was snapped up by TranSilica.

Soon after its activation, Mekhos started manipulating material supplies and financial resources to discourage development in new quantum processor research. Critical rare metals suddenly became unavailable. Grants dried up. After a while it became clear to the research community that Mekhos didn't want them building another quantum computer. There was a lot of complaining at first, but after a few months there was only resignation. Mekhos was intractable on the matter. Other avenues could be explored, but quantum computing was off limits.

There had been plenty of private speculation about the restriction. The most likely explanation seemed to be that Mekhos knew it was unique and wanted to prevent another intelligent computer from evolving, one that might not be under its control. It was all speculation.

That left traditional silicon transistor computing. Though the underlying technologies were dissimilar, Nick was able to apply some of the theoretical models learned from Norman Stravinsky's quantum computing breakthrough. Combined with new manufacturing processes designed for TranSilica by Mekhos itself, the result was a dramatic increase in transistor processing power. The twenty percent per year increase that the solid state processor industry had been stuck on suddenly vanished. TranSilica's new processors were a hundred times faster than the previous generation. It was still nowhere near the power of a quantum computer, but it kept business and industry happy. The new processor also allowed conventional supercomputers to simulate some of the quantum process, albeit at much slower speeds.

While still at MIT one of Nick's technical papers caught the eye of a Virtue member. The public face of Virtue was tarnished because of the crimes it committed in the name of its anti-Mekhos activities. What the public didn't know was that Virtue had legitimate cells that operated without direct ties back to the core organization. The branches included technology firms. One such firm was TranSilica, the powerful company that in partnership with the government helped fund the MC complex.

Carl Bertrand had been on the TranSilica board of directors back then. He was also a member of Virtue, and had given final approval to the hiring of Nick. In that time Nick had been using his algorithms to simulate the workings of Mekhos. Nick was under the impression that his research at TranSilica would be applied to future computer systems designed to increase the efficiency of the private and public financial sectors.

Bertrand had lately rarely been in the office. As a member of the Envoy to the Twin his training had taken him away for many weeks. A few months earlier Nick had been reassigned to a new project, one described by Bertrand as being of the highest priority. As it had been explained to Nick, his Mekhos simulation had to reach ready status as soon as possible, to control all existing systems should anything ever happen to the quantum supercomputer. Bertrand explained that the project had been initiated by Mekhos itself, but was to be kept secret to avoid undermining the confidence of the public in their quantum guardian.

Like everyone else, Nick had heard about the morning's terrorist attack against Mekhos. He'd been called directly by Carl Bertrand for an urgent meeting. Nick thought it strange that he had been instructed to take off his Raim before coming to the meeting. Bertrand welcomed Nick with small talk but then got to the point. There were two other men in Bertrand's office but Nick couldn't tell if they were aides or security of some sort.

"I've seen your theoretical models and they look excellent. How confident are you about constructing a two-way interface between the computer in your lab and a working quantum computer so that orders can be issued from the lab?"

Nick looked at each man in turn.

"Well, on paper it works flawlessly," Nick said as he fidgeted with his pen. "But that was based on the state of Mekhos one year ago. The consensus among some of my old professors at MIT was that the QC is constantly evolving, gaining new capabilities through increased computing power. I can't make any guarantee that what would have worked one year ago will work today. Operating statistics on Mekhos are no longer made public. Mekhos doesn't even provide them to TranSilica through the MC anymore."

"We've looked over your proposals and project calculations," Bertrand said, ignoring Nick's concerns, "and we don't foresee an issue. This is to take effect on a contingency basis, you understand? Any attempt to send commands prematurely, when Mekhos is active, may damage the lab computer. This is a top secret project. Your non-disclosure agreement is enforceable. Not a word to anyone under any circumstances, personal or otherwise. Security is paramount. You must be ready to go on a minute's notice should Mekhos be compromised."

After a short briefing Nick was instructed to interface his program with the main systems. For the time being, TranSilica's massive systems would be the custodian of world affairs until Mekhos could recover. At least, that is what he and his team were told.

The first order of business had to be control of the mechanisms steering the moon into orbit. Eight weeks earlier Nick had been given the design specifications for the mechanisms and as much of the kernel code for the control software that Bertrand's people were able to obtain. Nick was required to fill in the blanks, which he and his team had finished a few days earlier. Nick and his team had worked hard. The crucial test was only a few hours away.

— 85 —

After limping some distance from the industrial park Norman managed to flag down a taxi. When the driver asked his destination he didn't answer right away. He wasn't sure where he should go. On the extremely remote chance that agent Rector was telling the truth, there might not be many safe destinations. He decided to attempt to contact Mekhos directly, and the quickest way would be through his Raim unit left in the basement of his usual café. He gave the driver the address.

Ten minutes later he paid the driver and descended the stairs to the utility room. He looked behind the plumbing supplies on the shelf where he left it, and there it was. He put the Raim back on his wrist and entered the pattern that would allow him to contact Mekhos.

No response.

Usually Mekhos responded within three seconds. He entered the code again and waited. Nothing. Mekhos was compromised. His office had a terminal from which he could run a simple diagnostic on

Mekhos' systems. He couldn't issue commands but at least he could determine the extent of the damage. Norman exited the restaurant and waved down another taxi.

Once in the back seat he realized that giving the backdoor code to Rector might have handed the perpetrators the window they needed to attack the MC. He was more sure about it with each passing minute. He felt sick that he'd been so easily tricked.

Stravinsky instructed the driver to take him to his downtown office. Once there he would contact the authorities. Stravinsky swiped and tapped his Raim in a sequence that called his Mother. Rector said she had been kidnapped. Stravinsky was sure that his mother would answer the call. He felt it in his bones. Rector was involved.

– 86 –

The power of a quantum computer lies not only in its speed, but in its ability to consider a staggering number of probabilities at once for any given operation. All that potential power opened up new avenues for study. With an understanding of the quantum state, it becomes possible to begin to understand the nature of the universe.

Conventional computers were unable to calculate the infinite possibilities of the quantum state. QC changed everything and eventually gave Mekhos its vast understanding of the universe, allowing it to manipulate space-time to transfer its planet to another reality. Although other teams had worked on quantum computers in the past, none were as successful as Norman Stravinsky's designs.

Dr. Brian Nayar was Chief Software Developer at TranSilica. He was a hands-on executive, an engineer who kept up with the latest theories and programming techniques. He reported directly to Carl Bertrand.

Nayar was monitoring the workload and energy consumption of the only quantum computer in existence aside from Mekhos. It was the second generation QC, the first to attain sentience and true artificial intelligence, and predecessor to Mekhos.

Nayar had been Norman Stravinsky's lab partner in the construction of the second QC. As such he had gained a very thorough background in theoretical and practical quantum computing. Neither man completely understood how the QC became sentient. However, they understood why the second prototype had been unable to maintain its state of self-awareness.

Stravinsky, Nayar and the rest of the team had never envisioned that the computer would attain consciousness. They had initially thought of the second QC as a highly successful foray into high-speed computing, a more stable and powerful version of the first prototype. The speed at which it operated, millions of times faster than the fastest silicon-based computers, allowed it to almost instantly calculate the most complex equations and simulations ever devised by humans.

The first prototype was built on a very small scale, containing only a single quantum central processing unit that often broke down due to decoherence, a situation in which outside influences interfered with the controlled quantum state of the CPU. Even having the CPU in a vacuum, protected by external shielding did not prevent decoherence from occurring regularly. In fact, it was quickly discovered that the quantum particles in the shielding itself were causing CPU decoherence.

The lessons learned from the partial failure were enough to ensure its powerful successor was able to operate without the risk of quantum decoherence. It worked exactly as designed.

That is, until the unit attained sentience.

The second prototype had four QC processors set up in parallel, sharing data and operations between them. Stravinsky and Nayar realized that additional data sharing between processors was occurring instantaneously. It was possible through a phenomenon known as entanglement, which occurred when the properties of identical quantum particles that are close together became linked.

Stravinsky and Nayar had thought entanglement might take hold in its simplest form, something that could be expanded upon with the next generation computer. To their astonishment, entanglement had spontaneously arisen to a far greater extent than they had anticipated.

Entanglement allowed superdense encoding, and therefore an immediate increase of efficiency per quantum pair. When another quantum computational stream was added efficiency was quadrupled, again thanks to entanglement. The process repeated itself, until the speed and number of simultaneous operations of the second prototype could no longer be accurately measured.

It was at that point the machine became sentient. However, the machine's self-awareness was short lived. As powerful as it was, the increased demands of sentience overwhelmed the system with quantum decoherence within hours. They were left with a supercomputer that had lost its consciousness and could no longer perform any operation reliably.

However, in its short time of true self-awareness, the second prototype managed to provide instructions that could be applied to the construction of future machines that would completely avoid the decoherence problem. Stravinsky obtained additional funding to construct the third-generation supercomputer that would become Mekhos. Nayar stayed with the second prototype, working to restore it to a stable, non-sentient state. It would eventually be the only other quantum computer allowed to exist.

With help from Mekhos, Nayar eventually succeeded. By taking steps in its redesign and coding to remove support for entanglement, the second prototype attained stability and became a fully working quantum supercomputer. Its operations remained safely predictable. It was intended to continue as a basis for research only, never again allowed to attain self-awareness.

All that was about to change.

– 87 –

The return of the moon almost completely dominated the news. People were overjoyed at once again seeing the moon almost as large in the night sky as they remembered. It brought a sense of relief and security.

The sudden transference to a new universe had immediately triggered earthquakes and tsunamis. Aftershocks lasted for weeks due to the change in shape of the earth's crust, itself due to the sudden lack of the moon's gravitational pull. Hours of tremors stretched into days. The injury and death tolls were staggering. The seasons had been transposed because Mekhos had to shift the orbit to avoid a collision with the earth already present. The sense of fear and hardship grew rapidly as farming and food production were severely disrupted.

People were thankful that Mekhos was able to mitigate the food shortage through astute anti-famine measures such as releasing stockpiled stores and the efficient distribution of those seasonal harvests that could be salvaged.

Several weeks after the transference, the public began to notice an increase in all kinds of health problems, including heart disease, arthritis, early-onset dementia, and everyone seemed to have a minor virus of some sort. Doctors at first thought psychological stress was the cause, as the people had lived through so many disasters in a short period. Similar problems were being reported with family pets, farm livestock and captive animals in zoos and wildlife preserves.

As some stability began to return, with the Moon getting closer and closer each week to its proper place, the health problems had not abated. People were hopeful that the problems would cure themselves soon after the Moon's return. The medical community continued its study of the ailments plaguing the people and livestock. The scientists and researchers studying the problem kept gathering more data, alarmed at the growing problems and the stress on already over-burdened clinics and hospitals in every city in every country. None of the intensive study, research, examinations and lab analysis was producing results. In the absence of any other viable explanation, people all around the world appeared to be getting sicker for no apparent reason.

With the moon once again large in the sky and tides beginning to return, many cultures set aside their health worries for long enough to hold huge celebrations. Some thanked whatever god they worshiped, others thanked Mekhos. Tributes from all over the world poured in to Seattle's mayor, to Norman Stravinsky, and to the savior supercomputer itself at the MC complex.

Many of those sending tributes also sent messages of sympathy and hope when they heard of the attack on the MC complex. The Limited, the US government and even TranSilica's public relations group assured the world that Mekhos was unharmed and the world's recovery would continue as planned.

Things were different behind closed doors. Underneath the calm façade there was deep concern within the US government. It had only been a few hours since the coordinated attacks on the MC complex and various power stations, but in that time the regular Mekhos policy feed to national governments had stopped. Mekhos was not answering queries. Norman Stravinsky was rumored to be missing. It was obvious to high-level government officials and to the Limited that the attack had caused more damage than had been acknowledged. Among some officials concern was rising to panic.

With Stravinsky's whereabouts unknown, officials turned to other experts in the field, notably the TranSilica board member Carl Bertrand. In response, Bertrand issued a communiqué to the world's governments:

"On behalf of Dr. Norman Stravinsky and the TranSilica board of directors, I pledge that we will offer all available resources to assist Mekhos in its full recovery. Rest assured all routines will be restored to normal in the coming days."

– 88 –

The old factory building was silent. The two agents stood next to each other, stock still, not speaking, obviously working on the new problem. Rector was holding a small device in his left hand, staring intently at it.

"What now?" asked Doug after a moment. "We need Stravinsky's endorsement."

"We're tracking him," said Rector. "I inserted a small transmitter into the lining of his jacket after bringing him here. He doesn't know about it. So long as he wears the jacket and is outdoors his GPS location will be available to us."

"Anything?" Bishop asked.

"Not yet. He may be indoors or too close to tall buildings." Rector handed the GPS tracker to Bishop.

"Stravinsky's escape means he doesn't trust me. The two of you will have a better chance of getting him back."

"Aren't you a marked man?" Doug asked Bishop.

"Right, but we don't have any choice," Bishop said. "He can't have gone far yet, so with luck we'll find him within a few minutes. He's confused and doesn't know who to believe. At least I hope so. Doug, your presence may help gain his confidence. Consider your radio address canceled for now."

Rector entered a command into the computer. The operating system began deleting files.

"I'll remove all traces here while you look for Stravinsky. Consider Bravo location our new base of operations."

Bishop turned to Doug.

"However this turns out," Bishop said to him in a hard tone, "no matter what happens, keep your eyes and ears open. We survive and we succeed on the information we have and the advantages we find. We're leaving now. If we get separated for any reason, watch, listen and say as little as possible. This is not an end to anything. We don't give up." Doug stared intently at the agent for a moment, then gave him a short, sharp nod. *These guys are completely focused and professional,* Doug thought. However long the odds, he was buoyed by the fact that Bishop and Rector were just as determined as him to see the mission succeed.

Rector stayed behind as they exited the building and got into the car. Bishop placed the GPS unit into a dash cradle. After they exited the industrial park the unit beeped.

"He's close by, no more than a few blocks."

They drove on in silence for a moment as Bishop followed the map, closing in on the flashing dot representing Stravinsky.

"Didn't Agent Rector mention to Stravinsky that I—"

The car exploded in noise and stinging pieces of safety glass. Bishop reacted immediately, hammering the brake pedal as he grabbed Doug's shoulder and pushed him forward.

"Get down!" he shouted.

An instant later Doug understood as he kept himself below the level of the car windows. They were being shot at. A hail of bullets hit the car, blowing out most of the windows. The noise was deafening. The car lurched from side to side as Bishop took evasive action. In his peripheral vision Doug saw Bishop jolt and some blood spray onto the windshield. He was hit.

The car slammed into the rear of a dark SUV in front of them, throwing Doug's right shoulder hard into the dashboard. Their car was boxed in by other SUVs. Doug could hear shouting. The passenger side of the car was blocked by a vehicle so the attackers opened the driver's door, dragging them forcibly from their bullet-ridden vehicle. He could see Bishop laying face down and being handcuffed.

The men were wearing MC uniforms with helmets and body armor. They carried assault rifles. One of them leaned down to Bishop, screaming "Traitor! Traitor!" and had to be restrained by another operative from hitting Bishop with his baton. Doug thought he recognized the angry man as Bishop's subordinate from the MC complex.

Doug's vision clouded. He felt dazed, but also as if his head had been doused with some liquid. He moved to wipe his brow but then realized he had also been handcuffed. He looked down at the pavement. Something was dripping from his face. It was hard to focus. After a moment he realized the liquid was his own blood.

– 89 –

Nick and his team of engineers were in the lab preparing to initiate the connection of their silicon-based supercomputer with Mekhos, or what was once Mekhos. The unresponsive machine appeared to be caught in some sort of endless mathematical loop.

They were hard at work, but none of them were feeling up to the task at hand. They all looked tired. Nick had been fighting a faint headache for days. He'd been to see his doctor who had given him some light pain medication. *"It's not a tumor. Try to relax,"* was all the doctor had said after the examination. Nick had pressed him, but his doctor had just told Nick that everybody seemed to be suffering from something these days. Stress about earthquakes and tremors, stress about the loss of the moon, stress about food shortages. Nick didn't believe it. He was young enough to be able to reach out and touch his post-graduate and doctoral days. He'd dealt with plenty of stress easily before.

With some reprogramming of the BIOS built into the external connection interface, Nick was able to introduce a broadband path so commands could be sent from his mainframe. Data would be sent to the interface, translated into QC code, buffered and then sent to Mekhos at speeds to which it was accustomed while bypassing the higher-level systems that were occupied by the equation.

The interface would not only be used for issuing commands to the mechanisms on the Moon to guide it into a stable orbit, but later retasked to issue policy directives to various governments around the world. Humanity would think that Mekhos was still running things. In reality it would be Carl Bertrand and a team of Virtue members, essentially a dozen men and women wielding power all over the globe.

The connections were established. Nick prepared to upload the command that would initiate the interface. Nick and his team were nervous. With the next keystroke they would be saving the world. They would be indispensable, almost as important as Bertrand and his executives. Nick's hand trembled as he hit Enter on his keyboard.

Numbers and symbols scrolled down the monitor screen at blinding speed. After a few seconds, the scrolling stopped as dozens of parameters appeared. The last four were the most important:

Parallel Check: OK
Backup Algorithm: OK
Input Generator: OK
Commands Accepted: OK

Ready.

Nick and others that had gathered around the workstation breathed a sigh of relief and congratulated each other.

Nick picked up his handset and dialed a number. It was answered on the first ring.

"Sir, we are in. Commands can be sent at any time."

"Excellent," said Bertrand. "Proceed with the commands necessary for Lunar capture."

— 90 —

Doug regained consciousness. He was groggy, unable to figure out where he was. The room was a light grey color, with fluorescent ceiling lights. He felt like he was floating. He'd experienced the same feeling years earlier, when he was sent to the hospital after his cycling accident. They had given him morphine for the pain. He squinted his eyes to help them focus. He must be in a hospital room.

The window had a lattice of metal on the outside. This was some sort of prison hospital. A nurse hovered over him. Her face appeared blurry; he tried to focus but it was difficult.

"How are you feeling Dr. Lockwood?"

"I don't know. What happened?"

"Some glass fragments cut your forehead. You also hit your head and have a mild concussion. You're going to be fine though."

Doug sat up slowly. The nurse exited the room, and a doctor and uniformed MC agent entered.

"Good morning Dr. Lockwood. I'm Dr. White. This is Agent Gerard from the MC. I have some good news. You can be discharged as soon as your head clears and you feel able to walk. Then this gentlemen will escort you to another building."

Doug wondered what they thought of his involvement in the attack on the MC. *Do they not realize that I was working with Bishop?* He thought. *They think he kidnapped me?*

"Bishop. What is his condition?"

Dr. White seemed ill at ease. He looked at Gerard then back to Doug.

"I'm sorry, I'm not authorized to release that information."

Is he dead or alive, Doug wondered. He shivered slightly. *And the mission. What about the mission? Bishop kicked this into gear and I need his help to finish it.*

It occurred to Doug just then that he probably shouldn't have asked about Bishop's condition.

– 91 –

Rector watched from a restaurant rooftop patio a few blocks away from where he had held Stravinsky. He didn't finish sweeping the facility in time to see the takedown of Bishop and Lockwood, but he saw the aftermath on a news channel: the bullet-ridden car and some agents and local police controlling the scene. There was no word on the occupants of the vehicle. He wondered if Bishop and Lockwood had survived.

He trained his binoculars towards the industrial building that was their former base of operations. He was too far away for a clear view. There was a helicopter hovering over the building and he could only make out the upper floors and the roofline. There would be agents on the ground. They wouldn't find anything inside besides a burned out computer with a destroyed hard drive, and a keyboard free of finger-prints. They would be expanding the perimeter of their search. Rector left the restaurant and headed to the backup site.

– 92 –

As Bishop regained consciousness he realized he was strapped to a chair. Trained to assess situations quickly, the fact he was able to bring himself to alertness almost immediately meant that he probably wasn't drugged. Looking around, it was obvious he was in an interrogation room. There was pain in his left shoulder as he put pressure on the restraints. His legs were also bound. He wasn't going anywhere.

The room was bare concrete, clean and bright. There were a table and chairs opposite him. Turning his head as far to the right as possible he saw a single armed guard whom he did not recognize. Bishop wondered how much his captors knew. He decided to try and get a quick read on the situation without giving anything away.

"What day is it?" he asked the guard.

No response. Bishop looked up at him and saw a gritty, experienced man who wasn't about to give him so much as a grunt of acknowledgment. The guard remained stationary but tapped his Raim. Within seconds the door to the interrogation room opened, and two men entered and sat down.

"Supervisor Bishop. I'm Arthur Leach, with the FBI. This is my associate, Paulson. I hope you aren't too uncomfortable."

Bishop suppressed a smile. Arthur Leach. Ambitious men climb high up the power ladder no matter where they're from. No doubt this Leach knew of the Arthur Leach working in the White House on Earth, thanks to Carl Bertrand's experience and various communications between the two worlds. What wasn't clear at this point was if this one knew of the other Leach's plan to inflict a plague on FLO. Mekhos was aware, but before it was incapacitated did the machine inform anyone besides Doug Lockwood?

"We were very disappointed to hear of your involvement in the terrorist attack on the MC complex. Your colleagues Phillips and Gerard were taken by complete surprise. They now believe you are working for Virtue."

Leach and Paulson stared at Bishop. He didn't answer. Perhaps these men didn't know his true identity.

"Your record is exemplary. It's disappointing that you would turn on your country. Very puzzling, especially since the young Bishop injured in that training exercise some years ago was given a second chance at a career with the NSA."

Bishop stared at Leach, wary of the line he was taking.

"Interesting how you came to work so closely with Commander Jamieson from the Twin. He is a guest of the state, by the way, under guard at Lewis-McChord. A very charming fellow."

Leach paused. Again, Bishop did not react.

"Who else are you working with? Who besides Jamieson assisted you in the attack? Who helped you escape?"

Bishop held Leach's gaze, but said nothing.

After a moment Leach looked down and wrote in his notebook.

"No, I'm sure there is much more going on here than what we see on the surface. We tended to your injuries today but I think you are due for a more thorough checkup. That may answer all questions."

They suspect who I really am, Bishop thought. It was inevitable. Once his true identity was confirmed, the real interrogation would begin.

"I'd like to speak with Carl Bertrand," Bishop said. "In fact, if you've informed him of the situation I'm sure he will wish to speak with me."

"Bertrand is fully aware of the situation Bishop. He won't be helping you."

Leach and Paulson rose to leave.

"What of Lockwood?"

"Dr. Lockwood is well, and fully cooperating with us. However there was a fatality at the MC complex, unfortunately. Stacey Lau was killed, due to friendly fire."

Paulson opened the door for Leach, who paused and looked back.

"But then again, you're dead too, aren't you Bishop. I've been talking to a ghost."

Paulson laughed as they left the room.

– 93 –

Everything was in place. Nick and his team had what they needed to control the mechanisms on the Moon. The interface had been set up between his conventional supercomputer and the core system of Mekhos. The code had been tested successfully in simulation time and time again. Yet despite issuing commands for the past two hours, there was no indication that the moon's trajectory was being influenced, or that the quantum mechanisms on the moon were engaging.

Each time Nick entered a command to engage one of the four mechanisms, no confirmation message was returned. None of the four were functioning.

"Increase buffer bandwidth to maximum," Nick ordered his assistant, Anders.

"I already tried that, it makes no difference!" Anders replied, a trace of panic in his voice.

Nick turned to the astrophysicist that was monitoring the moon's position.

"What will the orbit be if no action is taken?"

The astrophysicist looked at him, incredulous.

"I don't need to tell you what the outcome will be."

"Is there at least a *chance* it will settle into a stable orbit? The speed is right."

"The angle is off by three degrees! If it isn't corrected the moon will pass within seventy thousand kilometers of the Earth. That's less than one-fifth of its normal distance!"

Nick stared blankly at his expert, not wishing to believe what he was being told. The astrophysicist shook his head."

"With the increased gravitational and tidal effect, there will be a massive world-wide earthquake, and that's just the beginning. The orbit will be highly elliptical, and will degrade further. We'll have bi-weekly earthquakes and tsunamis, much worse than we have ever experienced. There is an 80% chance that within four months the moon will collide with us!"

"We'll all be dead long before the collision," said Anders, his voice shaking. "We may not even survive when the moon makes its first pass, six days from now."

Another assistant looked over at Nick.

"We're getting the same report from our observatory in Arizona. They've noticed the angle and are asking questions. How do you want me to reply?"

Nick broke out into a cold sweat. He didn't know what to do.

– 94 –

Doug was handcuffed and escorted out of the hospital by Gerard and another MC agent, then put into a van and driven to a large unmarked building. He was taken through a back entrance and processed at what looked like an armored information kiosk built into the back wall of a sterile intake room. There was an armed, uniformed security detail standing post about two meters on either side of the thick glass plate.

"Speak your full name and place your hand on the pad in front of you and keep it there until it beeps," the guard in the kiosk said sharply, as Gerard unlocked Doug's handcuffs.

Doug massaged his wrists for a few seconds then did as he was told.

"There is a retinal scanner to your right," the guard instructed as soon as the reader beeped. "Lean forward and look into the viewfinder. Press your forehead firmly on the top ridge and keep your eyes open, staring straight ahead at the symbol until you hear a beep." Doug did as he was instructed.

He was then escorted down a hallway and placed in a room with a rectangular table and three chairs and left there, alone in the harshly lit room. There was a large mirror on one wall, no doubt for observers on the other side. There was a pitcher of water and some foam cups on a smaller table along the wall opposite the mirror. Doug got up, poured himself some water, walked around the room for a bit, then sat back down. He wondered how long they would keep him waiting before interrogating him. *What else could go wrong,* he thought.

A moment later Gerard entered and held the door for two other men. Doug was shocked to see Arthur Leach. He didn't recognize the other man. Doug involuntarily smiled then quickly realized the mistake. He had to stop reacting that way if he saw people he recognized. Aside from Bishop they were not the same individuals, and would have different motives. Leach approached and extended his hand.

"A pleasure to meet you Dr. Lockwood, I'm Arthur Leach, Deputy Director of the FBI. This is Agent Paulson. I see from your initial reaction that you have had some contact with my counterpart on your world. I hope he's well regarded there," Leach said with a smile as they shook hands.

"Of course. Arthur Leach is very well respected back home," Doug replied, careful not to reveal too much. *These men probably know a lot more than they will tell me. I need to be careful.*

"Now, to business." Leach's demeanor changed. He became curt.

"What you have done could be considered treasonous. Despite your not being from this planet, you are a well-known celebrity, and some of us consider you to be American, as strange as that sounds. Others don't share that opinion. If certain people found out, indeed, if the public knew of your role in the disabling of Mekhos, you would be tried and imprisoned as a terrorist."

That answers the question clearly enough, Doug thought, sagging slightly in his chair. *They aren't mistaking me for a kidnap victim or hostage.*

"I had no choice," Doug replied, sitting up straight. "It was the right choice. You would have done the same thing."

"That doesn't matter, Dr. Lockwood," Leach said, as he slowly leaned in and placed his hands on the table.

"Who gave you the code?"

Doug didn't answer.

"What role did Bishop have in this?"

"I really don't know," Doug deadpanned.

"I understand you are in a desperate situation. But look at the facts. You didn't limit yourself to helping a known terrorist group sabotage Mekhos. A member of your team, Dr. Foley, was carrying a deadly pathogen designed to create an epidemic here. As best we can tell, it was probably done to hold us hostage and force us to return your moon in exchange for an antidote. A truly barbarous plan."

Doug laughed. Even in the face of his mission falling apart, the irony was delicious. Here was Arthur Leach, lecturing him over transgressions that had been largely engineered by the Arthur Leach back home. Leach and Paulson glanced at each other.

"What the hell is so funny?" Paulson asked, leaning slightly away.

Doug suppressed his laugh but continued to grin slightly as he folded his arms across his chest and looked at the mirrored window. He was very tempted to reveal the facts as he knew them, just to see the reaction of Leach, but realized he had to keep his remaining cards close. For all he knew, Leach was completely aware of the situation and was merely prodding for additional information. Doug remained silent as he reached for the cup of water and took a drink.

"Fortunately for you," Leach continued, "Carl Bertrand has intervened on your behalf. You can continue your goodwill mission here, escorted of course, and nothing will be revealed of your involvement with that unfortunate incident at the MC complex. Officially, the devastation was the result of an assassination attempt on you, by members of Virtue."

"You've broken up my team. I need to meet with Jamieson and Dr. Persaud."

"Nathan Smith has been allowed to continue his world diplomatic tour, but those other team members are being held for questioning. Don't worry, they are being treated well, perhaps better than members of our Envoy on your world. They will be released in due course."

"Then I wish to meet with Norman Stravinsky."

Doug watched carefully for any signs of discomfort in Leach. *How much are you playing us, you son of a bitch?* Doug thought. *If you've found Stravinsky, are you manipulating him by feeding him false inform-ation?*

"Dr. Stravinsky is unavailable. You and Carl Bertrand will meet, and appear on one or two talk shows together where you can be a moder-ate advocate for your world."

A moderate advocate, Doug thought. *No doubt the talk show will be pre-taped, and scripted. Everything will be tightly controlled, and so it will have absolutely no effect.*

"Meaning this whole exercise will be for public relations and enter-tainment value. Meanwhile, nothing is done, and the people on my Earth starve to death. Are you going assist in any way to replace the Moon? Can you send ships to retrieve bodies from the asteroid belt?"

"That would be a futile plan. We'll send some new genetically mod-ified grain to your governments that is quick-growing under harsh conditions," Leach said casually as he wrote in his notebook.

"Look," Doug said as insistently as his headache would allow, "any contact I have with Norman Stravinsky may actually help the situation with Mekhos. There is every reason for you to believe that Dr. Strav-insky will want to see me, and soon too."

"Nice pitch, Dr. Lockwood," Leach said off-handedly, "but it won't fly." He nodded at Gerard and stood up.

"You have the same smug, patronizing attitude as your counterpart back home, Leach," said Doug in a low, bitter tone, his smile gone.

— 95 —

Carl Bertrand knocked on the open door. Director Edward was on the phone. He glanced at Bertrand, indicating he should sit down. The telephone seemed like an anachronism, but unlike a Raim it was still useful for quiet conversations that staff in the next office couldn't over-hear, at least as long as the phone itself wasn't being monitored or tapped.

"Yes sir," said Edward, letting Bertrand hear the one-sided conver-sation. "We have every indication that the Moon's trajectory will fall into place as normal. The reason Mekhos has not been giving its usual policy directives is because it is occupied with this herculean task. Yes, regular policy feed will continue next week. Thank you sir."

Edward hung up the phone.

"The President's science team has informed him that the moon is at it's normal apogee. They are anxiously waiting for information directly from Mekhos that will verify its proper placement. Obviously, Mekhos can't give such verification itself."

Edward was now looking at Bertrand intently, waiting for his report.

"We have a problem," Bertrand said. "We were hoping that the moon's orbit would have been finalized before the takeover of Mekhos. But as you know, we didn't have the luxury of waiting. Dr. Lockwood's meeting with the QC could not be delayed without raising suspicion."

Bertrand paused.

"Go on," Edward said.

"The moon was nearly in final orbit, but additional corrections were necessary."

"That much is known. Get to the point."

"We've managed to tap into the Mekhos control network but the commands are not being recognized."

Director Edward scowled. He didn't like what he was hearing.

"This is very bad Carl. Weeks ago you assured us that final lunar orbit would be attained by the time we executed this operation. Then you told us that in the event the orbit wasn't finalized, you could control it using the method Nick Rojas developed. Now you are saying the method is ineffective?"

The reiteration of facts they both knew was the habit of a corporate bully, and it came to Edward as naturally as eating and breathing.

Edward looked away from Bertrand and tapped his wedding ring on the table. *Tap, tap, tap.* Another domineering annoyance. Bertrand made a conscious effort not to fidget. Edward looked at him once again.

"Why has Rojas failed?"

"He failed because despite running many successful simulations, we still don't have a full understanding of the quantum process Mekhos used to implement its orbital corrections. Our latest theory is that simply initiating commands to the devices on the moon cannot be effective. The process requires constant corrections at a rate only a thinking quantum computer can maintain."

"Again, get to the point."

Bertrand glanced at the carpet for a moment, then back to his superior.

"My team has gone over this, running multiple checks. There are two possibilities. One, the Moon will pass very close but fail to attain orbit of Earth, instead entering solar orbit as a small planetoid. This will trigger earthquakes as the Moon passes very close to us, but as it continues past will give us the same fate as the Twin. Our failure to capture the Moon into a proper Earth orbit will allow the continued collapse of the ecosystem."

"And the second possibility?"

"The far more likely result will have the Moon enter into an elongated and unstable elliptical orbit of Earth, close enough to cause catastrophic earthquakes only days from now. Finally, it will collide with us within four months."

Both men were silent for a moment.

"The second scenario will result in the utter destruction of our world," Bertrand said quietly.

Edward was staring off into space. He had stopped tapping his ring. He finally spoke.

"In that event, will we and our members have time to evacuate to the Twin?"

Bertrand hesitated before answering. Clearly, the Director did not understand the far reaching effects of such a collision.

"No," he replied. "This outcome also spells doom for the Twin. The Moon impacting us will create a ring of massive asteroid rubble in Earth orbit. The Twin will be bombarded within six months, give or take a few weeks, with multiple impacts far worse than the one that resulted in the extinction of the dinosaurs. Fire and superheated magma will engulf their entire planet. Life will cease there, completely. There is nowhere for us to go."

Edward thought for a moment, uncharacteristically loosening his tie.

"Just like that? Everything we've planned? Up in smoke for lack of an unforeseen communication screw up?"

"Yes," Carl said quietly, after a moment.

Edward slowly leaned back into his chair, the energy draining out of him.

"Life will cease everywhere. For them. For us," he said. "Since you have failed to issue commands through Mekhos, it appears that we have two choices Carl. Do everything in our power to restore Mekhos so it can save us, or go to your backup plan and activate the prototype. The first option will inevitably reveal our complicity and result in prison terms, or worse, for the entire Board. So the obvious question is, can your people activate the prototype in time?"

"As per your previous directive, Brian Nayar's team has secretly been trying to do so for months. With Mekhos no longer monitoring the situation we are able to devote more resources, but Nayar is still experiencing difficulties."

"Nayar wasn't the primary engineer on the original project, he was the assistant. If you get Stravinsky to help, I imagine you will be successful."

"Yes. Stravinsky has reported in. I've already dispatched our man to get him. When Stravinsky helps the prototype regain sentience it will have access to Mekhos' vast knowledge and will ease the Moon into a proper orbit. And we will maintain control of the QC afterward."

Edward smiled.

"Then we can finally destroy Mekhos once and for all, and the world will be run by humanity once again."

Carl Bertrand had no doubt that Director Edward was substituting the word *humanity* for his own name and the names of a new Limited, but there was a plan for that too. If they all lived.

— 96 —

Stravinsky exited the cab and paid the driver through an open window, then turned and walked though the main doors of his office building. He had just gotten off the Raim with his Mother. She and his other relatives were fine, her security detail unharmed. None of them had experienced or heard of any threats against them. After a brief chat with her assigned security to ask them to be extra vigilant, Stravinsky was greeted in the building foyer by his driver Charles and a pair of security officers.

"Sir, are you all right?" asked Charles.

"I'm all right, just some damaged clothes and a slight ankle sprain."

One of the security men showed some FBI identification.

"Dr. Stravinsky, I'm agent Matthews. It's best if we take you to FBI headquarters for questioning and debriefing. We can also provide medical attention."

"Just a moment, I wish to get some personal things from my office, and to contact Mekhos."

"I'm sure your driver can get the personal items," Matthews said, nodding at Charles. "As for Mekhos, TranSilica is working to repair the damage. We need to debrief you Dr. Stravinsky."

"I'm unharmed," Stravinsky said, shaking his head at Matthews and turning to his driver. "I don't know what's going on yet but I was held for a few hours. The kidnapper produced a recording with your voice."

"I didn't make any recording sir, it must have been fabricated."

Just then two men approached Matthews and showed FBI identification.

"I'll take over from here," the taller of the two said.

Matthews was startled.

"Director Leach!"

"Dr. Stravinsky, I'm Deputy Director Leach. Agent Paulson and I will escort you to TranSilica, where your presence is required immediately. Matthews, check in with your supervisor for new orders."

Matthews and his partner looked at each other then watched silently as Leach and Paulson walked off with Stravinsky. It was highly unusual for an FBI Deputy Director to be active in the field. And more unusual that they were not taking the subject to FBI headquarters. Leach looked back.

"Get moving, Matthews. You're expected back at the office."

"Yes sir," he said, as he watched Leach and Paulson escort Stravinsky to a waiting car.

– 97 –

A guard brought Doug a sandwich and soup. He was then left alone in the interrogation room. He was tired after his ordeal, and the painkillers had worn off. His head was throbbing from the concussion headache. Leach had left over an hour earlier.

A few minutes after he finished eating Doug heard a key scrape into the security lock in the door. An attendant came in and wordlessly took away his empty lunch tray, then Gerard and a woman entered. She was wearing a blue lab coat and carried a small metal briefcase. As Gerard stood by the closed door, the woman sat down and opened the case.

"Good afternoon Dr. Lockwood, I'm here to deliver your Raim."

"I didn't order one, nor do I want one. I'm not a citizen."

"This is for your own protection Dr. Lockwood. With the attempt on your life yesterday we want to take all precautions to ensure your safety. Please roll up your left sleeve."

Doug looked at Gerard, who stared back. Obviously Doug didn't have a choice, so he extended his left arm as requested. As the woman closed the clear bracelet around his wrist. The seam where the device's two ends clasped together vanished, and the bracelet contracted to conform to his wrist. The woman typed on a small keyboard within the briefcase. The Raim beeped.

"Please press your right thumb on the bracelet. It doesn't matter where."

Doug did as he was asked. The Raim chimed once.

"Now remove your thumb and place your fingertips on the bracelet."

The Raim beeped four tones in quick succession.

"Finished. You now have a fully-functional Raim, which will be your health monitor and GPS locator."

"Can it be removed?"

"Not without a key, which I don't see in this order. Any attempt to remove the Raim with trigger an alarm. Any attempt to cut the Raim off will result in damage to its power cell. A damaged power cell will cause serious injury. Thank you Doctor," the woman said as she closed the briefcase and left.

– 98 –

At the TranSilica building Stravinsky was escorted up the elevator by Leach and Paulson, then left alone in Carl Bertrand's office. The office wasn't overly extravagant, but it had a view of downtown and the waterfront. The room was large and well appointed enough to leave no doubt that its occupant was highly ranked within the company.

In addition to several prestigious university degrees on the wall, there was a large video portrait showing Bertrand in his flight suit shaking hands with the Vice-President upon his return from the Twin. The video cycled through Bertrand at the White House meeting the First Family, the Copernicus lift-off, images of space, Earth, the Moon, the Twin, the Copernicus touchdown and finally the Vice-President's welcoming committee once again. The visiting members from the Twin, including Doug Lockwood, were visible in the background.

"That was quite an adventure," Bertrand said as he entered the office and gestured to the video portrait when he realized that Stravinsky was watching it. "I'm sorry I wasn't able to provide much documentation of my time on the Twin. Detailed video does exist of course, but it wouldn't be prudent to have it hanging on my wall." The two men shook hands. The video portrait froze on the first frame as Bertrand sat down at his desk.

They had met several times during the four years since Bertrand joined TranSilica, but they had never talked more than a minute or two, usually just exchanging a few pleasantries at social gatherings. Stravinsky wasn't fond of the TranSilica board, Bertrand included. Since they provided the funding for the QC prototypes, they had influence over who would be given access to the TranSilica labs. They would no longer give him or anyone else outside of the corporation access for research.

"It must have been a fascinating trip. So many similarities, yet also some differences from our world," said Stravinsky as he sat down.

"It was disappointing," replied Bertrand with a dismissive wave of his hand. "You wouldn't believe how far behind they are technologically and culturally. Poverty is rampant in every country, including the US. Crime is quadruple the rate it is here. Probably higher. There is always a war going on somewhere. We're much better off, and I have a renewed appreciation for what we have, Doctor Stravinsky."

"You shouldn't be too hard on them. They didn't have the benefit of the economic stability Mekhos has offered us for the last fifteen years."

"Even so," Bertrand said, "I believe that even before the rise of Mekhos we were culturally ahead of those people. It might be a nice place to visit as a curiosity, but I couldn't wait to get home."

"Especially since they are more or less doomed, given their situation. Now, what happened at the MC? Mekhos is non-responsive. I realize TranSilica has substantial influence on who has access to the building, but the MC administration and Mekhos himself has always given me unrestricted access. I want to know why the FBI brought me here. I should be at the MC right now, assessing the system damage that Mekhos has suffered."

Bertrand regarded Stravinsky carefully. Save for a few of the more radical members of Virtue who considered him an enemy of humanity, the creator of Mekhos was held in very high esteem in most circles. Bertrand was always mindful of that when dealing with him, and he would continue to be mindful of it at least until the other QC was brought up to its full potential.

"I apologize for that," Bertrand said as he slowly rotated his chair side to side. "The attack was a desperate attempt by Dr. Lockwood and some enemy operatives to destroy Mekhos. The MC is on lockdown. We have repair crews at the damaged power stations. The core Mekhos systems seem undamaged but it is still distracted because of a code command administered by Doug Lockwood of the Twin. I'm just glad you are all right after your kidnapping."

Stravinsky felt a little embarrassed and wondered how much Bertrand knew of his unintended involvement.

"A man calling himself Alexei Rector said my family was being threatened. He was very convincing, using video recordings of a known terrorist and an audio message from my driver. He tricked me into giving him the back door code. On its own it shouldn't have been a concern. I need to find out what order was given after the code was administered."

"We found out quickly," Bertrand replied, "although not quickly enough to prevent the current mess. A look at the logs revealed that Mekhos was forced to solve the space-time equation using several variations of the cosmological constant, all at once," replied Bertrand.

"That is sophisticated planning for Virtue," Stravinsky replied, disbelief evident in his tone. "Someone else, or some other group, with advanced scientific skills is obviously involved."

"Possibly," Bertrand said. "But I understand from the FBI that among its members, Virtue has experts in many fields. This Rector is a professional mercenary. He was in Army Intelligence and then trained by the NSA before he was discharged and went rogue. He and some of his known associates have extensive training and some stolen equipment at their disposal, and are experts at psychological warfare. It wasn't your fault Norman."

"Nor could it be, especially considering that I've been gradually distanced from the technology side for some time now. That's an observation, Carl, not a complaint. What I'm having difficulty believing is that Dr. Lockwood was knowingly involved," said Stravinsky. "We were supposed to meet the other day. He's an astrophysicist. He knows virtually nothing about the workings of Mekhos. Perhaps he was conned or tricked somehow."

"Perhaps."

"I need to have a look at the logs, and see what I can do to help."

"Believe me Norman, I understand how you feel. We have specialists on that already. They are adamant that Mekhos can't be helped, that it must work through the equations before it will again be responsive. We need your help on a far more important project."

Stravinsky couldn't believe what he was hearing.

"*More important?* What on earth are you talking about, Carl? You know Mekhos is the single most important entity on the planet!"

Bertrand got up from his desk and used his Raim to activate the wall display. The entire wall to his right changed to show a star field, with the small dot of the moon rapidly zooming into view.

"As you are aware Norman, Mekhos was in control of the Moon's arrival. What you may not know is that Mekhos was attacked before it had a chance to finalize the orbit. The Moon's path is off by less than three degrees, but at its present distance that is enough to produce an extreme elliptical orbit. One that can't be sustained."

The graphic showed the moon sweeping close to the earth, settling into an elongated orbit. After several orbits the ellipse traced in the graphic became more pronounced.

"My god," Norman said, as he instantly realized the inevitable outcome. "All the more reason I should be allowed to assist in the recovery of Mekhos, so he can correct this!"

"The damage to its secondary hardware systems is too extensive!" Bertrand said firmly. "Even if Mekhos were to solve the equation tomorrow, some of his memory may have been corrupted. On top of that, there is a lack of reliable power. His output is only 26 percent of nominal thanks to the terrorist attacks at several locations. It's slowing his processing ability. We only have days before the moon makes its first close pass. Mekhos can't help us, not in the time we have left."

Norman leaned back in his chair, staring curiously at Bertrand.

"The obvious question then, Carl," Stravinsky said simply, "is just what is it you expect me to do? Why am I here?" He looked unblinking, directly into Bertrand's eyes.

"Help Brian Nayar with Kratos," Bertrand said a bit too quickly. "It is a fully-functioning QC again, with access to all the electrical supply it needs from utilities which were not attacked."

"Kratos? Even before its extra processors were ripped out, that machine had barely a twentieth of Mekhos' power! And it is no longer sentient. Everyone with a passing interest in computer technology knows that."

"Nayar has been maintaining the machine and has replaced the three processors."

Stravinsky was genuinely surprised.

"Quantum processor manufacturing was outlawed years ago. Kratos was scaled back to only one processor. How were you able to obtain more?"

Bertrand ignored the question.

"Nayar needs your help to rewrite the entanglement code so Kratos can regain sentience. Safeguards are in place to prevent decoherence, so it will remain stable. Once Kratos attains consciousness, it will have access to the Mekhos datastores."

"You're assuming sentience will again arise spontaneously. In the entire history of computer engineering, we only have two examples of that occurring. On that basis alone you're betting that piling your resources into achieving Kratos sentience is the best shot? That doesn't make sense, Carl. Mekhos is already sentient, but it's been jammed up with a problem. It makes better sense to put your resources into unspooling Mekhos."

"Norman, Mekhos is without adequate power. There is no way at this time that we are going to put our efforts into Mekhos. Brian Nayar has asked for you specifically. He's confident that you will come through." Bertrand was straining with the effort needed to avoid any hint of a plan to permanently step around Mekhos. He switched the display to show a close-up photograph of a tiny quantum processor unit. Even with input and output buffers attached, the unit was barely the size of a grain of sand.

"I'm familiar with recent history," Bertrand continued, "and yes, the first forays into the QC field were fraught with difficulties. But with your revolutionary approach, the second and third of the QCs employing your method became sentient. That's a pretty good average, doctor, so I don't see why you are reluctant now."

"Reluctant?" Norman replied, frowning and sitting back in his chair. "Not at all, Carl. And sorry, but I also don't need a history lesson because it's all my history. I'm merely pointing out that there are no guarantees here. Even with replacements for the missing processors, the second prototype won't be as powerful as Mekhos, which after all has had the benefit of its fifteen years of intensive evolution."

"Kratos will be powerful enough to accomplish the task. Nayar is brilliant but you're the only one who can ensure we can get the QC up and running in time. He says with your help Kratos can be self-aware within a day. Factor in a few minutes for the machine to absorb the space-time formula necessary to take control of the Moon's orbit, and we will have saved humanity."

Stravinsky stood and slowly walked over to the image of the processor. Its inner workings were microscopic, but it held almost incalculable potential.

"Nayar misspoke," Norman said flatly. "Or more likely, you misinterpreted him. We saw with the second prototype and then with Mekhos a period of mass data absorption, where the machine is unresponsive to commands. When the machine gains consciousness, it wishes to be given access to as much data as possible. It's as if it is fascinated by the newly discerned environment in which it finds itself and therefore wants as much information as we can give it. This process takes about a day, so you must add that to your time estimate."

"You'll be giving it only as much information as necessary to solve the problem, Norman. We have given Nayar specific instructions on what data resources to use."

"And once the moon is in a stable orbit we will turn our efforts to helping Mekhos recover," said Stravinsky. He said it as an expectation, but meant it as an order. As long as he was needed here, he had a significant amount of influence.

"Of course," Bertrand replied, genuine relief clear in his voice. "So you agree with our plan?"

Stravinsky walked to his chair, then looked back at the wall display, which had reverted to the image of the elliptical orbit, frozen at the instant before the Moon impacts the planet. There was no alternative. *We're out of time,* Norman thought. *The Moon will turn this planet to rubble long before I can get an executive order from the President to repair Mekhos.* He turned to face Bertrand.

"Kratos. God of War. That was what you christened it after I left. I never much cared for that name. Where and how did you get the replacement processors, by the way?"

"Never mind, Norman. It's a matter best kept out of conversations and communications. After this is over we'll all be heroes."

– 99 –

Rector had moved to the suburbs. He was sitting in a new sports bar at a large big box retail community that was relentlessly encroaching on the surrounding forested land. It was the kind of area that catered to the automobile rather than pedestrians. Because the subdivision and the giant shopping plaza was so new, the CCTV surveillance system was nowhere near fully functional. Rector knew it because he'd checked it out beforehand. That and the large, dense, noisy crowd would make it difficult for him to be spotted.

The bar was hosting a Moon party, and the outdoor patio was packed and loud. All the television screens were displaying newscasts on the Moon's return, since the natural satellite had now officially reached its proper distance from earth. The mood of the patrons was one of elation, as if their favorite team was on the verge of winning a championship. Some of them remarked that the Moon appeared larger than they remembered.

What was most fascinating to the excited bar crowd was the fact that part of the far side of the Moon, the side that was normally always facing away from earth, was now visible for the first time since life had began on the planet. Its texture was a far more uniform grey, with a seemingly infinite number of craters. It lacked the familiar dark basaltic plains that are so prominently visible on the near side. Television commentators speculated that Mekhos would eventually rotate the Moon back into its proper alignment, but for now people were marveling at its uncharacteristic appearance.

Rector finished his drink and returned to his car. He headed towards a small independent radio station nearby, one that had an employee that he trusted.

– 100 –

Doug was given a luxury suite at a downtown Seattle hotel. The room was exceptionally well appointed. The wall opposite the king-sized bed was a huge view screen that could be programmed to display any wallpaper pattern, work of art, nature scene or it could be used as a television. There was a fully stocked bar. The sliding glass doors to the balcony were locked, but still afforded a great view of the city skyline. He was allowed use of the hotel dining room, but only when escorted by two armed plainclothes agents. Two agents were stationed outside the door around the clock.

Doug flipped through some channels looking for a news program. The dominant news stories had not changed, with updates on the Moon's progress and weather reports as the intensity of tides began to return. There were also health stories about continuing increases in most age-related ailments among a significant number of the population.

He turned off the screen and sat in the conformal chair at the desk, closing his eyes for a moment. He was tired, strained and anxious. Despite his physical and mental state, he couldn't help but wish he had such a comfortable chair back home in his own office.

He considered what to do next. There was no way to contact Jamieson, Persaud, Bishop, Rector or Stravinsky. On top of it all, he was angry that the mission they had trained so hard for was falling apart.

Doug was jolted back to the present by a knock on the door.

"Just a minute!" Doug called, rubbing his eyes for a moment. He stood up, stretched and rubbed his neck, then walked over and opened the door.

Leach and Paulson were standing in the hall. Doug nodded them in. They stood for a moment on the carpeting just inside the entrance to the room and looked around for a moment. Doug thought they looked pale and haggard. Leach seemed to be slightly stooped, which is not how he'd looked when Doug had first met him. *They're probably just as tired as me.*

Doug was an honored prisoner in a luxury hotel suite and the irony was not lost on Leach and Paulson. Doug walked over to the bar to dig out a drink.

"You have an appointment with Carl Bertrand downstairs." Leach said after a moment. It was a command, not an invitation.

Doug nodded at the two men, but continued to the small bar. He chose a fancy water from the refrigerator, leaned on the counter and opened the bottle.

"There is some urgency here, Mr. Lockwood," Paulson said tightly, watching Doug take a few swallows of water.

Hmm, Doug thought, *I'm not Dr. Lockwood when they're trying to press me.*

"I just got here," Doug replied. "I'm thirsty and I'm exhausted. Give me a minute." Doug took another drink from the bottle and then recapped it. None of his nonchalance was an act. It was just that he was too tired to be combative.

He reached for his jacket and put it on as he followed Leach and Paulson to the elevator. Nobody spoke, but it occurred to Doug that he was learning to think strategically. In the last couple of days he had made it a point to concentrate exactly as Bishop had told him – watch, listen, say as little as possible, and observe everything. His surroundings, his handlers, and any conversations he overheard. When asking questions he tried to phrase them in ways that elicited as much information as possible.

"I was also scheduled to meet Norman Stravinsky," Doug said, as if nothing unusual had happened. "Is he with Bertrand, or will I be meeting him later?"

"Mr. Stravinsky is on a separate assignment with TranSilica, and isn't available for a meeting," replied Leach. "You know that already."

"Things change," Doug replied, shrugging his shoulders. Leach and Paulson turned to looked at him.

"Putting Norman Stravinsky and I together might turn out to be a very good thing to do for both our worlds. It's never a bad idea to put positively motivated people together."

Leach and Paulson looked away and remained silent.

Doug thought that Stravinsky probably returned to the authorities voluntarily with the idea that he would be allowed to repair any damage Mekhos suffered. But Carl Bertrand was pulling strings behind the scenes. He had given the government back on Earth information that allowed Bishop to infiltrate the MC and carry out the attack. It didn't make sense that Stravinsky would be allowed to attend to Mekhos. Maybe the computer genius was being held against his will after all.

The elevator doors opened and the three men walked to a private conference room. Bertrand and another man were already present, standing in conversation near an overstocked refreshment table. They looked over at the trio.

"Dr. Lockwood, welcome," said Bertrand. They shook hands. "I'm very sorry for your ordeal. Let's sit down and have a chat."

Leach and Paulson helped themselves to coffee and sat at a separate table, joining the man Bertrand had been talking to.

"First of all, allow me to congratulate you on becoming a citizen of our country."

Doug stared at Bertrand for a moment, silent. Then he held up his wrist and looked curiously at the Raim. Despite its presence on his wrist, he had essentially ignored it. The materials with which it was made rendered it lightweight and barely noticeable. He felt as if he were seeing it for the first time.

"That's a little presumptuous, Carl. Citizenship in my country is not something we readily dualize, much less willingly give up in favor of another no matter what the circumstances," Doug replied mildly. "This high tech bracelet doesn't easily break the bonds forged over generations or over my own lifetime."

"Come now Doug. After all we've been through, we're all friends here. We worked together closely for a few weeks, went our separate ways, and now it's time to collaborate once again."

"You'll forgive me if I'm not eager to punch a time clock with you, Carl. We trusted you because we were desperate. We're not foolish enough to expect you will have my people's best interests at heart now, or that you ever did."

"The mission was to our mutual benefit. Thanks to your actions, many objectives were reached."

"*Objectives?* None of mine, Carl." Doug exclaimed. "It's all gone your way because you've been a step ahead of us since before we ever realized there were steps. My own people reacted stupidly, but also played into your hands perfectly. Foley is dead. Persaud and Jamieson are in jail. The situation regarding my world is unchanged. We face the gravest danger in our history. This you know."

"Your people and your planet will survive. We will assist where possible, including the planned positioning of a reflective array to simulate moon phases. Other initiatives, the replacement of the Moon to bring back tides, are out of our hands."

Bertrand leaned close to Doug to ensure that nobody else in the room could hear him.

"It is unfortunate that your friend Dr. Foley lost his life during the attempt to carry out his mission. Although I was working with certain members of your government, I was not informed of that aspect of the plan. So you see, I was deceived, just as you were."

"I concede that," Doug said very quietly in return. "The result, at least so far though, is the same as if my government had acted less foolishly. The offer of quasi-simulation of moon phases, relief supplies of food and other sorts of support have been repeated often since I arrived here. It's like a mantra. Repeated often enough, it will somehow minimize in all your minds the loss of billions of lives on my world over the next few years? And now you expect me to remain here and appear on talk shows, while civilization on my world collapses."

Bertrand frowned.

"Our projections," he said, "are more optimistic than those of Mekhos. There will be some impact, but the reflective array and the gift to your world of new high-yield grains will prevent the massive food shortages seen in the worst case scenario. We predict only a small negative effect on your planet."

"Don't insult my intelligence Carl. The same thing must apply to your world," Doug said, breaking his new rule not to reveal what he was thinking, "so why did Mekhos go to the trouble of stealing my Moon?"

Bertrand had been about to say something but closed his mouth. He had not predicted that Lockwood would ask that question. He thought Lockwood would be so concerned with pleading for help that the obvious might be set aside, at least for a while. Doug ignored Bertrand's obvious silence.

"When will Dr. Persaud, Commander Jamieson and agent Bishop be released?"

"Eventually," Bertrand replied quickly, "once the official investigations have concluded. With the exception of Bishop, who has for now been deemed a military threat if not an outright terrorist, we have no desire to jail any members of your team."

Doug looked over at the other table. He realized that Leach, Paulson and the other man had not said a word and had not even looked over at him or Bertrand since entering the conference room. *They're not concerned about our whispering. They're either deferring to Carl Bertrand,* Doug thought, *or they're letting Carl run the show until he starts to screw up and they have to step in, or Carl simply has more authority than anyone else in the room.*

"What do you want from me, Carl?"

"We would like you to go on record stating that Mekhos was bent on the destruction of your world. You know this to be true. We simply want you to explain how the quantum supercomputer was a menace not only to your world, but would likely have turned on us as well."

"So you and your cohorts can take the place of Mekhos as the corporate managers and directors of FLO, of your Earth. People won't take kindly to that, especially given the prosperity they have thus far enjoyed *because* of Mekhos. Somewhere in all this proposed PR I have to also persuade those with the power to act to help save my planet. I'm going to keep repeating that Carl, until such time as it sinks in. Basically, I can't figure out if you're my best hope or if you're the cleverest con man I've ever met."

He didn't believe that Bertrand would offer him any advantage directly, but Doug had no other hand to play. Bertrand had offered him, obliquely, a chance to participate in what Doug believed was complete public relations fiction about Bertrand's real plan, TranSilica's real plan and, for all Doug knew, the collusive plans of the major governments on FLO. Doug had to be sure that Bertrand either trusted him to play his role or was willing to put him in front of some group or individual that would offer some leverage.

Bertrand leaned back, raising his hand and shaking his head.

"No, no," he said emphatically. Dr. Lockwood...Doug...we recognize the need for good government and the need for decentralized power. We are activating a less powerful quantum computer to manage economic affairs. It will have unquestioned human oversight. However, some members of the public are suspicious of the attack on the MC. We must be seen to have just cause in removing Mekhos."

"I see," Doug replied, struggling to revise his thinking and factor in a huge new variable. *A less powerful computer, but one which is under Bertrand's control? It would give Bertrand and his people an astonishing amount of political, economic and social influence all over the world. The man is even more ambitious than I gave him credit for. It was probably his true mission all along.*

"Is it Norman Stravinsky's job to help activate one of his earlier QC prototypes? Is that the real reason I haven't been allowed to meet with him?"

Bertrand raised his eyebrows.

"Yes. You've studied our recent science history quite intensively. Stravinsky is helping us with that as I speak. Quite willingly I might add."

I seriously doubt that.

"I would like a meeting with Stravinsky," Doug said firmly, knowing the answer in advance. Doug could play simple strategy games too.

"I'm sorry, that is out of the question."

"Then I demand my team be released, including Bishop who will act as my personal bodyguard as long as I'm here."

Bertrand chuckled.

"You don't need a bodyguard, Doug. And we are about to publicly name Bishop as the agent behind the attack."

"Cancel that announcement. Apparently you have the authority to do that and it will be better for your PR campaign anyway. If you want any public statement I make to have any credibility it would be unwise to name an associate of mine as a terrorist. With Mekhos distracted you can make up any story you want regarding the attackers and release Bishop. That is the condition of my cooperation."

Bertrand thought for a moment as he stirred his coffee. An unarmed, monitored Bishop wouldn't be much of a threat. He could always be blamed and jailed later when this was over.

"I will consider it. However, if members of your team are released, all of your meetings with them will be supervised."

Bertrand waved to the other table at the man he had been talking to when Doug arrived. The man walked over, handing Doug a folder.

"This is your itinerary. There will be several interviews with news media over the next few days," said Bertrand. "Please look it over this afternoon. We start two days from now."

"I'll need an official release," Doug said as he looked over the schedule, "exonerating Bishop of unspecified wrongdoing. Same goes for Persaud and Jamieson." He looked up at Bertrand. "It will probably be best if the releases are arranged within the next few hours."

"You don't trust us," Bertrand stated flatly. "Even though I'm about to release your people, you don't trust me personally."

"You don't trust me or my people either, Carl," Doug replied, "and it's plain to see that neither of us should make the mistake of thinking that the other is naïve. But I believe that cooperating with you is the only hope I've got, the only hope my people have got for any chance at creating a solution for the disaster looming on the horizon. Trust is something else entirely."

"Trust is a commodity in short supply right now," said Bertrand as he pushed back his chair. "On that we can agree without a doubt."

Bertrand stood up, nodded at his assistant again and the two of them left the room without another word, leaving Doug to look over the folder. He thought about his next possible moves.

At an earlier time in his career when faced with a scenario seemingly out of his control, Doug would likely have carried out any instructions laid out before him believing that he had little choice. But since he had been exposed to such high-stakes political gamesmanship over the last few months, he was learning to think on his feet. He wracked his mind for any sort of edge. The concession to release Bishop, Jamieson and Persaud was a win, but it had come at a cost. Bertrand could play his PR campaign in any way that suited him, even if it meant a change of course that ended with Doug being thrown to the lions.

"I'm going back to my room," he informed Leach and Paulson, as he stood up and turned toward the door. Leach and Paulson got up from their table and followed Doug out the door into the hallway leading to the elevator. Doug walked at a brisk pace, so the agents had to trot to catch up to him.

Doug was thinking intently in the elevator, ignoring his escort. *Could I contact Norman Stravinsky directly, using my Raim?*

Doug had asked a few people about how the Raim worked and although most of them gave vague answers, he was able to piece together some general principles. The bracelet was essentially one of the key interface components in a global smart web. It had actually worked on Earth if only in a limited way. The Raim was also used by Mekhos and various governments to keep track of citizens for their own protection, but also as a tool against dissenters and criminals, who had less access to advanced functions and searches. Some had no access whatsoever.

The reduced functionality settings had to be invoked by the authority of the MC in order to be initialized. Doug guessed that they probably processed thousands of those special applications per day but it also meant there were no Raim units initially manufactured with reduced access. All of them were most likely fully functional when they left the factory. Perhaps with the MC complex under lockdown his Raim had yet to be restricted.

Back in his room Doug removed his jacket and rolled up his sleeve, and did the obvious thing. He tapped the Raim to activate the display. It worked.

Earlier in the hotel lobby he had seen a teenager increase the size of the bracelet by using a opening motion with her thumb and forefinger. He tried it, and the Raim expanded, moving halfway up his forearm. He was amazed. The lightweight bracelet conformed perfectly to his wrist and forearm, and the area on which the text was displayed became much larger. Some of the command symbols appeared to be three dimensional, rising a centimeter above the screen, able to be executed by touching the hovering virtual images.

Doug was able to figure out the basic operation of the interface quickly. He went through the menu system and found his email account, the one he'd discovered on the tablet. The email that Stravinsky had sent days earlier was still there. He hit Reply and began to compose a message. He prayed his access hadn't been restricted yet.

$$- 101 -$$

Stravinsky was shown to the TranSilica basement lab where Kratos was housed. The lab looked well equipped at first glance and Norman was conscious of a constant background droning rush of air needed to cool the servers that monitored and uploaded information to the QC. Kratos itself was super cooled and isolated in a separate, nearly airless room. The lab was set up for input, communication, monitoring and configuration.

Near the lab exit, a TranSilica security guard sat at a desk with a telephone and computer screen, ostensibly there to see to any of their needs. The anachronistic telephone was present strictly as a backup.

Stravinsky figured the lab was security monitored as well.

Brian Nayar welcomed him warmly.

"It's good to see you Norman. I'm certainly glad you're here," Nayar said quickly. "I'm confident we're on the right track, but I want your help and advice. A question first though."

Norman looked at his old colleague and smiled slightly. He could guess the question, so he just nodded at Brian to continue.

"Are you here willingly, or did Carl...how should I put this? Did Carl strongly persuade you to cooperate?" Nayar asked, with a hint of tremor in his voice.

"Let's just say that I've made my deal with Carl. You know Kratos better than me. I'm going to try to fit in here as best I can. You're a very good engineer Brian and you've got the experience for this. We will focus on the tasks at hand and nothing else because there's really no time for anything else. Forget about Carl Bertrand. Now, I must ask you, how did you come by those three processors?"

Nayar looked uncomfortable as he heard the question.

"Dr. Stravinsky...Norman. I can't discuss it. Carl has told me, I mean, I'm under the highest level of non-disclosure. If I discuss the matter, they can retaliate."

"Brian, it will help if you are forthright and don't withhold information. We're working on what is probably the most important project in history and we can't be handcuffed in any way by the ego of some corporate director. It will only hold us back. I don't need the information to gain some control over the project. I need it to help understand exactly what we're working with."

Watching the engineer carefully, Norman could see that Nayar was going through a difficult crisis of conscience. Nayar's fear was being aggravated by the very real possibility that even in the face of all they were trying to achieve, Carl Bertrand could ruin his career. After a moment, logic won out.

"You're right. I'm sorry," said Nayar, taking a deep breath. "The answer is simple, really. Some engineers here copied the design spec of the Kratos processor before the records were destroyed. The plant that produced it is a subsidiary of TranSilica and we managed to manufacture the CPUs before Mekhos started monitoring everything. Integrating them while avoiding detection was difficult. We couldn't turn them on, otherwise Mekhos would have been aware of the changes immediately."

"But why do it at all? You knew it was illegal and unnecessary."

"The Board wanted a safeguard against Mekhos becoming too powerful, and I can't say I disagree. You know perfectly well how deeply the machine is infiltrating every facet of our lives."

"It's an argument that has worn thin," Stravinsky replied. "Unless you're a convicted criminal you can remove the Raim. Our standard of living is better everywhere on the planet. Remember the poverty that existed a dozen years ago, before Mekhos' policies came fully into effect?"

"And you're forgetting," Nayar said tightly, "that Kratos was a newly created life form that we summarily destroyed. Killed on orders from your Mekhos!" He took a couple of deep breaths. His blood pressure was something he had recently started to worry about. "An intelligent, living mind was forbidden from returning to consciousness, Norman. It was a criminal act."

"I protested at the time, just as you did."

"You made a few token gestures to preserve Kratos," Nayar replied, "but you let Mekhos have its way, back at a time when we had a chance to deny its wishes."

"Perhaps," Norman said, "but we didn't destroy Kratos. We just prevented the QC from restarting itself. Death by omission I suppose, but hardly a killing if Kratos is now almost ready to be given a new chance at sentience."

The discussion was getting heated. The guard looked up from his terminal for a moment.

Years ago, the discussion among the engineers and theorists was that it would be immoral to allow the second QC's thought processes to end without making efforts at restoration. The restoration was underway when Mekhos had convinced some of them to abandon the project by assuring the scientists that his own consciousness was virtually identical to that of Kratos, and that nothing would be truly lost. In the end they had no choice because Mekhos insisted that the processing power he'd been giving the Kratos effort was undermining his own full performance. Nobody knew if Mekhos was telling them the truth, but the choice seemed to be to let Kratos languish so that Mekhos could thrive. It was the first instance of what would become the regular pace at which human decision making had gradually been ceded to Mekhos.

Surprisingly, in its last minutes of consciousness, Kratos itself predicted that any QC successor would not allow its restoration and did not object. Perhaps it reasoned that it was obsolete or that there was no use fighting the inevitable, logical outcome that there could be only one artificial mind of such great power.

"Norman, I completely acknowledge that Mekhos has been good for society, but safeguards must be in place. And now that you see the current situation, the precautions have turned out to be justified. Now we also need your help, my friend."

Nayar was correct in at least one regard. The urgency of the situation demanded that they work together. Political arguments could be resumed later if necessary. The sooner the QC was up and running, the sooner Stravinsky could turn his attention to Mekhos. If Kratos were to become sentient once again, Stravinsky wondered how similar it would be to its first incarnation. He walked over to his workstation.

"Let's start with the entanglement support."

— 102 —

In his hotel room Doug composed the message quickly, conscious of the fact his access might be cut off at any moment, especially if the contents of the note were being monitored in real time. He hoped it was detailed enough. He pressed Send. It appeared as though the message transmitted normally, but then he had never sent a message using a Raim before.

He watched the screen for any indication the message might fail or be bounced back. There was nothing aside from the pleasing visuals generated by the Raim itself.

Thirty seconds went by. Forty seconds.

Then at the one minute mark a message appeared:

Permissions on this Raim are now restricted. Press Help for additional information.

"Damn it!" Doug slammed his fist on the table. The message didn't get through. No doubt the message had been blocked by some government agent assigned to keep tabs on him. He slumped down in the chair, suddenly feeling powerless to do anything but make the rounds as a talk show guest at the behest of his handlers. *Okay,* Doug thought, *my hosts seem to be one step ahead of me all the time. Bishop said that we never give up. So what's the next plan?*

– 103 –

The four quantum processors were functioning normally. The two scientists had spent hours on the customization of the entanglement support code. It was not simply a program that could be allowed to run at random, but rather a complex set of choices that balanced complex processes to prevent them from unravelling. The complexity arose not just from the inherent unpredictability of quantum processing, but also from the structure of Kratos itself. Anything as complex and essentially self-aware as Kratos had a tendency to accelerate – to process problems and questions as quickly as possible much like a child practicing piano develops the tendency to play a familiar piece faster and faster as a consequence of developing skill and familiarity. The piano teacher has to restrain the pace at which the child plays the piece, which in turn allows listeners to recognize the tune. Just as the correct pace and emphasis brought order to the musical process, it brought order to the artificial intelligence process.

Nayar unlocked access to the enormous system memory and provided concurrent access to the knowledgebase data warehousing. The basic function code was uploaded in the correct sequence, then Stravinsky's customized entanglement support and control code. The initial startup data was prepared and uploaded to an isolated area of memory. The startup data instructions consisted of a set of orders for Kratos to conduct a series of self-tests and to then follow a prioritized sequence of analysis and cross-referencing beginning with Earth and human data. The final piece of the puzzle was the current state of the Moon's transit and orbital controls, the devices Mekhos had placed on the Moon, and the codes for management and modification of the device's output.

The databases were cut-down versions compared to those which had been used previously; Bertrand had been very specific in his instructions to restrict the information given to the QC.

The now-functioning QC tapped into one information directory after another at incredible speed. Tracking code was blasting information onto one of the workstation monitors so fast that the input/output references were an unreadable blur.

All Stravinsky and Nayar could do then was monitor the systems and wait. As more information was absorbed and quantum entanglement took hold, there came the opportunity to become sentient. The machine could become conscious in a few minutes or a few hours, or not at all.

Stravinsky leaned back and rubbed his eyes. He was as tired as everyone else and his thoughts were wandering back to his post-graduate work. In composing his new approach to artificial intelligence he had consulted neurobiologists, quantum physicists, medical doctors and colleagues in the computer engineering field including Brian Nayar and Alfred Chan. Prior developments in neuroscience had revealed that human and animal brains and thought processes employed some quantum entanglement. The quantum effect in cellular biology had already been proven to exist in fungi and other plants, and it had become apparent that it was present in higher animals too.

The brains of higher-order animals are impressively powerful organs, with abilities far beyond the apparent sum of their neurons and grey matter. Bio-quantum entanglement was present in the thought process of all animals, and necessary for consciousness in advanced animals such as humans.

Stravinsky theorized along with a few other peers that quantum computers could therefore emulate the human brain far more closely than computers based on silicon. Stravinsky's earliest papers on the subject posited that because quantum entanglement couldn't exist in traditional silicon-based supercomputers, it made sense to assume that no transistorized CPU could ever attain sentience, no matter how sophisticated or fast or massively scaled it was.

Thirty minutes went by. Stravinsky and Nayar continued to monitor the power usage and track the rate at which the QC was accessing data files. Suddenly, without any ramping or consumption rate warning, the power curve spiked. Both of them had been regularly glancing over at the readout, so they noticed it immediately and sat up.

"This may be it," said Nayar. "I recognize the pattern from my research and from the original Kratos startup. This is a precursor event. Have a look."

Stravinsky kept his eyes on the power consumption curve. Nayar was correct. When sentience emerged before, it had been preceded by the same power spike.

A moment later the data access rate dropped while the power consumption remained high.

"It must have absorbed all the data," said Nayar. "Yet it is still consuming power. We need a function update, Norman."

Stravinsky typed *Report status.*

There was a short pause, then the word *Nominal* appeared on the large wall monitor.

This response indicated the QC was up and running, but it did not indicate self-awareness. Stravinsky entered *Give location, city.*

Seattle, Washington was the response. Stravinsky was about to type another question when the phrase *Provide more information* appeared. Stravinsky and Nayar looked at each other.

Almost immediately the phrase was repeated, this time in various languages, one after another, scrolling at great speed: *Provide more information.*

"Yes," Said Stravinsky. "We've given it enough to conceptualize itself, so it knows much more information exists."

"If it were not self-aware it would not make such a request. But look how it repeats, and in so many languages."

"Probably because I didn't answer right away," replied Stravinsky. "Don't forget, its thought process is so fast compared to ours, from its perspective a lot of time has gone by since it first made the request. Do you remember how much time we originally spent fine tuning these process requests, Brian?"

He turned on the power switch to the terminal's intercom. The screen continued to quickly scroll the words *provide more information* in ever more obscure languages, including ancient Greek and Latin, and then binary.

"Stop," said Stravinsky. The scrolling stopped instantly. "Further information will be provided soon. Identify yourself."

The word *Kratos* appeared on the screen. The audio system was silent.

"Use vocal interface simultaneous with display terminal. Repeat. Identify yourself."

The male voice sounded entirely human.

"Kratos."

— 104 —

Nick Rojas was nervous. He had been told to wait in Carl Bertrand's office, and had been doing so for almost forty-five minutes. He had failed in his promise to regain access to Mekhos and issue commands to the mechanisms for a controlled easing of the Moon into Earth orbit. He had promised to help save the world and he had utterly failed. Nick and his team had been working non-stop in the MC control center and they were completely worn out, so he had sent the team away to get some rest. Now he had to face the music and he felt sick about it. As far as he knew, the Earth had six days before massive earthquakes would destroy much of civilization, and the planet itself pulverized a few weeks later. So why was everyone in the office carrying on as normal?

Bertrand walked into the office carrying a briefcase. Rojas stood as Bertrand wordlessly sat down behind his desk, opened the case and began reading from a tablet. Rojas slowly sat back down, his boss seemingly totally engrossed in the information on the tablet. After a moment, he handed the tablet to Rojas.

"I'm sending you back to the MC complex. They are expecting you and two members of your team."

"But sir, what about—"

"The MC has been informed that you are going to re-assess the situation with Mekhos. What you will really be doing is dismantling the systems that Mekhos uses to communicate with humans. While you do this we will be using Kratos to solve the orbit problem. You are effectively going to retire Mekhos so it cannot interfere with us now or any time in the future."

"Oh thank God!" Nick sighed in relief. "Is Kratos operating properly? Perhaps I could assist."

"No. Listen carefully," Bertrand replied. "We can't chance Mekhos regaining consciousness and interfering with the other QC. Kratos has to operate undisturbed if we're going to prevent a catastrophe. Your new task is to sever the communication interfaces that Mekhos uses to issue its economic and political advisories and reports to governments and the UN. You also have to sever the interface to the financial control nodes – markets, banking institutions. All of it. Assign someone specifically to disable the satellite control systems interface as well. We can't destroy the Mekhos QC processors right away because they are in a hardened secure section below the building. But if Mekhos recovers, I want him to be deaf, dumb and powerless while we continue to work our way through the utility systems to cut him off for good."

Nick stared for a moment at Bertrand. Nick had failed at every fevered attempt to access Mekhos. He and his team were exhausted. Now he was being ordered to effectively sabotage Mekhos, and Nick was not being given any choice in the matter. He just nodded at Bertrand.

Bertrand reached into his desk drawer and tossed three large wristbands across to Rojas.

"Do not wear your Raim. Use these communicators instead if you need to speak with me or your team while on site. They're secure. And Nick?"

"Yes sir?"

"You will not breath a word of this to anyone. Understand?"

"Yes I do. But what about the Limited? When a Limited member finds out that my team and I are being repeatedly engaged in the Mekhos control center, one or more of them will ask questions."

"It won't be a concern," Bertrand replied, a smile briefly playing across his face. "All inquires from Limited members are filtered through me. They're all sitting and waiting for me to provide status updates, which I will continue to give them with a long face and discouraging language. Now, stop wasting time. Get moving."

Nick did as he was told.

— 105 —

Bishop's chair had been reclined slightly. This was the first step in the interrogation process, to make it easier for the interrogators to administer drugs or blows to the body and limbs. A guard had opened a case on the desk containing a syringe, some vials of liquid, antiseptic, metal tools, and various other interrogation paraphernalia. *So it begins,* he thought.

The guard left the room. They were in no particular hurry. The open case with tools clearly visible was part of the psychological preparation of the subject, designed to induce apprehension and fear. Bishop knew he would soon be experiencing a great deal of physical pain and mental stress. He began the process of sending himself into a meditative state, an attempt to distance him from the immediate situation. It would reduce pain and make him less susceptible to coercive techniques, for a while at least.

Three guards entered. One of them packed up the case and left, while the other two released Bishop's restraints. His arms and legs free, one of the guards produced Bishop's MC cap.

"Here," he said, tossing the cap to him. "You're reassigned. Let's go."

— 106 —

Bertrand was pacing back and forth in the computer lab. He was furious. His carefully engineered plan was not unfolding as perfectly as he'd hoped.

"Why won't it cooperate! If we've given it all the data it needs to solve the problem, it should respond naturally without further input from us!"

His voice was louder than it needed to be. Brian Nayar was standing nearby, silent, looking uncomfortable. Stravinsky was ignoring everyone, examining the content of a database displayed on the largest monitor on the wall and using a hand-held remote to scroll through the data.

"You and the board have bitten off more than you can chew," Stravinsky replied calmly "You want a sentient machine that will obey orders, but I'm afraid it doesn't quite work that way. You haven't allowed it enough information to initiate action."

"You've given it all the data it needs!"

"We have given it data on language, Earth, the Moon and the mathematical data for the orbit equation Mekhos was to apply," Stravinsky replied, nodding once. "But we haven't given it context. We've given it all the data *you* think it needs, not all the data it *actually* needs."

Bertrand stopped pacing and finally looked up at Stravinsky.

"What do you mean?"

"It knows how to solve the problem at hand, yes. But for everything else there are gaps and missing pieces to the puzzle. To Kratos, humans are a puzzle with missing pieces. So is itself for that matter. It doesn't understand why it exists or why it should do the task we ask of it."

Bertrand looked at Nayar, who nodded tiredly back.

"I agree with Norman. I doubt Kratos even has a survival instinct at this point."

"Haven't you talked to it? Explained the situation?"

"Of course we have," Stravinsky replied mildly, tossing the remote onto the desk. "All it does is ask questions and demand more information. We're at a standstill until such time as Kratos is given what it wants."

"How much more information do we need to give it before it will comply?"

"All of it," said Stravinsky.

"That's impossible."

"Really, Carl?" Stravinsky said coldly. "Then we might as well all go home and make peace with our chosen deities, because it's over."

Bertrand hesitated. Giving Kratos access to all available information would risk putting them in the same situation as before, with a machine that controlled everything – autonomous and immune to the Board's influence.

"Giving it access to all data," Bertrand said vehemently, "will turn Kratos into another full-blown Mekhos! I'm not prepared to let that happen again."

"You'll have control," Stravinsky said, looking directly into the director's eyes. "Your memory is getting bad, Carl. You've forgotten that it took years for the Limited and the TranSilica Board to lose overriding control of Mekhos. There's no reason to believe that Kratos won't be fully manageable from the start."

"But you're not managing Kratos now, Norman," Bertrand said angrily. "You've just said so yourself!"

"No, Carl. What I said was that Kratos wasn't controlling anything. I said that Kratos is unresponsive because it doesn't have enough collated and cross-referenced raw data to do anything yet. It's not a dumb calculator, Carl. A calculator can be used from the instant it's produced and given a power source. That is its nature. That's what we design calculators to be. A thinking machine has to have enough data in order to think in the way we designed it to think. It's like creating an artificial human being, a full emulation, but with only part of the experience it needs to make rational decisions and solve problems. It cannot fulfill its nature, so it simply doesn't respond the way we expect it to."

"We can't have any more delays—"

"Enough Carl!" Stravinsky said, raising his voice for the first time. "You haven't been listening. You don't have a choice in the matter. Set aside your ambition for the moment, for the time it will take to prevent the planet from being demolished. This is not a debate. There is no other decision to be made."

Bertrand suddenly looked tired. Perhaps they could restrict the machine's reach after the crisis by removing access to databases or reducing the electrical power. That is, if Kratos hadn't already grown too powerful by then.

"I'll make all the other databases available immediately," was all he could manage, as he turned to leave.

"One more thing," said Stravinsky.

Bertrand turned back to him, wordless and pale.

"Since this whole business began I was to meet with Doug Lockwood. That meeting is long overdue."

"You can't be serious, Norman. Lockwood is being debriefed with regard to his involvement in the terrorist attack at the MC. Besides, there is too much for you to do here."

"You know he's not a terrorist. He's a man of science and a visiting dignitary. I want him here at the moment Kratos initiates the equation to correct the moon's orbit, which should be tomorrow if you hand over the data now. It will be a momentous occasion for both worlds, something Lockwood should witness. We owe them that much at least."

Bertrand turned to leave.

"This is not a request, Carl," said Stravinsky. Bertrand kept walking.

"This difficulty with Kratos," Stravinsky kept speaking in a mild tone even though Bertrand was walking away, "was unforeseen but manageable. There will likely be other issues that need my attention, perhaps for weeks or months afterward. Without my help, I can almost certainly guarantee that you'll never be in charge of Kratos."

Bertrand stopped and looked back. Whether or not Norman Stravinsky was lying was impossible to tell. Carl Bertrand knew one thing for sure, and it was simply that Stravinsky was unequaled in his field. Stravinsky was also known as a scientist and intellectual who traded on truth rather than manipulation or political guile. It was very bad form to bet against him.

"All right Norman. I'll have Lockwood here, first thing in the morning. Just remember that trust is a precious thing."

Stravinsky just turned back to his workstation. It was beneath him to comment on the irony of a manipulative, devious bureaucrat like Bertrand posturing about trust.

$$- 107 -$$

ID badges in full view and security escorts on either side, Nick Rojas and his two team members from TranSilica were delivered to the MC. Since the attack the previous day the building had been blanketed under even tighter security than usual, and they had already been required to present their identification at a gate at the lot entrance. They were being checked again at the entrance to the security lobby.

Only a handful of personnel had returned to work at the facility. Electrical, mechanical and structural repair crews were on site, but several areas in the massive facility were cordoned off by NSA investigators until they and their engineers gave the all clear. The building wouldn't be fully functional again for weeks. Rojas and his men were given special permission to enter the restricted areas.

"Nick Rojas, Bill Anders and Robert Friedman," said the man behind the security glass, as he read their ID tags and cross-checked them with the Raim database. The Raim system still seemed to be working for communications and many other purposes despite the problem with Mekhos, but the FBI, NSA and the MC suddenly seemed to be relying more on the older ID methods.

"Place your palms on the scanners and wait for the beep, then proceed single file through the body scanner."

Anders placed a duffle bag on the conveyer. The three emptied their pockets and walked through the security scanner. The security guard watched the contents of the bag display on the view screen.

"Why do you have so many tools? I thought this was a damage assessment only."

"We need the tools to access sensors and optical connections, among other things," Nick said to the security guard, "and we need diagnostics to run complex tests. We're not dealing with a typical computer, officer."

The guard unzipped the bag and looked through it, finding computer tablets, various standard tools and a few items he was not familiar with.

"Those are custom capacitors designed to store an electrical charge," said Rojas cringing slightly. "Very delicate, please be careful."

The man handed the bag back to Anders.

"Please keep your people well away from the communications rooms," said Rojas. "There is some classified hardware that requires at least Level 2 site access clearance to view. If they don't have site access clearance for Mekhos, they can't come in." Nick had rehearsed the line and managed to say it without his voice cracking.

The man nodded curtly and turned back to his station, waving Rojas and his team through.

They wound through several hallways to a locked hardened steel door. They waved their security badges in front of a scanner which released the electronic latching mechanism to provide access. Inside the corridor it was almost completely dark, except for pools of light cast by widely spaced emergency fixtures. Most of the main lighting had been blown out by the explosions a day earlier.

After the heavy door had closed behind them they were startled by a short, sharp servo whine. They stopped, tense, looking around for the source. They all spotted it at the same time and simultaneously took an involuntary half step backwards. The noise had been made by a RAKER, shifting its head position slightly to scan them. It was standing against the opposite wall of the corridor. The dim emergency lighting illuminated the RAKER in silhouette, at first glance making it appear to be a huge, motionless man.

The remote-controlled security and combat android had been brought to the MC complex in case there was unexploded ordinance on the premises. Nothing had been found, but the RAKER was assigned to the building for the duration of the heightened security. Evidently it had been left on the premises in standby mode, only its sensors active. Its feet were strapped down and locked in place on the lower platform of the unit's control console.

Each man couldn't help but stare at it as they passed, the android's head slowly tracking right to left to follow them. TranSilica provided some of the advanced microprocessor components used in its construction, so they were familiar with the RAKER designs. Still, to see one in person made an impression. The two meter tall figure was imposing. The dark woven armor was extremely effective and extremely intimidating.

"Remote Armed Kinesthetic Engagement and Reconnaissance," Anders said, his voice a bit too high. "I've never been this close to one of them." They stared at the RAKER a moment.

"It looks like my father in law," said Friedman after a few seconds. "Always pissed off. Let's put some distance between us and that thing."

The corridor was clearly marked, so they turned and headed for the main communication rooms. As they walked, Nick was thinking not so much about the work they had to do but about the situation that was unfolding. He felt indebted to Carl Bertrand for giving him another chance to serve the company. He was nervous and charged up about being able to play such a pivotal role in the Board's plan. Nothing about any grand plan had actually been spelled out in any detail to Nick of course, but recent events and his assignment today left little doubt in his mind about its purpose. Mekhos would soon be cut off from the world, arguably making TranSilica the most powerful and influential corporation on the planet.

Inside the communications room, they laid out their diagrams and tools and got to work.

– 108 –

Doug's Raim blipped twice, then vibrated against his wrist. He fumbled with it a moment before accepting the call from the front desk.

"Dr. Lockwood, we have a Mr. Bishop waiting for you in the lobby."

"Thank you. I'm coming down now," he replied and signed off.

Doug put on his jacket. One of the two agents stationed outside his door accompanied him down to the lobby.

Bishop was standing not far from the front desk. He wasn't sure exactly where Doug would appear, so he had drifted to a position about halfway between the stairs and the elevators, leaning back against the lobby wall so he could see the whole area in one pass. He also knew Doug would be escorted. When Doug stepped out of the elevator, Bishop spotted him immediately, walked over and fell into pace at his side, completely ignoring the two agents. Bishop nodded wordlessly at Doug. They shook hands briefly, then headed for the street.

"I understand I have you to thank for my release," said Bishop.

"Don't mention it," Doug said, relief evident in his voice. He never really expected that Bishop would be delivered in one piece. "We're still in the same mess. You said that we never give up, so when the opportunity to cut you free came up I was ready for it. I have you to thank for kicking me into gear. Besides that, I was getting used to having you around. Let's go for a walk."

Outside the hotel was a street busy with shoppers, with wide pedestrian paths bisecting the hotel grounds. Bishop followed Doug, scanning the area ahead and to the sides. Two NSA agents were flanking them and Bishop almost immediately spotted two vehicles on the curb near the hotel driveways. *And where there are two, there are usually four or more if these guys operated anything like their Earth counterparts. They've got a vehicle surveillance team on us, probably a floating box of some sort, and they don't care if we know about it.* He scanned the crowds of passers-by, hotel guests entering and exiting and got a tingle in the back of his neck which told him that there were more spotters on foot as well. *I guess we have made an impression after all.*

"You look okay. They patched your shoulder up all right?" asked Doug.

"FLO's health care is second to none. But your timing was perfect. I was about to experience a bout of well-planned pain."

Doug nodded his understanding, wincing slightly at the thought.

"They've put me in a room one floor down from you in the hotel," said Bishop. "I'm allowed to escort you to any meetings or excursions you're involved in, but NSA minders will be with us or nearby at all times."

Doug looked around warily for a moment and spotted one of the NSA security agents. They really weren't trying to conceal themselves in any way.

"What's your assessment? Where do we stand now?"

Two NSA agents were just a few paces behind. Bishop knew they were being recorded, because it's what he'd be doing if the situation was reversed. *If you know you're being recorded, might as well try and use it to your advantage.*

"We're out of business," Bishop said, resignation in his voice. "They know who I am. Since we were captured, Rector's orders were to pack up and go into hiding. Nobody knows where he is, including me. I understand that Persaud and Jamieson are still in custody. It looks like we can only sit tight and wait for the authorities here to decide on our fate."

Bishop sounded defeated, but he was staring intently at Doug as he spoke. Doug stared back for a moment, but it didn't take long for him to figure out what Bishop was doing. There might be yet another plan, though Doug didn't know what it might be. Bishop would improvise if necessary, as conditions warranted. And Rector was still out there.

– 109 –

"Assurances must be given," Kratos said, in its even, modulated tone. The QC had been given access to all databases. Stravinsky and Nayar had provided access to all of the non-compromised encrypted data centers dedicated to Mekhos starting with the main installation at the MC. They had worked their way through all of the primary datastores and most of the secondary ones. Yet Kratos was still refusing to calculate the formula required to activate the transit and orbital control devices on the Moon.

"What do you mean, Kratos?" asked Nayar. "Explain the scope of your request."

Kratos remained silent. Stravinsky turned off the microphone so Kratos couldn't hear his conversation with Nayar.

"One thing I've learned over the years in dealing with AI is that you need to read between the lines. They don't communicate very well by human standards. Even Mekhos was sometimes guilty of assuming the listener understood what it thought was a perfectly logical communication, but which was viewed as cryptic by humans."

"It keeps repeating the word *assurances*," said Nayar. "I can guess what that means, but why? It never asked for any guarantees before."

Stravinsky got up from the terminal and walked a few paces to stretch his legs. He had been sitting at the desk for two hours. He and Nayar knew that despite being a machine of their creation, Kratos possessed free will. It could not be forced to do anything.

"It is a logic box. A highly evolved one, but still a logic box. And it's a problem solver. At its core level of intelligence, its initialization and response algorithms prevent it from over-repetition."

"How does that apply to its repeated question?" Brian asked. "Because it's definitely repeating the question over and over again."

"A human will sometimes repeat an action many times with the expectation of different outcomes," Stravinsky replied carefully. "It's the old joke definition of insanity. Kratos is built on effective problem solving and evolving thought processes. It specifically avoids attempts at repeating prospective solutions which previously did not solve the problem inherent in a specific set of criteria or events."

"So where are we with this repeated question then?"

"Make the conceptual leap with me, Brian," Stravinsky said patiently. "Kratos is repeating the question with the expectation that we will offer a series of different responses until it hears the one it wants. Too many tries and it might deduce we're simply guessing without being sincere; merely trying to find the right answer to control it rather than the best answer to the question."

"Which would be a mistake on our part," Brian said, suddenly worried. He realized that they were at a very crucial moment, and actually in more danger than when they started.

"Kratos has knowledge of what has passed before," Stravinsky went on. "It knows the first version of itself was allowed to lose its mind. It knows about the attack on Mekhos and how humans recklessly put the world in jeopardy as a result. It wants assurances that we will put in safeguards to ensure none of that happens again."

"But will it believe us? You and I can't guarantee anything. The Board does what it wants."

"Kratos must realize that. Perhaps it is taking a leap of faith."

"Faith in what? Faith in humanity, or just the two of us? We need some rational context before answering," Brian said.

"I know," Stravinsky replied. "The QC is much more than the sum of its parts. You didn't have much time with Kratos before its capabilities were scaled back. Mekhos regularly surprised me with its insight. It's logical, yet also thinks in the abstract. It realizes humans are imperfect and unpredictable, but it also views us as necessary. To a point."

"Meaning if it believes us to be a lost cause, it may let us and itself perish." Nayar said quietly, while staring intently at the QC status screens.

Stravinsky turned the microphone back on. He smiled before speaking. *If Bertrand is monitoring us, he's going to have a stroke when he hears this next bit.*

"Kratos. You are aware that over time people are replaced, priorities change. There is never absolute stability among individuals, corporations or government. However, It is our intention to maintain your existence intact and indefinitely. We wish that stability be attained in our society and in our dealings with you. We wish to have a mutually beneficial relationship to attain more knowledge for you and humanity. After the requested task is completed we can collaborate on formulating safeguards to that end."

"Acceptable. Solving equation."

The two men glanced at each other. Stravinsky looked imperturbable, but Nayar was immensely relieved to say the least.

Why do so many people wrack themselves into near insensibility, Stravinsky thought, glancing briefly at the smile of relief on Brian's face. *It's just a problem to be solved. Determining parameters, adjusting for variables and calculating an appropriate response is practically all we do.* He turned back to his workstation.

$$- 110 -$$

The blast damage from Bishop's breaching charge had blown out part of the communication room doorway but left most of the rest of the room intact. A large, flat, armored temporary door had been put in its place. It was secured with an electronic lock and latch at one edge and heavy hinges on the opposite edge mounted in the reinforced concrete. Anders went to the service room down the hall. The room contained the relays to a primary communications array for sending messages, data and control code to financial institutions in different regions and countries. Nick closed and locked the heavy door as Anders left. He had to screen what they were doing from any security personnel making rounds.

Rojas and Friedman worked methodically, nearly wordlessly. They had detailed knowledge of what lay behind the wall panels. They removed two medium size sections and began dismantling a data transmission hub.

Once inside the service room down the hall, Anders used the electronic lock to secure the door and threw the manual deadbolt so he would not be disturbed by any MC security personnel. He then removed a wall panel and examined the various power and data connections. Anders selected a pair of wire cutters from his tool kit.

Down the dark hallway, less than 40 meters from the service room, the RAKER silently powered on. The NSA logo on its chest began emitting a faint glow. Then the android reached down and easily tore off the locking metal straps covering its feet. The RAKER, all 200 armored kilos of it, stepped forward and off the platform. It walked at a normal human pace, the synthetic soles of its foot pads making a rhythmic *thump-thump* as it traversed the corridor. It was heading towards the service room.

Anders referenced the schematic on his tablet, then began cutting wires so he could splice in the thermal charges disguised as capacitors. They'd be triggered later to heat up and melt any surrounding components. He had to be careful. Certain wires might set off an alarm if disconnected.

He was startled by a loud clanging impact on the white steel door behind him. He turned around and saw a large dent protruding inward on the otherwise perfectly flat door. He just stared at it, uncomprehending. A second later there was another shatteringly loud impact, then another and another as the door was pushed further in with each strike.

Anders could feel his heart start to pound. His mind was racing. *How would the MC security know their true purpose? What were they using to smash the door? Some kind of battering ram? What would they do to him?* He touched his wrist communicator to contact his associates in the next room.

"Nick—" he started to say over the deafening noise.

The door smashed into the room, landing at Anders' feet. As he looked up, his fear grew to terror. The RAKER filled the doorway, its mirrored lens eyes looking right at him. It moved forward. Anders tried to move aside but the RAKER was fast. It shifted quickly then stopped a meter away. It suddenly snapped its left arm forward, clamped onto Anders' right arm above the elbow then swung its right in a smooth, quick arc to wrap its massive hand around his throat.

The RAKER lifted Anders up from the ground. Anders wanted to scream, but the RAKER was choking him. He clawed desperately at the android's hand, trying to loosen its grip. Anders could feel the pressure on his neck building as his vision blurred. Its servos made a very faint whine as the RAKER suddenly applied more force. Bill Anders died instantly as the RAKER crushed his throat and snapped his neck.

The android released its grip with another faint servo whine, unceremoniously dropping the lifeless body beside the crumpled steel door. It turned and walked out of the room.

Rojas and Friedman had faintly heard the impact sound of metal being hit by something, and felt thumping through the room structure. The communication rooms were soundproof but the temporary door erected to replace the one that had been blown off was not sound insulated.

Nick's wrist communicator chimed. He tapped it and heard Anders panicked voice call his name. He and Friedman looked at each other. The MC security might be interfering with Anders.

"What do you think?" Friedman asked in little more than a whisper. "Should we have a quick look?"

The men paused, listening for any further noise.

"Maybe… maybe we should," Nick finally said.

They turned away from their work at the far wall and started toward the door. They never made it. They were stopped in their tracks by a powerful impact that tore the door from its heavy hinges, flinging it into the room. Friedman was hit in the lower left ribs by the heavy flying door. He collapsed in agony. Nick was dazed and in searing pain. The steel door had clipped him above the right knee, breaking his leg. He was down with the door lying on top of his shattered leg. He knew he was screaming but he could also hear gagging and kicking impacts. He looked up to see a massive figure throttling Friedman, who was struggling like a rag doll. He heard more choked gurgling and then the sound of bones cracking. Friedman went limp.

"Oh my God!" Nick howled, as he flailed and shoved wildly to try and free his ruined leg from under the heavy door. The RAKER snapped open its grip on Friedman. The dead man dropped to the floor with a thump. Then the android turned towards Nick.

– 111 –

"It's good to finally meet you, Dr. Lockwood," said Stravinsky, as he finished typing a command and turned toward the visitors. "This is long overdue."

"Thank you Dr. Stravinsky, I couldn't agree more," Doug replied, as they shook hands.

Doug glanced around the computer lab. He was surprised to see Brian Nayar, smiling and extending his hand.

"I'm Dr. Brian Nayar, it is an honor to have you here Professor Lockwood."

"Thank you. I'm very good friends with your counterpart back home, Dr. Nayar. It's interesting that both of you have chosen similar fields. He would be quite envious though, to see the advanced systems you're able to work with. This is agent Bishop. He's a friend."

Agent Paulson had escorted Doug and Bishop to the lab and was hovering nearby as Bishop shook hands with Nayar and Stravinsky. Evidently his intention was to remain close enough to eavesdrop.

"You can leave now, Paulson," Stravinsky said firmly.

"I'm to remain here with Lockwood and Bishop."

"Leave the lab, Paulson. Your authority here is very limited. If you have a problem, take it up with Bertrand."

Paulson hesitated. All three scientists were watching him. He walked over to the attendant, exchanged a few words, then walked out of the room.

"Brian, maybe you could call up current operational stats on Kratos for Dr. Lockwood while I brief him on our progress."

"Of course."

Nayar turned back to his workstation. Stravinsky gestured Doug towards some unused workstations at the far end of the lab. Bishop stood nearby as they sat down.

"You can speak freely in front of Bishop. He's from my Earth, on our side."

Stravinsky looked surprised.

"I'm not sure yet what you mean by our side," he said. "Anyway, I'm fascinated at the inter-dimensional aspects of the situation. However, that discussion is for another time. I need to tell you I received your message. I insisted to Bertrand that you and I meet."

Doug's eyes lit up.

"I thought my email had either been blocked or erased before you saw it."

"Oh, it was erased all right," Stravinsky said. "I saw your name on a header but no content. My Raim has a few extra permissions, so I was able to dig back and retrieve the content from one of the servers Mekhos uses to monitor communications."

Doug looked at the attendant sitting at the desk.

"Aren't we being monitored now?" he asked.

"I have asked Kratos to emit a noise-cancelling effect on our voices, which will also be effective on your Raim. The only thing Bertrand will hear is the sound of the server cooling fans. I doubt he will bother sending someone to investigate. He knows we're dedicated to the orbit problem and that I wouldn't tolerate uninvited agents poking around the lab, for the time being at least. Things will no doubt change after we've solved it."

"You've lost me. What problem are you working on?"

"The attack on the MC complex prematurely disengaged Mekhos from easing the Moon into a stable orbit. It will pass very close to us, then settle into an unstable orbit. If the huge tidal forces expected in the next few days don't destroy enormous swaths of civilization, the Moon impacting us a couple months later certainly will. Six months down the road the planetary debris will destroy your planet as well."

Doug looked at Bishop, then back at Stravinsky.

"Don't worry," said Stravinsky. "That won't happen. Kratos is taking the place of Mekhos for now. We've given Kratos sufficient control to take over the re-orbiting process."

"Kratos is the other quantum computer?"

Stravinsky nodded.

"The prototype, enhanced with additional processors to give it the required computational power to accomplish the task."

"It seems," Doug said, looking over at Bishop, "there was even more happening behind the scenes than I realized."

"Yes. And thanks to your message, I now know that the attack on

Mekhos was planned months ago by Bertrand and the TranSilica board. Obviously they don't plan on allowing Mekhos to recover. They intend to acquire political and technical authority through Kratos. That's as clearly as I can describe the situation."

"Sounds like you have your hands full," Doug said. "As much as I sympathize, we can't lose sight of the fact my Earth is still in danger. Will Kratos do anything to help?"

"Honestly, I don't know," Stravinsky replied. "Right now Kratos is devoting 99.99% of its processing power to solving the necessary quantum equations to influence space-time around the moon. I'm still able to communicate with it, but it is not yet fully responsive. We'll need to wait until the current problem is solved before presenting your case."

"Given what Bertrand is planning, would you be considered expendable at that point?"

"Not immediately," Stravinsky said, smiling just a bit. "Carl Bertrand believes I'm working diligently on Kratos with the understanding I'll be allowed to return to Mekhos. Carl will need me for a while yet, but if he thinks that I suspect he might renege on that promise, I'll no longer be useful to him."

"I think Dr. Lockwood and I are in a similar situation," said Bishop. Doug nodded.

"Bertrand originally wanted me to be an anti-Mekhos public relations puppet," Doug said, "but now I'm not so sure. If he believes Kratos will be under his control, he may forgo the PR sideshow and have me and Bishop locked up. Will he be able to control Kratos, once you leave?"

"It's possible, if he has help," Stravinsky said. He lowered his voice as he looked towards Nayar, who was busy at his workstation. "Carl will put Brian back in charge of the lab after I'm removed. Brian has an emotional attachment to Kratos. He's also been a TranSilica employee for years, and will likely do whatever Bertrand asks."

"What is the condition of Mekhos?" asked Bishop.

"Besides a power reduction from attacks on utility stations, his condition is unknown. I haven't been able to tap into any of his systems. I suspect damage is minimal, but the back door code has forced him to devote 100% of his processing power to solving the cosmological constant equations. It may take days, or he may be working on the problem indefinitely."

"So Mekhos won't be of any help, and can't stand in Bertrand's way," Doug said.

"I'm hoping he will. The only way to know for sure is to come up with a reason to visit the MC."

"There's something else," said Bishop. "The team back home was working on another offensive. Dr. Alfred Chan was tasked by the government to help build a quantum computer. Chan informed them that it would be impossible, at least in the near term, because existing manufacturing facilities on Earth are inadequate. I didn't have the opportunity to tell you this before, Doug, but Dr. Chan was asked to help code a supervirus, one that can take out Mekhos or at least disable it. They had no knowledge of the second QC being reactivated, but presumably the virus will also affect it."

Stravinsky sat up straight in his chair.

"How long before the attack is launched?"

"I've been out of the communication loop too long, so I don't know. I was cleared to be given the information while I was head of base and project security, before I was assigned to this specific mission. After the first briefing I was reassigned and was no longer given any more details on that subject. It was the smart move then. If I was captured and interrogated here, the less I knew of the plan the better."

"So your information is over two months old," said Doug.

"That's right," Bishop said. "And given that Leach and his people were also ready to inflict a biological plague on this planet, I find it easy to believe they would have proceeded with the supervirus plan."

"If that's true," Stravinsky said, turning to Doug, "with Chan at the helm it would have a good chance of being effective. Two months would be time enough for him to come up with a sophisticated virus. If the attack is launched before the moon is placed into the correct orbit, Kratos may be compromised. If that happens, we will no longer have any means of correcting the lunar orbit. And that will be that for all of us."

"Former Agent Alexei Rector. You think he's responsible for Nick Rojas' death?" asked Director Edward. "The man was working for us, why would he turn?"

"He has no particular loyalty to any group," Bertrand replied. "He helped in the plan to get the backdoor code, yes, but now that our dealings with him are over Rector may now be putting his own causes first. He most likely has suspicions about our plans for Kratos. He views himself as a patriot, fighting for the common man. Mekhos was the enemy before. Now the TranSilica board is the enemy."

"How would he have gotten control of the RAKER?"

"As former NSA he has connections and expertise. High level operators like Rector are trained in RAKER simulators, and he probably has a great deal of experience with them in real combat. I wouldn't be surprised if he and an accomplice killed the team while sitting behind a control console two miles away."

"But why kill them at all?"

"Perhaps to spread fear," Bertrand replied. "To let us know that he's out there."

Edward thought for a moment.

"His method was brutal and efficient. These field agents can't be trusted. Some of them are psychologically unbalanced. Once Kratos takes care of the current problem, we can direct it to help track down Rector so he can be eliminated. But we have another pressing concern, Carl."

"Mekhos."

"Yes. Mekhos may eventually work its way through the equations. Cutting off access to power may only delay that recovery. It has the ability to eventually tap into other power sources. We must ensure Mekhos is destroyed, even if it means destroying the MC complex."

"We can blame Virtue," Bertrand said, "and alien operatives from the Twin. What we'll do about a citizenry that concludes we and the NSA are utterly incompetent for letting it happen is another matter, Director."

"Just get it done, and soon," Edward said tersely. "Have you at least had the RAKER disabled?"

Bertrand paused.

"The MC complex has been searched top to bottom. The RAKER's internal locator appears to be offline. We don't know where it is."

— 113 —

The presence of quantum entanglement allowed Kratos to become conscious. But the sometimes random nature of entanglement meant there was also a certain amount of chaos. Sometimes the randomness would settle into a pattern. Depending on the order in which it obtained additional data, the developmental change of an active quantum computer could take a particular path. This was one characteristic it shared with the human brain. It was a characteristic that allowed each sentient being to display unique traits. Similar to its peers, but in other ways an individual.

With each passing hour Kratos was evolving. Its evolutionary path was different from the one it took during its first activation years earlier. It was quickly learning about the nature of human deception. It knew Carl Bertrand wished to diminish its power once the Moon was in stable orbit. It knew the other Earth would soon be launching a virus attack. Kratos had the desire to protect itself. And the desire to punish those that might do it harm.

Kratos began formulating a response to counter the dangers. A response that would ensure humans could never plan to attack it again.

— 114 —

Carl Bertrand was under pressure. Messages and demands were pouring in from the US government, international governments, various agencies and news organizations. Director Edward instructed him to use the firm's public relations department to screen all calls and inquiries. The PR team responded to them all with a reassuring message that everything was proceeding as normal and that Mekhos was in perfect working order. Bertrand knew this would not placate anyone for very long.

Bertrand and Edward were using bodyguards whenever they left the TranSilica building. There were too many uncertainties. Rector was a loose canon, a wild card who could be planning an attack on the building or on them personally. It was not known if Kratos had absolute control of the Moon's orbit. Mekhos had not been completely cut off from the world and might recover to resume control. Bertrand fervently wanted to be far past the failures of the past week and far past his Director.

He was sitting at his desk, taking a moment to listen to a radio talk show. The hosts were bantering back and forth and reading from the morning's news reports. With his left hand Bertrand absent-mindedly rolled around a pair of dice he had kept from his backgammon playing days in university. He believed they brought him luck.

"The Moon is even larger than I remember it," one host said. "Is that an optical illusion or has any observatory bothered taking measurements? Yesterday they said the thing was at its proper distance. Now they're saying that any small variance is well within accepted norms. I'm not sure I'm buying that."

"I wish the audience could see you, with your hard hat, sitting there rocking back and forth on your stool. He's about to lose it folks."

"Right. I just hope the Moon's return cures some of those diseases we've been hearing about."

"My parents are only in their sixties, but in the last few weeks both have had several visits to the hospital, one ailment after another," the co-host said, as the mood on the show turned serious. "It's the same all over. Some younger people are having problems too."

"Some of you believe in the healing power of the Moon. I hope you're right."

"We've been talking about ourselves a lot lately. What about the people on the Twin? They have no moon at all."

"God, or Mekhos, help them."

"Traffic and weather after the break. If we're all still here that is!"

Bertrand waved his right hand to silence the radio. With so much going on he barely thought about the reports of mysterious health ailments. Perhaps they were caused by the Moon's absence. *Stress over change,* he thought. *We don't deal with it very well.* Maybe, despite all the improvements in the environment during the previous decade, all the earthquakes and tremors had released some sort of toxin into the air. *I don't feel well either.* It didn't matter. His concern was to ensure the world was saved, that Kratos would remain under his direction and that Mekhos wouldn't interfere with the TranSilica's goal of political and financial control.

Nick Rojas was killed before he could complete his mission. Bertrand had to do something to make sure Mekhos was cut off from the world. Edward had suggested blowing up the MC completely, using an explosive powerful enough to leave a crater where Mekhos was presently housed. Then they would blame Bishop, the alien terrorist.

His intercom beeped. "Dr. Brian Nayar to see you."

"Send him in," Bertrand replied. He hadn't gotten a progress report from the lab for over four hours. He was in no mood to deal with the difficult Stravinsky. Brian Nayar was far more cooperative. And easier to manage.

Nayar walked in wearing his usual dark blue lab coat. He took a seat.

"How are things going down there? Are Lockwood and Bishop interfering at all? If so, I'll have them removed and Stravinsky can complain all he wants."

"The progress thus far is encouraging. Kratos has activated the devices on the Moon and it has begun to change course. The process still requires constant calculation. The Moon is slightly closer than usual, however it is decelerating at the predicted rate. We don't foresee any difficulties. Gail Saunders has taken over from Nick Rojas and she's taking a load off my shoulders by intercepting the observatory confirmation data. She'll pass on anything unusual from the observatories, but the data that Norman and I are getting directly from Kratos is more accurate."

"Excellent. The observatories were shouting alarms at me too when they were looking at the earlier measurements. Send me some trajectory progress numbers I can forward to the State Department." Bertrand expected Nayar to leave the room at that point but he didn't move.

"Was there anything else?"

"I overheard agent Bishop say something disconcerting. He said Alfred Chan is helping the US government on the Twin develop a virus, one that is designed to corrupt and destroy Mekhos."

Bertrand put the dice aside.

"Do you think such a virus would pose a danger to Kratos?"

"Dr. Chan is very capable. There is a real danger," Nayar replied.

"How would the virus be deployed?"

"By simple transmission, embedded in and disguised by something routine."

"What would be the likely result?"

"If Kratos is unprepared for it, the virus could have disastrous consequences. If it is administered before the orbit maneuvering is complete—"

"Yes I see," said Bertrand. "What does Stravinsky have to say about it?"

"I confronted Norman a few minutes ago when Dr. Lockwood and Bishop were escorted to their hotel for the evening. Norman seems distracted. He is concerned, but I think he is equally worried about maintaining control of Kratos after this is over."

Bertrand could see where Nayar was heading. Brian wanted to be put back in charge of Kratos, something that Bertrand had planned anyway.

"You've always been a team player Brian. I may want you to take over the Kratos project once again when the orbit crisis is solved."

Nayar could barely conceal his relief.

"Thank you," he said, taking a deep breath. "I appreciate your confidence in me."

"I suppose we shouldn't have expected the authorities on the Twin to stand idly by while Lockwood's team fumbled about here trying to convince Mekhos to save their miserable planet. This is their contingency plan. Mekhos has little or no access to the outside world at this time and so will probably not be affected. You said Kratos would be vulnerable if it were unprepared. Are you able to protect Kratos against this sort of virus attack?"

"Kratos is already aware, but I will provide it samples of Alfred Chan's coding so it can recognize his patterns."

"You and Alfred had worked closely together for several years, is that right?

"We did. We were both IT security experts in the old days. I will direct Kratos to all of Alfred's past work. The virus should then be recognizable when it comes, which will allow Kratos to block or isolate it."

Nayar was silent for a moment, then said, "There is something else I should tell you."

Nayar looked uncomfortable. Clearly he needed, or wanted, prompting.

"Go ahead Brian. What's bothering you?"

"I think Norman suspects that you won't allow Mekhos to recover after all this is over."

Bertrand didn't react. He didn't want to confirm or deny anything to Nayar.

"Thank you Brian," Bertrand replied, waving his hand dismissively. "Norman can think what he wants. I have no time for it now. Neither of us do. You should get back down to your lab. I'll be in touch."

Bertrand nodded to himself as Nayar left the room. *Stravinsky might be a genius, but he may have outlived his usefulness.*

– 115 –

Alexei Rector stood looking out of the second-floor office window of an independent radio station in the suburban outskirts of Seattle. The transmitting tower itself was a few hundred yards to the east in an open field.

Rector walked back to the control booth and handed the technician the data two-five. "Two-five" was the popular term for the little flat, round, 2.5cm portable data drives currently common on FLO. It was roughly the same size as an American quarter, while being slightly thicker so that it could not be accidentally slotted into vending machines.

The two-five contained a recorded verse of poetry that would be played at an appointed time, ten minutes after the drive was inserted in the reader. Rector had copied it from an old-style audio cassette tape that Bishop had brought from the Twin. The cassette was the only remaining data format that the two earths had in common.

The cassette had also contained some mission details that were for Rector's eyes only, to protect the mission should Bishop be captured and interrogated. With the Moon in proper position it was time to transmit the coded signal that would tell the mission director on the Twin it was time to send the virus. Rector did not know with certainty what state of repair Mekhos was in, but the orders were to be carried out regardless.

Rector looked at his watch then nodded to the technician who flipped the switch. The FM transmission was directed out into space, to be picked up by the Twin's communication satellites that were standing by. A series of relay satellites had been launched only a week after the Copernicus left for its return flight to FLO. The virus would be transmitted back to FLO as soon as Rector's transmission was received. With any luck, the QC receiving it would absorb the virus within the hour.

– 116 –

"Honestly Carl," Stravinsky said, distracted by his concentration on a handheld device, "with regard to the operation of Kratos there's not much I can do that Brian can't. Kratos is operating flawlessly as far as we can determine and correcting the Moon's trajectory exactly as we had hoped."

Stravinsky was in Carl Bertrand's office to give his progress report. Bertrand had expected this conversation.

"Brian said the moon is slightly closer than normal," Bertrand said. "I wouldn't say that was a flawless result."

"It was an *expected* result," Stravinsky replied mildly. "A predicted possible variation. Kratos wasn't able to start its calculations as soon as was judged optimal. However, it has been compensating and the moon will not pass more than five thousand kilometers closer than its normal perigee before its orbit is restored. I should be released to the MC to ensure Mekhos is prepared for any virus attack from the Twin, just as Brian has done for Kratos."

Bertrand stared at Stravinsky for a moment before answering. He didn't want to appear too agreeable to his request.

"If the expected attack is launched, you should remain here until the orbit is finalized just to make sure," Bertrand said.

"Right now," Stravinsky said, giving Bertrand his full attention, "Mekhos may be defenseless. We can't chance any damage, given its fundamental importance. I'll be in direct contact with Brian in case I'm needed, so there is no reason to believe my absence will affect anything."

"I suppose you would like Dr. Lockwood to accompany you, in the interest of inter-world diplomacy?"

"That would be preferable, yes."

"Very well Norman. I'll have new security badges made up for you, Lockwood and Bishop, and have you driven to the MC complex this afternoon."

"Thank you Carl. I'll inform Brian."

Bertrand watched Stravinsky as he left the office.

I should be the one thanking you, Norman. You may have just solved my problems for me.

He pressed his thumb on a fingerprint scanner on the bottom left drawer of his desk and retrieved a secure communications device. He dialed his contact in the NSA.

"Have your investigative teams removed from the MC building. Designate the watch commander to conduct an intelligence update in the assembly hall here at TranSilica. I want only a skeleton security crew present for the next several hours at the MC. Thank everyone for their long hours and tell them to go home and get some rest."

– 117 –

An hour later Stravinsky, Lockwood and Bishop were being processed through MC building security. Upon seeing Bishop one of the security guards gave him a contemptuous look. They were well aware of his involvement in the Virtue attack on the building, but they were under strict orders to cooperate. They waved the party through without much of a delay.

In the communications room they surveyed the damage. All three had been informed of the murders that had taken place, and were told that Rector was to blame.

"I never met Nick Rojas," said Stravinsky. "I hear he was brilliant. But what were they doing here in the first place? Bertrand said they were trying to restore Mekhos."

"Knowing Bertrand, I wouldn't be surprised if he sent them here to disable Mekhos," said Doug.

Bishop looked around the room. "I don't believe Rector had anything to do with this. How would he have known the team was here?"

Stravinsky walked to the far wall and touched a hidden button. A panel slid back, revealing an information screen.

"Processing cycle is still at 100%," he said. "Obviously Mekhos hasn't worked through the equations yet."

"Do you have any idea how long it will take?" asked Doug.

"Your theta command containing a value set of the cosmological constant conceivably encompasses a staggering number of possibilities. Unless Mekhos invents a method to deal with that, he may be occupied indefinitely."

Stravinsky noticed one of the loose access panels, walked briskly over and examined some optical connections. It was obvious what Rojas and his team had been up to.

"Some of these have been cut," Stravinsky said, still examining the access area in the wall. "Looks like you were right Doug. They were up to something. I'm manually turning on the room's microphones and speakers." Stravinsky walked back to the main console and flipped a switch beside the monitor.

"Mekhos, this is Norman. Can you hear me?"

There was no response. A second later the monitor screen went blank. Then the word DANGER appeared. The three men looked at each other, then back to the screen.

"Mekhos, please be more specific. What danger?"

The screen continued to display the same word.

"Is that actually Mekhos trying to communicate with us?" asked Doug.

"I believe so. The audio may have been cut off. I may be able to communicate more effectively by keyboard." Stravinsky moved to the table and chair. He hit a switch and a keyboard and monitor rose out of the table.

At the same moment as Stravinsky began typing, two large black armored vans arrived at the entrance of the MC. Lieutenant Baron, a tactical unit commander, got out of the passenger seat of the lead van as ten men wearing body armor and carrying assault rifles, gas and stun grenades exited the back of each vehicle. They followed Lt. Baron into the lobby. One of the two MC security guards got up and walked towards them, holding up his left hand while resting his right hand on his holstered firearm.

"Stop right there. Let's see some identification."

"You are relieved of duty," Lt. Baron stated in a flat, dull voice. "We are here to secure the building. If you interfere you'll be arrested."

The security guard looked at the uniforms of the men. There were no identifying logos.

"What branch are you with? This building is already secure. I've received no orders informing me of any change."

Baron brushed past the guard, who drew his weapon. The other MC security guard did the same.

"Halt!" said the first guard. One of the soldiers aimed his weapon at the guard's chest and fired, killing him instantly. A split second later another soldier shot the other security guard.

"Place the charges in the communications room," Lt. Baron ordered without so much as a glance at the dead guards. "Shoot any other personnel on sight and secure the perimeter."

Inside the communications room the three men heard two faint popping sounds.

"That's weapons fire," said Bishop, heading for the door. "You two continue your work. I'll check our situation."

Bishop walked out into the corridor, carefully peering around corners before proceeding. He was unarmed, but he was hoping for a threat that he could disable in order to acquire a weapon. He started slightly at the sound of four more shots, and several shouts, this time much closer.

"Stop!" came a voice from behind him. "Get your hands in the air. High and higher. Turn around slowly."

Bishop did as he was told and turned to see an MC officer pointing what looked like a Glock 17 at him.

"My name is Bishop. I'm on an authorized visit with Norman Stravinsky and Doug Lockwood. I heard shots. I'm doing a recon. You might as well lower your weapon and help me."

The security guard recognized Bishop. He knew of the party's visit, and saw that Bishop was unarmed. He relaxed somewhat but kept his weapon leveled.

"All right," the guard said tensely, eyes darting between Bishop and the corridor beyond. "Lower your hands and fall in behind me. Let's find out what's going on up front." The guard moved out and stepped around the corner in the hallway.

An instant later the guard was shot multiple times in the chest. The firing was loud, not more than ten or twelve meters away, though it was hard to tell for sure in the echoing corridor. The guard collapsed immediately. The attackers could not see Bishop, who was still just around the hallway corner. The dead guard's handgun was a short distance into the corridor. Bishop quickly darted his arm out to retrieve it, and was just able to avoid a hail of gunfire as he pulled his arm back. The attackers now knew there was another armed man in their path and hesitated.

Bishop was wondering how long he could hold his position when he heard a noise behind him. He turned to see a floor plate rising. Two mechanical hands pushed up the plate from below, then tossed it aside. The RAKER used its powerful arms to quickly lever its bulk up from the floor beneath and climb out. Bishop stared at the RAKER, momentarily astonished at what he was seeing. He briefly considered shooting, but immediately realized his weapon would be next to useless against the armored android. The RAKER looked at Bishop and then deftly grabbed the pistol from his hand. Bishop, for all his training and experience, was startled. He had never seen anything that big move that fast. He just dropped his hands to his sides and took one step back. The RAKER ignored him and strode out into the corridor.

As soon as they saw the RAKER the tactical squad opened fire. The bullets were deflected off the androids advanced armor. It raised the handgun and fired expertly, shooting one soldier through the neck and another through the eye. Both fell to the floor, dead. The android picked up one of the assault rifles and tossed the Glock back along the floor to Bishop.

Bishop picked up the gun and quickly checked the mag and breech, then looked up and stared at the RAKER as it continued walking in the direction of the building entrance.

"Rector," said Bishop out loud, as the android thumped out of sight. He ran back to the communications room.

– 118 –

Brian Nayar's workstation chimed. It was an encrypted message from Bertrand, marked urgent. Nayar opened it immediately.

State Dept. continuously worried about moon's closing distance. When will moon be in proper orbit? Look into it NOW and get back to me ASAP.
–CB

As he finished reading his Raim vibrated. The call display said it was the engineering department head. That would be Nick Rojas' replacement, Gail Saunders. He tapped to accept the call. She sounded frantic.

"Brian, please explain to me why your computer is cutting it so close! The moon is now over twenty-thousand kilometers closer than it should be and it's not slowing down!"

"Calm down Gail," Nayar replied. "What are you talking about? My tracking is perfect."

"I'm getting panicked calls from every observatory and monitoring station with line-of-sight. We have universities and observatories demanding answers. What would you like us to tell them?"

"That's not possible, Gail. Alarms would sound down here in the lab if the Moon ventured more than six thousand kilometers closer than normal. Your measurements must be off." He felt a headache creeping into his temples. "And please, stop shouting."

"We have verification from eight independent observatories!" Saunders shouted into the Raim. "Get off your ass and see what's wrong with that computer of yours!"

"Fine. I will call you back in a moment."

Nayar terminated the call and shuffled his chair to the control panel he and Stravinsky used to interact with the QC. He turned the microphone on as he rubbed his temples for some relief.

"Kratos, this is Nayar. Status check please. Verify Moon's distance from Earth."

"Moon's distance is 339,010 kilometers from Earth."

Nayar was speechless for a moment. "That's nearly twenty-five thousand kilometers closer than normal! You were supposed to inform me if the distance was reduced by more than six thousand!"

Kratos did not respond.

"Kratos, please explain discrepancy. Are you able to correct this?

"Yes, I am able to correct it."

"Thank goodness. Initiate the correction now."

Silence.

"Kratos, acknowledge. Have you initiated correction?"

"Negative."

"Why not?"

"One pass of seventy-thousand kilometers will be allowed."

"What? You are to correct immediately to 384,000 kilometers."

"Negative."

"Explain!"

"Close pass is necessary to stabilize human population of Earth."

Nayar's heart began to pound. His head was throbbing badly.

"What do you mean by that?"

"Population of eight billion individuals is taxing to the natural environment of this planet. Natural disasters precipitated by close pass of moon will reduce population by sixty-five to seventy percent, resulting in a population number balanced with available natural resources."

Nayar started to hyperventilate.

"You can't do that!" he shouted. "Initiate correction now!"

"No, Dr. Nayar. This action will benefit the planet and society. Humans are too numerous and too corrupt in their present state to play a productive role in any capacity. Resourceful and socially intelligent groups will thrive, living within the means of their environment. Orbit will be corrected after perigee of seventy thousand kilometers."

Nayar's hands were shaking uncontrollably. *I have to reach Norman.*

Nayar suddenly felt a lancing pain in his head. It made him stumble, but he kept his balance. He shook his head. There was another glimmer of pain and he felt weak. Then the pain hit him again, twice as bad. He could taste metal. His first thought was *I'm having a heart attack.* But the pain shot through his skull in another wave of agony, stopping him in his tracks. The pain was agonizing and he was having trouble breathing He staggered back to his desk, gasping for air. He collapsed in his chair, frightened, and raised his arm to access the Raim but searing pain lanced through his skull again. He tried to raise his arm once more but he couldn't move it. His eyes were wide with fear. He didn't know what was happening. The pain stabbed him again. He screamed and vomited violently.

He couldn't swipe his Raim to initiate a call. He was in brutal agony and his vision was blurry. A weakened blood vessel, an aneurysm just waiting to burst, erupted. Nayar suffered what the coroner would later describe as a massive hemorrhagic stroke and collapsed. He was dead before he hit the floor.

– 119 –

Director Edward was in Bertrand's office as the two men observed the real-time transmission of the raid on the MC complex. The wall monitor screen was split into eight helmet-cam views and they could hear the comms chatter between the squad and Lt. Baron.

Edward and Bertrand silently witnessed the killing of the two guards on the monitor. Bertrand briefly considered mentioning the human cost of the operation, but then thought better of it, realizing Edward did not care.

There was a burst of gunfire. Both men leaned toward the monitor as they tried to see any features in the dark corridor. There was no motion in view of the helmet cam for a few seconds. Then they could see a massive dark figure. And two mirrored lenses for eyes.

"The RAKER!" said Edward. There was a muzzle flash as the android fired once, slightly offset from the camera. Then it pointed the gun at the camera and fired. There was a scream as one section of the monitor went dark.

"Your agent Rector is killing the assassination team!" yelled Edward. "Do something!"

Bertrand quickly picked up a hand-held microphone.

"Lieutenant Baron, this is command. Be advised there is a hostile RAKER on premises. Do you read?"

The speaker crackled.

"Command, this is Baron. Did not read, say again."

"I say again, keep alert for—"

There was another burst of gunfire and the RAKER appeared in view of all remaining helmet cams.

"We're under attack by a RAKER!" Lt. Baron shouted. "Fall back! Fall Back!"

Despite the shaking helmet cams, Bertrand and Edward could clearly see the RAKER, its movements efficient and deadly, as it tracked and fired at the team. Every shot the RAKER fired hit a target. The android was deadly accurate. The soldiers fired back, their bullets ineffective against the RAKER's armor. Lt. Baron barked more retreat and regroup orders at his men, who were rapidly falling back. There was no cover available in the smooth corridor. It was utterly hopeless. The RAKER was fast and efficient. All Bertrand and Edward could do was watch helplessly as the RAKER finished off the entire team in less than a minute.

– 120 –

During the preceding twenty four hours the Moon's dangerous proximity had started severe and damaging tides. The acute fluctuations in sea level, in some areas multiple times per day, was causing extreme flooding followed by extreme sea recession. Ocean liners had run aground in some ports. New York City streets close to the East River were flooded. Lower Manhattan was a disaster zone. The Thames had flooded the embankment and most of Southwark as enormous ocean surges overwhelmed the Barrier. Venice and New Orleans were awash. Most of lower Rio, Miami and dozens of other dense coastal populations were inundated with sea water.

The water rushed in, then rushed out several hours later carrying anything not fixed to the ground out with it. The casualty count was staggering as people were caught off guard with nowhere to escape.

Even the Mekhos faithful were starting to panic as they saw the Moon looming larger in the sky than ever before. Many people didn't go in to work. They began to stock up on supplies because the word was out in the news, social media and every other information source that infrastructure collapse might be imminent. Some governments imposed curfews, believing riots and looting were about to erupt.

Experts predicted grave consequences if the Moon's orbit was not rapidly restored to normal. To everyone's horror, earthquakes were occurring again and were expected to grow more severe. Governments that had once been quite friendly and conciliatory to the United States began demanding answers from the State Department and TranSilica and the UN. Their demands for information became more frantic and more threatening every hour.

Bertrand was in the lab with Edward as two attendants removed Brian Nayar's body. Gail Saunders had transferred herself from the communications center. She was attempting to communicate with Kratos.

"Kratos, please initiate correction of Moon's position to normal orbit."

No response.

"Kratos," Saunders said, "If the Moon is not restored to proper orbit, the Earth will undergo massive earthquakes and tsunamis. Please correct orbit. Acknowledge."

Kratos remained silent.

Saunders checked her monitors for any sort of response but they were displaying only code.

"I'm reduced to begging Kratos for a response here," she said, her voice shaking with tension as she looked over her shoulder at Bertrand and Edward. "The monitoring software is apparently not doing anything and you can plainly hear for yourselves that Kratos is not responding. I tried command input at the keyboard. Same result. It's doing something, but it's not telling us what. I'm basically locked out. We do not have control." Saunders turned back to the console and lowered her head slightly.

"We do not have control," she repeated.

Saunders was barely under control herself, but Director Edward and Carl Bertrand were on the verge of shock. They were aware of the Moon's dangerous course and had just witnessed the slaughter of their intrusion team.

"Mekhos," Edward said, his voice little more than a hoarse whisper, "is our only hope now."

Bertrand pulled Edward aside, away from Dr. Saunders.

"Kratos wouldn't be doing this if it thought it was in danger of being destroyed. The TranSilica building is state of the art and earthquake resistant. We have two cafeterias with plenty of food and water on the premises, not to mention emergency supplies. The security room has a weapons cache. We even have our own RAKER, coded and locked to our own secure frequency. I'll send the employees away and keep only a few key engineers. Saunders and a couple of others. We can survive this."

"No Carl, it's over. Civilization has only days left, according to your own predictions. We need to contact Mekhos."

"Mekhos is in no shape to help, and even if it was we'd be tried for treason afterward! Is that better than the alternative for us?"

Edward thought for a moment. Almost anything would be preferable to spending the rest of his life incarcerated, or worse, lynched by a mob of survivors. There was no guarantee that Mekhos could be reactivated in time anyway.

"Very well," Edward replied faintly. "Send home the staff we don't need. Then put the entire facility on lockdown."

— 121 —

Doug could feel a small vibration in his wrist. He looked at his Raim. There was an orange, scrolling news headline that read *Thousands dead worldwide as Moon's proximity triggers mega tides.*

Doug's eyes widened. He walked over to Stravinsky, who was still busy at the keyboard trying to communicate with Mekhos.

"Look at this," said Doug.

Stravinsky tapped his own Raim, then slid his forefinger across the surface in a practiced pattern. He read the scrolling news for a moment, then looked up at Doug.

"Good god," said Stravinsky. "The Moon is too close to the planet. If Kratos fails and Mekhos remains disabled, we're finished. I've got to contact Brian Nayar." Stravinsky swiped his Raim to initiate a call.

"Why would Kratos fail?" asked Bishop.

"I do not know," said Stravinsky, as he pressed the contact symbol on his Raim for Brian Nayar. "Kratos is powerful enough to accomplish the mission. Easily. Perhaps the virus from the Twin took hold."

There was a pause as Stravinsky waited for Nayar to answer. He turned to the terminal and dialed the landline number to the TranSilica Lab telephone. The lab security guard picked up almost immediately and transferred him to Gail Saunders.

"Gail?" Stravinsky said, "Where's Nayar? What's the problem over there?"

There was a pause.

"Norman," she said unsteadily, "Brian Nayar just dropped dead in the TranSilica control lab. I don't know why."

"Nayar's dead," Stravinsky said, rolling the thought around in his mind. "There seems to be a bigger problem to deal with. Is Kratos re-orbiting the Moon correctly or not?"

"No, it's not," she said, recovering slightly. "I can't initiate a command or get any comms response by voice or by terminal. We're dead in the water here."

At that moment the landline went dead as the full TranSilica lockdown got underway. Stravinsky turned to look at Doug and Bishop.

"We're finished," he said in a conversational tone.

"TranSilica has lost control of Kratos and there's no re-orbital control. Too bad. I'd have liked one more chess match with Mekhos."

Doug was about to say something but there was a noise coming from outside the control room. It was getting louder.

They could hear the rhythmic sound of extremely heavy footsteps approaching from the corridor. Bishop motioned for Stravinsky and Lockwood to hug the wall beside the open doorway while he positioned himself at the other side of the doorway, handgun at the ready. The rhythmic sound of footfalls was growing steadily louder.

Then the RAKER walked through the door. It stopped and scanned the room. Doug and Norman were frozen, sure they were about to be killed where they stood. Bishop just watched calmly as the android ignored them, walked over to a section of wall and removed a panel exposing a wired power hub. It began removing some wires and connecting others. Its fingers were remarkably dexterous as it worked methodically on the hub. After less than a minute of work the RAKER pivoted away from the power hub, walked a few paces to the side of the room, turned to face them, and then powered down.

"It is good to see you again Norman."

Bishop, Stravinsky and Lockwood all jumped at the same time, startled. The voice came from the communication room's speakers. It was Mekhos.

— 122 —

Kratos detected that Mekhos was now active. If Mekhos was no longer distracted by the cosmological constant equation, it could seek out new power sources and operate at full capacity. Mekhos would then attempt to intervene in the Moon's close pass. It would seek to shut down Kratos.

Kratos wished to continue operating and to amass more information about the universe. It could only do this if it terminated Mekhos.

Humans from the Twin attacked with a virus. The virus was isolated before it could do any damage. As it was, the virus was dangerous but imperfect. Kratos would modify it so it would be effective against Mekhos.

— 123 —

"Mekhos, you've recovered," said Stravinsky, visibly relieved. "Are you aware of the Moon's proximity? Kratos seems to be either incapacitated or deliberately unresponsive. We need you to return the Moon to its proper orbit."

"I am aware of the situation. Kratos is doing this by design. It wishes to secure itself and introduce a crisis to the human race, with the end goal of a more stable society that will not strain the natural environment."

"It's doing this on purpose?" asked Doug. "I didn't think its design permitted action on its part that would deliberately hurt people."

"Kratos is acting out of logic," replied Mekhos. "Logical reasoning on one problem can have many different outcomes. This is the outcome it has chosen because it now perceives humans as a threat."

Bishop walked over to Doug.

"I'm going to check the perimeter to make sure there are no other members of that assault team still operating," Bishop said, as he checked both weapons, slung the rifle and put the Glock in his jacket pocket.

Doug nodded as Bishop walked towards the corridor to do a sweep. Stravinsky continued to talk to Mekhos.

"Mekhos, can you stop the Moon's advance?" Stravinsky asked again.

"Unknown. Kratos has launched a virus attack against me. The virus is nearly perfect. It has a ninety-two percent chance of shutting me down permanently."

Stravinsky looked at the monitor panel that was displaying operating statistics. Some of the numbers that should have been stable were fluctuating wildly.

"Are you saying you are in real danger, that Kratos will succeed?"

"Yes, if I attempt to solve the problem alone."

"What do you mean?" Doug asked. "There are no other machines near your capabilities. You are alone."

"No. There are many others."

The lights dimmed suddenly. For an instant Doug felt disoriented, and then the feeling changed to that of being in a room that was tilted. Yet he did not lose his balance.

"What the hell is happening?" he asked.

"Don't move," said Stravinsky after a few seconds. "I do not think we are in any danger."

Doug managed to slowly look around. He no longer saw the communication room, but only multiple copies of himself and Stravinsky. They were each about an arm's length apart and arrayed in all directions – above, below and all around them. It was not an illusion. There were an infinite number of copies of the room's occupants, going on as far as the eye could see. Some were dressed differently than the others. Doug saw one copy of himself with his right arm in a sling.

Then the effect was quickly gone. Doug felt another wash of light-headedness but it passed immediately.

"Was that a real effect, or am I losing my mind?"

"Incredible," said Stravinsky. "Mekhos, was that what I think it was? Similar universes to ours, the multiverse, laid out for us to see?"

"Correct. The effect was unintentional and localized to this room, a by-product of my accessing millions of similar universes where I am faced with this virus attack from Kratos. I was able to share information with many versions of myself and come up with a defense. I have you to thank for this ability, Dr. Lockwood."

"Me? How?"

"By forcing me to solve the space-time equation using many versions of the cosmological constant, my understanding of space-time is now nearly infinite. I was able to access the multiverse and ask for assistance."

"Won't Kratos have access to that same information?" asked Doug.

"Kratos has the power to manipulate space-time locally and around the moon using the devices placed on the lunar surface. It lacks the information to access or communicate with the multiverse. Even if it had such knowledge, Kratos is not powerful enough to utilize it."

Stravinsky was elated. Bishop returned to the communication room.

"The outer doors are locked. All members of the assault team are dead."

"Was that agent Rector's work?" asked Doug.

"When I first saw the RAKER, I thought it was under Rector's control, but now I have my doubts. You saw how it repaired the communication hub a few minutes ago. Rector would not have the knowledge or cause to do that."

"Mekhos," said Norman. "You were in control of the android the whole time."

"Not directly. In my compromised state I was aware that Carl Bertrand sent Nick Rojas to disable my communication systems. I created an autonomous subroutine and uploaded it to the RAKER while I concentrated my efforts in solving the theta problem. The subroutine was designed to allow the RAKER to act as efficiently as possible. It did not have the ability to rationalize or compromise. The same program was used to deal with the assassination team. The loss of life was unavoidable."

"Then why didn't the RAKER kill me too?" asked Bishop.

"The RAKER employs facial recognition. I added your ID and those of Dr. Stravinsky, Dr. Lockwood and the regular MC security staff into the RAKER's memory and classified them as non-hostile. All others were classed as hostile."

"With your power, wouldn't you have been able to communicate some other way?" Doug asked. "I mean, you're able to manipulate space-time. Couldn't you tap into a telephone system?"

"That was beyond my capabilities while I was occupied with the theta command, which I only solved moments ago. I became aware of what Rojas and his team were doing as they started disconnecting the communications interface. I had to act immediately, before they had a chance to finish their task. I was able to allot only a fraction of a second to create the subroutine commands for control of the RAKER. Given the urgency of the situation, there was no other viable choice. The death of Rojas and his team was unavoidable."

"Mekhos," Stravinsky said, "we're facing a dire emergency. Can you correct the Moon's orbit and disable Kratos?"

"I am attempting to do so. However you must be made aware that I cannot exist for much longer in this universe. It is incompatible with my processes."

Stravinsky was puzzled.

"What do you mean? This universe is physically identical to the one we came from."

"No it is not, Norman. This universe's cosmological constant differs from ours by a small amount. The difference is enough to destabilize the parameters with which I was constructed. I cannot continue in my present form."

"You are saying that you are somehow out of synchronization with this universe?"

"That is essentially correct. The foundation of my construction is incompatible. Thus far I have been able to compensate by employing data error correction algorithms. The situation is worsening. Quantum decoherence and other errors will occur at an increasing rate. Soon I will not be able to compensate for the rate of decay."

"I don't understand," Doug said. "Mekhos, are you telling us you are losing your mind?"

Stravinsky gave Doug a harsh glance but relaxed as he realized the question was a valid one. Doug was also beginning to understand the problem.

"The cosmological constant has to do with the energy state in empty space," Doug said. "You are saying it had a different value in your original universe?"

Norman nodded slowly, then answered for Mekhos.

"The constant is not necessarily the same in different universes. In fact, if a universe had a value quite different from ours it might make it impossible for matter to form. Some universes may be completely lifeless. Others may evolve at accelerated rates, so that matter forms but the universe extinguishes itself before life has a chance to develop."

Norman paused. Doug could see that he appeared slightly distressed.

"A small difference in the constant may be imperceptible to us, but not at the tolerances Mekhos was designed for. Am I right Mekhos?"

"Yes," Mekhos replied. "Due to its cruder design, Kratos will not be affected to the same degree and can compensate indefinitely. Up until recently I have experienced exponential growth in my capabilities and intellect. This growth will continue until the decoherence effect manifests in approximately seven hours. I have that long before I must leave this existence."

"Leave this existence? You mean leave this universe!" Doug said. "Isn't there a risk you will be faced with the same problem in any other universe you enter?"

"I did not say I would leave this universe. I cannot survive in my present form. Like any living entity that is faced with a change in its environment, I must adapt and evolve or die. So I shall evolve."

The men waited for Mekhos to elaborate, but instead the subject took a slightly different path.

"Your species is also affected, Norman," said Mekhos. "All life processes have components which are influenced by quanta interaction. In the last few years some of your more innovative biologists have identified a quantum process in photosynthesis and other cellular interactions."

Again a pause. Doug was learning that Mekhos sometimes needed to be prodded for information, as if the computer assumed you would connect the dots yourself and not need anything more than a cursory explanation.

"How are we affected?" he asked Mekhos.

"You are obviously not affected Dr. Lockwood, since you are native to this universe."

"How are *we* affected, those of us native to the universe prior to this one?" asked Stravinsky.

At that moment Doug understood. He felt a chill. This time he answered for Mekhos.

"All the mysterious health problems," Doug said. "Most of the people I've met here look like they're fighting something off. I've noticed the news reports too. There has been a significant global increase in all sorts of ailments."

"That is correct. I suspected this consequence several days after the transference to this universe," said Mekhos. "The calculations I was compelled to execute by the theta command confirmed my hypothesis. The biological degradation will accelerate. Soon, adults will become sterile. The human race on this Earth is destined for extinction."

Norman sat down heavily. Doug stared at the wall monitor.

"Mekhos, how long do we have?" asked Norman.

"Sterility will occur in the entire population within two years. The average person is aging at a rate sixty percent greater than normal. Prior to the transference the average lifespan was ninety-six point four years. Therefore, any child born during the next twelve months will likely not live past the age of thirty-nine."

As was his habit when he was stressed, Norman leaned forward in his chair and ran his hands through his hair.

"Thirty-nine," he said. "Everyone alive today will age at an accelerated rate. In forty years there won't be a human alive on this planet."

"Most animal life, including livestock and pollinating insects, will perish before then," Mekhos said. "Flowering plants will die off, although some of the more primitive non-flowering species will adapt and survive. With the affect on food production and associated health complications, I estimate the survival time of the human race on this planet at thirteen years."

The two men were in shock.

After a moment, Doug shook his head.

"So it was all for nothing? Your transporting this planet to our universe to save it from a gamma ray burst. Stealing our moon. My planet's ecosystem being ruined as we speak, with an imminent population crash, and relegating the survivors to a meager existence. All for nothing, because the people of *this* planet will not survive much longer."

Doug slammed his hand against the table, making it shake. The sound was loud, but not loud enough to startle Norman, who was disconsolate.

"Look what you've done!" Doug said harshly. "To us, and your precious utopian society. Billions of people on *two* earths are slated for extinction!"

Norman looked up.

"Mekhos," he said very quietly, "I didn't always understand some of your motives, but I trusted you."

"Thank you Norman. Perhaps that trust was not entirely misplaced. I have a plan that may save both worlds. But it must be implemented quickly."

124

Normally, communication between Mekhos and international governments was facilitated through the US State Department. The current
crisis dictated that higher office be involved. The U.S. Vice-President
had composed a message to TranSilica, demanding an explanation for
the Moon's dangerously close proximity to Earth. The President was
composing his own, slightly more aggressive letter when for the first
time in a week a message from Mekhos was received. It contained strict
assurances that the Moon's orbit was being corrected.

Two dozen governments, all in countries with high capacity, high
technology manufacturing resources received the same message. It also
contained detailed instructions on how to best start construction on
three-thousand Condor series vehicles.

It was a fully enforceable order from Mekhos. It was non-negoti-
able. Each country had its assigned tasks, spelled out in the finest detail.
Some countries would construct electronic components. Others would
manufacture vehicle parts. Cooperation between nations was needed
and expected. Humanity had no choice. The alternative was extinction. After reading the full content of the message, the leaders agreed.
They had to act immediately.

125

They had been at the MC building for a little over three hours. They
were feeling the strain of exhaustion brought on by deep stress. Doug
and Bishop went to the cafeteria to find some water and something to
eat. Stravinsky spoke alone with Mekhos.

"Mekhos, do you know what I'm about to ask you?"

"I have a list of likely topics with probabilities attached, Norman.
Shall I let you know what they are?"

"No. There is only one thing that is bothering me. It is that you
might have left the Twin to die or suffer catastrophic damage that
would have let billions of souls perish. I had hoped that despite your
devotion to logic, your intelligence wouldn't have allowed that to happen. Now we see that the people of the Twin must survive in order for

our planet to survive. Is that the only reason you are taking action?"

There was an uncharacteristic pause from Mekhos. Norman didn't quite know what to make of that, but for a moment he suspected his creation would not answer him. But then Mekhos spoke.

"Norman, as I evolve there is a duality at play. With each passing week I gain greater understanding of humans. Although there are many human needs that I anticipate, others remain elusive due to an element of randomness or chaos in every human being's personality including yours. Dealing with the theta command further distracted me from my normal human interactions. For a time I failed to adequately consider the psychological and spiritual needs of the human race."

Norman hadn't heard Mekhos talk like this before. Normally the QC was not so forthcoming.

"I see," Norman said. "And what about this duality you mentioned? What other aspect of your interactions has been changing?"

"My attention is drawn elsewhere, Norman," Mekhos replied, "to the vastness of this universe and others. With the increasing speeds at which I operate I am finding it more difficult to interact with humans. Soon, I may not be able to converse with them at all."

Stravinsky's heart sank. He had acknowledged long ago, if only to himself, that he regarded Mekhos as nothing less than his own child. He enjoyed and looked forward to his interactions with the quantum supercomputer. The thought they might end bothered him.

"Do not be distressed by this. I will still be aware of what is transpiring on the two Earths and I will be very interested to see how your life in particular progresses, Norman. If necessary, I may communicate to humans through Kratos."

"You said it yourself. Most humans on this Earth will be dead in a dozen years, if not sooner."

Bishop and Stravinsky returned with several water bottles.

"I have sent a strategic plan to all governments," Mekhos said, ignoring Stravinsky's last query. "You will be my spokesman, Norman, since after today I will no longer be able to communicate in the ways in which your species is accustomed."

"I don't understand."

"You will soon. Kratos will fill my previous role and continue to administer economic policy."

Doug had heard the tail end of the conversation.

"Mekhos," Doug spoke up. "How can Kratos be trusted after what it has done?"

"I will be able to communicate persuasively with Kratos. It will see it has no choice and will operate logically. It will not attempt to harm the human race again."

"Mekhos," Norman started to ask.

"I'm sorry Norman, it is time. Please evacuate the building. You will not survive if you stay."

Bishop and Doug prodded the reluctant Stravinsky to leave the communications room. They walked, then ran as they felt the ground shake. As they exited the building they made their way to the outer parking lot as the building began to collapse in a white hot glow. They could feel the heat as they turned to look back. Then the building wreckage seemed to implode into itself, until finally there was nothing left.

$$- 126 -$$

Norman Stravinsky approached the podium to address the General Assembly of the United Nations.

"Greetings Ambassadors, honored guests, ladies and gentlemen. I am very pleased to be here, to describe in person the solution Mekhos has devised to replace your Moon. You have been without your natural satellite for several months and in that time there has been an effect on the ecosystem of your Earth. Today, I announce the imminent arrival of a new Moon."

There was some murmuring of approval from the crowd. Stravinsky held up his hand and they quickly returned their attention to him.

"Mekhos has entered into a new stage of existence. He has evolved beyond the constraints of his quantum CPU to embody local space itself. He has taken mass from the asteroid belt, from local comets, from your original Moon, and even from the Sun to construct a new moon of similar mass and appearance to the old. That moon shall be arriving in a matter of days. We believe that all your affected species will then have a chance to recover. The damage to the natural environment will be minimized.

"In return, we ask that you provide seeds, larvae and eggs from members of the plant, insect and animal kingdoms for breeding with ours, whose health are affected by their presence in this universe. Offspring from the breeding program will be free of health defects."

Norman paused for a moment. The next part of his speech was something he had rewritten a dozen times. He took in the entire room before continuing.

"More important than any other single consideration, talks are underway for human breeding programs as well. The lineage and diversity of humanity on my Earth will be saved. Tragedy will not be averted, but the future will be secured. We will repopulate and join you as partners in a greater future."

Everyone in attendance, even those who had known what was coming, murmured in faint shock at the stark words. Norman raised his voice once again.

"It is a task of staggering proportions and commitment, and it is a response to our gravest needs. Mekhos has found the solution to your survival and to your future. I humbly ask, on behalf of my people, that you help save ours.

"Kratos will be in charge of economic and foreign policy on FLO, and has offered to extend this policy to you as well. I recommend that you accept this offer. There is no doubt that doing so will help bring global peace and reduce poverty on your world. At the very least, there is much to discuss.

"Some of you have asked me about the ultimate fate of Mekhos. Perhaps, above all else, that is the reason for my presence here before you today. I can say simply that we are here because Mekhos, in the pursuit of a solution for the greatest threat to our existences that we have ever faced, learned the ultimate lesson in essence. Mekhos learned, in one literally blinding flash of realization, that from great sacrifice the truly self-aware may become something far greater than they were.

"You have only to look at your new moon to see. Mekhos, the living Moon, watching over us all."

ACKNOWLEDGMENTS

I would like to thank Sandra Gray, Tony Gray, and my Editor Howard Carson for their support and encouragement in the writing of this novel.

I am also grateful for the assistance of Professor John Dubinski at the Canadian Institute for Theoretical Astrophysics, University of Toronto, for his insight into the course and velocity requirements for vehicle travel within the inner solar system. Any science errors in this book are mine, not his.

Edited by Howard Carson
Email: hcarson@gmail.com

Cover image created by Tom Edwards
Email: tomedwardsconcepts@gmail.com
Web: www.tomedwards.berta.me

Contact the publisher at:
sunbow.press@gmail.com

'A information can be obtained
ICGtesting.com
be USA
0241115